PACIFIC STATE

THE SUNDOWN SERIES : BOOK TWO

GRANT PRICE

Black Rose Writing | Texas

ISBN: 978-1-68513-340-5
PUBLISHED BY BLACK ROSE WRITING
www.blackrosewriting.com

Printed in the United States of America
Suggested Retail Price (SRP) $23.95

Pacific State is printed in Book Antiqua

*As a planet-friendly publisher, Black Rose Writing does its best to eliminate unnecessary waste to reduce paper usage and energy costs, while never compromising the reading experience. As a result, the final word count vs. page count may not meet common expectations.

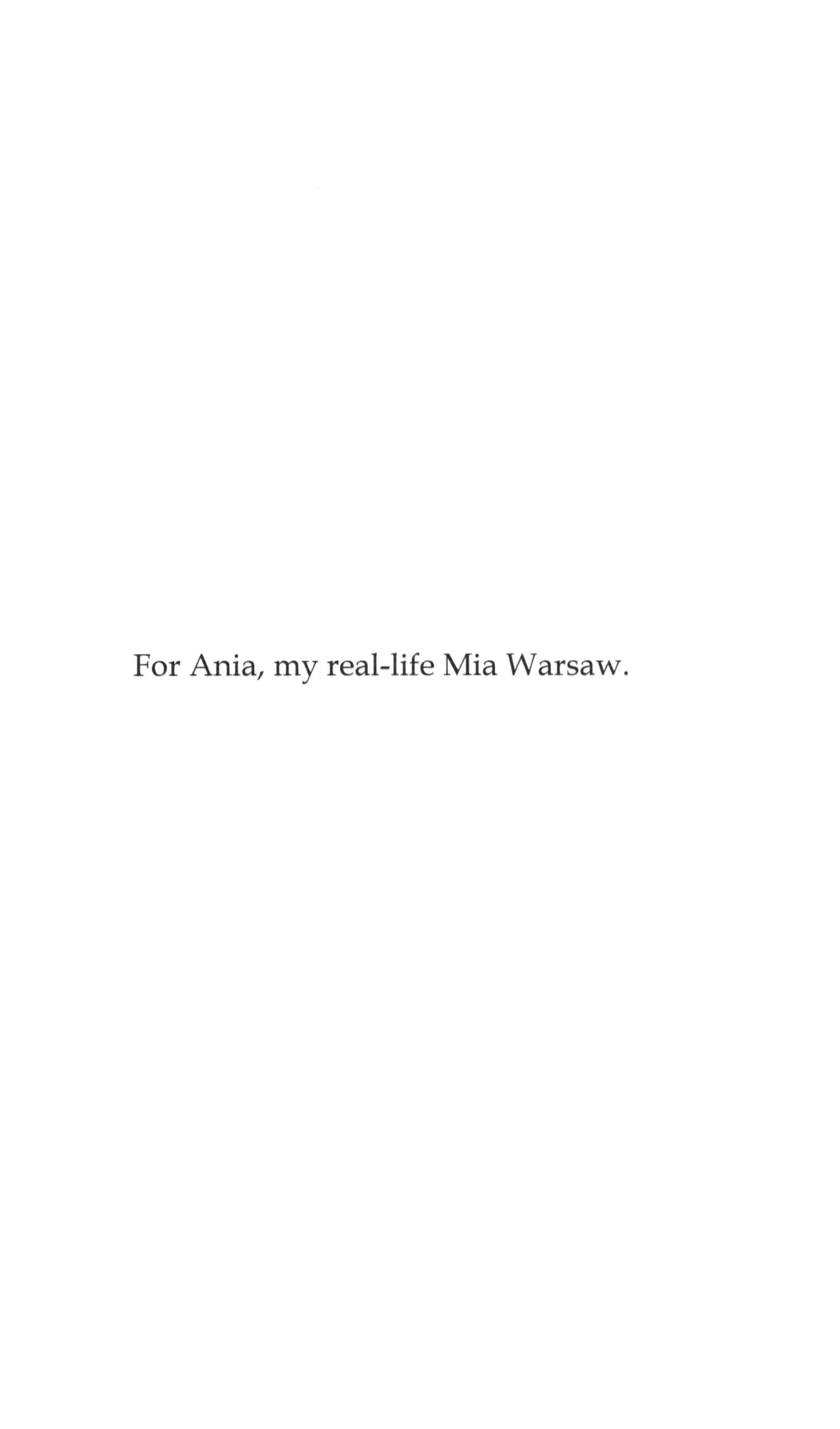

For Ania, my real-life Mia Warsaw.

"A clever blend of realistically presented future concepts, rebellious characters and heart-racing action. If you enjoy fast-paced sci fi with fascinating technology details, this book is for you."
–Los Angeles Book Review

"Clever world-building, plenty of tension and balances its characters on a knife edge…fans of dystopian science fiction will definitely enjoy this!"
–LoveReading (Books We Love)

"Fast-paced, action-packed and authentic…never a dull moment."
–Readers' Favorite (5/5)

"Crisp, precise and well rounded. Pacific State is like a modern-day version of Neuromancer…and so much more fun!"
–Anna Mocikat, author of Behind Blue Eyes and Shadow City

"Price is redefining sci-fi. Gone are the days of cardboard characters, artifice and an overemphasis on technology. What we get instead is a dissection of the human condition in a reality that is twisted just far enough to serve the story. Playful, exhausting and crafty, all at once."
–Ben Scharf, Andere Filme

PACIFIC
STATE

*"The factory which works all night is a sign of the victory
of a ceaseless, uniform and remorseless time.
The factory continues even during the time of dreams."*
–John Berger

ONE

A MORAL KIOSK

1 'He took my child from this world,' said the woman. 'Now I ask you to take his world away from him.'

A bulb threw spoiled light onto a grim room. Windows taped, walls nicotine, floor pockmarked with the brittle dried skeletons of insects. In the corners, single-use plastic lay piled like forgotten sculptures. The air was a curtain of dust and cloying sweetness. It was a hopeless space that had been built without ceremony, occupied without ambition, then abandoned and left to rot.

In it, a woman who hadn't had the misfortune to experience such squalor in life.

In it, a woman and a girl for whom squalor was their life.

The woman who didn't belong wore a muted dashan gown whose sleeves pooled on either side of her chair. Designer violet eyes glowed faintly in the semi-dark. She was the oldest in the room, though it would have taken a tissue sample to prove the fact, because her skin had been crisped and stripped at great expense. Even so, she didn't wear her artificial youth as a vain person would. It was part of her, just as her wealth was part of her. Her hands rested in her lap, her eyes on her audience. She had no mind for the decay around her, for she carried enough in her soul.

'I no longer believe in this system we have created,' she said. 'It has been good to me, but now it has taken away the only thing I would never have given up. From an early age my daughter Lulu showed a talent for music. She heard things others could not. She responded to it with her body and mind. Before the end, she believed she was close to transcending the limits of the time to which we are bound. I don't pretend to understand what she meant, though she tried to explain it to me many times, and even had our consciousnesses share a Haight pool in an attempt to transfer her experience to me. I tell you this only so that you recognise what her music meant to her.

'Her move to Wraptstar wasn't for fame, carbon, comfort or sponsorship. She wanted her channel to provide tranquillity amid the noise. She wished to show that beauty could still exist, even thrive, in a world that had become barren and nihilistic. For a child to think like that? I would call it a miracle of cognition. Perhaps her precociousness reflects on me and how I raised her. Perhaps it doesn't.

'When Lulu played her Cristal Baschet, people stopped to listen. I mean truly listen. Her songs were chromatic paintings dipped in light. When she pressed her fingers to the glass, she continued a conversation that had started a million years ago and which has no end. Her message depended on her mood. It could be beautiful. It could be humorous. It could be melancholy. What the music always did was demonstrate a level of empathy a girl her age had no right to comprehend. And her audience loved her for it.'

For the first time since the woman had arrived in the room, a crack appeared in her façade. The hands that rested in her lap trembled, and the movement sent waves along the delicate sleeves of the dashan gown. An intake of breath, loud and sharp. Then stillness.

'Luc Benz found her through Wraptstar. I had never met him, though I was well aware of his reputation. Few can twist the system as he can, and even those living underground have heard the name of his father. I don't know if Lulu knew much about him. She didn't think like you or I do. She wanted only to touch people, and an intimate audience with a man who has the resources to assist thousands in need would have appealed to her. If she had only told me her intentions. If she had only confided in her mother. You may have heard about what Benz does to young women who are invited to his penthouse. You haven't? Then I will tell you.'

The woman looked to the ceiling, then back at her audience of two.

'Benz is not a surgeon, yet he practises anyway. He refers to it as his 'outlet'. Subcutaneous grafts and osteo-plants are his focus, using parts sourced from black resellers around Berlin so they can't be traced. No new technology. That would be a waste of carbon. He has zero interest in providing the girls he works on with any genuine enhancements. His satisfaction is derived from the act itself. Occasionally, his surgery is successful and his patient survives. That is worse than dying, because it means he can open her up again. When they found Lulu's body under a pile of refuse in leech town, it showed three grafts she hadn't had before, plus a ten-year-old HH-omnipol chip inside her skull. It was the chip that killed her, the coroner said. His notes also stated that the surgery for the three grafts was inferior to the point of torture, and from the marks on Lulu's body he suspected it was performed without anaesthetic.'

The woman stopped again. This time her hands did not tremble. Her designer gaze held firm. 'You have heard my story,' she said. 'So I trust what I say next will not shock you: I am willing to pay you whatever you ask to kill this man.'

***

A silence, drawn out to the point of discomfort.

The other woman in the room stirred. From her black ripstop nylon vest she withdrew a straight-sided parejo that was cut at the bottom and pushed it between her lips. The girl sitting next to her proffered a battered cartridge lighter, and the woman leaned in so the tip of the parejo touched the dirty flame. Through velvet smoke she squinted at the woman who had been Lulu Chao's mother.

'You took a risk coming to this place.'

'I do not care. I've already lost everything that mattered.'

'Then why come at all? Why not swallow a handful of Oblivion pills and be done with it?'

A crease appeared on the woman's artificially youthful skin. 'I heard you could be callous with your words, but suggesting to a grieving mother that she kill herself exceeds all expectations.'

'You think I should welcome you with open arms?'

'Simple courtesy would do.'

'Answer me this: when were you last in a neighbourhood like this one?'

The woman hesitated. 'Longer than I care to admit.'

'Admitting is better than not.'

'Then it is years,' said the woman. 'Does my answer satisfy you? I know what you're thinking: that mine is the problem of a rich person, involving another rich person. That if someone rolls a stone, it will roll back on them. Why should you have anything to do with it? But I am not here for me. I came to speak to you on behalf of Lulu. She never knew hardship because I hid the true nature of existence from her. I did it because I've seen what this world has turned into. I have observed with my own eyes, year after year, how malaise has taken hold like the rot in this room and how morals have eroded to the point that they no longer exist. The infrastructure is swaying and ready to collapse, more so than many at the top are willing to believe.'

She looked into the eyes of her interrogator. 'You should understand that better than anyone, Mia Warsaw.'

The half-smoked parejo fell to the floor, where it lay smouldering. The girl watched it, as if the smoke might give her a clue as to what would happen next between the two women.

Mia Warsaw sat unmoving. Faye Mao had surprised her twice, and knowing her name wasn't one of them. The first was that she had come to the meeting in person. The second was that she had owned up to what she was. A growther. A peddler of polite fiction. A citizen who had likely become rich off the misery of others, albeit one who had now suffered the greatest emotional loss there was. Mia didn't hate the woman, didn't feel much of anything toward her, but she would not make their conversation a pleasant one simply because civility dictated she should.

'You think you know me,' she said.

'I know only of your feats,' said Mao. 'The matter with Minister Bülow. Your stint in the Ziranese Liberation Army. A standoff with Heizer's strikebreakers.'

'That was all a long time ago.'

'How about the demise of Athos? Is that recent enough?'

Mia said nothing.

Next to her, the girl smiled. 'Most gens think she's dead by now.'

'When the broker told me it would be you,' said Mao, 'I was tempted to call it off. I know you despise my kind.'

'Yet you're here anyway. And you're asking me to kill a man. A man with whom I share no connection.'

'I am. Lulu wasn't the first and she won't be the last. Not unless someone does something about it.'

Mia could feel the girl's gaze on her. 'Go to the bulls. That's what they're there for, at least for people like you.'

The flawless skin wrinkled again. 'I took you for aloof, not a fool. The police in my precinct are bankrolled by Habanik Entertainment Corp. Habanik is owned by Benz's father, Eccard. I have asked myself several times why they haven't simply killed me yet and staged it to look like an accident.'

'Is that why you have a Barbarossa junkhead standing sentinel outside?' asked the girl. 'It's pretty, but you know they'll just slag it if they wanna get at you bad enough.'

Mao interlaced her fingers in her lap. 'I realise that. It's there to buy me time. I wish only to live long enough to see Benz dead. Then they can do what they want with me.'

Mia stuck out a booted foot and planted her heel against discoloured plank vinyl. 'You may have lost your daughter, but you still have more than most.'

'I don't see it that way.'

'It makes little difference to me how you see it.'

Now, finally, desperation showed in the woman's violet eyes. 'Won't you help me?'

'Why should I?'

'I will pay you. The broker said it was what you wanted.'

'You think this is about putting carbon into an account? You're wrong.' Mia levered herself out of the chair. She stood over the woman. 'Dead wrong.'

Mao stared, her body rigid, as if any movement would shatter her into a thousand bloodless shards.

'Are you going to kill me?'

Mia smirked. 'Not today. But you should leave now.'

With the utmost dignity, Faye Mao gathered her dashan gown around herself and stood. The raw silk edge of each sleeve left trails in dust as she made for the door. Beyond it lay the single titanium-laminate biped that she trusted to shield her from an entire city's casual violence.

'Chotto matte,' said the girl. 'Wait.'

Mia turned to her. Janeane was a gossamer blonde who had worked a polygon window on the Spree circuit until one night she'd gone to the cheaptainment block people called the Trident to throw herself off its roof. Mia didn't believe in fate, but she'd been up on that roof, too, after losing the last of her neweuro on a pajatso board. Instead of jumping, Janeane had seen her, talked to her, asked her for a job. Mia had said she wasn't the Ministry of Labour, but the kid had insisted that every mercenary could use a good thief. She'd disappeared for five minutes and returned with an unlocked cash slate holding more neweuro than Mia had seen in weeks. That had been six months ago.

Faye Mao paused at the door. Her designer eyes were blank, resigned. 'What is it?'

'I have a question,' said Janeane. 'How old was Lulu when she died?'

'Sixteen.'

The kid glanced at Mia. 'Tensix. Maybe a year younger than me.' She said it simply, like there was nothing to it, but the subtext was clear. Then she stood and drifted to the wall at the back of the room, leaned against it and hitched a leg up underneath her. The centre was left to the two women. Separated by a few metres, yet worlds apart, watching and waiting for the other to blink first.

'Is this your daughter?' asked Mao.

Mia ignored the question. 'What do you want?'

'I want you to give me justice.'

'That word no longer has any meaning.'

'Then give me my revenge.'

Mia took in the hardness of the other woman's face, saw a mother's pain weaponised and ready to be unleashed on her daughter's executioner. Janeane's words echoed inside her head.

Mao took a step closer. 'You were once a symbol of resistance against econopaths like Luc Benz. When you took the Minister of Transport hostage, you showed that even criminals thought to be untouchable could be held to account. Benz is no different. In many ways he is worse. He should suffer as he has made his victims suffer. My own personal revenge is scant motivation to take a person's life, I grant you that. But proving there is more to this crumbling world than evil alone?'

Violent violet eyes burned into Mia, pinning her to the spot. 'This is your calling, Mia Warsaw. And I beg you to do it.'

Mia blinked.

'Okay,' she said. 'You'll have what you came here for.'

Faye Mao did not speak as a tear grazed her cheek. Her chest rose and fell and the dashan gown shook on her elegant frame.

'Thank you,' she said finally.

'The broker will handle the fee. Until it is done, I recommend you lie low. And invest in several more automatons to protect you.'

Mao nodded. She looked with gratitude to Janeane, who winked, then left behind the grim room and the business she'd transacted there.

As the door closed, Mia dropped into the vacated chair and rubbed her temples and didn't speak for many minutes.

The street was in a bad part of town, home to cold-blooded citizens with hostile intentions. Grit in the air, the stink of oily food and grain alcohol seeping between the cracks of shutter-fronted refugee-run chow joints and dive bars. Any transport on two, four or six wheels was so ramshackle it wasn't worth the effort of stealing. Mia Warsaw saw the looks that the derelicts gave Janeane, and she kept the kid close as they followed a rubberised paving strip to a kingCab depot two blocks up. Under her coat she kept a hand on the hilt of a fully charged Daisy, an electrified anti-riot baton that could drop an anabolic dysmorphic in a heartbeat.

Janeane seemed oblivious to the attention she was receiving. 'Are we gonna do it?'

Mia's gaze flickered to a man who squatted in a doorway, holding an ancient box terminal whose reader was worn shiny with use. There were gouges in his face where his grafts had been forcibly removed. He pointed at his terminal and whispered his spiel in a broken voice as they walked by.

'There's no 'we' in this,' said Mia.

'Says you.'

'Correct.'

'Why'd you take me with you, then?'

'I wanted you to see how that kind of person thinks and acts.' Mia paused. 'But I judged her wrong, at least in part.'

'Far as I could tell, Ms Mao isn't much different to you or me, except for the threads and her personal guard dog to keep the bad guys away.' Janeane's expression hardened. 'Besides, I already know what too much carbon can do to people. Clients showed me that when I was working my window.'

Ahead, a fly stumbled out of an Indo-tech reseller, then froze as he saw the kid approach. Mia gripped the Daisy a little tighter and opened her body more. Even as the fly made to speak, Janeane skipped around him like he didn't exist. He watched her go, then shook his head and shuffled on. He hadn't noticed Mia at all.

They reached the corner and found a depot absent of kingCabs. Two passengers waited at the blast gate, hands deep in the pockets of vinyl jackets. Quick eyes gave Mia Warsaw and Janeane the once-over and labelled them as probable non-threats. A beat-up track sentry patrolled the depot's perimeter, its packed camera head scanning in full revolutions. An overhead display flashed a message in red: ARRIV FIVE MIN.

'Rollerboy's seen better days,' said Janeane, eyeing the sentry. Then she noted the look on Mia's face. 'Shoulder?'

'It's aching a little.'

It would never be right, thought Mia, not unless she paid a whitecoat to open her up and replace flesh with high-density Plastex. But she didn't have the carbon for a procedure like that, didn't have the carbon for anything. She was in debt all over town. To a dermaclinic for the work they'd done on her face. To a second-rate implant artist in Gesundbrunnen to switch out her bio-ID chip. To various vendors for weapons, clothing, accommodation. And most of all to Mantis, the broker who had stepped up when she'd been bleeding out and found a reliable scalpel jockey to sew her back together. After regaining the use of her arm and learning to shoot straight again, she'd hit the streets only to find work scarce. Six hard months of scumjobs and she'd barely been able to settle the vig. Now, though, Mantis had put her onto the revenge fix against Benz. If she managed to pull off the job, she could pay her debts, load up a truck and kiss Berlin goodbye.

It sounded good in theory.

Janeane shuffled her feet. 'When that cannon tagged you, did you think you were gonna die?'

'I told you already.'

'Aw c'mon. I like to hear it.'

'I didn't think about dying. I didn't notice I was hit until I was on the roof of the train.'

'But you got the cannon even after it shot you?'

'Yes.'

'Pure geznet.'

On the forecourt, the track sentry halted at the blast gate and its camera head locked on to the new arrivals and scanned their ID chips. Janeane stuck out her tongue. Rubber treads bit into asphalt and the sentry rolled on.

'That Benz guy —'

Mia clicked her tongue.

'Désolé. You got a plan in mind?'

'Not yet.'

'Wanna talk it over?'

'No.'

'So what you're saying is you're uncomfortable about the job.'

'I'm not a mercenary.'

'The way I understood it, that ain't what Ms Mao was asking you to be. More like an avenging angel.'

Mia looked at the roller sentry, which was exploring a pile of rags on the far side of the depot. When it extended a probe, the pile stirred and a man's face appeared. 'Are all kids your age this perceptive?'

'Maybe. I don't know many kids.'

A breeze made its way over the forecourt and Janeane brushed away white-blonde strands from her eyes. 'When I was doing the polygon thing,' she said, 'there were plenty of clients I wanted to pull a trigger on. You could tell the ones, even before they started coming on fierce. Ugly energy. You knew you'd be in for it once the show got underway. Sometimes I tried to melt into the visuals or get off the stage as soon as I'd pitched a few shapes. Other times I figured it was my turn. Why should the other junos have to handle them and not me? I know now that ain't the right way to think. It puts the burden on me and the girls instead of the client. But maybe it's how this kid Lulu thought. Maybe, like Ms Mao said, Lulu had the idea that her music could calm his ugly energy and protect the others who came after her. Shouldn't have been her cross to bear, but there was no one else to do it. Then there's you. This ain't your mess, but you're doing it anyway. Because it's your turn.'

Janeane raised a leg and tucked her foot against the thigh of her other leg. 'How I see it, anyway.'

Mia squinted at her. 'Is that so?'

'Plus,' said the kid with a smile, 'once we do this job, we're gonna have all the scratch we need.'

'There's that word again.'

'Don't pretend you don't need help.'

They both fell silent as the track sentry passed them again. The overhead display indicated that the transport would arrive in one minute.

'Well?' said Janeane after the automaton was out of earshot.

'Yes, I need help. But we're not stealing credit slates here.' Mia's mind moved fast. 'If daddy finds out who cut his son's thread, we'll be exposed in a big way.'

'You're saying it needs to look natural.'

'Or like an accident.'

'Know anyone who does that kind of work?'

'No. But I know someone who may know someone. If he agrees to talk to me.'

'Why wouldn't he?'

'History.'

A six-wheeled kingCab that looked more like a tank than a taxi pulled up at the blast gate and discharged five people. A chime sounded and the gate opened, and a message spelled out in red crawled across the overhead display: PLS EMBARK.

'So who is this guy?' asked Janeane, waiting as the other two passengers took their seats inside the cramped gun-metal grey transport.

'His name is Ramirez,' said Mia. 'But people call him Lucky.'

2 In his technique the fighter wasn't exceptional, but it didn't matter because he had something his opponent didn't: the willingness to put himself in harm's way. It showed on the parts of his body that weren't covered by jade-green armour. Scars where blades and spikes had scraped flesh. Tight white points where the body had knitted itself back together. Pink welts, deep clefts. Perhaps he'd been quicker in his youth, more able to rely on deftness over plain bravery, before having to adapt his game to his slowing body. Or it could just as well have been that he'd always fought this way. Confident, patient, a true predator. It made him a pleasure to watch. As he turned circles in the floodlit amphitheatre, his eyes never leaving his opponent, he breathed air that was foul with sweat and copper, and he heard the ecstatic screams of the men, women, fluids and nons who thronged the pit. He did not care that they screamed not for him, but for the carbon they would make in the event of his triumph, his maiming or his death. He did not care, for he was certain he would win.

Owen Resler watched the fight in silence. He had not bet, so he had nothing riding on the outcome. Punic — whether legal, semi-legal or illegal — was the most popular sport in Berlin, the Conurbation, Frankfurt, Hamburg and Munich, yet its appeal was lost on him. There was blood and there was pain and there was death, and that was supposed to add up to casual entertainment for citizens like him. A line had been crossed a while back without any voices being raised. Now he was part of it, watching.

'Alessi is slower than the damn Mars programme.'

To Resler's left was Joel De Witt, flawlessly dressed in a dynamic suit whose iridescent threads were the colour of money. He was still a young man, but his hair was grey. One of his eyes was a milky shroud, a pattern-rec fluid implant that he'd had fitted after being bumped to senior offset trader.

'Hustle, damn you,' shouted De Witt.

Resler watched as the scarred samnite fighter raised his short sword to parry a blow intended for his throat. With a practised insouciance he dropped his guard and beckoned, but his opponent, wary of a trap, backed off.

'Who'd you lay your action with?' he asked.

'On the refu. Alessi.' De Witt rubbed the skin of his cheeks. 'Don't ask me why.'

To Resler's right, the third man in the group, Ivo Esteban, issued a dry laugh. 'Because you know better. That's always why.'

'Casse-toi, Ivo.'

'Back at you.'

In the pit, Alessi retreated over the silicon floor. His opponent, a youthful scutarius who carried a body-length shield on a Nagema-Vulkan cybernetic forearm, stalked him. When the scutarius attacked, Alessi caught a blow on his leg greave and staggered back, but managed to bring his short sword up to defend himself before the other man could cleave him in half.

'And he calls himself Ace,' said De Witt in disgust.

'How much did you bet?' asked Resler.

'Two stacks.'

'You've got more in the bank than you have sense behind the eyes,' said Esteban.

De Witt ignored him. The scutarius was merciless in pursuing Alessi over the silicon, and now he was wise to the samnite's trick of lingering in the kill zone. He used his shield, the tool unique to his class, to force Alessi back against the corrugated metal net that enclosed the pit. With nowhere else to go, Alessi put his faith in a wild swing that missed, and the scutarius punished him by slamming the shield into his exposed, sweat-streaked chest. The noise of the crowd solidified into a death chant, but the scutarius, aware the fight was being broadcast on Wraptstar, didn't go in for the killing blow. He wanted to remember this time under the lights, this fight when he went from unknown face to rising star. He'd had six fights on the Punic circuit already, all of which had ended in victory, but they hadn't been in a place like this, this palace, where suits from around the city had come to bet on him and will him to beat the legendary, yet fading, refugee fighter Ace Alessi.

'That kid had better watch himself,' said Esteban.

De Witt looked away, his face sour. 'You ain't funny. He's got it sewn up.'

But Resler saw it, too. As the scutarius took in the adoration of the crowd, he dipped his Nagema-Vulkan arm and the shield dropped with it. Ace Alessi shifted his weight onto his front foot.

'There,' said Esteban.

Alessi's sword was a blur, leaping over the scutarius's shield, into the younger man's throat and out the other side. The samnite put a boot against the large shield and twisted the sword and pulled it free. The scutarius dropped, lay on his side, no longer moved. Silicon absorbed the fluid that leaked from him. The crowd roared for their man.

'Samnite victor,' announced an invisible voice. A clean-up crew entered the pit and dragged the fallen scutarius over the silicon by his pale legs. Ace Alessi raised a hand and the illuminated metal studs on his helmet glowed red. He made his exit through the archway at the rear of the amphitheatre, and as the lights came up the audience thinned out as the stage was reset for the next bout.

'Did you see that?' said De Witt. 'I knew the bastard was good for it.' He touched his index finger to the terminal built into the arm of his chair and grinned at Resler and Esteban. 'A twelve-stack. Ain't bad for an afternoon's work.'

Resler said nothing. He'd never had a twelve-stack of carbon in his life. He glanced at Esteban, who only smiled. His suit, too, was made of dynamic polyamide, though it was of a lower quality than De Witt's. Resler knew Esteban didn't care about such things. He never had.

In the pit, two roller-cleaners sprayed down the silicon, and the chemical tang reached their seats and made the inside of Resler's nose itch.

'Ready to leave?' he asked.

'Since we got here,' said Esteban.

De Witt jumped to his feet. 'Onward, my loyal somatophylakes.'

In the building's foyer an attendant no older than the dead scutarius handed them their overcoats and bowed and then lingered some. When he saw no tip was forthcoming he retreated with a scowl.

Resler eased his coat over his tired frame. No, not tired. He couldn't think like that. The ache in his back and in his forearms was what success felt like. On his eye-over, miniature green numbers informed him of the time. No longer early, not yet late. He breathed the foyer's austere air, pleased to be away from the scent of blood and near-sexual desire. 'What's next?' he asked.

De Witt cocked his head. The opaline eye swirled. 'I got us a reservation at Piquant. Cab's waiting outside. So chop chop.'

***

Piquant Bytes paired New York tropical with minimalist cuisine. Expensive, soulless, middle-man chic, hot for another few weeks until the chasing crowd moved on to the next thing. Housed in a short stack of low-slung cantilevered slabs overlooking the Spree, its armour-reinforced sliding entrance remained shut except to those with enough clout to secure a reservation. Once inside, guests were led over an ultramarine brook and along a gravel path that bisected a garden of monsteras and calatheas. Each table was positioned in such a way that no two parties were in each other's line of sight once seated. The firm responsible for the interior was now redesigning the home of Thijs van Zilverhuizen, the Climate Bank President, who lived in a fortified compound south of Frankfurt.

'How'd you swing this?' asked Esteban as a roller-waiter deposited them at their table. The air was cool and misted and smelled of peppermint.

De Witt lounged against the top-end muskin booth. 'I know a guy. Plantologist. Ended up getting the green gig here after his vine installation at Hearts & Napalm won a bunch of awards.' He paused. 'Shame the prollos burned that place to the ground.'

'Fitting, though,' said Esteban.

'Are these plants real?' asked Resler. He reached out, touched a monstera leaf. It felt genuine enough, not that he had anything to compare it with. The only greenery he ever touched was the biotecture stuff growing on the outside of his cube in Niederschöneweide.

De Witt shrugged. 'Who cares? If it looks legit, that's good enough. Shall we get started?'

Through his eye-over, Resler dialled into Piquant's frequency and the menu flashed up. He identified the cheapest beer on the menu and put his order through without offering to take care of drinks for De Witt and Esteban. He was back in credit since starting at Scopo, but months of living on the red line had taught him a couple of things. Like not picking up the tab unless he had to.

He dissolved the eye-over and looked at De Witt, who sat with his head back against the muskin, his expression vacant as he, too, read through the menu. Strong-jawed, syringe-sculpted frame, not a hair out of place. The S13 Academy graduate belonged in a place like this. He, Resler, didn't. Not yet. Addresses like Piquant made him feel like an imposter. But that was part of the game. The more he played, the better he would become and the more comfortable he would be participating in the fantasy that all was fine and life was good.

He hoped to hell that was the case, anyway.

De Witt spoke without looking at either of them. 'You want sonic seasoning?'

'For a three-O percent markup?' Esteban shook his head. 'All they do is pipe muzak into your chip and you're supposed to think the food tastes different. I've done it before. It's not worth it.'

'He's right,' said Resler, seizing the initiative. 'That's for prollos. Circular file it.'

Now De Witt looked. And grinned. 'Our former anti-establishment genius is speaking Whicolla like a pro already.'

Resler's cheeks coloured and he said nothing more until the roller-waiter brought their drinks.

Esteban raised his glass and looked to Resler. 'Well done on making the cut,' he said. 'Scopo culls nine-O-five percent of its probation people. But not you, Owen. You're on your way.'

'Gracias,' said Resler. He could think of nothing else to say.

'Welcome to the club,' said De Witt, and he drained his glass of whiskey. Resler took a sip. The beer was the first alcohol to touch his lips since he'd started at Scopo. He didn't need to be furry behind the eyes when he woke at dawn for another day of sifting data.

'How's that joy button working out for you?' asked De Witt. 'Better than a forehead plate?'

Resler's fingers strayed to his temple, where his SynSult dope plate had been embedded four weeks previously. 'That's an understatement. I have the heartrate of a coma patient when I'm fracking, and I can deep-dive on data for hours without fatigue. The tech I used when I was doing hackwork wasn't anything like this.'

'Scopo give you a good price?'

'A quarter-stack of carbon each month. Should be paid off within two years.'

'Not bad for bleeding edge.'

'I don't see it that way,' said Esteban. 'You need that temple dot for your job.'

Resler shook his head. 'They didn't force it on me. I could've gone for a forehead plate on a much lower tariff.'

'Sure,' said Esteban. 'And then you would've been in the nine-O-five percent that was culled. It's a pay-to-win model.'

De Witt grinned. 'You know the game, Ivo. That's how it is.'

'This is a SynSult Series Six,' said Resler. 'All the hackwork guys dreamed of having one. If I have to pay a little for the privilege of using it, so be it. Besides, by using a SynSult I can do twice the work of the white-collar in the next cubicle. It's only a matter of time before management fast-tracks me and I'll pay the debt off in full.'

'Except every data head with half a brain has the same idea,' said Esteban. 'If you're all wearing gold, no one stands out.'

Resler glanced at him, annoyed. 'Are you going to sit there and pretend it's any different at Amordium?'

Esteban frowned, said nothing. De Witt laughed and ordered another drink.

When the food arrived on plates of wood cellulose, Resler stared. Barely three mouthfuls with a smear of sauce. From starving on welfare to spending a week's salary on nothing. He glanced at De Witt and Esteban, but their faces showed no surprise. And why would they? This was normal for them. This was the world he had joined. He had to embrace it, or he would be out. If that happened, he didn't know if he could survive on poverty row a second time.

'I have to tell you what we're trialling down at the big firm,' said De Witt. 'But you gotta keep it quiet. Ain't corpcon-worthy yet.' He stabbed at a disc of celbeef on rice with a chopstick, plucked it free with his teeth. He spoke as he chewed. 'Ever heard of Castheiser?'

Resler gave him a blank look. Esteban shook his head.

'It's direktsoft for a neural plant, straight out of the Beijing labs.'

'Already sounds expensive,' said Esteban.

'Hear me out. It's a little sensitive to set up, but once you get it configured properly you can say goodbye to Whicolla and relays and sprint-vaults forever.'

Now Resler was listening. 'How do you figure that?'

'The best way to describe Castheiser is that it's an autopilot for your brain. Say you have a meeting and there are ten action points on the agenda. Once you give Castheiser permission, it'll take over and steer the conversation in the direction it needs to go. It's algorithm-based, but honto intelligent. If everyone in the room has Castheiser, that meeting will be over in less than a minute. You go in, Castheiser speaks, and you come out with the goods.'

Esteban's chopsticks, holding two cubes of sweet potato tied with a shaving of burdock root, hovered in front of his mouth. 'And meanwhile you sit there, listening to a piece of software manipulate your mouth?'

'Oh, no. You blank it all. It's like going into micro-sleep.'

Esteban lowered the chopsticks. 'You're joking.'

'Not me. It's gonna revolutionise the workplace. Productivity through the damn roof. Look, the Athos collapse left a lot of unclaimed real estate on the table, and S13 has been grabbing as much as it can. That's no secret. But now we've got to assimilate it all, quick. If we roll out Castheiser company-wide, we'll get it done in weeks.'

'You're saying you're willing to give control of your mind to a program just so you can get out of a conversation?'

De Witt threw back his fresh glass of whiskey. 'Why not?'

'Why not?' Esteban's eyes burned. 'While you're floating in that abyss, anything could happen.'

'It's an office. What's gonna happen, Nostradamus?'

'Maybe some disgruntled worker from downstairs comes in and shoots up the place. It's happened three times at S13 this year already.'

De Witt shook his head. 'Furthest he can reach before security smokes him is the hogpile, and I'm sure some of those dead-enders would consider it a mercy if he came in spraying.'

'Jesus, Joel. You can't say that.'

'Look, it ain't about some no-hoper going postal. If installing Castheiser means I don't have to listen to idiots spouting about apricating, zeugmarkets and planvarication for the rest of my life, I'd rather have a minute's sleep.'

Esteban turned to Resler. 'Help me out, Owen.'

Resler didn't answer immediately. He saw what Esteban was saying, but taking sides against De Witt was like betting against the house. He plucked a sliver of celmeat from his plate and chewed. It had no flavour.

'If it improves efficiency, I guess I'm for it,' he said. 'Meetings are productivity killers. If white-collars were free to actually get their work done, we might have a chance of meeting the Preservation Act's goals.'

Esteban shook his head. 'The Act is rigged, Owen. You know that better than most. Don't pretend otherwise just because you wear a suit now.'

He was cut off by De Witt bringing his hand down against the table. 'Enough. You wanna talk stupid and get eyes on you, you do it elsewhere, away from me. You know, you sound more like a dust jockey every time I see you, Ivo. Are you sure you don't wanna hang up your tie for a pair of shit-stained overalls? There's plenty of samizdats out there. I'm sure your management skills will come in handy.'

Esteban shook his head and turned his attention to his plate. Satisfied, De Witt leaned back against the booth. Resler picked up his beer and drank and watched the monstera leaves trembling in an artificial breeze. The peppermint mist clogged his nostrils. Spectral green digits in the corner of his eye-over showed he had five hours before he needed to be back at Scopo's headquarters near Warschauer Strasse.

When a roller-waiter deposited another whiskey at the table, Esteban buttoned his jacket and stood.

'Don't say you're abandoning me already,' said De Witt. 'I was only joking around before.'

'I have to get back across the river.'

'But your shift doesn't start for hours.'

'Four hours.'

De Witt sighed. 'Look, I'll spring for a couple of drinks. Then you take a blitz pill and you're good as new. You won't have enough time to sleep even if you do go home now. What do you say?'

Esteban shook his head. 'I have to get out of these clothes.'

'You sure?'

He nodded and turned to Resler. 'You coming?'

De Witt groaned. 'You're not taking the golden boy, too?'

'Up to him.'

Resler looked from Esteban to De Witt. He was tired. He'd just spent a fortune on nothing. The digits in the corner of his eye-over never stopped turning over. And De Witt made him anxious.

'Best if I call it a night,' he said. He pinched the fabric of his sleeve. 'They still have their eye on me. They'll know I'm wearing the same suit and that doesn't look professional.'

'Smart,' said Esteban.

De Witt scowled. Then his features cleared. 'Suppose the polygon girls ain't too far from here. Got a few stacks of carbon burning a hole in my chip thanks to the great Ace Alessi. I reckon they'll be pleased to see a captain of industry in their midst.' He drained his whiskey and stood. 'Let's get to it.'

Outside, Resler and Esteban said their goodbyes to De Witt, and watched as the lights of his kingCab receded along the Spree's north bank. They crossed the road to where an eVelo dock burned aquamarine against nu-crete grey. They each unlocked a bike from the dock and keyed their chip to its frequency.

'Thanks for bringing me along,' said Resler.

Esteban fixed his gaze on the Plastex awning that stretched from one bank of the river to the other to protect the water as it passed through the heart of Berlin. Graffiti troupes had gotten to most of it, and the Plastex was bruised red and blue and purple and yellow.

'I'm gonna give you some advice, Owen,' said Esteban. 'Don't get stuck on the hype train. Ride it long enough and you'll realise there's no end station. It just goes around in circles. Joel knows it, deep down, but he has no stomach for the alternative, so he pretends we're still moving forward. I know you've had a tough time of it this past year and that a person will give up all kinds of beliefs if it means they can eat. But I'll just say this: the world doesn't need another yes man.'

Before Resler could respond, Esteban climbed onto the bike and jerked the starter. He nudged the bike onto the road and gunned it, leaving Resler alone with the start of a headache spiking behind his eyes and sourness in his throat.

He took the eVelo's helmet from under the seat and smelled the greasy foam as he pulled it on. He threw his leg over the saddle and set the destination. A four-O-minute ride in light traffic. That left just enough time to grab a couple hours' sleep before he had to leave again.

A message from the bike appeared on his eye-over. *SaneBike: live your electri-city. Good morning, Mr Resler.*

As the machine spirited him through sodium-lit streets, Resler wondered what was good about any of it.

3 Scopo Tower was an autoclaved graphene breeze block, its dreadnought silhouette a negative space in an overcast sky. Among the workforce, the building's windowless bottom half had earned the moniker Hell, while the biotecture-skinned, glass-fronted top half was known as Heaven. Scopo Tower was the flagship of Natelligence, a tech campus that attracted talent from across Germany and beyond, its resident firms working on everything from weather manipulation to histosol cultivation to the use of Clostridium thermocellum in consolidated bioprocessing. Many enterprises that found their start at Natelligence ended up being bought out by either Habanik, S13, IG Band or Faber. A few, like Scopo Industries, remained fiercely independent.

Owen Resler emerged from Frankfurter Tor maglev station feeling like he'd been taken apart and put back together with half the pieces missing. Sleep had been fleeting, and he'd wasted precious minutes knocking back ersatz in the vague hope it would shift the block behind his eyes. He had sleep repression pills in his jute duffel, but they were a last resort. Even a couple could throw off his sleep cycle for a week.

When he reached the Natelligence campus he fell into line with the other suits on a floor conveyor that tracked under a Plastex canopy to Scopo Tower. As tailored adverts played on strategically positioned lightwalls, a thousand artificial eyes scanned him and his colleagues, reading for flesh, fabric, metal and chemicals. Resler watched as a man ahead of him wearing an uneven bottle-blonde mohawk was abruptly pulled through the conveyor's phase-light barrier by a security guard. The man wriggled free and turned to the guard with a gloved fist raised. There was a small explosion and the guard dropped to the floor, blood erupting from his mouth in a geyser. The fist, some kind of bionic spring-mount, clattered to the ground. An alarm sounded and the conveyor stopped and, as the suits looked on, the man cradled his handless arm and made a run for it. Another guard unholstered his sleek black Scopo-issued suppressor and fired three times and the man fell to the ground with his arms outstretched.

The conveyor started again with a jolt. Murmured words travelled through the suited ranks. Resler's gaze lingered on the guard who had been struck by the loaded fist. There wasn't much left of his face.

***

In the immense lobby of Scopo Tower, Resler squeezed into a pneumatic tube with several other workers and logged a digiticket over his neural chip for the pneumatic to take him to floor tenfour. Dead centre of Hell. It stopped three times on its way up, each entryway and connecting corridor identical. Tenfour was set out in a grid of cubicles, each of which consisted of transparents on three sides and a Plastex door on the fourth. Resler activated his eye-over and followed a solid blue line to the nearest vacant.

His cubicle was large enough to accommodate a bioceramic desk, a gelchair and a flat, dish-like console, and small enough that if he extended his arms fully he would have been able to touch the transparent walls to his left and right. He placed his duffel in the desk's only drawer and thumbed the biolock, removed his jacket, then settled into the chair, which moulded itself to the contours of his body. From a cradle to the right of the console he took the alu-clad terminal line, thin with a needle point, and found the gap in his shirtsleeve that exposed the metal cavity embedded in his forearm. He pushed the terminal line home. There was no feeling, but he shivered anyway. The line established a neural connection between him and the console and monitored his heart rate while he was fracking. It would also disconnect him from the system in the unlikely event that his SynSult plate failed. Most importantly, it showed every management head in the Tower that he was plugged in. At Scopo, people tended to disconnect their terminal lines only when necessary. For the duration of his probation, Resler hadn't taken his out even to do the mandatory minute-long, desk-bound mobility exercises that were supposed to minimise carpal tunnel syndrome and other physical ailments. He hadn't wanted to give the execs any excuse.

A platypus tube snaked down from a neat hole in the ceiling, and he pulled it toward him and sucked on the plastic and grimaced at the chlorinated water that filled his mouth. The tubes were flushed and disinfected every time an employee vacated a cubicle, but it made no difference to the taste of the water, which was basic grade.

When he activated the console, the transparents glowed with information. The one to his left showed a list of available jobs in the communal pool, as well as those already being worked on and by whom. The one to his right displayed his heart rate, efficiency rating — currently sitting at eight-O-nine-point-three — the internal communication channels, Scopo's update feed, and, at the bottom, the minutes he'd spent plugged in.

The transparent in front of him was where he worked his data. Assisted by AI and his dope plate, his job was to seek out sensitive details, or 'pertinents', from data sets generated through the use of Scopo's products, the primary one being a smart adaptogen that bound itself to pathways in the host's brain in order to mirror neurons and suppress empathy. The adaptogen was a hit among the high-ups and mid-levels, because it allowed them to make decisions without being held back by their conscience. According to rumours, the board at Habanik popped the thing like it was a roll of stevia drops. Buried in the adaptogen's small print was a consent clause that gave Scopo the right to rip geographical, communication and biometric data directly from its users' neural chips. All of that data needed sifting, isolating and packaging before it could be sold on to whoever was willing to pay the asking price. There was so much information that in Resler's first week he'd dismissed too many strings as irrelevant and been flagged by a quality assurance handler. Now, even if he was sure the data was useless, he threw it in a data hole that he'd constructed on the sly within the system so he could retrieve it without having to sift the raw cubes again.

As he finished setting up, Allison, Scopo's semi-smart AI, materialised on the update feed. Androgynous in appearance, it spoke through a perma-smile.

'This announcement is brought to you by Daisy Electric Nightsticks: shockingly good self-protection. A minor disturbance this morning on conveyor B2. A terrorist provisionally linked to the Ebisu anti-technocratic cell was neutralised by members of the Scopo security team as he attempted to gain entry to Scopo Tower. During the altercation, the terrorist injured one of the responding guards, who has been transferred to New Charité for treatment and is expected to make a swift recovery. Donations are welcome.'

Resler grimaced. Swift recovery. The man's face had been mash and bone. Why lie? No one cared about the guard either way.

He scanned the job list in search of an activity he could handle without grief, but he'd been slow to get started. The good options were taken. He selected a job at random and several data cubes appeared on the transparent in front of him. When he opened the first cube, strings of information unspooled at lightning speed and he felt the SynSult plate at his temple focus his mind like no street drug could. As he watched the transparent, the strings slowed and already his eyes were being drawn to knots that could prove useful to Scopo. He still marvelled at the SynSult's capacity: without it the data would overwhelm him, distend his brain, cause death by information overload. Up in Heaven there were frackers who could handle twice as much data as he could. One day, he thought. If he kept his head down.

His last thought before he gave himself over to his task was that Scopo allowed its employees to maintain just enough agency to function as it wanted them to, and nothing beyond that.

***

He had been making good progress when a notch blinked on his eye-over. He pulled back from the console, saw that the ID belonged to his sister. Despite risking the system flagging him for inactivity, he paused his work and waited for his dope plate to go into standby, then accepted the call.

Ina appeared on a thumbnail-sized display in his left eye, her image captured by a camera in her office. The detail was minimal, but he thought she looked pale.

'Are you okay?'

'Owen, you don't have to sound terrified whenever I call you.'

'So you are okay?'

'I'm fine.'

A brief silence.

'I haven't seen you,' she said.

'I've been busy.' It sounded lame even as he said it.

'And I haven't?'

Ina worked at Zoologischer Garten, for a legal clinic that used what little resources it could muster up to assist the tide of refugees coming in from Spain, Portugal, Italy, the Balkans and Turkey. Their homes and livelihoods had been scoured out of existence by the sun and the heat or else submerged by rising waters. The cities that continued to function in the south didn't have space for everyone, so those with the means migrated north to where technology shielded urban centres like Berlin from the worst of the changes that were happening elsewhere. Before he'd joined Scopo, Ina had tried to get him involved in the clinic's work, but Resler had resisted. He hadn't told her why, but dealing with that amount of misery on a daily basis would have tipped him over the edge at a time when he was barely holding on as it was.

'I didn't say that.'

'So we can meet?'

'Why? Is it urgent? Are you in some kind of trouble?'

On the thumbnail, the flicker of a smile appeared on Ina's face.

'Ever hear of the Doomsday Troop, Owen? The ones who spray the city black and red? You'd be too pessimistic even for them. I just want to see my brother once every few years, that's all.'

He blinked. 'You're right. I'm sorry. How about dinner? Oh, which reminds me: we had a table at Piquant Bytes last night.'

'That's great.' Ina's tone lost its warmth. 'Didn't take long until you had more carbon than sense, did it?'

'Please,' he said through a grimace. 'I didn't mean it like that. I just thought you'd be interested. I don't want to argue.'

'Who's arguing?'

'Not me.'

A brief silence followed. Then Ina spoke.

'Instead of dinner, why don't you drop by the New Dawn?'

'You mean so I can see how the other half live?'

'If only it were half.'

She was baiting him. Head up to the tent city known as Amerika and be confronted by misery in all its many shades, or refuse and confirm Ina's suspicion that he was just another heartless suit looking out for number one. There was no way for him to come out on top.

'Listen, I have to get off this call. I'm supposed to be working. Let's work out a time later.'

'Fine. When do you finish?'

'I don't know. Eight or nine.'

'Christ, Owen. When do you start in the morning?'

'Around six-thirty.'

The thumbnail didn't move. She was staring. 'I hope it's worth it. I really do.'

The link died and Resler's eye-over dissolved. Transparent screens surrounded him. A glance at the one on his right revealed that his efficiency rating had fallen by two percentage points while he'd been on the call. The internal communication channel flashed for him to sign a new addendum to his pension plan, which he did. Allison appeared on the update feed to announce the company's value on the global stock markets.

Resler opened cubes and sifted data, keeping the gold and throwing the rest into the hole.

***

An hour later, an alert came through that his two-O-minute lunch break had begun. He pulled out of the system and the SynSult went into standby and he yanked the terminal line from the metal cavity in his forearm. When he stood a wave of blood rushed to his head and his legs became weak and he had to grip the edges of the desk to stop himself from falling. His vision clouded and he counted the seconds until it cleared. The transparents locked themselves down.

He left the Plastex cubicle and followed the hard blue line on his eye-over. A pneumatic took him up two floors, where he joined a long corridor with perma-active lightwalls that displayed generic Scopo ads or else messages from Allison that employees could key into as they walked by. Resler kept his comm channels closed, listening instead to the shuffle of his shoes on rubberised flooring and the swish of fabric. He was wearing his power suit, a static midnight blue three-piece cut by an Armenian tailor in Kreuzberg. He wore it only when he needed a psychological kick, which averaged out at three days a week.

The canteen contained ranks of soft white bioceramic tables large enough to seat six. Barely-there muzak dribbled from concealed speakers. Esteban had told Resler it was the same at Amordium, explained that the colour white deprived a person of their senses and their identity. Resler could attest to that. His mind worked differently when he was inside the tower. The outside world became non-existent. Work was all that made sense.

He shuffled past the queue for pill lunches, went to the dispenser and drew up the brief menu on his eye-over and selected a four-part tray lunch. Two savoury blisters, one sweet, one gelwater. When he extended his finger to the dispenser's nub, a miniscule black number on his eye-over fell slightly. The dispenser thrummed and a hatch opened and the tray lunch was pushed into his hands. He went to the nearest table and the two men and one woman already seated there greeted him with a nod.

One of the men spoke as he chewed. 'Zenzen North Star, oceanboil, zerosum for Scopo, no-brainer.'

'Sent up the ladder?'

'Post-probation? Minusnull chance.'

The other man grinned. 'Move the needle, turn heads.'

'No belts, no qualis, no XP. Risk squared.'

The woman shrugged. 'Take offline. Liner opendoor. Pain gain offset. Then fish or cut bait.'

'Stable.'

The woman turned to Resler, who was trying not to be noticed. 'Input welcome,' she said with a smile.

He cleared his throat. 'No savvy big picture.'

The man who had spoken first took up the slack. 'Semi-low-hanging fruit vis throatchoke in situ FFM. TechBiz belly-up, solid assets, rudderless and ripe. Killer soft seamless for Scopo portfolio. Run it up the flagpole double-you-dee-why-tee?'

Resler blinked. Whicolla was a jungle and he had no machete. Underground they had laughed about it. Here he needed it.

'Savvy.' From the little he'd understood, the man wanted to know if he should tell management about a Frankfurt tech firm being in a financial hole. He didn't care either way. 'Affirmative. Greenlight.'

The man smiled. 'Merci l'ami, j'apprécie.'

Resler nodded. The three soon left, and he turned his attention to the line for pill lunches as he ate. There, employees even lower than him on the food chain tore the caps off reuse bottles and titled their heads back as they shook the pills into their throats, then tossed the bottles into the returns unit and hustled for the exit. The digits in the corner of his eye-over showed that he'd been on break for almost a quarter of an hour. A leisurely lunch. One of the perks of being a fracker.

He was back at his desk with twoten seconds to spare. The Whicolla exchange lingered as he plugged in the terminal line. Sooner or later he'd have to learn it properly, though he didn't know how he was supposed to find the time. Subscription software patches weren't an option: Whicolla evolved so quickly he'd have to pay for lexicon upgrades every couple of months on top of a basic monthly fee. He didn't have that kind of carbon.

A name came to him. Castheiser. De Witt's direktsoft suite that cut through Whicolla like it was nothing. There was no chance of getting his hands on the full version, but maybe there was a demo, a trial, or a Brazilian knock-off he could lean on until he brought his business-speak up to standard. On his five-minute evening break he would call De Witt and see what the man could do. Joel had been good for a favour ever since Resler had dragged him through his studies and gotten him into the S13 Academy. Joel had secured him the Scopo interview, put in a good word with the superintendent of his Niederschöneweide printcube, and was now enthusiastically teaching him how to act like a suit.

De Witt always came through.

***

Resler held on to the thought as he worked through to evening. At six-midi he paused the console and felt the SynSult ease up, and the ice in his brain thawed and he was back in the real world with all the sensations that came with it: the chair cushioning his body, the fabric of his suit resting against his skin, the recycled air cool in the temperature-controlled box. With the transparents off he could see into other cubicles, where nameless colleagues were locked in to their tasks. Some sitting, others standing. One man had already shut down for the day and was shouldering his bag. The discomfort at being the first to leave was evident on his face.

Resler activated his eye-over and called up his index, and the name JOEL DE WITT burned green among white lines. Electrons flowed over a million extrinsic semiconductors on the neural plant at the base of his skull and the call connected before he'd had a chance to compose himself.

'Busy day, Owen. Speak fast.'

The eye-over connected to a camera in De Witt's office and showed him from a side-on angle. Taut, lean, in a different suit to the night before. Attention on something in front of him that Resler couldn't see. All business.

'Last night you talked about that directsoft suite. Castheiser. Do you see any way of getting me a copy?'

'Not on S13's carbon. I'm rising, but I ain't that high yet.' A floating pane entered the camera's field of view and De Witt batted it away. 'What do you need it for?'

'My Whicolla. Still struggling with it.'

'But that's a good thing, baby.'

'Sure. I'll leave you to it. A bientôt.'

'Wait.'

A notch blinked on Resler's eye-over. He opened it. Standard VCF file, one-time use, no name.

'What's this?'

A tight grin appeared on De Witt' face. 'Pure gold dust. Datatect way down underground. Plug a call and they might be able to hook you up. If they answer.'

'How'd you get it?'

De Witt turned and winked into the camera. 'Don't share it with anyone.'

He yanked the call.

Resler leaned back in his chair, felt the tug of the terminal line in his forearm. Without thinking, he disconnected it. The VCF, a white rectangle edged in cold blue, revolved on his eye-over. Six months ago he'd been on the breadline. Eight months before that he'd been a sensor data modeller with what he'd thought was an anti-growther group, but which had turned out to be a front for Athos. Now he was sitting in Scopo headquarters wearing a SynSult Series Six and carrying a contact card for a grey tech dealer.

Times changed and they changed fast.

'Mr Resler.'

Resler jolted in his chair. On the transparent to his left, a man with black hair and pocked skin watched him through perfectly circular orange ocular modifications. His dress was simple: a collarless navy shirt buttoned to the throat and a red square-bottom tie.

Line Manager. Resler didn't know him by any other name.

'Touch base, no heart line. Enlighten.'

Resler thought fast. 'Three-O sec unplug moment, soft reset. Complete.'

He scrabbled for the terminal line and inserted the needle-like point into the metal cavity at his forearm. 'Good to go.'

Sweat collected at the collar of his shirt. Line Manager watched him without speaking. Then: 'Cashing in post-probation golden ticket?'

Resler shook his head. 'Negative.'

Line Manager turned to something off-camera, then back to Resler. When he spoke again, it was in plain language. 'Now that you are firmly part of the family, I wish to give you a chance to prove yourself, Mr Resler. I'm sending you the details of an account in Frankfurt. Sun-woo Holdings. Have you heard of it?'

'No, sir.'

'Sun-woo could provide Scopo with a significant capital injection for our next-stage expansion plans. I want you to collect all the data you can find — in house, Vertoo, partners, archives — and extract the pertinents so our psychologists can work it into a suitable profile for the pitch team. Deadline EOB Saturday.'

'This week?'

'Correct. And you'll be going with the team to Frankfurt for the presentation.'

Resler nodded automatically.

'Strive,' said Line Manager, slipping back into Whicolla. 'Laser focus.'

'Affirmative.'

The transparent blanked. Resler breathed. Frankfurt. That was what people in his business called an opportunity.

He opened the file that waited in his dashboard and scanned the information. What Line Manager wanted would usually have taken a full week of work. He had three days, plus what remained of the current one.

He thumbed the biolock on the desk drawer, retrieved his duffel and searched through the pockets until he found a brown cylindrical container capped with a white lid that he had to press down and turn to open. He shook out two white pills, his throat tight, and swallowed them with a mouthful of water from the platypus tube. He coughed and hit his chest with his hand. One pill was enough to repress the need for sleep for ten hours. Two would have him flying until lunchtime tomorrow. If, after that, he'd made enough headway, he might be able to snatch a couple of hours' rest in the communal bunk room on the eighth floor. Either way, he could forget having a normal sleep cycle for the next few weeks.

He wiped his work slate clean and drew up the Sun-woo account. A scan of the in-house database retrieved three cubes of data. As good a place to start as any.

When he opened a cube and got to work, the SynSult Series Six kicked in and cooled his mind, and the tangible world faded away like an afterthought.

4 Marzahn was automatic town, streets like wide open landing strips. Sunlight plastered warehouses, drive yards, cranes and towers, turned the district into a single great grey-white block that would have hurt the eye were it not for the fact that the city's ever-growing tide of citizens expanded in any direction but this one. Here was the dominion of road trains and robots, of capital drones and mimics in armoured eVelos scudding over tarmac rivers, of fortified walls erected to protect grain silos and data centres. Marzahn was not a place to which human beings came without good reason.

Two women stood on the roof of a dead Soviet platten. The cloud cover was a dirty ribbon pinned against a hard blue sky, fragile and almost genuine. In one direction the high-rise overlooked a checkyard whose electrified gates opened every half-hour to allow an eight-wheeled AI-controlled prime mover to slide into a covered berth. There, the grain vehicle would be scanned for deficiencies, before being shunted to the main depot a kilometre further down the road or else scheduled for repairs. In another direction the Soviet offered a view of a quadrangle formed by four smaller residentials, also in the concrete prefabricated style, and it was on this no-man's land that the younger of the two women trained a dull black Galileo monocular, while the other screwed a suppressor onto the muzzle of a Khyber-copy long-barrel rifle.

Mia Warsaw rested the rifle on the roof edge and took a yellow-brown parejo from her pocket, bit it and spat the plug into the gutter next to her foot. A flame touched the rolled synth-tabac and its smoke rose to join the clouds overhead. She glanced at Janeane, who lowered the monocular and scratched the back of her neck.

'You're sure your guy Ramirez will show?'

Mia shrugged. 'Mantis said this is where he would be.'

'And Mantis is never wrong, right?'

'Not never. But almost never.'

'How come you introduce me to women like Lulu's mom, but not Mantis?'

'First, Mantis is a non. Second, you don't deal with Mantis unless you have something to offer in return.'

'Ah. Like your six months of servitude, you mean.'

Mia didn't bother to respond. She held out her hand for the monocular and Janeane dropped it in her palm. She focused the lens on the quadrangle. Grass and fissured concrete. No bodies, no movement. The buildings were about as green as basalt. After the Preservation Act was passed the residents of Marzahn had been offered a cut rate on biotecture pods built in their thousands south of the river, and most had taken the deal. The ones who hadn't soon changed their minds when the streets emptied and the pavements were ripped up and the road trains came in from the docks and the superfields like rolling thunder. Even so, it was likely some of the residentials were still occupied, even if every window was either boarded or smashed in.

Mia checked her timepiece. They had been on top of the Soviet for two hours already. So far their luck had held, but the sec-drones wouldn't miss them forever. Despite what she'd said to Janeane, her faith in Mantis's intel was waning. She rested the monocular next to the Khybercopy long-barrel, both of which she'd bought with the advance wired to her off-grid account by Faye Mao. The unique code for the rest of the carbon was locked behind an impenetrable Mercy door, where it would stay until the job was done. She pulled on the parejo and watched as Janeane tested the spongy roof cladding with her boot. The kid wore a blue mesh skirt with an asymmetrical cut, and Mia could see uniform white lines on the inside of her left calf and a jagged cleft in the right shin that had come courtesy of a john at a polygon show.

'You want to go through five floors and get impaled on a rebar, keep at it.'

Janeane waved a hand, kept prodding the roof. Mia shook her head.

Then, out of the corner of her eye, movement. She flicked the parejo into the gutter, hissed at the kid and picked up the Galileo and trained it on the concrete square. Two men emerged from the blasted entrance of a residential on the quadrangle's east side. Mia figured them straight away for Dutch syndicate ballers because of the lattice tattoos on their necks. They wore sweeper coats over vests with interlocking discs of silicon carbide ceramic, and their appearances differed only in that one had his long greasy hair scraped back in a ponytail while the other kept his free. They looked bored, like they'd been to the spot countless times before and would do so countless times again. From a distance they appeared unarmed, but no one wore an ankle-length coat in thirty-degree heat without good reason. The man with unbound hair was missing the index finger on his left hand. In its place was a shard-like Overrider, advanced tech that could kill the energy to a whole tower when jammed into its central system.

'Is one of them Ramirez?' asked Janeane.

Mia shook her head. 'Mafia.'

'Mean brothers.'

Mia continued to watch. The syndicate men took up a position along the colourless skeleton of a railing. The way they stood made it obvious they were waiting for someone.

'Hey,' said Janeane, pointing.

Mia refocused the Galileo onto a single-rotor drone that flew in low between the buildings. It paused over the men, its peashooter barrel covering them as it ran an ID chip scan.

'They're so taufed,' said Janeane.

The syndicate man with the Overrider cocked his head and his eyes flashed, and the drone pulled up and turned and made for the horizon.

'Did he just get on that bird's channel and tell it to fly someplace else?' asked Janeane.

'Seems that way.'

'Then I don't wanna tangle with them, Mia.'

'You won't have to. Now be quiet.'

In unison, the men looked to the only building whose entrance Mia couldn't see from the roof, its shadow taking an isosceles-shaped slice out of the concrete. From the shadow stepped a man. She panned the monocular up, taking in heeled boots and black pants, billowing shirt and hunting vest. His face was all sharp angles, his salt-and-pepper hair wild and curling. She clocked the Agitator printshot lodged in the small of his back, doubted he'd be able to reach it in time if the confab went sour. He carried a black case in his hand.

'That him?' asked Janeane.

If it's not then someone's doing a damn good impression.'

'He looks beat up.'

'You must have pretty good eyesight to see that from here.'

But the kid was right. Something had wrung the easy confidence out of Gian Ramirez since the last time she'd seen him. The man the subterraneans had once christened 'Lucky' looked like a player who was about to gamble away his last stack of carbon and already knew he wouldn't win. As he approached the railing, the syndicate man with the ponytail held up a hand and Ramirez stopped and set the case on the ground. Words were exchanged that Mia couldn't hear, and while they talked she slid the monocular onto the Pic rail of the Khybercopy long-barrel and picked up the rifle and rested it on bipod legs on the roof ledge. She leaned over the weapon and panned with the scope until she had all three men in view.

Janeane crouched at her side. Her words emerged in a whisper. 'What are you gonna do?'

'I have three shots. They'll have me fixed after the second. It's going to be interesting.'

'Why do you need three?'

'First shot'll be off. Happens when you remove the scope.'

On the quadrangle the black case was with the syndicate men. The one fitted with the Overrider bent down and touched the shard to the biometric lock, which flashed blue and died. He popped the lid. Gloss-black ingots lay stacked against the case's cushioned frame.

The kid leaned over the lip of the Soviet until her feet were off the ground. 'What's in there?'

'Brickbats. They're going to see you.'

She ducked back down. 'Brickbats?'

'Neodymium or praseodymium. You use it to create stable magnets. Put it in a non-volatile thermal-assisted switching MRAM and you have a robust memory source that needs little power and will keep ticking over even if the lights go out. After the Chinese bottlenecked it, the price of NdPr went through the stratosphere. Those ingots will be worth a lot in the right hands.'

'Gotcha.'

From his coat the syndicate man with the Overrider took out a box-shaped scanner and crouched next to the case. Mia watched as he aimed the scanner at the ingots and read the results. He muttered something to his colleague, then rose and casually turned his body so he was standing side on to Ramirez. Ramirez's shoulders and head were down, his hands deep in the pockets of his hunting vest.

'The deal's dead,' said Mia. She hesitated, then relaxed her grip on the Khybercopy and stood.

'What are you doing?' asked Janeane, still crouched.

'Making a decision.'

The kid looked from her to the quadrangle and back to her. 'What happened?'

'My guess is the brickbats are counterfeit, and now they know that.'

'And?'

'You know what happens when you try to rip someone off in this town.'

Shots whipped over concrete. Mia lifted the rifle and looked for the shattered body of Ramirez through the scope. Instead she saw the syndicate man with the ponytail lying on his side with a smoking hole in his head. The other staggered away, his Overrider hand smashed and bloody, a spotted trail following him like claret touchpaper. Ramirez stood over the ingot case, his hunting vest raised to reveal his hand passing through its lining, and in that hand was an Agitator whose plastic body had been filed down to the size of his palm. He discarded it, retrieving the other printshot at the small of his back and lining it up on the retreating man, who had reached the entrance of the closest residential. As his fingers closed around the door handle Ramirez whistled and the man turned. There was a single shot and the syndicate man's eyes closed and he crumpled.

'J'y crois pas,' said Janeane. She was up and leaning into the void. 'Did you see that?'

'I saw it.'

Ramirez looked at the body for a long moment, as if expecting the man to rise from the dead and draw on him, then took a clip from his jacket and opened the Agitator's body and pushed it home.

'Shit,' said Janeane, pointing. 'Look.'

Mia lifted her gaze from the Khybercopy and trained it on a shape that skimmed between the façades of the Soviet blocks. A drone, the one the syndicate man had overridden, its single peashooter barrel primed. Ramirez hadn't noticed it. He stood over the case, his attention on the counterfeit brickbats whose surfaces were slick with blood and sunlight.

'I can't watch,' said Janeane, and she clamped her hands over her eyes.

Mia brought the Khybercopy to bear on the drone. Her movements were fluid, the rifle becoming an extension of herself, a finger resting against print-plastic. Her existence was reduced to a circle viewed through one eye. The crosshair flew ahead of the drone. An impossible shot to save the life of a man she'd given up for dead seconds before.

She fired.

The drone bent in mid-air. When it hit concrete, the noise carried to the roof.

Beside her the kid jumped up and down and slapped the roof ledge. Mia panned the scope over the concrete square, where a man in black stood without moving. His augmented gaze found her and now she could see how he had discarded the haunted expression like a cloak, and there was the real Ramirez with his brilliant eyes and careless beard, and when he flashed a smile it shifted something in her chest. He touched a finger to his temple and she shook her head to tell him she wasn't carrying the same chips as before, and he nodded and waved at her to come down to where he waited with two dead men and a smoking drone.

***

'How did you make that shot?' asked Janeane as they followed the stairwell down through the creaking Soviet.

Mia shook her head. Then she remembered. 'The scope. It wasn't dialled in.'

'Pure geznet. He's the luckiest guy I ever saw.'

The kid skipped ahead of her, then turned and laid her palm flat against the handrail to block Mia's path.

'Were you gonna let him die?'

Mia shifted the bag that held the Khybercopy onto her good shoulder. 'I misjudged. He looked done. Like I said, I had three shots, and those syndicate guys would have been zeroed after the second. They could've brought all kinds of artillery down on our heads before I stopped them. Better him than us.'

'But wasn't he your friend?'

She shook her head. 'More like a colleague.'

'That's honto cold.'

'I didn't ask for your opinion.'

The kid remained where she was, a challenge in her eyes.

'It was his deal and his knot to unpick. What happened would've played out whether we were there or not.'

The girl frowned, an imperfect ridge in near-flawless skin. 'And if someone was gonna kill me? Would you shrug your shoulders and walk away? Better me than you?'

'That's not the same. I thought Gian had played his last hand. You, I get the feeling there's a lot you still want to live for.'

'So you'd take the shot if it was me?'

Mia closed her eyes. 'Yes. Happy?'

'You bet.'

Janeane turned on her heel and continued down the stairwell, and Mia followed.

Outside, Ramirez had dragged the man with the ponytail into the shadow of the building where his colleague lay and stripped them of their vests. The black case sat shut beside them. When Ramirez saw Mia and Janeane, he came to the middle of the quadrangle. A grey metre separated them.

'Mia Warsaw.'

'Hey, Lucky,' said Mia. There was more gravel in his voice than she remembered.

His gaze flickered to her exposed shoulder. 'What happened to your arm?'

'I got shot.'

'Hanging around with terrorists will do that.'

'If the Vanguard are terrorists then you're a politician.'

Ramirez grinned, soft and easy, and his attention shifted to the kid. 'And you?'

'My name is Janeane. Ain't got a last name.'

'What's your story?'

'Oh, I used to be a polygon girl, but Mia stopped me from killing myself, so now I steal stuff for her when she needs it.'

Ramirez raised an eyebrow and looked at Mia, who made no apology for the kid.

'Okay, mijita.' He stuck out his hand and Janeane took it. 'Gian Ramirez. Whatever you used to be don't have to make you what you are now.'

She nodded, then looked beyond him to the bodies. 'Can I try on a vest?'

'Be my guest. They ain't gonna bite.'

She skipped away, a spinning top on a concrete lake, and Ramirez and Mia watched her go.

'You babysitting now?' he asked.

'Anyone who was a polygon girl and survived can take care of themselves.'

'I don't doubt it. How old is she?'

'Tensix, tensev. Never asked.'

He shook his head, turned back to Mia. 'I gotta say: you're the last person I expected to see.'

'I have a job for you.'

'You mercking again?'

Mia shook her head. 'I'm in debt to Mantis. Been working it off for months.'

'That's a tough hole to be in. What about the Vanguard?'

'Once I do the job, I'll be free to leave Berlin.'

'Word among the subterraneans is that your group had something to do with Athos's flatline. Is that right?'

Mia didn't miss a beat. 'Athos collapsed because an old man refused to give up his seat at the table. Simple as that.'

'Suit yourself.' Ramirez glanced once more at Janeane, who was trying on a vest five times her size. 'So what's the job?'

'Bringing a son of a bitch to justice.'

'Your forte.'

She nodded. 'But I need help.'

Ramirez scratched the back of his neck, then reached into his jacket and withdrew a flask and took a drink. The ground leaked heat around them. He offered the flask to Mia, who declined it. 'The ingots in that case were supposed to be my out. Sell them to those bastards, walk away with a cash prize. I haven't got the stomach for the life anymore.'

'Seems like the opposite from where I'm standing, Lucky.'

'If I truly was lucky, they wouldn't have figured the bats for fake until I was way underground. Can't seem to catch a break lately.'

'You mean aside from not getting blown away by that drone?'

'Fair enough.' The half-smile on his face froze and for a moment there was only pain in his eyes.

'What's wrong?'

He massaged his temples with a sweat-streaked hand. 'Ain't slept in a while. Got a headache like you wouldn't believe. Anyway, tell me about the job.'

'Later,' said Mia. Somewhere, an AI would have recorded the single-rotor's demise and was dispatching either a machine or a human to investigate the cause. 'You okay to come along with us?'

Ramirez shrugged. 'As long as it's safe.'

'It's that.' She whistled and Janeane looked up.

'We going home?' the kid shouted, dropping the vest. Mia nodded.

'Where's home?' asked Ramirez.

'The theatre,' said Mia.

5 As the sun died and LED signs flared, Owen Resler hopped the maglev to leech town before switching to a creaking S-Bahn bound for Zoologischer Garten. The SynSult plate at his temple drew looks from some in the carriage, and when Resler refused to dial a wafer-slice of carbon over to the electric wallet of a stinking transient, the man shouldered him and growled that he didn't belong. Resler was tense after that, but the other passengers left him in peace until he reached the Garten, and when he stepped onto the platform he disappeared into the crowd.

At the southern exit he gave a few neweuro to a scarred man wielding two fully charged Daisy batons, and his temporary bodyguard led him safely through Amerika, the forever metastasising city of tents and polycarbonate cubes that clustered around the Garten. When they reached the double blacktop of Kurfürstendamm, the man turned and retraced his steps without a backward glance at Resler. There were more lights than people on both sides of the street, pointing the way to augstores and food joints and cheaptainment stacks. Place that had once been some of the most expensive in the city — Kurfürstendamm, Wittenbergplatz, Savignyplatz — had taken a hit when the city's business elite had decamped wholesale to Potsdamer Platz, and another more fatal one when the first waves of refugees from the burning south had crashed against the bulwark of West Berlin and drained into its streets. Now the district was dominated by Spanish, Italian, Greek and Turkish influences. Resler walked by the rubble of the Memorial

Church, a hollow tooth no longer, and the scorched skeleton of its modern counterpart, and he activated his eye-over and found that the polizei were no closer to apprehending the People's Own bombers than they had been when the group had killed scores of citizens and refugees the previous year.

He turned into a street clogged with illegal single-use food containers, drawing more looks from the pedestrians he passed. Six months ago I had far less than you did, he wanted to tell them. But he kept his head down until he reached the entrance to a familiar walk-in legal clinic, its flashing 24/7 sign painting green the faces of those who lingered in the fetid air. He sent a ping to Ina to let her know he had arrived. A grime-streaked doorway to a residential block offered a likely place to wait. He slipped his hands into his pockets and directed his gaze to the metal-fronted tech reseller across the street and tried to ignore the fatigue that had dogged him since Line Manager had assigned him to the Sun-woo account. The time on his eye-over showed that it was after ten. Beneath it was a new set of digits: the hours, minutes and seconds before he had to be back at Scopo. Always too few. He dissolved the display. He wanted to be free, if only for an hour.

'Ehilà.'

Resler turned, found himself face to face with a refu. Unshaven, unwashed, bloodshot eyes. Some kind of Ital-tech implant built into his throat.

'Come va? Help you with somethin'?'

'No.'

'What you want here?'

'I'm meeting someone.'

'A girl, right? Fancy guy flash the carbon, tell some figa you gonna change their lives, 'cept all you wanna do is ball. Right?'

Resler's hands sat damp and useless in his pockets. 'I'm not here for that.'

'I gonna keep your plan a secret, amico. But you gotta do somethin' for me. You gotta break me off a piece.'

'What are you talking about?'

The refu's eyes were like cyclones trapped behind glass. 'What you think, man? Carbon. Only language the world speaks.'

'You want me to pay you.'

'Don't play dumb, amico. You're wastin' my time.'

Resler's exhaustion spoke for him. 'Yeah? You got a job you need to be at?'

The refu's hand dipped to his belt and withdrew a butterfly blade that whipped through the air and stopped centimetres from Resler's face.

'No, but you do. And you ain't gonna be doin' it so well when I take your eyes.'

Resler backed up until he was touching the door.

'Natale.'

The refu spun around and the blade disappeared, and Resler saw his sister. Ina was a head shorter than the refu, but she showed no fear as she walked toward him.

'Cosa c'è che non va, Natale? What's happening here?'

The refu ran a hand through his thinning hair, said nothing.

Resler cleared his throat. 'We were talking about my work.'

The refu turned, his bloodshot eyes showing first disbelief, then relief.

'Is that right?' asked Ina.

'Ah, yeah,' said the refu. It sounded more like a question than a statement.

'Just looking out for me,' said Resler. 'That's all.'

Ina's eyes narrowed. 'Making sure no harm comes to my brother in a rough neighbourhood?'

'Your brother.' The refu blinked. 'Right. Didn't want no lowlifes trying their luck.' He made to clap Resler on the back and Resler moved out of the way.

'That's fortunate,' said Ina. 'Because you know what happens if a refugee is arrested for a serious crime like, say, armed robbery. They'd end up in a hard labour colony so fast it'd make their head spin.'

The refu's face was grey.

'No crime here,' said Resler. 'Just two guys chewing the fat.'

Ina glanced at him. 'You ready?'

'Sure.'

'See you tomorrow, Natale,' said Ina, and she took Resler by the arm and steered him out of the alley. When Resler looked back the refu was staring after him, hostility radiating from every pore.

'He won't thank you for that,' said Ina, as if reading his mind. 'Natale's a proud kind of killer.'

'Uh huh,' said Resler.

They turned onto Ku'damm, a glass artery where loudspeakers and lightwall ads and the noise of machines made conversation difficult. Ina kept a firm grip on Resler's arm, and brother and sister were silent as they fought their way through the press. Stationed at intervals along the street were polizei sentinels with chests daubed in S13 Yellow that scanned the streams through multi-format lens clusters. In the crowd were many citizens who wore suits of static thread, heading home in the airless evening to containers and pods that were cheaper to rent because they were in a third-rate area of town.

As Resler was about to ask where they were headed, Ina pulled him into an insect-fry shop that stank of palm oil and za'atar spice. She raised a hand to a woman in a stained apron behind the fibreboard counter and made her way to a booth near the window. Once seated, she stabbed at a cracked touchscreen menu mounted on the wall.

'Chilli grasshopper okay?'

'Sure,' said Resler. He looked around. Overhead, an illegal fan churned heavy air. On a wall, a fixed screen broadcast one of Generator Joe's classic synaesthescapes. They were the only customers in the joint. 'Mash if they have it.'

'That's the only way they do it.'

The woman in the apron brought them two glasses of beer and when she left Resler didn't know what to say. He hadn't seen Ina for months, not since his first week at Scopo. Both their faults. Him because he couldn't stand the judgement in her eyes. Her for not wanting to speak that judgement aloud. Now, when he looked at her, he saw the fatigue lines in her skin and he wanted to reach out and take her hand and tell her he was glad to see her. She was an island of calm in the storm that was his life, and her simple presence meant more than she could ever know.

'You look tired, Owen,' she said with a half-smile.

'Thanks.'

'Are you tired?'

'I'm getting by.'

'Guess there's even less chance of getting a straight answer out of you now.'

Resler frowned. 'Okay, you win. I'm exhausted. I was assigned a major project last week and I've been working on it non-stop since. A team will be presenting my data to a customer in Frankfurt, so I can't afford to drop the ball. Otherwise I'm out.'

'Is that what your overlords said?'

He ignored the jibe. 'Not exactly, but it's easy enough to read between the lines.'

'Are you on the pills?'

'Trying not to. But it's difficult.'

Ina nodded slowly. 'We have clients at the New Dawn who used to work good jobs. Suit jobs. Some pushed it too far with the sleep suppressants. After a while, the body and mind can't handle another artificial bridge between waking and sleeping. Know what happens? You go blank. When you wake up, you find you've lost everything. Either that or you forget to breathe. Then you don't wake up at all.'

'I didn't come here for a lecture, Ina.'

She brushed a length of hair out of her eye, tucked it behind a tattooed ear. 'I'm not here to give you one. We're just talking about work.'

'So tell me how things are going at the clinic,' he asked, desperate to get off the topic of Scopo.

'Had time to read the news lately? It's getting worse. More refugees are coming up from the south every day. It's too hot. The ones who can afford to live in the controlled biotectures are okay, but they don't reflect the reality of things on the ground. Those who were making just enough carbon to buy what they needed to beat the heat are having to stretch their resources more and more, so many of them are packing up and heading north before they lose all their bargaining power.' She sighed. 'Sometimes I'm not sure how much longer I can do this for. Part of me wants to drop it all and run. Especially when I read about what's coming next. They say Italy will be another Sahara within a decade.'

'Surely the government could overlook the tech embargoes if it's this urgent? The water conflicts were nearly ten years ago. They need help.'

Ina smiled without humour. 'Even if we opened the trade routes now and sent them the best Chinese meteorology tech we have, it'd be too late. Anything south of the Dolomites and the Pyrenees is irreversibly damaged. You can set up cloud seeding and number-two-crop superfields and vertblades and all the rest, but nothing will grow there any more. Then there's the fact that every city has its own ruling council, and each one is looking to turn a quick buck that they can squirrel away for when the infrastructure collapses once and for all. That's the chief problem, Owen. No one gives a shit about other people, because they can barely keep their heads above water themselves.'

'So what's the plan? We just keep letting them in until we're overwhelmed?'

Ina's expression became dark. 'Scopo really has taken you out of the loop.'

Resler frowned. 'Either tell me or don't.'

'You have thousands upon thousands of people streaming north in search of somewhere more hospitable to live, right?'

Resler nodded.

'Well, here's the thing: by the clinic's calculations and many others you can find floating around the Vertoo slabs, less than one-tenth of those refugees make it to Germany's border. The ones you see hanging around Zoologischer Garten? They're the tip of the iceberg.'

'So where are the rest?'

'You've heard of that cabal of corporate mercenaries building a wall around the Alps?'

'You're saying they're hiring refus to do the job.'

She stared. 'We're not talking contracts and works councils here, Owen. They're being forced to do it. On a massive scale.'

Resler shook his head. 'I don't buy it. Slavery next door, in Switzerland of all places. If the refus are building the wall, then they're getting something for it. Food, board, sanctuary, whatever.'

Ina shrugged. 'You know how the business world works. Profit first, ethics later. Your own damn employer produces a drug to repress a person's conscience.'

'It's not a drug. It's a smart adaptogen.'

'That's hardly the point.'

The woman in the apron came to the table with two plates of chilli mash and a bowl of amaranth, and Resler took a pair of metal chopsticks from the communal pot and gave them a spray with a small bottle of disinfectant he carried in his jacket. When he offered it to Ina, she shook her head. They ate with their heads bowed, accompanied by the vague sounds of the synaesthescape on the screen and the louder buzz from outside. Resler didn't realise how hungry he'd been until he found himself scraping metal against wood. Ina looked up, used her sticks to push some of her mash onto his plate.

'You don't need to do that,' he said.

'Eat.'

When they were done, Resler sat without a thought in his head, the stress of the day and the week that had preceded it fading to nothing, and he knew if he closed his eyes and leaned back against the booth cushion he would be able to sleep, at least until his twisted circadian rhythms jolted him awake.

'Are you okay, Owen?'

Head slightly tilted, eyes hard, lips bloodless. Ina had always looked at him this way. As a child when he'd shown her how to break into their Britz high-rise's rudimentary IoT system and unlock the door to the roof. As a hotshot data modeller when he'd thought he was pushing back against the system but had been working for it the entire time. As a shell of a being who had resorted to trawling through garbage in order not to starve. And now, as a newly minted member of the successful set, anxious, miserable, weary to the bone.

'It's not what I expected.'

He looked up. Ina had a knack for this, getting him to speak aloud the fears he otherwise barely acknowledged.

'Will it get better?' she asked.

He thought of De Witt and Esteban. 'Maybe. What I hate most is that I can't be grateful. There are people struggling all over the city, and I don't just mean the refus who come to your clinic. I mean citizens, innocents who haven't put a foot wrong a day in their lives, but who have a boot against their throats anyway. Forever just one slice of carbon away from losing everything. Then there's me. A suit. Carbon balance in the black, employment forthcoming.'

He sighed, his eyes following a smear of orange grease on his plate. 'But that's all I have. I work, I sleep. Except much of the time I don't sleep because I have to work. You know, I've met Joel a couple of times recently, and he makes it sound like I'm a money guy now. But the places he takes me to? I can't afford them. I don't fit. I don't believe their rhetoric. When I spoke to that refu today—Natale, was it?—I wanted to tell him I might look like a suit, but appearance is all it is. Smoke and more smoke. No substance.'

'You shouldn't be looking to Joel for answers to anything existential, Owen.'

'I'm not. But I can count on him when it comes down to it.'

'What about Esteban? Have you spoken to him recently?'

'Yeah.'

'And?'

'I think he gets it. You hear it in the way he talks. It's like he's already mentally checked out and is waiting for something to give him the final shove out the door. Me, I've only just checked in.'

'No one says you have to stay, Owen.' Ina took a swig of beer from her glass.

Resler's anger spiked. 'What's the alternative? Begging for data rips all day just so I can buy a flash-dried pack of scran? I refuse to go back to that.'

'There are other paths.'

'I'm open to suggestions. Let me see: number one would be to work with refus.'

'You're being hostile.'

'I don't know the meaning of the word.'

She brushed her hair behind her ear. Beads of sweat clung to her clavicle. 'Sometimes it can be enough to know that there's someone out there who cares for you.'

Resler's anger died as quickly as it had flared. He slumped. 'I'm sorry,' he said, wiping his forehead. 'I'm not myself right now.'

'Forget it.' She punched the touchscreen and a request for payment appeared. She winked at him. 'Just get the bill and I'll forgive you.'

***

Outside, the late-evening rush showed no signs of abating. LEDs burned like stars. Resler activated his eye-over, read the miniature digits on the left of the display. Six and a half hours until Scopo.

'Do you need to go?'

She was at his elbow, her eyes on the eVelos and kingCabs and isolated private transports that were like electrons orbiting the atomic city nucleus.

He nodded. 'I wish I didn't.'

'Get some sleep. It'll do you good.'

'How do you do it? Whenever I see you, things don't seem half as bad.'

'That's what sisters are for.'

'I only wish I could say the same about brothers.'

'You have your uses,' she said, and drew him close. He held her, the only person in the world who understood him, and wondered if she, too, was thinking of their parents whose faces were little more than a pencil sketch to him. On the corner of the street, a polizei sentinel scanned them with its lens clusters, their embrace now recorded for eternity and ripe for weaponisation if the need ever arose. But in that moment Resler didn't care, because it was better than anything he'd felt since the last time he'd seen her.

'You want me to get you a kingCab?' he asked when they broke apart.

She shook her head. 'I'm going back to the clinic.'

'You work as much as me.'

'The difference is I want to do it.'

They retraced their steps, and at the entrance to her street he watched her go. She walked alone, between knots of refugees who sat or stood or lay against dirt-blackened paving slabs, and she showed no fear and they showed no hostility. With reluctance he turned away and headed for Zoologischer Garten. Uncomfortable as it was, it was cheaper to hop the S-train across town than to de-rack an eVelo.

The voice was soft in the crowd, but he heard it fine. 'Nice SynSult. Series Six, is it?'

He halted. Leaning against a pillar was a woman in a dirt-spattered jumpsuit, its dynamic threads blinking. She was tall with a wave of orange-crush hair, and her eyes were half-hidden by a cheap ultraviolet visor that matched her cut.

'Right,' he said, looking left and right, wary of a street con.

'I had a Series Four for a while. Loved going deep on that baby. AIs were all too eager to assist.' She had a clipped accent.

'What happened?'

She grinned a set of greyish teeth. 'The floods. They told us we could withstand a one-in-one-thousand event, but the water swallowed everything anyway.'

'Danish?'

'Dutch.'

'What was your specialism?'

'Ocular tech engineer. Shrouds, boosters, modular eye-over re-rums, that kind of thing.'

Resler said nothing, unsure if she was pitching or shooting.

She laughed. 'Don't worry, cowboy. I'm straight. Just interested in your dope plate, that's all.'

'Have you managed to find something here?'

'Not until my case is processed. And I'm at the back of the line.' She shrugged. 'I make ends meet over in Amerika. Basic assemblies any tech monkey could do, but it's keeping me in neweuro until the man upstairs makes his decision on whether I'm allowed to stay in Berlin.'

Resler swallowed. 'Any idea how long it'll take?'

She shrugged again.

He looked at her, all sardonic smile and hard eyes under tangerine Plastex, and he wished he could do something for her. But he was nothing. No one. 'Buy you a cup of chicory?'

'No, you're okay. You looked like you were in a hurry before.'

He nodded, turned to go, paused. 'What's your name?'

'Henrietta Bes,' she said. 'And you?'

'Owen Resler. Got an eye-over?'

'Only thing the flood didn't wash away.'

They exchanged unique IDs and he saved it to his index. 'Stay in touch,' he said.

She winked. 'See you around, cowboy.'

Resler joined the crowd that streamed toward Zoo, and as he re-played the conversation in his head a dull ache started in his chest. Bes's story was a common one. Highly qualified, living in Amerika, biding her time until the chance came to prove her use shoring up Berlin's fragile economic ecosystem. That was why he had to clock up the hours and make the grade at Scopo. If he lost his job, there were a thousand others waiting in line to take his place, and likely for a lower salary. He'd been told that on his first day.

At the station he found an auto-dispensary selling NRI meds and bought a blister, then threw back the two pills inside and dropped the packaging in the recycler. He made his way up to the platform, where the air was heavy with sweat and ozone, and watched generic light-wall ads for a syringeless melanin booster as he waited for the pills to take effect.

By the time the train pulled in and he stepped aboard, he no longer felt anything.

6 Once, long ago, it had been called the Delphi, a theatre for silent films. On the wrong side of the tracks during the division of Berlin, the building had been shuttered and its rooms and halls stuffed with crates of vegetables, stamps, linen and weapons. Later, a succession of entrepreneurs had tried to restore the theatre to its former glory, but after the Preservation Act was passed it became too expensive to bring such structures in line with the new environmental standards, so the theatre's final owner had abandoned it and left it to rot. The Delphi had been due for demolition for more than two decades, but the only measure taken in that time had been to swathe it in canvas tarps that snapped in the breeze and became more bleached with each passing year.

On warped stage boards Janeane skated on self-propelling blades that left gouges in wood, never looking as though she might fall.

'Hey, Lucky,' she shouted. 'Watch this.'

She flashed forward and launched herself into the air, spinning, her arms straight like arrows. When she landed a cloud of dust rose and the wood creaked and the girl laughed as though there could be no more joyous act in the world.

'Fantastic, mijita.'

Ramirez watched from a fold-down seat whose upholstery had been eaten away until only the wooden core remained. He brought his hands together in lonely applause, then leaned back, his legs resting on the top of the seat in front, revealing heeled boots with silver toe-caps and a scorpion blind-embossed into the synthetic leather.

'That kid is something,' he said.

Two seats down, Mia Warsaw sat with a mug of chicory coffee cradled in her hands. The liquid sent steam rising to rafters that were invisible in the semi-dark of the Delphi's main hall. Her attention, too, was on the stage. 'If you touch her, you lose your hand.'

'Hey.'

She shifted her gaze to Ramirez, whose dark eyes flashed a warning.

'That ain't me, Mia.'

Mia shrugged. 'Pretty girls make hombres do baichi things.'

Ramirez shook his head. 'Not this one.'

From his belt he pulled free a flask and unscrewed the cap and drank. After arriving at the theatre, Ramirez had doused himself in greywater and tied back his long, curling, salt-and-pepper hair, revealing a slice of chrome about the length and width of an index finger at the top of his forehead. Mia thought he looked haggard.

'For your coffee?' he asked, extending the flask. She shook her head. He slotted it back onto his belt, then made a show of looking around the hall, taking in the rusted scaffolding and muted archways. 'How'd you find this place?'

'A colleague underground put me on to it.'

He flashed a smile, tipped his head to the ceiling. 'Still in contact with Mantis, then.'

'Still.'

'Could've saved me a few problems if I'd had a way to get in touch with them.'

Mia didn't take the bait. She sipped her coffee. It tasted like dirt.

Ramirez lurched forward in his chair and dropped his boots to the floor, then hit her with a look that meant he was about to be straight.

'Who's the star-crossed son of a bitch you're after?'

'Luc Benz.'

'The greenwash king.'

'And heir to the Habanik throne.'

'Big contract. Dangerous. How'd you wind up with it?'

Mia told him about Lulu Mao, the doomed Wraptstar girl who had played beautiful music and suffered and died on an operating table, and about Lulu's mother Faye, who was putting up a serious fee to dispose of the man responsible for her daughter's death. When she finished speaking, Ramirez was hunched down in his chair as if protecting himself against something.

'Four operations,' he said. 'No anaesthetic. The girl shouldn't have had to endure that. The bastard.' He shook his head as though to clear it. When he spoke again, his voice was sharper. 'How much do you stand to make if you pull it off?'

'One-five-thou stacks. Fivedred upfront.'

A whistle. 'Most I've ever heard of for a wetwork job.'

Mia shook her head. 'It's more than that. It has to look natural. If I go in all guns blazing, I'm dead. Even if I erased Luc, his father would come back at me with everything he has. I already spend every day looking over my shoulder. I don't need another demon lurking there.'

'Here's an idea: why don't you take what the client gave you, pay your debts and disappear? Fivedred stacks are a good deck of carbon by almost anyone's standards.'

'Is that what you'd do, Lucky?'

'No. All I'm saying is this ain't an amateur-hour job. You have to get every detail right. Guys like Luc Benz are born wary.'

'This isn't without precedent, Gian. Take Klaus Koje. One of the most protected men in the city, but he went down just the same as any other street slinger.'

'Bullet between the eyes, wasn't it?'

'So everyone says.' Mia took a breath. 'I'm going after Benz, but I need your help to make it work.'

He laughed, brief and harsh, and on the stage Janeane stopped and looked at them with a question in her eyes, and when neither of them spoke she resumed her dance.

'Why should I help you?' he said. 'After what you did?'

'For the money.'

His eyes burned. 'You think you can buy me.'

'I told you from the beginning it wasn't a permanent thing.'

'Us or the job?'

Mia waited a beat before she responded. 'Both.'

Ramirez stared. Then he sighed. 'Dios mío, you're cold. I ain't surprised, but part of me hoped that when you saved my life for fun, maybe you'd changed.'

Mia finished the last of the chicory and set the mug on the floor.

'You haven't asked about the others,' said Ramirez.

'Because they're dead.'

'Yeah, they're dead. Maybe they wouldn't be if you'd stuck around.'

'I'm no one's guardian angel.'

Ramirez nodded toward Janeane. 'Except hers.' Stained fingers worked the cap of the hip flask again, brought it to pinched lips. He coughed and wiped his mouth with his shirtsleeve. 'Not long after you left I lost Bodine and Mitre in a standoff with the bulls in a warehouse down in Lankwitz. I barely made it out myself. At that point I was ready to kiss the city goodbye and see if a samizdat might have a place for me in the dust. But Cycle kept needling me, told me that if I left then the corpos had won. You know how she was. Revolutionist to the last.'

'What happened?'

'Bit off more than she could chew on a central terminal. Overloaded her dope plate and fried her synapses like worms in the sun. By the time I got to her she was long gone. The smell, tía. You don't forget it, not even after a fistful of adrenergics.'

'I'm sorry. She was a straight one.'

'Don't give me that,' he said quietly. 'Why would you be sorry? If you'd cared about any of them, you wouldn't have pulled your disappearing act.'

On the stage, Janeane slid to a halt. Skin flushed, sweat dripping from her temples, breathing hard. When she saw Mia watching she beamed.

'Gonna go change,' she shouted. She kicked off the blades and padded across the destroyed boards to a doorway at the back.

'Enough of memory lane,' Mia said, turning her attention back to Ramirez. 'You asked why you should help. Either you do it for the money or you do it because girls like Janeane and Lulu shouldn't be the plaything of a sadist in his ivory tower. Pick one. Makes no difference to me.'

'Why don't you ask Mantis for help?'

'No more favours. I can't afford them.'

Ramirez nodded. Then he winced, just as he had back in Marzahn. Jaw rigid, eyes screwed shut. As she watched, he exhaled a long breath and a hand reached to his forehead and rubbed at the skin surrounding the chrome.

'What is it?' she asked.

His eyes flickered open. 'My luck ran out.'

'What do you mean?'

He tapped the chrome sliver. 'This thing is disintegrating. It was only supposed to last five years. Been in there for ten. I put it off for too long. It's causing headaches like you wouldn't believe. Some days I wake up and it takes a few minutes before I can move my legs.'

'How long has this been going on?'

'A few months.'

Mia grimaced. 'Can you do anything about it?'

'Found a neurosurgeon at an unlisted clinic beneath the city who said he could put me under the knife. Wants way more for the procedure than I can scrape together. That's why I tried the manoeuvre with the brickbats. Wouldn't be so baichi if I wasn't desperate.'

'Would your cut from this job cover it?'

He looked to the empty stage. 'Yeah.' A note of resignation in his voice.

'So you're in?'

Ramirez continued to look at the stage. He bit his lip, then muttered something under his breath. When he turned to her, he looked drained of energy. 'I'm in.'

She extended a hand and he eyed it and then shook it. She wasn't foolish enough to think he would ever forgive her for leaving, but then she wasn't in the market for Gian Ramirez's forgiveness. So it didn't matter.

'Any ideas on where to start?' she asked.

'I have a few.'

'I'm all ears.'

'We need more muscle. You're good, but Benz can afford the best. You know the kind: augmented to the gills, riding the three-O line, empathy dialled to zero. Every instinct geared toward turning living things into dead things. And that's without factoring in what Benz has going on under his own hood. We won't know that until we spend a little of your advance on some hot data.'

Mia nodded. 'You got anyone in mind for us?'

'Sure. Johnny Seven. The OMA.'

'He's still alive?'

'Just about, last I heard.'

Another voice spoke behind them. 'Who's he?'

Mia and Ramirez turned to find Janeane lounging two rows back, her hands interlocked behind her head.

'You move quiet, mijita.' Ramirez scratched at his beard, bemused by her. 'How long have you been listening?'

She grinned. 'Long enough. Who's Johnny Seven?'

'Ex-military. A good guy. We've worked together a few times. Only problem? Esté como una cabra. Totally crazy.'

Janeane lifted a tanned leg, the one with the neat white lines etched into it forever, and rested it on the top of the seat in front of her. 'Why?'

Ramirez glanced at Mia, who gave a slight nod. 'He landed a liquidation job out in the dust. Some samizdat settlement making too much noise. Maybe they knocked off a road train, maybe they took in someone they shouldn't have. I don't know. Johnny gets dispatched with a detail of automatons and when he arrives he finds a few families working some weak farmland. Men, women and kids, all just barely hanging on. Has to be the wrong place, right? Johnny runs it up the line, but he's told to carry out his orders. The automatons — Barbarossa bipedals, those big seek-and-destroy things — move in and start torching the tents. When he sees kids running out with flames on their backs, a switch goes off inside old Johnny, so he gets behind an organ gun and goes to town on the Barbarossas. Seven pieces of milspec hardware reduced to slag in less than a minute. Then he turns the gun on the burning children. People say it proves he's insane, but I think he did it out of compassion.

'After his court-martial, they put him in online exile, but his brain patterns were so messed up the program froze. He unhooked himself, blazed through a bunch of guards on his way out. Been on the wanted list ever since. Just like your guardian here.'

Janeane hadn't taken her eyes off Ramirez as he spoke. 'The seven in Johnny Seven. It's for the junkheads, right?'

'Nothing gets past you, mijita.'

'And what about OMA?'

'One-man army. Just a little joke among the lowlifes.'

'Do you know where he is?' asked Mia.

'Maybe.'

'Another outlaw for the posse,' said Janeane, looking beyond the pair of them. 'Geznet.'

'Oh?' said Ramirez with a faint smile. 'What's your speciality?'

'I learned a few things on the Spree. Like how to make rich people with extreme egos feel like they're unique.' Her gaze widened a little as it settled on the chrome at Ramirez's forehead. 'Do you have a brain augmentation or something?'

'Kind of. Part repair job, part neuroprosthetic. The repair job because someone shot me in the head. The neuro because when I woke up I could no longer move my arms or legs. I have an intracortical interface with neurotrophic electrodes that work with the striatum to decode my neuronal signals. That's why I'm not in a wheelchair. It was bleeding edge at the time, though there are better ones around nowadays. I get blue-light interference sometimes. Stops me short, causes the occasional seizure. Still, nothing I can't handle.'

'How the hell did you survive getting shot in the brain?'

He winked at her. 'Just lucky, I guess.'

Mia clicked her tongue at the kid. 'That's enough. Go and heat up some food, will you? I want to speak to Gian alone.'

Janeane shrugged. She stood and stretched, then threaded her way along the row on silent feet until she was swallowed by the dark.

Ramirez looked at Mia and she shook her head. 'What she says and what happens in reality are two different things. She's not going anywhere near Benz.'

He nodded. 'For the best. But I know a man who relishes this kind of thing. Ever heard of Disco Volante?'

'No.'

'Con artist, emphasis on the art. The Ishtar Gate theft.'

'That was him?'

'Sure. Bankrolled by an Iraqi repatriation committee to pull it off. Thousands of bricks dismantled and shipped in one night. The word was out all over town that it was his handiwork, but the polizei could never pin it on him.'

'What's his fee?'

'For him it ain't about the carbon. It's about the ballet. This dance is just tricky enough that it might interest him.'

'Unused tools collect rust.'

'What? And you think we're at the top of our game right now?'

Mia said nothing.

'We'll also likely need a technocrat,' continued Ramirez. 'But that's Disco's department, if we get him.'

'Who do we approach first? The con man or Johnny?'

Ramirez thought for a moment. 'Volante. He's the mastermind.'

She squinted at him through muted light. Tired, drawn, grey. 'Sure you want to take this on?'

He drew himself up and squared his shoulders, and she felt sorry for him because the gesture achieved nothing.

'Yes. Don't ask me that again.'

He stood, made his way along the row, then paused and turned to her. She saw that his eyes were bright with anger and was glad for it. 'Don't tell the girl,' he said. 'She doesn't need to know.'

'You got it.'

Then he was gone, and Mia Warsaw sat alone in the dead theatre. She lit a parejo, its eye a firefly in the dark, and as she smoked it she thought more about Luc Benz and what she would do when she caught up with him.

TWO

TOWNS CALLED MALICE

7 Frankfurt was all money. More so than Munich with its movetech and savant schools and neo-traditionalist art market, more so than Berlin with its hot ideas and logistics, more so than Hamburg with its port and access to cooler shores. It even eclipsed the Conurbation — the supercity comprising Düsseldorf, Cologne, Essen, Dortmund and Duisburg — and all the carbon that bled out of it. Frankfurt was money because Frankfurt had always been money, from the time of the Holy Roman Empire to the Wirtschaftswunder and on to the present, and its cerebral streets and crystalline scrapers were home to men, women, nons and fluids who worked teneight or even two-O hour days and popped sleep repressors like they were capsule dinners. There was only one motto to live by in Needle City: keep moving or be trampled.

Resler could taste opportunity in his lungs the moment he stepped onto the scraper's secondary glider platform. It was open to the elements, offering an unfettered view of downtown: endless boulevards of white facades and ballistic windows, supernova lights and sculptures. Biotecture skins perfectly tended, gen-trees turning uniform branches to the sun, Sapa terraces cut into strips of vivid green and maintained by a small army of bots. Even against the backdrop of a full-blown eco-crisis, where rewilding and proliferation were encouraged, nature in Frankfurt bent to the will of its human master. Resler had never seen anything like it. Berlin was a slum by comparison, a refu-ridden backwater whose twin currencies were desperation and chance.

Once the eight other members of the Scopo pitch team had disembarked, he followed them into the scraper and along a dusky walkway lined with bamboo trees. The people he passed were of a different calibre to what he usually saw in Berlin. Their clothes were sharp, dynamic, built for total function, and many wore pattern-rec fluid implants, just as De Witt did. When they walked, they moved fast. In their presence Resler felt like more of a fraud than ever.

No, he told himself. He deserved to be here. His work was good, and the pitch guys had told him as much. For two straight weeks he'd sourced and sculpted the best pertinents from an endless lake of data, and it was his canvases they would use to persuade Sun-woo that Scopo was a horse worth backing. He hadn't slept more than four hours at a time since Line Manager had given him the job, but it didn't matter because now his efforts would pay off. They had to.

Inside the pneumatic at the end of the walkway, Resler found himself staring at one of the pitch team's two gophers. Copper-inlay brows, purple lip rings, a blackout blouse that clung to her. Way out of step with the appearance of the other team members. When she caught his eye and smiled, he nodded and looked away and focused on the slicked hair of the man standing in front of him. He could smell the product in it. Cedarwood and vanilla, too heavy.

When the pneumatic stopped the group emerged into a corridor of tulip lamps and panelled wood polished to a high sheen. Resler hung back, letting the rest of the team go on ahead. The gopher did so, too, falling into step with him while keeping her eyes front. He was about to break the silence when she spoke.

'First time in Needle City?'

'Yeah.'

'My second rodeo. Place leaves me cold. Give me Berlin any time.' She spoke as though she didn't care who heard what she had to say.

'You don't like it when things are clean?'

'Sterile. I don't like sterile.' Her gaze flickered to his temple. 'You a data head?'

'What tipped you off?'

She grinned. Around his age, he decided. Much more comfortable in her own skin than he was.

'How do these things usually work?' he asked. 'The pitch, I mean.'

'On the level?'

'Sure.'

'We go into the boardroom, the senior suit does the pitch, we get out. Neither of us is gonna say a word. Most you can expect is to be glared at by whichever C-suite abruti is sitting at the other end of the table.'

'Oh.' Relief mingled with disappointment.

'Still beats sweating in the basement of the breeze block.'

'That's where they put you?'

'Worse. That's where I chose to be put. If you're gonna be in Hell, why not be in the seventh layer?'

'I guess.'

'What do they call you?'

'Resler. Resident data head. You?'

'Ngozi. Subterranean hardware alien.' She paused, as if contemplating something. 'Say, I guess you helped shape the package for this little jaunt.'

He scratched his neck. 'I guess I did.'

'A little brittle around the edges right now?'

'Is it that obvious?'

She smiled, said nothing.

Ahead, the pitch group congregated before an entrance barred by double black Torggler doors. As Resler and Ngozi joined them, the doors concertinaed outward and the group filed into an antechamber of faux-marble flooring, strelitzia plants and gelcouches. At the far end was another door, watched over by a dark-suited assistant wearing ocular plants. Ngozi ghosted away to speak to the other gopher, leaving Resler alone with his nerves. Near him paced a man in a sharp black suit. Crisped skin, anabolic frame, the works. He halted, looked to the coffered ceiling, exhaled through pursed lips. 'Bullshit,' he muttered. When he noticed Resler watching him he shrugged a pair of massive shoulders.

'Futile,' he said.

'No savvy,' said Resler.

'New hire?'

Resler nodded.

The man's gaze strayed to the SynSult plate at his temple. 'Fracker.'

'Affirmative.'

'Tense?'

Resler shrugged. His expression sent a different message, and the man was smart enough to see it.

'No fear,' he said. 'Rapid brain dump. Tartan paint labour, box-check. Margins razor thin, Scopo zero-sum, Sun-woo circular file the deck quick smart. Savvy?'

Resler nodded and thanked him, and the man resumed pacing.

He ran the Whicolla back through his head. If he'd understood it correctly, then Scopo didn't expect Sun-woo to put its financial weight behind the company at all. The meeting was simply a formality. He'd spent two weeks killing himself for nothing. And now he saw it: of course Line Manager hadn't selected him, a novice, to lay the groundwork for a major investment deal. He'd been given the job because he'd unplugged his terminal line twice that day and he'd needed to be punished for his lack of commitment. Thankless drudge work, dressed up to look like an opportunity, and he'd bought into it wholesale.

That was the game, said a voice.

Go to hell, said another.

At the far end of the chamber, the assistant with the ocular plants stirred. 'Ms Sun-woo will see you now.'

The Scopo team smoothed their suits with pale hands, cleared throats, shared a few muttered words. The assistant opened the door, revealing a boardroom with a sweeping, minimalist table occupied solely by a woman dressed in a luminous red jeogori shirt and grey chima skirt. The man in the sharp black suit led the way. Resler conquered his desire to run and brought up the rear.

When the door eased shut behind him, the sound of the latch touching the mortise exploded in his ears and made him deaf to all conversation that followed.

***

The corpse drawer was illuminated by soft pink strip lights mounted behind galvate panels. Resler lay fully clothed on a thin mattress and stared at the Plastex ceiling that was no more than half a metre from his nose. His eye-over was off. The pitch team's glider back to Berlin had been grounded due to a dust storm north of Frankfurt, and Allison at Scopo had booked a bank of drawers in a capsule hotel close to the grey slick that was the Main river. With a rare gap in their schedule, the team, minus Resler, had headed down to the old town with its shrink-wrapped facades to drink endocannabinoid-laced apple wine and score Abyssinian tea gel caps and browse the metal girls and boys in the famous Dom/Römer Club.

Empty, exhausted and ignored, Resler muttered a command and the strip lights dimmed until the drawer became a velvet outline. He wouldn't be able to sleep. The suppressants he'd been abusing prior to the pitch would still be in his system for another week at least. He considered pinging De Witt or Esteban to lay bare his disappointment, but held off. Joel would only urge him to get back on the horse, while Ivo would tell him things he already knew but didn't want to hear. So he stared at the ceiling through irritated eyes and listened to the blood rush through his ears.

A low chime roused him. He lifted his head, looked at the entry plate by his feet, saw a red LED eye glowing in the dusk. There was someone outside.

He muttered for the lights to switch on, then manoeuvred his body around until his head was at the entry plate. He pressed his thumb to the biolock and the plate slid open, and he poked his head into the void and saw Ngozi standing with one foot on the rung of the ladder leading up to his drawer.

'Ça va?' he said, his mouth instantly becoming dry.

'Oui, ça va bien. Were you sleeping?'

'Trying to, but no dice.'

'Zizz dots will do that.'

He nodded, then eased himself out of the drawer and climbed down the ladder to where Ngozi waited. She'd swapped the blackout blouse for a deep red wide-lapel suit with contrasting triangular shoulder plates and a tape collar. The copper inlays at her brows shone under the ceiling spotlights.

'You didn't go with the others,' he said. It was a lame observation.

'They're not my people and I'm not theirs. I get the feeling you know what I mean.'

He said nothing. Just because she spoke her mind didn't mean all bets were off.

'I thought you would've been out celebrating, though,' she said.

'Why?'

She spoke slowly, as if to a child. 'Because of the deal.'

'What deal?'

'Don't tell me you haven't heard.'

'My eye-over has been off since we checked in.'

She laughed and slapped him on the arm.

'Sekhmet, man. You're gonna flip. Get this: the pitch? Ms Sun-woo liked it. She liked it a lot.'

Resler waited for his brain to catch up. 'I was told it was a dead rubber.'

'Not anymore.'

'So they're going to invest?'

Ngozi shook her head. 'Better.'

'Better how?'

She bit her lip, watched him. Resler grinned, loose for the first time in many weeks.

'Tell me,' he said, 'and I'll buy you a drink.'

They both heard the invitation for what it was. It would have taken less than a second to switch on his eye-over and find out the news that way. But that wasn't what he wanted.

'You're the one who'll need it,' said Ngozi. 'Ms Sun-woo took the pitch to heart. She's not interested in investing. She wants to buy Scopo.'

Resler leaned against the bank of tubes, his legs unstable, a hundred thoughts and questions blending into a superhighway blur.

'What does that mean?' he asked finally.

'You were the lead fracker for the pitch, weren't you?'

'I was the only one.'

'Then I hope you're ready to go to Heaven, Resler, because you're gonna be looking down at us all from your corner office.'

As she spoke, he saw her expression change. Her realisation at what this meant. That if he did go upstairs, there was a strong chance he would end up corrupted like the rest. And one day he might recall the gopher with the copper inserts where her eyebrows had been and decide to interfere in her life in some way. Then the moment passed and her expression changed again, apprehension giving way to a breezy sensuality, and she clutched his hand and pumped it.

'Well done,' she said. 'In case no one says it later. Well done.'

'Thank you.' He didn't want her to let go of his hand. When she did, he had to stop himself from reaching for it again.

'You ready to buy me that drink?' she asked.

'Yeah.' He laughed and shook his head. 'You bet.'

***

At the New Cocoon Club Resler maxed out his slate on a private pod and a bottle of mezcal, which they drank straight from jicara cups and killed the burn with celorange slices dusted with worm salt. Over jagged waves of AI-tempered algo, Ngozi told Resler about her past. The loss of her parents in the first water conflict way down south, her forced relocation to Berlin, the difficult years she'd spent bouncing between pajatso parlours and dive bars along the Mehringdamm strip, her neweuro wage never enough to make ends meet, then the studies she'd lucked into to earn the qualifications she'd needed to rise above the suck.

'I've been in their world for five years now. Guess that kind of makes me a growther. And you know what?'

'Let me guess,' said Resler, dropping an orange rind onto a plate full of them. His head was thick. Despite not being much of a smoker, he'd ordered an atomiser and a couple of vials of Djasalm on his never-never slate — the one he shouldn't be touching — and the nicotine was pulling his veins tight and making him want to say foolish things. 'You got more satisfaction tending bar and dealing pajatso.'

'Right. The cliché. But it's true. The subterraneans have way more to say than the suits. Only thing this gopher job has ever given me, other than carbon credit, is fear. Fear of missing a day, fear of pissing off the wrong person, fear of waking up and seeing a redline on my eye-over. Not that they'll be able to fire me for anything I've done at the breeze block.'

'Huh? What kind of things?'

'Oh, you know. Unplugging the terminal line, copping Zs, dead-filing data.'

'How'd you get away with that?'

'Their security is a joke. Two-layer Tectaline defence and a Westenra daisy chain, nothing more. And Allison? Dumbest AI I've ever met. Once you're inside central you can poke around as much as you want, erase vidlinks, fabricate records. With that dope plate of yours, you could shut down the whole building for a week without breaking a sweat.'

'Good to know.'

She shrugged. 'Enough about me. Let's focus on Owen Resler. You don't act or talk like a suit. How'd you get roped into this?'

Resler tried to ignore the nicotine and collect his thoughts. 'I've always had a head for data,' he said. 'Tapping into my building's central as a kid, building Vertoo crawlers, reworking Wraptstar algorithms, that kind of thing. Good enough to be scouted a few times during my studies. But I wasn't interested.'

'Why not?'

'Because when you see an eVelo barrelling down main street with ten guys all trying to get control of the handlebars, you don't reach out your hand and try to hitch a ride.'

'Neat.'

'You know what I mean. Propping up the old life when we're in full-blown climate mitigation mode is madness. It's the way they pretend everything's going to be fine or that they're doing it for society which gets me. I'd have more respect for the heads of the Big Four and all the other dwarf players if they said straight up that greed is their only motivation. And the fact that citizens continue to believe their lies about climate neutrality and all the rest? Well, they're fools and I don't have time for them either.'

Ngozi stared. Resler supposed that if she could have raised her eyebrow, she would have.

'All very pretty,' she said. 'Yet you work for Scopo. See the contradiction?'

He nodded. 'I get it. I'm the worst kind of hypocrite. Before Scopo I was with an underground group. A cell down in Teltow cooking up prediction models that could be used to prove big polluters with a clean image were falsifying their data. Turned out Athos was bankrolling us from the start. Their people manipulated us into putting those data packages together so they could tank their competition and eat what remained. All we did was give them the cutlery.'

'Tough break. And when Athos fell, you found out?'

'Right. Suddenly the tap was switched off. Not that we were making bank, but you have to keep the lights on when you're working with tech. We couldn't do that anymore. The group disbanded. Some went further underground, a few made a try of it in the dust.'

'And you?'

'Honestly? I felt guilty as hell. There were times when I wanted to go to the roof of the Trident and take a header off it. I came close, especially after the food ran out. Welfare's no joke. Then a friend came to me with the Scopo Academy opening and I grabbed it. I was desperate.'

Ngozi eyed him. With what? Pity, disgust, understanding. The drink had loosened his tongue and he was blowing his chance.

'Sad story.'

'I'm rambling,' he said. He reached for his jicara, raised it. 'Here's to being a cog.'

She raised hers. 'Here's to doing what we have to do to survive.'

He nodded and drank, embarrassment sending blood to his cheeks. Over the lip of his mug he watched as she finished her mezcal, then looked at him in a way that couldn't be mistaken.

'Are we gonna get out of here soon?' she asked.

Resler coughed. 'Where to?' he asked, but received no response.

Outside he hailed a kingCab, and as they climbed in Ngozi spoke into the cockpit intercom. 'Take us to a short stay,' she said. 'Whichever is closest and has a room available.'

Then she was on him and he was melting into her, and neither saw how expertly the driverless vehicle navigated Frankfurt's austere streets nor listened to its warning about how the neighbourhood where the short stay was located could become rough after midnight. When it pulled up outside a two-storey nu-crete block swallowed by creeping vines, Resler paid and Ngozi grabbed his hand and dragged him to the hotel's armoured door, which opened as it read his ID chip. Then they were inside, following a set of steps up to a room with a biolock and a double tatami and no window or wet cell.

In stale air they made love. Both were drunk and tired, but their movements were frantic because they knew this was a night snatched from the growthers, an event so unusual as to be almost unique. They found within one another the things each had been looking for—

softness, understanding, authenticity — and when they were done they lay there, breathing hard, with sweat on their skin and satisfaction in their hearts.

***

Later, as Ngozi slept, Resler went down to the hotel lobby and emerged into a cobalt dawn. Foot traffic was still light, but there were more eVelos on the road than there had been an hour previously. The smell of atomised tobacco clung to the threads of his shirt. His head was thick, his throat raw. He checked his work account via his eye-over, but no one from Scopo had reached out during the night. He didn't know what it meant, if it needed to mean anything at all. Now, removed from the excitement of Ngozi, the doubt was beginning to creep in. The pitch team could claim the coup for themselves; after all, they were the ones who had sold the firm to Ms Sun-woo. Line Manager could also take the credit for assigning him the task in the first place. And perhaps the deal would fall through. Or maybe the higher-ups would call it for what it was, a fluke, and he would be passed over until he proved himself a second time. Things weren't anywhere near as clear-cut as they had seemed back in the New Cocoon Club.

He rubbed each eye with the heel of his hand and yawned. They needed to get back to the corpse drawers before the other team members woke up and started asking questions. That meant he had to go and wake Ngozi.

A notch blinked on his eye-over. Scopo ping, C-Suite seal. When he opened it, the synthesised voice message that it contained couldn't have been more to the point: *Sun-woo Holdings coordination meeting with lead data fracker. Thursday, ten-O-O sharp.*

There it was. Lead data fracker. An acknowledgement.

As he crossed the lobby again, Resler tried to slow his breathing. Maybe now, he thought, things would come good. Maybe now he would be in a position where he could change things, just as he'd envisioned back when he'd first started tinkering with data as a kid. He would prove to Ina and Esteban and all the rest that he'd been right to take this path.

He was about to make the system work for him.

8 Charlie's was a blind tiger beneath the old East-West Berlin crossing point, its phantom line watched over by holographic soldiers barking stock commands in German and Russian. It occupied a snarl of mothballed nuclear bunkers that had been turned into dance floors, darkrooms, drug pits and AR cells. The place had never been busted by the authorities because the man upstairs didn't know about it. Plates, trackers, augmentations and handhelds had to be turned off before descending into Charlie's embrace. Its clientele was a mix of artists, rewilders, bohemians and intellectuals, each as nihilistic as the next, and once inside they tended not to emerge again for days.

Mia Warsaw had never heard of the place. Janeane had.

'A suit took me once,' she said, flanked by Mia and Ramirez. They stood alone in a dim street a few hundred metres from the crossing point, in front of a store wrapped in a security shutter. Mitte was a limb of the city that slowly died after dusk, the lightwalls switching off at midnight. 'Some big art guy on business from money city. Sekhmet, was he fat. Paid my release for a day and a night, which didn't come cheap. We went off grid, made our way into the U5 tunnels with a couple of ronin so he could dig the Cornish murals.'

Mia watched the kid as she talked. An overhanging strip spat out light that painted her a pale blue. Her platinum hair was scraped back and up in a Kanagawa wave and she wore what looked to Mia like an assortment of buckles and straps under a vinyl jacket. Sometimes the kid seemed like she was from a different planet.

'All day long the fat man kept talking about the Reichshof. Know it? Everyone does. Guess he was planning to work through a few kinks with me there, only he didn't get the chance, because when we made a stop at Charlie's I dosed his drink. He barely made it out before he collapsed. I skipped after that, hauled ass back to my window. Never heard from him again. Maybe his heart gave out while he was under.' She shrugged.

'You've lived some, haven't you?' said Ramirez. Clad in a black short-sleeve knit, black pants and boots, the grey at his temples and in his beard seemed to glitter in the quiet light.

'Sure,' said Janeane. 'But living on my own terms is something I'd like to do more of.'

'Amén a eso, mijita.'

Mia ran her hands over her tac-suit, checked everything was locked down. Her shoulder ached. 'Shall we do this?'

'Absolutely,' said Ramirez. He led them into an alley adjoining the street. The ground was covered in trash, illegal single-use. Further along were metal bins on wheels that leaked foul liquid onto cracked concrete, and it was in front of one that Ramirez halted. With both hands, he manoeuvred it aside to reveal a fingerprint sensor built directly into the wall. When he thumbed it, there came the sound of metal on metal and the bin next to him opened, its metal face rising like a gull wing to reveal a cramped alcove. A barely-there diffuser gate hummed quietly.

Janeane whistled. 'How much did the printcred cost you?'

'Enough,' said Ramirez. 'Switch off your augs if you got them and let's get inside.'

The kid sauntered through the diffuser into the alcove.

'After you,' said Ramirez, motioning to Mia.

She took a final look along the alley, then joined Janeane in the alcove. When Ramirez slipped inside, the gull wing closed shut, leaving them in momentary darkness. There was a grinding noise and a jolt and the floor began to descend. A light switched on, revealing un-treated walls held back by graphene nets.

Mia balled restless hands by her sides. This wasn't her style. Charlie's contained too many unknowns, and she had no weapons to deal with them. Ramirez had warned her about the club's zero-tolerance policy, said that a concealed carry meant a mindwipe or a plain old slug to the back of the skull. And their sensors were top spec, as good as the ones installed in the Nerthus towers. Mia supposed it meant no one other than security was armed, but that didn't mean she had to like it.

The untreated walls gave way to a round chamber adorned with ultra-bright décor. Murals, signs, slogans in Sütterlin script, streaks of fluorescence that merged and split apart. The elevator locked into the chamber floor and as they stepped out Mia found herself looking at a huge man who lounged on a raised throne next to a closed Torggler door. His eyes were heavy with shadow, his lips a perfect bow of pea green. Strips of golden silk were wrapped tightly around his sculpted body.

'What do you seek?' he asked. His voice was deep, synthesised.

Mia spoke first. 'We have business.' She felt Ramirez stiffen beside her.

The man glared. He crossed tanned shaven legs that disappeared into thigh boots and shook his head. 'Not here.' He gestured toward the elevator, his command for them to leave.

Mia frowned, sized him up. He was tall, over two metres, and powerfully built. Without a weapon she wouldn't be able to take him.

Then Janeane spoke. 'Chotto matte, monsieur. You didn't ask what kind of business.'

Pea-green lips made a pout. 'And so?'

'We're here to dance and be free. That's our business.'

'Are you certain of that?'

'In this reality? You bet.'

The man's demeanour changed. 'Have you been here before?'

'Yes. Run my ID if you wanna check.'

He shook his head. 'You know the rules?'

'No augs, no tech, no discrimination, no corp talk, nothing without consent.'

The man nodded. He spoke a command that was inaudible to them, his throat mod lifting the frequency well beyond the boundaries of human hearing, and the Torggler rolled open and the music and the heat and the smell of sex and synth-smoke and cheap alcohol stole into the chamber. Janeane took the lead, blowing the man on the throne a kiss before she skipped through the door, and Mia and Ramirez followed her.

***

It was a warren inside. Twisting tunnels connected caverns in which painted bodies pulsed to chaino, while in smaller alcoves, away from the pounding music, pleasure seekers lounged on gelcouches and smoked Djasalm cigarettes to take the edge off their chemical highs. With plants and cosmetic augmentations having been killed prior to entry, all bodies and faces were old-world dark, and blue ceiling spots and the soft red glow of dispensers and roller-servers were the only sources of light.

Concrete steps took Mia, Ramirez and Janeane down two levels to where the air was even thicker. Men, women, nons and fluids brushed past them as though they didn't exist. Janeane flitted ahead and disappeared before Mia could call for her to wait, and when she heard her name being shouted she turned to find Ramirez lingering in the entrance to a vacant alcove. She shouldered her way back through the crowd, hearing the discontent in the voices of those around her, and felt her body sweat inside her tac-suit.

In the alcove, Ramirez eased himself onto a defective gelcouch with his eyes screwed shut. Mia crouched beside him, making sure to keep a watch on the entrance.

'You okay?' She had to shout to be heard.

'Just a flash. It'll be over in a minute.'

'The kid took off.'

'She'll be fine. Charlie's is made for her generation.' There was a sheen on his forehead and neck and the salt-and-pepper hair was plastered to his scalp. He wiped his mouth with the back of his hand.

'Where would Volante be?'

'In a place where he can be seen and adored.'

Three women with ritual scars across their cheeks stumbled into the alcove and sized up the two people dressed in black. They turned and left without a word.

'Lucky,' said Mia, 'I get the feeling we aren't welcome.'

Ramirez gave a dry laugh. 'They don't like outsiders. They can smell it on us.'

'What's the problem?'

'This is their sanctuary. We're breaching it, reminding them of the world upstairs. Best thing we can do is to keep our eyes on the floor and not draw attention.'

With a grunt he rose from the sofa and took a box of pills from a pocket at his chest and popped one. 'There's a big cavern at the end of this tunnel. It's where the VIPs have their fun.'

Mia frowned. 'I thought the idea was that everyone gets the same treatment.'

'Si, claro. But like on any farm, some animals are more equal than others.'

They plunged back into the crowd, and now Mia moved with the people instead of against them. This could have been her destiny, she realised. Just another dissenter for whom revolution amounted to a word, driven underground to chase chemicals and forget the reality being shaped by people whose names were known by all. Instead, she'd taken a stand, first learning from men like Ramirez how to shoot and how to survive, then putting her convictions to the test. She hadn't wanted to become a mercenary, had wanted only to send a message, but that had changed after Bülow, the transport minister, had accidentally taken a piece of shrapnel to his brain while she'd been holding him hostage. For a while the Abbot, a doctor turned freedom fighter, had offered her the glimpse of a different path with the Vanguard, but the Abbot was no more. So now here she was, in the pleasure trenches with the dissenters but not part of them, seeking a con artist to help her pull off a killjob so she could pay her debt to Mantis and the rest.

As Ramirez had described, the tunnel opened into a high-ceilinged cavern with a sunken bar at its centre. Surrounding it was a dance floor where lost souls submitted to one another or swayed to themselves. The floor was overlooked by two circular platforms, each of which had a corrugated metal staircase blocked by an electrified gate leading up to it. Mia and Ramirez regrouped at the sunken bar, where a bare-chested tender pinned them with a quizzical eye. Ramirez ordered two waters and paid with the touch of a credit slate.

'You see him?' asked Mia.

'Platform on the left. El anciano.'

She followed his gaze. It wasn't hard to identify the con artist. Disco Volante was a fat man with thinning grey hair who wore a static beige coat over a black shirt and a red silk cravat. His features were refined, soft, untouched by hardship. He lounged on a plush seat with his feet on a low tempered glass table, holding court to a latex-clad man and woman half a century younger than him.

'Joder,' said Ramirez, tightening the grip on his water bottle. 'I wouldn't want to go three rounds with his boy.'

Mia shifted her gaze and became cold. Sitting opposite Volante was what she took to be the old grifter's ronin. Two metres high and rising, anabolic muscles that were perma-tense, plates of metal along the forearms, chest inlays, ports, biojacks, the whole package. Drab grey utility pants covering his legs, empty dual shoulder holsters the only garb on top. In contrast to the battleground of scars that covered his body, the man had a seraphic face with no visible augmentations. The combination was an unsettling one.

'Recognise him?' asked Mia.

Ramirez shook his head. 'I'd say ex-military. Colossus is definitely edging the three-O cut-off point. Augmented to the gills.'

Mia didn't respond. The man didn't need to go anywhere armed; he was already a weapon. She clicked her fingers and the tender glared at her but came anyway.

'Yeah?'

'Baijiu. Bottle.'

When he brought it, she looked at Ramirez.

'You thirsty?' he asked.

'Pay the man, Lucky,' she said.

While he did as she asked, she took the bottle by the neck and pushed her way through the bodies that pressed against each other on the dance floor. She halted at the electrified gate that blocked the way to Volante's platform and shouted the con man's name. Volante and the ronin turned their heads toward the source, the latter rising from his seat, and Mia saw he was even taller than she'd estimated. His eyes were nebulae that took in her face and the web of scars at her exposed shoulder and the bottle in her hand, and he moved to block Volante from her line of sight. Then a flicker of recognition crossed Volante's face when he saw Ramirez push his way through the crowd and he muttered something to the ronin, who took his seat again with evident reluctance. The electrified gate died, and Volante beckoned for Mia and Ramirez to come up.

At the top of the steps Mia paused and listened. Something was dampening the music. Aural gauze cocooning the platform, maybe. She glanced from Volante to the ronin to the man and woman who wore looks of hazy confusion at the disruption. There was no trace of fear on Volante's face. And why would there be, she thought, when he had an executioner in his corner? She felt Ramirez behind her, heard his laboured breathing, knew that if anything happened he would likely be of little help.

'You're Mia Warsaw,' said Volante simply.

Mia said nothing.

'And it seems we have a mutual acquaintance. Gian Ramirez, my most felicitous of friends. It's been far too long. Here to briefly escape the horrors of this anthropogenic existence?'

'Not exactly, Disco.'

'I see. I have a question that may betray my lack of manners, but I would be remiss not to ask. Should I be worried that a thief and a—what is the best way to put it?—a soldier of fortune have plumbed the depraved depths of Charlie's to track me down?'

The ronin stared at Mia. She held the bottle of baijiu tighter.

'No,' said Ramirez. 'You have nothing to fear, Disco. That is my word.'

Volante turned to his man. 'You see, BB. Words trump ultraviolence ninety-nine percent of the time. Mr Lucky here is a friend and his word is worth its weight in carbon.'

The ronin didn't move an inch. His eyes remained on Mia.

'So,' said Volante, rubbing soft hands together and resting them on his ample lap. 'What brings you here?'

'A job offer,' said Mia.

'Requiring your skills,' added Ramirez.

'You're aware I am effectively retired?'

'Sí.' Ramirez glanced at Mia. 'But that's only because there were no longer any jobs big enough for you.'

Volante raised an eyebrow, then turned and clapped his hands at the latex-clad man and woman sitting across from him. 'My dears, I'm afraid our paths must diverge. I do trust you have enjoyed yourselves. Perhaps we shall meet again some day.'

The man and woman remained seated, their altered minds slow to catch up. BB stood, and he had to duck his head to avoid the pentangle light that illuminated the platform.

'You heard the man,' he said. His voice was soft, childlike. 'Leave.'

They rose and stumbled to the stairs, leaving drinks and pills and vials scattered across tempered glass, and when they reached the dance floor the gate became electrified again.

Volante watched them go. 'How large and varied the corporeal buffet remains even in my advanced years.' He gestured at the vacated seats. 'Do make yourselves comfortable.'

When Mia sat, she made sure she was facing BB. She placed the bottle of baijiu on the table.

'Kind of you to bring refreshments, but as you can see we have plenty,' said Volante. He smiled, the only relaxed figure on the platform. 'And so. Your job.'

Ramirez glanced at BB. Volante caught the meaning.

'BB is with me, Gian. I trust him with my life.'

'What's his deal? A savant?'

'Far from it. BB is the product of the Prince Consort's Own, a failed British eugenics programme,' said Volante. 'He was to be the tip of the spearhead of the new empire. We all know how that turned out. Still, their loss was his gain. Heightened senses, speed, agility, strength and pain tolerance.'

'See much of the civil war?' said Ramirez, addressing the ronin directly.

'Enough,' said BB. His face was unnerving in its perfection.

'Did you get out before they locked down the island?'

'Why so many questions?'

'Politeness never killed anyone.'

'No, but I've been known to do so.'

Volante pulled a handkerchief from his jacket and mopped his brow. 'Now, now, boys. I'm all for peacocking, but only if it's in a spirit of enjoyment. So play nice. BB, these people just want to get to know their potential new business partner. That's not too much to ask, is it?'

Mia watched the ronin. Every fibre in his body was tense and ready to go. She shifted her weight, testing the water, and his attention was on her straight away.

BB spoke without looking at Ramirez. 'I flew a Gossamer fixed-wing out of London before the nationalists toppled the government.' He lifted a forearm to show off a steel polymer graft surrounded by hard flesh. 'They strafed me with everything they had on the way out. I nearly lost both my arms guiding the Gossamer down into Le Havre. Rearranged my insides, too. The docs had to take me into max-aug territory just to keep me alive.'

Volante reached for a bottle of Chateau-Pont resting in an ice bucket and poured three glasses. Neither Mia nor Ramirez took one. 'Scientists all over the land are desperately searching for ways to make human beings more resilient to endo-electronics and augmentations,' said the con man. 'There must be a reason why the body shuts down when foreign bodies exceed thirty percent, but not even the smart AIs at the Big Four have the answer. Can you imagine the furore if the threshold was raised to thirty-one percent?' He raised his glass to the light and studied the ruby-red liquid. 'In my opinion it is only a matter of time before we smash through that particular ceiling, though I fear I shall not be around to see it.'

'Perhaps three-O isn't a bodily limitation,' said Ramirez. 'We weren't meant to be machines. Maybe it's the spirit saying 'no more'.'

'Who knew you had a theological streak within you, Lucky? I like it.'

Ramirez tapped his head. 'Ain't like I don't have my own chrome dome.'

Volante nodded and drank the Chateau-Pont. 'And so back to your job offer. Speak freely. Our elevated status excludes us from being overheard.'

So it was an aural gauze, thought Mia. That didn't mean their conversation wasn't being put to tape, and dropping names was never smart anyway. 'We're going after an executive who specialises in deep carbon offset,' she said. 'His father's a head honcho in Berlin. This exec has been slicing up girls at his penthouse on Potsdamer Platz, and that only ends when he stops breathing. But it's not a simple cleaning job. It has to look natural.'

'I believe I know to whom you are referring,' said Volante. 'I've heard the rumours. Is this about the money or the man?'

'Does it matter?'

'I suppose not. But an opportunity to understand what motivates Mia Warsaw is no quotidian matter.'

'My reasons are my own.'

Volante smiled, and the fleshy face became softer still. 'Very well. What is the reward?'

'A thousand stacks of carbon credit. Equal split to all.'

The old man whistled. 'A plentiful sum. The benefactor is guaranteed to pay?'

'The code to the account is locked behind a Mercy door deposited with an Epsilon holdman. If we do the job and the client reneges, the holdman will open the door and give us the code. If she dies, same scenario.'

Volante nodded and looked beyond the platform to the massed ranks below. 'A delicate job,' he said, more to himself than anyone else. 'Requiring a steady hand to guide it.'

Mia watched him. So far she'd seen bluster, ego and little else. Gian had vouched for him, but Gian was in a corner and a man like that was more willing to take risks. Pull the plug, said a voice. Cancel the contract with Lulu's mother. There are other ways to work off what you owe.

None that would settle her debt in one swoop, though.

BB spoke. 'Disco? May I speak?'

'Great empires are not maintained by timidity, my boy.'

'Do we need this?'

Volante frowned. 'What else would you propose we do with our time? Shall we be forever enslaved to cheap intoxication and the temptations of the flesh?'

'Why place yourself in harm's way?'

'Because therein lies the thrill. How else to find satisfaction on this burned-out husk of a planet? Besides, I have you to watch over me.' Volante turned away from BB, looked at Ramirez and Mia. 'I would expect everyone to do as I ask. No questions, no overrides, no vetoes. I don't work that way.'

'You're the maestro,' said Ramirez, telling the man what he wanted to hear.

'I also want twenty-five percent of the payment upfront. No negotiations.'

Ramirez glanced at Mia, who nodded. 'Done,' he said.

'And BB comes along, too.'

'Whatever helps you sleep at night,' said Ramirez.

'A final thing: if I don't think the job can be done, then I walk. And I keep the twenty-five percent.'

Mia nodded again. 'Fine.'

Volante beamed. 'Then, and I say this with no little fanfare: you may provisionally count me in.' He made a point of looking at BB, who grimaced.

'We don't need this,' he said. There was a pleading tone in his soft voice.

'Necessity's role in this scenario is negligible, my boy.'

'Disco.'

Volante waved a pudgy hand. 'I'm afraid to say you're embarrassing me. If you're unable to respect my decision, you may go back to the penthouse and wait for me there.'

As BB stared at Volante, Mia saw the anger rippling under the surface of the ronin's skin and wondered how the old man could remain so calm. But Volante had evidently played the game before, because after a few moments BB's eyes dulled and his shoulders dipped.

'I would prefer to stay with you.'

'Good,' said Volante. His hand touched BB's cheek, as if comforting a child. 'We have nothing to fear but fear itself.'

Ramirez watched them and shook his head. 'You boys are loco.'

BB's hand shot across the table and wrapped itself around Ramirez's wrist before he could react. He jerked Ramirez forward enough to grab him by the neck and push him down against the table.

'Don't call me crazy,' he said softly.

Moving on instinct, Mia swept up the baijiu and cracked the cap and flicked the bottle, and a stream of alcohol leapt across the table and doused BB. In the same movement, she pulled her lighter from her pocket and clicked it and a purple cross danced between two poles. BB didn't move. Ramirez remained pressed against the glass, powder taking to the air as he struggled for breath.

'Human skin burns quick in alcohol,' she said.

'Not his face,' said Volante, and for the first time Mia saw that he was scared.

BB smiled and the table erupted. Ramirez flew backwards, onto the platform floor, and before Mia could do anything the lighter was slapped from her grasp. BB loomed over her, muscles jumping, and she was frozen because he'd moved too fast for her and now she had no play.

'What now?' he asked, the voice more childlike than ever.

Then the easy malice left his face and he became rigid, and Mia watched as a delicate arm holding a blade curled around his neck.

'Better be cool, ami,' said Janeane, standing on the chair behind BB. Her eyes met Mia's and she winked. Her hair was wild, her skin smeared with glitter and kohl.

'Don't you dare deface him, little girl,' said Volante, his eyes on the blade.

'So tell him to be cool, old man.'

'BB, calm yourself.'

BB remained rigid, his eyes burning into Mia's.

Volante's tone became more insistent. 'Billy, please. This isn't necessary. Give yourself a relaxant.'

BB blinked, as if waking from a deep sleep. His shoulders dipped and the tension left his body. He looked around the platform. 'The man called me crazy. It set me off.'

'Please now remove the knife from his throat,' said Volante.

The blade disappeared into a textile fold and Janeane jumped down from the seat and offered a hand to Ramirez, who was still lying on the floor.

'Miss me?' she asked.

Ramirez clambered to his feet with a groan and massaged his neck. 'Sure did.'

Volante watched Janeane. 'How did you get up here, girl?'

The kid pointed at the ceiling. 'Ain't so difficult to shimmy along those pipes if you can balance. I saw you all getting cosy, thought I'd come and say konbanwa.'

Volante dabbed his brow with his handkerchief. 'What's your name?'

'Janeane,' she said with a mockbow. 'Family names are overrated. I'm with Mia. You're Disco Volante?'

'At your service,' he said, his consternation giving way to faint amusement.

'And this hunk's your bodyguard?'

'Something like that.'

'No hard feelings, monsieur,' she said to BB. The ronin nodded, his gaze placid, an automaton in standby mode.

Janeane turned to Mia. 'Are we on?'

Mia hesitated. Gian was fading. Volante thought he was the star of a kino product. BB was beyond unstable. And she'd just allowed herself to be outmanoeuvred with ease. But when she looked at the kid who had tamed a giant and saw the ghost of another girl hovering above her, she knew there was only one answer.

'We're on,' she said.

9 The meeting was set to take place at any time between seven and tentwo, so to avoid getting caught in the morning meat press Resler made his way to the Natelligence campus in the milky rheum of dawn. After returning from Frankfurt he'd briefly considered taking a loan from Joel DeWitt to buy a dynamic suit, but instead he'd settled for having his static threads drycleaned and his brogues buffed to a mirror shine in a salon in Little Hanoi. Too nervous to eat or drink, his stomach was tight and sour by the time he stepped off the mono and into the tunnel to Scopo Tower. His duffel—containing his pills, a duffel and a dust mask—hung like a dead weight from his shoulder. Despite the hour, he wasn't alone on the floor conveyor, and the small crowd to which he belonged was divided between the artificially pepped and the bone tired.

With his eye-over activated, Allison directed him to the ninth floor of Hell and he followed a blue thread only he could see to a cubicle that looked like every other one he'd occupied in the past seven months. He placed the duffel in the bioceramic desk drawer and thumbed the biolock, then booted the console and settled into the gelchair. Three transparents blinked into life. He threaded the terminal line through the opening in his shirtsleeve and into the port at his wrist. Beyond the transparents he could see colleagues trickling into the office. Faces tight, shoulders rounded.

He scanned the job list. He was early. Plenty of tasks he could do on autopilot. He pulled a data cube from the stack and tried to lose himself in his work.

***

The ping from C-suite came at five before midday. Anticipation turned Resler's tongue electric, made it difficult to swallow. He put his cubicle into standby and took the pneumatic down to a crowded lobby and went to the bank of four matte black exec tubes that would shoot him up through the breeze block to Heaven. The convex doors opened as he approached, his biometrics already synced with the system, and he hopped into a tube alone and the door spun shut with a hiss.

A small screen showed the floor number in luminescent green. As the pneumatic traversed the levels, so Resler's excitement grew, and when the elevator finally halted he was ready to experience his first taste of Heaven. He emerged on unsteady legs into a plush lobby of bamboo and laser-cut stone. The only furniture was a sweeping Løvgren boomerang reception desk that cost eight times' Resler's annual salary, attended by a man of indeterminate age who had been auged to the gills. Red-orange oculars, terminal spike in place of his right index finger, cheek inlays, polymer hair swept up and around the skull like a cyclone to hide the many incision marks and scars that came from being repeatedly chipped. Resler made his way over to the Løvgren, trying to work some saliva around his mouth before he spoke.

'Hello. I have an appointment.'

The receptionist stared at a spot ten centimetres above Resler's head. 'Name.'

'Owen Resler.'

'Voice match.' A thin metal rod with a ball on the end rose from the desk until it reached eye level. 'Look into the retinal scanner.'

The red light made Resler's eye twitch.

'Confirmation. Third stage: pinpoint neural ID scan. Remove your jacket and roll up your sleeve.'

Resler tried to not grimace. 'Is that necessary?'

The man's red-orange oculars smouldered. 'Roll up your sleeve.'

Resler removed his jacket and draped it on the Løvgren, then unbuttoned his shirt cuff and folded back the sleeve to expose his forearm. From a rack on the desk, the man took a cylindrical tube about the size of his palm and pressed the end of it against Resler's forearm. Resler hissed as the tube delivered the pinpointer into his bloodstream. The receptionist replaced the tube and handed Resler a square of self-adhesive gauze, and he patted it down where a tear of blood was beginning to show. The gauze became hard and bright, and he folded down his sleeve and buttoned the cuff, then slipped his jacket over his already numb arm.

'Neural ID confirmed.'

'Satisfied?' asked Resler. He knew he should keep his mouth shut, but pinpointers were an archaic — and painful — way to make sure a person was who they claimed to be.

The receptionist looked past him. 'C-suite will see you now.'

'Nice talking to you.'

The doors at the far end of the lobby slid into their frame without a sound and Resler strode into a room decorated in the Sustainable Moderne style: cork and 3D-printed steel, one-way dynamic glass windows, more bamboo. Seated at a long low table in the centre of the space were a man and a woman. Features nondescript, no visible plants, static suits and shirts, black on white, with solid grey ties to indicate their C-suite status. Opposite them was a single vacant seat, which Resler assumed was for him.

He felt rather than heard the doors slide shut behind him.

***

'Take a seat,' said the woman. Her voice was sandpaper.

Resler did as he was told.

'You are here as an employee of Scopo,' said the woman. 'We are working tirelessly to shape and innovate the business world of tomorrow, today. We can achieve that only through the ongoing commitment of our stellar workforce.'

Resler, unsure whether he should respond, settled for a nod.

'You've been with us only for a short while,' said the man.

'Yes, sir.'

'Your test scores in your interview were in the nine-O-ninth percentile. Impressive.'

Resler nodded again.

'After successfully concluding your probation period,' continued the man, 'you were given the opportunity by a superior to compile a portfolio of pertinents that would form the backbone of the Sun-woo Holdings account pitch.'

The woman took over. 'This involved much overtime, which speaks to your character both as an autonomous individual and as a member of the team. Professional and personal growth comes from seizing the opportunities presented to us in the business arena. At Scopo, we prioritise the ongoing development of our liveware as part of a sustainable human resources policy.'

'Your pertinents were presented during an investment pitch with Ms Sun-woo of Sun-woo Holdings,' said the man. 'The outcome of the pitch was unexpected. Sun-woo now intends to purchase Scopo, whether as a friendly takeover or, if no agreement can be reached with the board, as part of a hostile acquisition.'

Resler willed himself to speak up. 'Why hostile?'

'That is not your concern,' said the man.

For the first time since Resler had entered the room, the woman blinked. 'We think of Scopo like a family. From the top of the tree through to its roots, we value stability as we make inroads into markets that are frequently marked by turbulence and uncertainty.'

'Okay,' said Resler.

'We also make sure to reward talent. This is the best way to galvanise our liveware to dedicate themselves fully to Scopo, in accordance with our mission statement.'

There was a pregnant pause as the woman stared at Resler. He resisted the urge to shrug.

'"To give human beings the cognitive freedom to make bold decisions and co-create a more efficient world",' she said.

'Oh,' said Resler. 'Yes.'

The man spoke up again. 'The company wishes to acknowledge your stellar efforts on the Sun-woo account with a bonus.'

Resler blinked. 'A bonus?'

'All Scopo employees who go above and beyond to solidify the company's foundations and ensure its continued alignment with its North Star must be remunerated accordingly, with an aim to facilitate their professional and personal development,' said the woman.

In the centre of the table a hatch opened and a robotic arm emerged. It deposited before Resler a mirror-like black card whose corner was embossed in silver with the logo of Xiu Sheng Glider. The robotic arm withdrew and the table sealed itself.

Resler stared at the card, confused.

'Mr Resler,' said the man. Resler looked up. 'Despite your exceptional performance, in such situations it is customary to thank the employer when one is presented with a bonus.'

'Thank you,' he said automatically. 'Forgive me, but what is it?'

'This is your access card for interstitial glider flights within Berlin's business zones. The card will provide you with three flights free of charge, after which you will be required to pay a nominal charge for each subsequent flight.'

'A subscription fee naturally applies,' said the woman. 'To be settled monthly. Once you key in your biometrics, the carbon will be deducted from your balance.'

Resler looked from one blank face to the other. Xiu Sheng subscriptions were extortionate. That was an open secret in the business world. 'But I can't afford something like this.'

'It is a gift, Mr Resler,' said the man. 'For your hard work.'

There, finally, he caught the tone. An unsympathetic thread running through every word. The room's recycled air no longer moved.

'Of course,' continued the man, 'you are under no obligation to accept the gift. That is your prerogative. But it would constitute a breach of your contract.'

'"Executive benefits issued by the company to the employee must be accepted in full",' said the woman. '"Failure to do so shall result in immediate termination of the employment agreement".'

'What?' asked Resler, fighting his rising panic. 'But why?'

'Because it is stipulated as such in your contract.'

'That isn't an answer.'

'Mind your tone, please, Mr Resler.'

'You're putting me in an impossible situation. What did I do wrong?'

Silence followed. Sharp, shallow breaths. Skin damp, cheeks warm. He had come as a free man and they had made him a prisoner and he couldn't understand why.

'You may take it or leave it, Mr Resler,' said the man.

He looked at the card. A polished slice of nitingalvate with a Hanzi character stylised to look like wings. Find a way to pay for the subscription. Move out of his apartment. Cut down to one meal per day. Trade in his SynSult. Moonlight as an unlicensed techie in leech town.

'I can't,' he said. 'It's not possible.'

The woman stood, smoothed the bottom of her charcoal suit jacket. 'Mr Resler, your employment agreement with Scopo is hereby terminated. An extraction technician will be dispatched to your place of residence within five working days to remove any implants belonging to Scopo and seize all other company property. We are legally compelled to maintain your technical profile for three-O days, after which it will be deleted. We now ask that you collect your belongings and vacate the building. If you refuse to comply, we will summon a security team to escort you.'

Resler stared at the woman, waiting for her pale lips to widen into a smile and reveal this was all just a joke or a test and that they had a position ready for him in Heaven, where he could do his best work and change things from the inside. But her gaze was dead.

He forced himself to look each of his tormentors in the eye. 'I'll go. You don't need to call security.'

With difficulty he rose and buttoned his jacket. He glanced at the card, a gift that was anything but, then turned and left. On autopilot, he stumbled into the lobby, ignoring the man with the red-orange oculars and cyclone hair, and on into a black exec tube that spirited him down the spine of Scopo Tower to the ninth floor and the cubicle he'd left less than half an hour before. He retrieved his duffel from the bi-olocked drawer and was about to leave when his glassy-eyed gaze settled on the console. On instinct, he drew up a seat and booted it. The three transparents flickered to life around him. There was his pro-file and the job he'd been working on, and there was the data hole he'd created in his first week to help him become more efficient in his work. Something Ngozi had said in Frankfurt about how the Tower's secu-rity was shaky came back to him now. Moving fast, he threw the raw data cubes from the job into the data hole, then buried the hole deep in an unindexed subdirectory. He logged out, shut down the console and left.

With his duffel slung over a rumpled shoulder, Resler rode a packed pneumatic to the lobby, where a conveyor waited to spit him out into a jaundiced afternoon.

***

He walked away from the Natelligence campus in a daze, barely pay-ing attention to the traffic and the pedestrians of Friedrichshain, until a tractable kid with wild hair shoulder-barged him and told him to wake the hell up. He looked around, found himself standing in the shadow of the Babel-like autonomous retail space that was C-State. Hanzi signs he couldn't understand were lit up with LEDs strong enough to hold their own against the sunlight. Across the concourse, a never-ending stream of people flowed into and out of Warschauer maglev station. The circular roof above the train guideway was skinned with green perovskite solar cells. A tagger had managed to make it up there and leave their mark, and the city hadn't yet detailed a crew to wash it off.

He needed to speak to someone. Who? Ina would pity him. Esteban would tell him it was for the best. Ngozi he didn't know well enough.

He sent a ping to De Witt, then found a place to sit among the concourse food kiosks and cheaptech hawkers. A few people looked at him, a suit sitting on the ground, but he ignored them.

It took De Witt a full five minutes to answer. A matchbox-sized image materialised in Resler's eye-over. He was in his office, facing away from the external camera so Resler could only see him in profile.

'¿Qué pasa, buddy boy?'

'You got a second?'

'What's the problem? You sound more down than Athos stock. And how come I can't see you?'

'Joel, they fired me.'

De Witt inhaled, sighed. He leaned back in his cantilevered chair until he was almost horizontal. 'You're joking.'

'No.'

'What the hell happened?'

Resler told him. About the Sun-woo account, about Ngozi's prediction, about the meeting with C-suite and the Xiu Sheng card. When he was done, he understood the whole thing even less than before.

'Oh boy,' said De Witt. 'They gave you a white elephant.'

'A what?'

'A gift you had no chance of accepting, not unless you wanted to redline your carbon balance and spend the next two-O years working it off with a debtor gang in some algae factory on the Baltic coast.'

'But why?'

'Owen, think about it from their side. Scopo didn't wanna get bought out. They were sitting pretty. Half the suits in town use their product to override their good side and make money moves. You can guarantee they've got a bunch more innovations in the works, not that a grunt like you would find out until they hit the market. The thing is this: the Sun-woo takeover is gonna lead to restructuring. Always does. And some of those C-suite bods are gonna get canned because of it. They had the keys to the kingdom in their hand and then you yanked them away and threw them in the sewer.'

'I was only doing my job.'

'Yeah, and your failing is that you did it too well.'

Resler watched as De Witt closed his eyes and rubbed them. 'Never go all in on something if you can get away with a half-job. Count on the rest of the pitch team being given white elephants soon enough. Poor bastards. No severance pay, no pension.'

'Joel, what should I do?'

De Witt lurched back into a sitting position. 'What else can you do? Better start sifting the vacancy slabs in search of gainful employment.'

'Anyone who glances at my profile is going to see I was kicked by Scopo after half a year.'

'You've got a point there, amigo. Hmm, ever thought about going travelling? I heard the dust is nice this time of year.'

'Joel.'

'You're right, bad joke.' On the eye-over, De Witt glanced at something to his right. 'Listen, buddy boy. I gotta go. Time is carbon.'

'But what do I do?'

'Let's chat later. You, me, Ivo. We'll get some food, have beaucoup drinks, come up with a plan. Adiós.'

The connection cut. There was a sickness in Resler's stomach that had nothing to do with a lack of food. He had known this would happen, right from the start. This was the way they played. And it was why he'd avoided the life of the suit until it was his only remaining option. But to have his suspicions confirmed in this way was brutal. He looked up at C-State. Go inside, find a vendor willing to print him a gun, head back to Scopo Tower and start firing. He scowled. Sure, just like the guy with the bionic spring-mount. Security would plug him full of holes while he was still on the conveyor. Then Allison would issue an update calling him a disgruntled employee seeking revenge, his former colleagues would count themselves lucky, and everyone would move on with their day. Stupid idea. Besides, he had no idea how to shoot.

A notch of light appeared in the left-hand corner of his field of view. The caller ID belonged to Ngozi. He dissolved the eye-over without answering it and levered himself to his feet. From a grease-soaked kiosk he bought a tray of fonio porridge and ate it slowly, then forked over more neweuro for some stewed peach palm. He wiped sticky fingers on his suit pants and loosened the neck band on his shirt, and when the vendor stepped out of his kiosk and lit a Djasalm cigarette, Resler paid the man too much for one of his own and smoked it down to the fibre filter.

Then he walked the two hours back to his printcube, the sun on his back and the world on his mind.

10 Acid rain left wounds in leaves, edges ragged and purple. Between cracks in the canopy the sky glowed with the intensity of a god. In the Königswald forest it was easy to lose oneself, to forget that a diseased city was busy dying just a few kilometres distant. It was one reason why government fortifications had been strung up all around its borders: to stop citizens from remembering there was such a thing as nature, and that it was beautiful.

Mia Warsaw followed Ramirez along a path that was a suggestion scratched in dirt, on the trail of a one-man army. It was uncomfortably warm. They'd left Janeane casting dummy Vertoo data nets at the theatre and ridden the creaking S-Bahn to the Pichelsberg projects, where Portuguese and Spanish refugees lived together in modular box chains, emergency housing made permanent. There they'd paid a woman running an EV-converted junker to transport them to a secluded strip of the Königswald forest, waited for two roller sentries to trundle past, then used grapnels to climb one side of the nu-crete fortification and rappel down the other.

Ramirez spoke in a low tone as they walked. 'I holed up here with Johnny one time after a taufed job. The bulls were on us all the way out of town, but we managed to lose them once we hit the bamboo temps in Spandau. Even the polizei avoid that pit if they can help it. Anyhow, something changed in Johnny once we reached the trees. It was like watching a hurricane blow itself out. He didn't want to leave once the heat was off.'

'And your contact thinks he's here now.'

'Zhao Leng keeps his ear to the ground. He says Johnny made this his permanent home. Mosquito flyover coordinates place his camp two kilometres northeast of our wall back there.'

'What if he doesn't appreciate his peace being disturbed?'

'Well. Let's hope he's in a talking mood, not a shooting one.'

Mia's hand strayed through the slit in her jacket to the Agitator slung low below her hip. 'Yeah.'

Ramirez picked up his pace. 'Hang back a little, would you? No point lining both of us up for him.'

In the quiet of the forest, the sound of their boots on hardened mud was like a war drum. Mia's shoulder throbbed. She was still on edge after the encounter with BB. The way he'd disarmed her, rendered her defenceless before she'd had the chance to think. It confirmed a suspicion she'd held since becoming injured: she wasn't as quick or as confident as she used to be. The shooting match with the defence cannon on Autobahn One, so many months past, had shaken her more than she was willing to admit. During that long, terrible night bleeding out on a dirty mattress surrounded by strangers, she'd realised she had little to live for anyway. The green machine was still running, those closest to her were dead or disappeared, and the future held no surprises. In the end, it was exactly why she'd hung on, why she'd gone into so much debt to have the whitecoats sew her back together. The fact was she hadn't wanted to go out on such a miserable note. Now there was Janeane. She'd never had aspirations to become a mother, yet here she was playing guardian to a kid who thought they were both invincible. If they were going to survive the Benz job and get out of Berlin, she needed to be the old Mia Warsaw, the one who played an angle instead of weighing it up first and then missing her chance. But that was easier said than done.

'Ay.' Ahead, Ramirez was standing stock still on the track with his hand raised and his head angled downward.

Mia stopped. Her hand found the Agitator as she scanned the trees. 'What is it?'

'Wire.'

When he took a step back she saw it. A single strand of silver hair strung across the track, visible only where the sunlight touched it.

Ramirez turned his head and grinned. 'Another few millimetres and there wouldn't have been enough left of me to put in a matchbox.'

'Guess your luck's in.'

He began to nod, but his grin became rigid and his gaze found her chest. She looked down. A red dot, about the size of a neural chip, hovered over her heart.

'Don't move,' said Ramirez.

She breathed, low and shallow. The red dot twitched, a bug deciding whether to bite or leave her be. In her mind she saw Janeane, in the theatre, waiting for her to return. She had a fair idea of where the laser was coming from, but she didn't draw and fire, didn't drop to the ground, didn't make for the trees. She didn't do anything.

There was a low whistle. Then the leaves parted and a man appeared before them.

Johnny Seven had piercing green eyes, a buzzed skull and tanned skin. A head taller than Ramirez, he wore a milspec jacket and combats and held a Göl-Tek carbon-fibre carbine between hands that trembled. Sweat beaded on his forehead. Hard scars criss-crossed on exposed arms. He looked tightly wound.

'It's me, Johnny,' said Ramirez. 'Gian.'

'Yo sé,' said Johnny. His voice was raw, low. He tapped the side of his head with a finger. 'Spider eyes have been watching you since you abbed down the wall. Who's your friend, Lucky?'

'Mia Warsaw.'

'The guerrilla.'

His gaze found hers. The green eyes were hazy.

'What's on your hip?' he asked.

'An Agitator.'

'Rounds?'

'Three.'

He smiled. 'You'd have to shoot straight.'

'I've had practice.'

'I bet.'

'We're not here for fireworks, Johnny,' said Ramirez. 'It's work.'

'And maybe I'm the contract.' Johnny's attention remained on Mia, the red dot clinging to her breastbone. Half a chance, she told herself. Better than none at all. So do it. Do it before he takes the decision away from you.

'It's not like that,' said Ramirez. 'Betrayal ain't the only currency left in the world.'

Johnny blinked. The hands trembled some more and the Göl-Tek wavered. Then it fell.

'I wish that was the truth,' he said. He looked suddenly drained of energy.

Mia kept her hand on her gun.

'What kind of job?' he asked.

'Cleaning,' said Ramirez.

A nod. 'We'd better talk.' He swung the rifle onto his shoulder, turned and pushed aside heavy branches. 'My office is this way.'

***

An invisible route through the trees led them over a generous fire-break and around traps designed to alert or to maim. Then, like a mirage, a shipping container painted green and brown and gunmetal appeared in a clearing. Camouflage netting stretched from the roof to the ground on one side, providing cover for a generator, a stack of canisters and a scud bike. Sandbags created a rough perimeter around the container, which was subsiding into the forest floor.

'How'd you get that thing over the wall?' asked Ramirez. Mia could see he was struggling with the heat.

'It was already here,' said Johnny. 'I just added some home comforts.'

The container door screamed as he pulled it open. Inside was a basic cot with a two-season bag, a few empty plastic crates, some jury-rigged tech and a couple of floating screen bars. Gelwater pouches and blister ration packs hung from one wall, a military rucksack from another. Johnny mounted the Göl-Tek carbine on two vacant pegs. When he turned, he caught Mia's eye.

'You like? I lifted it before I was discharged.'

'I've never seen one before.'

'The army ain't looking for it. Most of my unit's either dead, in vats or on feeding tubes.' He went to a switch near the cot and punched it and a fan sputtered into life above them.

'Where are you getting the juice?' asked Ramirez, pulling up a crate and taking a seat.

'Contact electrification. Artificial leaves in the trees, all around. When silicate touches organic, the leaf structure transforms the mechanical energy into electrical. It goes straight down through the tissue to the stem, and I harvest it from there. Takes a lot of leaves, but leaves are what a forest has got plenty of.'

'Did the army teach you that?' asked Mia.

'Among other things.'

Moving closer to the container walls, Mia saw geometric patterns etched into the metal. Long, sweeping, intricate, the product of hours and hours of work. Her attention shifted again to Johnny, who was digging around in an old cool box he'd produced from under his cot. He threw a can of beer to Ramirez, but when he held one in her direction she shook her head. He shrugged, opened it for himself and drank. Then he dropped onto the cot and placed his forearm over his eyes. His hands trembled where they lay.

Ramirez took a pull from his can. Sweat dripped from his skin onto the container floor. 'How's things, Johnny?'

'Some days are good, others not so much. I still see what I don't want to see, usually at night.'

'Being out here helping any?'

'Sure.' He removed his arm from his face, pulled a tin box from a pouch on his combats and threw it to Ramirez, who caught it and opened it. 'These, too.'

'What are they?'

'Hexapantoline. They make me forget.'

'How many are you taking?'

'Per day?' He shrugged. 'I lose count.'

'Mierda.' Ramirez closed the tin and tossed it back. 'Hex is serious business. Are you speaking to anyone out here?'

'Like whom? The trees?'

Ramirez opened and closed his mouth. 'Old crews, maybe. Zanosh?'

Johnny shook his head. 'Didn't work out with that guy. Accused me of something.'

'What?'

'Killing his micro-biotope.'

'You're kidding. Zanosh? As in big, bad Zanosh who once took a police sentinel apart with his hands.'

'Right. But you have to look at it from his perspective, Lucky. The leaves on that thing were crackerjack.'

Ramirez stared. Then he laughed, enough to rattle his body. Johnny smiled and drank and looked over his can at Mia.

'Lucky,' she said.

Ramirez wiped his eyes. 'Sorry.'

'Tell me about the job,' said Johnny.

'Ever heard of Luc Benz?' asked Mia.

'No. Not so good with names. Only faces.'

From her jacket pocket she withdrew a denbar tube and flipped the catch, and the glassy nitingalvate screen unfurled and became rigid, and when she held her thumb to its rear the screen gleamed and welcomed her by the false name on her ID chip. She muttered a command, and the screen's miniature four-point phased array projectors boosted a revolving plenoptic image into the dead space of the container.

The three mercenaries looked into the face of Luc Benz.

It was the eyes that stood out. Laser-focused and withering, giving an edge to a face that was otherwise blandly handsome. Benz had a wide forehead and full lips, with no visible augmentations beyond a small, high-end respirator in his throat. His hair was streaked with International Klein Blue in the style of the New York celestial set. The plenoptic was a recent one, taken at a Habanik function where he'd received an award for philanthropy.

'Pretty boy,' said Johnny.

'A sadist,' said Mia. 'Officially, he's a carbon offset entrepreneur. Off the record, he performs illegal graft and chip surgery on young women. No anaesthetic. Keeps going until they check out.'

She muttered another command and Benz's head was replaced by the face of a young girl with high cheekbones, mercury eyes and platinum hair teased into a loose kogarashi cut.

'Lulu Mao. She was a Wraptstar who had built a following with her music. Benz experimented on her and had her body dumped in leech town. Her mother is paying us to go after Benz.'

Johnny's eyes didn't blink as he took in Lulu's features. 'How many has he killed in total?'

'The mother puts it at tensev girls and women. Likely more.'

A nod. 'We had a guy like him in Lepage Company. Tercero, his name was. Carried the flamethrower in my platoon. We all ended up damaged, but he was scrambled in the head from day one. The higher-ups knew about his issues, but they didn't do anything because Tercero was an efficient mother and always obeyed orders.'

Ramirez watched Johnny through the projection. 'Sounds like they had their perfect man.'

'Absolutely. So one day we're running perimeter in some no-man's strip up near Szczecin because a bot had tunnelled an insurgent chute under the wall and the Poles had managed to get five-O bodies through before we smoked the hole. On one of our rounds we stumble on a fresh chute, but this one isn't made for insurgents. We can see that right away. The bot that made the hole is thrown together from scrap and has the IQ of a rock. It's just lying there in the dirt, cooling down. One of our guys nips over and zaps it with a Daisy, burns its cards to hell. Then we get into position and wait.

'It doesn't take long before we hear them. Voices whispering under the earth. We know it's a refugee chute, so the plan is to wait for them to emerge, then round them up and take them to the nearest camp for processing. What do we care if a few refugees run the border? They're hungry and thirsty, same as we would be if we'd backed the wrong horse. So the first refu pops their head out and it's a woman. Bag of bones, dressed in rags. We're still in hiding, but she's smart. The bot isn't moving and it's too quiet. She ducks her head into the hole and shouts something.'

Johnny paused, drank from the can until it was empty. When he set it down, his hands were trembling more than ever.

'Before any of us can stop him, Tercero jumps up and goes over to the hole. He looks into the eyes of the woman and smiles as he pulls the trigger on his thrower. This line of plasma just, like, lights her up and continues on into the hole. Tercero is laughing and pouring it on, and we hear shouts as the flames reach whoever else is down there. Out of an entire platoon of bad lifers, no one moved. We were frozen listening to the screams.'

With a shaking hand, Johnny reached into his vest and pulled out a carton of Djasalm cigarettes. He offered them around. Ramirez shook his head. Mia took one. Johnny lit them up. Smoke rose to the fan in the container roof and danced with the vanes.

'What happened to Tercero?' asked Ramirez.

'We were ordered to camp at the hole that night. Stench of meat and nitro in every breath. Maybe that was what pushed us over the edge. None of us spoke about it, but when we moved out the next morning, Tercero was in a body bag next to the refus. Stab wounds, throat and chest.'

'Who did it?'

'All of us, some of us, none of us. Doesn't matter. We didn't stop him when it would've meant something. We only acted to preserve whatever conscience we had left.' He drew on the cigarette and stared at the geometric patterns on the container wall, and Mia saw clouds blossom in his eyes.

'What do you need me to do?' he asked.

Ramirez ran a hand through his hair and it came away wet. He coughed. Between the heat and the smoke from the cigarette, the air in the container was a chore to breathe. 'Straight up? We're going after the son of one of the most powerful men in the city, so I want you to cover our backs in case anyone gets the idea to put a barrel between our shoulder blades.'

'We have two others on board,' said Mia. 'A con man named Disco Volante and his bodyguard, BB.'

'What's Volante's deal?'

'Pulled the Ishtar Gate job back when,' said Ramirez. 'He'll set up a way to get to Benz without having to go in all guns blazing. We wanna make it look like an accident.'

Johnny nodded and ground the cigarette into the floor, then stood and arched his back. He went to the door and slipped out, and Mia and Ramirez rose and followed.

The forest air was sweet and cool, more authentic than anything a bloc purifier could manage back in the city. Johnny walked over to a pit still, his back to the pair of them, and cast an eye over the water that had collected there. Around him, leaf-filled branches were wrapped in plastic and tears trickled down the false skins.

Mia watched him, saw how his fingers danced at his sides. 'One more thing,' she said. 'There's a kid. Her name is Janeane. She's with us, but she's not part of the job.'

'The mijita looks young, but she can handle herself,' said Ramirez.

For several moments there was silence except for the shush of the trees. Mia's gaze shifted from Johnny to Ramirez, whose skin looked translucent against the green. A broken soldier and a dying man. She needed a miracle.

Johnny's shoulders rose and fell and when he turned the lines in his skin looked as deep as trenches. 'The girl. Lulu? I'll do it for her. It won't take the shadows away, but I think something up there brought you to me. A chance to balance the slate, maybe.'

Mia squinted. 'One question.'

'Yeah.'

'Can you keep it together?'

'Mia,' said Ramirez in warning.

'No,' said Johnny. 'She has a right to ask.' For the first time he smiled and the lines softened and he looked younger. 'I can't promise anything. But if I find myself in freefall, I won't land on any of you. '

Mia held his gaze. Here was a man who had nothing left to lose and also little to gain, but there was honesty in his words and composure in his actions. When the time came, she believed he wouldn't falter.

'Okay,' she said. 'Welcome aboard.'

Ramirez clapped Johnny on the shoulder and grinned. 'Better pack your things, ese, and say goodbye to the trees, because we're going back into the jungle.'

11

'I need you to get some data out of a hole,' said Resler.

If metalled eyebrows could have risen, they would have done. Ngozi settled for narrowing her gaze.

'Why?'

'Because Scopo owes me. I've been on welfare before and I nearly died. I'm not going through that again.'

They were on a lower walkway in leech town, in the fleabitten lounge of a zockpooler called Lucid State that smelled of cockroaches and synthetic tobacco. The Music of the Spheres drifted through the space like an iceberg, massive yet weightless. Aside from Resler and Ngozi, the lounge contained a handful of gamers who had either maxed out their credit or were taking a break after spending hours at the short-term dream machines.

Resler had ordered a beer for Ngozi and the cheapest of the cheap barley coffee for himself. He sipped it now, wondering if anyone had ever actually drank a cup for pleasure.

'C-suite said they had to keep my profile on record for a month for legal reasons,' he said. 'They also said they'd send out a techie for my SynSult, but that hasn't happened yet. If I can get the data I stashed in the subdirectory, I can sift it for pertinents and sell it on the underground grapevine. Thing is, I can't get back inside the Tower. But you can.'

Ngozi ran an acrylicked finger around the rim of her beer bottle. She wore a studded faux-leather biker jacket over a yellow blouse, and her gold-dusted cheeks were daubed with white dots from nose to ear. She had drawn looks of admiration from the punters when she'd entered the pooler.

Resler kept talking. 'I know what you're thinking. One night in Frankfurt doesn't mean a thing. And you're right. But I'm asking because I either get that data or I'm all done. I spoke to a friend of mine, Esteban, the kind of guy who can put a positive spin on anything. Even he said the white elephant gift is business seppuku. That means I'm dead in this town. White-collar won't take me because I'm damaged goods. Blue-collar won't take me because they'll figure me for a spy or a loser. So what else can I do?'

'Go black,' said Ngozi after a pause. 'There are groups underground that could use your skills.'

He shook his head. 'Scopo will have their eyes on me for the next tentwo months, easy, if only to make sure I don't turn up at Natelligence with a gun in each hand. How long do you think it'll be before they alert the authorities once they find me rubbing shoulders with nongrowthers? No, if I'm going to step outside the law, then I want to score enough to be able to buy a new identity and start again elsewhere.'

'And you think the data in the hole is worth that much?'

She was asking the right questions, thought Resler. 'It's Scopo. They have files on half the suits in the city. I don't know exactly what I threw in there, but we're talking about petabytes of information.'

Ngozi's eyes flashed in the gloom. 'If they catch you, they won't just lock you up, you know. They'll make an example of you, turn your every day into a waking nightmare. Theft and blackmail are way worse than murder in the suit world.'

A change in her voice. Subtle, but there. Resler read between the lines. 'It happened to someone you know.'

She lifted her beer as if to drink, then placed it back on the table. 'You don't wanna hear it.'

He looked her in the eye. 'I do.'

'It was my brother.' Her voice became a whisper, and Resler had to listen hard to hear her. 'He used to work for San-Paget, a subsidiary of IG Band. Xenotransplantation research, transferring living tissue from one species to another. You know when they put a pig liver in some rich guy's body so he can keep wasting air for another couple of years?'

'Sure.'

'Olu, my brother, made a discovery at San-Paget that scared the hell out of him. He made a copy of the information and ran.'

'What did he find?'

'I don't know. San-Paget's mambo men caught him before he could get out of the city.'

'And then?'

'They turned him over to the bulls and the bulls scoured his mind. He's still alive, a pair of hands to an admin AI, but he has no cognitive freedom. I went to see him once. That was enough. I could see in his eyes that he recognised me, but he couldn't speak. Couldn't move. Couldn't do anything. He'll be working that job until his body fails.'

'I'm sorry.' There was nothing else to say.

She nodded. 'Are you ready for that eventuality? For your body to endure after your soul is ripped from you?'

Resler swallowed. 'You know I can't answer that.'

A roller tender stopped at their table and a mechanical hand snaked out and took Ngozi's empty beer bottle. A green light pulsed on its flat top. She ordered another, then glanced at Resler.

'You want something stronger?'

He shook his head.

'My round.'

'I'm good with this.'

'Suit yourself.'

The tender disappeared and the Music of the Spheres filled the ensuing silence. Resler glanced at the thin crowd. Tractable kids with red lenses, consuming content direct from Wraptstar. Blue-collars for whom each day was a hustle. Transgressors who made their own rules. Even a harried-looking guy in a suit. He wondered how they all made the time to come here. Why weren't they working? Why didn't they rue the hours and minutes they were wasting? Did they know something he didn't?

The tender returned and deposited a fresh beer on the table. Ngozi stared at it as she spoke.

'You're asking a whole lot from someone you barely know.'

'I wouldn't have asked if I didn't think there was a chance you'd help me.'

'What if I get caught?'

'If there's even a slight risk, then I don't want you to do it. But like you said in Frankfurt: you have the run of their security.'

'Sounds like you've got it figured.'

He shook his head. 'Not at all. I don't even know what I'm going to say next.'

One table over, a tractable kid turned off his retinal for just long enough to kiss the peroxide-blonde boy next to him. As they broke apart the peroxide boy caught Resler's eye and asked him if there wasn't enough entertainment in the pooler for him already. Resler averted his gaze and drank a mouthful of the now-tepid barley coffee and felt hollow. It was wrong, leaning on Ngozi like this. He had no right. And he was about to say as much when she spoke.

'Fine.'

Resler closed his eyes for a moment and offered a silent prayer to no one. When he opened them, she was looking at him.

'When you sell the data,' she said, 'you give me half the profit.'

'I don't know how much it's worth or who I'm selling it to yet.'

The copper inserts blazed as they caught the light. 'Half.'

It wasn't as though he had any other options. He extended his hand and she took it and the warmth of her skin sent electricity through him. 'Deal.'

She drained her beer in three gulps and rose.

'Are we leaving?' he asked.

'Yeah. But not together. This is business now, Owen. Pure business.' She stood over him, the biker jacket exaggerating her silhouette. 'I'll come to your place with the data tomorrow evening at eight.'

'I'll be there.'

'I know you will.'

Then she was gone, leaving Resler with his half-cup of barley coffee in Lucid State's decrepit lounge, and on his eye-over he scrolled through his index for names who might be in the market for a few slabs of hot data.

***

In his printcube in the faint orange of early morning, Resler contemplated a one-time VCF file given to him by Joel DeWitt. It was all he had in the way of connections to the city's hard underbelly. Trying to rekindle the network from his off-grid days had proven to be a dead end. His ex-colleagues fell into three categories: gone legit, disappeared or dead. He'd tried the first himself and wanted to avoid the latter. The only other option was to disappear. And for that he needed carbon credit.

The file floated in his vision, a white rectangle edged in blue. All to gain, little to lose.

He opened the VCF file and it dissolved, never to be used again, as his eye-over pinged an unknown terminal. Three dots appeared, unfurling ad infinitum, and as Resler counted the seconds his anxiety soured to disappointment because the file was a bust. Now he would have to go to Zoologischer Garten, hire a bodyguard with the last of his cash and ask among the refus for a lead. It made him sweat just thinking about it.

The three dots disappeared from view, replaced by a hard blue line. There was no vidlink and no ID. His own name and number hung unmasked in dead space.

'Speak,' said a voice that was neither male nor female.

'I have some data to sell.' He paused. 'Sourced from Scopo Industries.'

'What do you have?'

'Uh.' Resler paused. 'I don't know yet. The data is en route to me. I'll sift it once it arrives.'

'Not the most compelling deal.'

'I know. But listen, I'm a fracker by trade. I know what kind of stuff I'm looking for. Part of the terms of use for Scopo's smart adaptogen states that Scopo can harvest data direct from the client's neural link. Most suits don't realise that, so they don't put up any barriers. All I need to know is whether you'd have a market for the pertinents.'

'I might. It'll take a week to put an auction together.'

A week was a long time, but it was better than nothing. 'Fine. The data will be too hot to store at my location. I'll need a hole to store it in.'

A notch blinked in the corner of his eye-over.

'That's a link to a back channel,' said the voice. 'Unlisted. Copy the pertinents into there and I'll put them behind a Mercy door. The cost comes out your end.'

'Right, fine.' Sweat beaded on Resler's forehead. 'But what's my insurance against you simply taking the data and cutting me out?'

'There isn't any. You were the one who contacted me. You can always take your information to the Trident and try to shape a deal with one of the clans.'

'I'd prefer not to.'

'If it puts you at ease, it isn't in my interest to rip off runners like you. Otherwise, my sources would dry up pretty quick.'

'Okay.' He made the decision. 'As soon as I sift the data, I'll send it across.'

'And when the auction is ready, I'll be in touch. Goodbye, Owen Resler.'

'Wait. What do I call you?'

Silence for a beat. 'Mantis.'

The connection cut and Resler wiped his forehead with his palm. More of a toe in the door than a foot.

Still, it was better than nothing.

***

By eight-midi, Resler had received no word from Ngozi and his imagination was in overdrive.

Through the single thin slat of scratched Plastex in the wall of his printcube, he watched a heatwave cook the city. The late sun threw Art Deco shadows over kinetic pavements and stacked nu-crete. The streets were near empty save for the occasional rapidTransit bus making its rounds. No pedestrians. He brought up his eye-over, found Ngozi's profile. Then he hesitated. What if she was in the middle of retrieving the data? What if Scopo's uniforms had scooped her up and were intercepting her calls? What if — and this was the one he found toughest of all to consider — she had changed her mind? It would only take a moment to find out if she had blocked his incoming pings, but he couldn't bring himself to do it. Because the truth was too heavy to bear.

Without her he was dead.

He turned his back on the sweltering city, went to the wet cell adjoining the living space and used some of his precious water ration to wash the sweat from his hands. In the mirror he saw skin devoid of colour and swept-back black hair that was glossy from the amount of times he'd run his fingers through it. Back in the living space he spent several minutes fixing himself a cup of chicory and a plate of fortified screwpine mash, but when he took up his position on the ledge by the Plastex window he found he couldn't eat or drink. As the food cooled, he watched the last sun fall away and high-efficiency lights wink on in a display of district-wide semaphore, and tried not to be afraid.

***

It was close to midnight when a dull chime carried through the printcube. Resler had been watching red digits do their dance in the corner of his eye-over. By the cube door, a small rectangular screen was lit up in clinical blue, and as he made his way over to it he wondered what he'd say when he found a cluster of polizei automatons crowding the surveillance eye.

Instead he saw Ngozi.

He punched the comm. 'Are you okay?'

'It's honto tropical out here, Owen. Let me in.'

For a second he considered asking her if she was alone, but instead touched his finger to the node. The screen went dead. In his mind's eye he saw Ngozi following the exposed nu-crete stairwell up to the eighth floor. He had just finished putting the cube back into a semblance of order when the striplight above the door glowed and he spoke the command for it to open. Ngozi swept into the cube, smelling of jasmine and smoke and the city, and she made a beeline for his only chair and dropped into it. Resler filled a beaker with treated water and she took it without a word and drank.

'This heat.'

'Are you okay?'

'With no small understatement: I have had better days.'

From a pouch in her navy-blue overalls she retrieved a stud that Resler recognised as an Aytaç helium drive, obsolete ten years and counting. His heart jumped as she handed it to him.

'Thank you,' he said, the sentiment utterly inadequate. 'What happened?'

'I managed to copy half the data onto there. I was going for the rest when a security gate came down like a ton of bricks. I barely had time to get out of central before the whole system went into lockdown. Scopo halted all company work. C-suite brought in an outside crew to run checks on everyone, Heaven and Hell both.'

'They let you go, though.'

She nodded. 'Took them long enough. They were looking for cloud and neural-wire footprints. Didn't even consider an old-fashioned data dump onto a physical carrier. Funny thing is that I think they would've kept us for longer, only they busted a few guys up in Heaven for siphoning off data. I wouldn't want to be them right now.'

Resler blinked. Already on cloud nine, yet still they wanted more. 'So we're in the clear?'

Ngozi went to the Plastex slat and cupped her hands and looked out over the district. 'For now. But Scopo will figure out soon enough that the ink trails don't match up. Once that external crew starts digging through old profiles, they'll find your data hole.'

'You didn't delete it?'

She spun around, hands clenched. 'I wasn't expecting security to hit me like that, Owen. Like I said, I barely got out.'

He raised his own hands, palms out. 'Just a question. I'm sorry. Really I am.'

She stared at him, chest rising and falling, on the verge of saying or doing something that couldn't be taken back. But the moment passed. Her breathing slowed.

'You got anything real to drink around here?' she asked.

He rummaged around under the sink for a bottle of pálinka and poured double measures into the only two glasses he owned and handed one to her. They drank in silence, winced at the roughness of the liquid. Then he took the Aytaç helium drive to the small console and static screen next to his bed and booted it.

'Let's see what we've got,' he said.

***

It was enough. Verbatim conversations, meeting protocols, names, timestamps, dates. Case after case involving C-suite execs from Habanik, IG Band, Faber and countless smaller players throwing back Scopo's smart adaptogen by the bottle to force through ugly business decisions. Water supplies poisoned, the Preservation Act bypassed, civilians tortured, competitors killed. It was a new Wild West out there.

Resler stepped away from the console, tired and sickened but elated. Ngozi watched him, her gaze troubled. There was only a dribble of pálinka left in the bottle.

'So many deaths,' he said. 'So much greed. Ever heard of Falko Wagenknecht? Chief data scientist at an IoT provider called Ynside.'

'Yeah,' said Ngozi. 'They do security for Nerthus.'

'Wagenknecht used Scopo to concoct a test to seal twothou unregistered residents inside their homes in a block in Britz just to see if the tower's carbon-capture pads were good enough to keep them alive. They weren't. All dead within two days.'

Ngozi's mouth fell open. 'This is dangerous, Owen.'

'Tell me about it.'

He poured the last of the pálinka into his glass, raised it in a mock-toast and threw it back, then went to the console again and opened Vertoo. It took tenfive minutes of hoop-jumping to uncover the un-listed back channel Mantis had given him, and on entering he was greeted by a blank slate-grey holographic slab.

'What are you doing?' asked Ngozi.

'My contact said to copy whatever good data I had onto this channel. They'll make a Mercy door for it so it's safe while they prepare the auction.'

'Can you trust them?'

'No.' He shrugged. 'But it's better to hide it there than have a blader in leech town sew your helium drive under my skin.'

A short while later the slab was blue and the copy process was complete. On the console Resler ran a fissure program to corrupt the original data, then placed the Aytaç helium drive under his boot and ground it into the printcube floor.

Ngozi stood, her eyes on the splintered remains. 'What's next?'

He looked around the space. 'I should put some distance between me and here.'

'Where will you go?'

'I know someone.'

'Your sister?'

'No. I don't want her involved.'

Resler activated his eye-over and pinged De Witt. It was four in the morning, around the time the serious suits caught the worm.

The connection went through, audio only.

'Qué pasa, Owen? Joining the dawn set?' De Witt sounded refreshed.

'I need to speak to you. Are you alone?'

There was a pause, the connection silent between the eye-overs.

'Sure. I'm alone. What is it?'

'Scopo.'

'What about them? They offer you your seat back?'

'No. Look, I'll just say it: when I checked out, I took some insurance with me.'

'What are we talking about?'

'Data.'

'Jesus. How much?'

'Enough. And it's good. If I find the right bidder for it, it should keep my carbon balanced until I work out my next move.'

'Owen, this is industrial espionage we're talking about here.'

'One way of putting it. But I call it getting even. Scopo doesn't know the data is gone yet, but they will soon enough. I'm not going to hang around at home waiting for a repo team to turn up. I need a place to lie low for a few days.'

'Like where?'

'Well. With you, I thought.'

'Wow, Owen. Man. Tell me you've just racked a line of Krokodil and this is feng feng chatter.'

Resler looked at Ngozi. She held her hand out, palm up, questioning. He shook his head. Joel's tone was off. Gone was the easy confidence. He sounded unsettled.

'This isn't a cutup, Joel. I need help. I know I've leaned on you before, but this is next level. If they catch me with this data, they'll liquidate me. End of story.'

'For Christ's sake.'

Another pause. Resler wandered over to the Plastex slat, half-expecting to see a bull drone hovering there. But there was only the dawn and a city shaking itself from slumber.

'Owen,' said De Witt. 'What kind of data is it?'

'You really want to know?'

'Yes.'

'Different levels of misery. A C-suite guy at IG Band used Scopo's adaptogen to carve out a deal with a city exec in Dortmund and use the Hengsteysee as a dumping ground for heavy metals and other industrial run-off. A whole department at Habanik used it to pilot a new immersive reality suite where citizens could actually kill each other for a nominal fee. That's a drop in the ocean.'

More silence.

'Joel?'

'Yeah, I'm here. Listen, Owen. When did you get your hands on this stuff?'

'Why does that matter?'

'Just tell me.'

'A few hours ago.'

'And you're at your cube now?'

Resler's blood ran cold. He turned to Ngozi, motioned for her to collect her things. There were questions on her lips, but he didn't have time to answer them.

'Of course not. I'm not dumb. I haven't been there since yesterday morning.'

'So tell me where you are, baby boy. I'll have a kingCab come and pick you up.'

'So I can stay with you?'

'Yeah, sure. No problem. Where should I send the cab?'

'Joel?'

'Yeah?'

'Go to hell.'

Resler cut the link and placed a block on incoming pings from De Witt's ID.

'What happened?' asked Ngozi, who was already by the door.

'A friend just tried to cover his own skin by selling me back to Scopo.'

'Asshole.'

Esteban, thought Resler. He should've called Esteban. Ivo wasn't a growther. Ivo had tried to warn him, just a few short weeks ago, about not getting blinded by the life. So much for that.

'You need to go,' he said to Ngozi. 'If Joel alerts Scopo, this place will be crawling with repo guys.'

'There'll be a record of me coming here,' she said.

'I'll delete it. Remember what I said about learning to break into central systems when I was a kid? First thing I do when I move into any new building.'

'But even you can't erase what the street eyes have seen.' She sighed. 'Guess I can hope that once Scopo knows you stole the data, they won't feel the need to poke around reams of surveillance footage to confirm it.'

There was a new sourness in Resler's stomach. 'Yeah.'

They stood facing each other. He wanted to reach for her, but that wasn't something they had.

'Where are you gonna go?' she asked.

'I know a guy.'

'Hope he's a safer bet than the one you just put your faith in.'

'He is.'

She nodded. Her lips trembled, as if searching for the right thing to say. 'Well. It's been eventful.'

When she raised her palm and extended it, he returned the gesture and their skin touched briefly and he felt her warmth.

'Take care of yourself, Ngozi.'

'Likewise.'

Then she was gone, leaving only the scent of jasmine in the air and a spike of regret in his chest.

He went to the recess next to his bed and pulled out his duffel and stuffed it with a few items of clothing, his hackwork kit from his underground days and an old photograph of his mother, father, sister and him. Then he went to the console and sidestepped his way into the printcube stack's central system and erased Ngozi's footprint. He wiped everything on the console and, once it was clean, carried it over to the Plastex slat and opened it and pushed the machine out into the dawn. He didn't hear it hit the ground. He shouldered his duffel and left the cube without a backward glance. It, along with Scopo, had been part of an existence he'd endured like a set of poorly fitting clothes.

It was easier to discard than he'd thought.

12

The air was unmoving, cut with the smell of dirt and synth-smoke. From theatre seats they watched a large man in a linen suit and a silk cravat traverse a scarred stage. His eyes, obscured by magniX goggles, were on the many screens that floated around him, each one displaying data only he could see. He paid the people in the seats no attention, though he was the one who had asked for them to assemble.

Mia Warsaw's eyes were on BB. The ronin sat near the stage, close to Volante. He was busy cleaning a Gauss rifle that was as long and wide as his forearm. It had a black and yellow cross-hatched paintjob and HIGH VOLTAGE stencilled down the body, with a set of four cylindrical flashtubes at the rear and a vertical forward grip for stability. Ramirez had explained to Mia that the flashtubes sent a huge squirt of current through to the electromagnetic coils housed inside the body, and that those coils accelerated a ferromagnetic slug to a fatal velocity. Unlike a printshot, it produced no smoke. The only sound came from the slug turning the target into liquid meat.

Mia hadn't seen BB fire it yet.

She glanced around the theatre. Johnny Seven leaned against a peeling wall, smoking and staring at nothing. Ramirez sat with his eyes closed, struggling to get control over his latest headache. Two rows back, Janeane lay sprawled across three seats, heavy black boots propped up on the lip of the chair in front. A broken chopstick hung from the corner of her mouth like a fishhook. When she caught Mia's eye she grinned.

'Trop chiant.' She nodded toward the stage. 'What is this, an exhibition?'

'You shouldn't even be here.'

She waved Mia away.

'Hey, Lucky.'

Ramirez didn't open his eyes. 'Sí.'

'Can you get him to speed it up a little?'

'No, mijita.' His voice was tight. The heatwave gripping the city was tough for everyone, but it was worse for Gian. His meals consisted of crushed up Betaubalin in a glass.

Janeane took the broken chopstick from her mouth, aimed and threw. It landed at BB's feet. He looked up from the Gauss rifle. Her smile was sweet. 'Hey, angel eyes. How long do we gotta wait for your sugar granddaddy to stumble back into the real world?'

BB's anabolic muscles rippled like live things under his skin. His voice was soft. 'That mouth of yours.'

'Yeah.'

'Did it ever get you in trouble?'

Mia's hand slipped to her waist. BB saw it.

'Not yet,' said Janeane. 'Got a few fellas into a spot, though.'

BB took a breath, visibly relaxed. 'Mr Volante will be with you when he's ready.'

'Quite right, BB,' said another voice. On the stage Disco Volante had stripped the magniX goggles from his head and was dabbing a red handkerchief at where the rubber had bitten into his skin. 'Your civility is commendable.'

'I learned from the best,' said BB. He returned his attention to the weapon on his lap.

Ramirez opened his eyes, leaned forward. 'What's the story, Disco?'

'I am currently putting the finishing touches to a plan that combines minimum risk with maximum outcome. It may be my greatest work yet.'

'You wanna share it with us?'

'All in good time.'

'So why are we here?'

'I gathered you all to discuss a matter of security. Lucky, would you claim proficiency in manipulating building automation surveillance?'

'If you're talking about the kind of systems we're likely to come up against to get to Benz, then no.'

Volante looked at Mia, who offered him a blank stare. He turned to Janeane.

'My dear? On the off chance?'

The kid grinned. 'Oh sure. Learned all about it painting polygons for rich piyan suits.'

'I shall take that as a no.'

'Take it however you want.'

Volante's gaze wandered some more, settled on Johnny. The soldier looked as though he hadn't heard a word that had been spoken.

'Johnny,' shouted Ramirez.

Hazy green eyes blinked, struggled to find the source of the sound. 'Yeah?'

'Know how to slide and glide building security?'

Johnny took a drag on his cigarette and spoke through smoke. 'Put a dope plate on the side of this head and you might as well drop me off at the morgue on the way to the job.'

'Pity,' said Volante. 'But it is as I expected.'

'What about him?' said Ramirez, nodding at BB.

'One does not use a hammer to write a symphony.' The con man's tone became all business. 'What I need is a technocrat. No jockeys, no burnouts. Neural linchpin should be a SynSult Series Four or higher, by my reckoning.'

'You planning on grappling with an AI?' asked Ramirez.

Volante smiled. 'Perhaps. All will be revealed.'

'When?'

'When we have our binary alchemist. Without them, the play cannot go ahead and the curtain will not rise.'

Mia grimaced. The self-congratulatory tone in everything the fat man said grated on her.

'Tell me, Lucky,' said Volante. 'Does anyone spring to mind who could take on the role?'

Ramirez shook his head. 'The three names I knew are in the ground. But refu town should have one or two options.'

'That kind of attention is best avoided if we can help it,' said Volante. He looked to his bodyguard. 'BB?'

'Not my world,' said the ronin.

Mia looked at Johnny, waiting, hoping for some kind of response. But he wasn't there. His head kept dropping and his mouth opened and closed as though he was speaking, though no words emerged.

'Then we have a problem,' said Volante.

Mia rose. As the theatre seat smacked against the backrest, the eyes in the room turned to her.

'I'll take care of it,' she said, hearing the resignation in her voice.

Before anyone could start asking questions, she made for the end of the row and left the hall via a side door. A dim corridor snaked through the building, which she followed to a small room that had likely once stored props but which was now where she slept. From beneath her cot she pulled out a contraband Han Flymotic console. Mid-level tech, boosted from a triad who had been too eager on the trigger over in Zossen district. She booted the Flymotic and spent many minutes completing the ten-step authorisation process that would allow her to gain access to the unlisted channel.

She hesitated before the glowing screen. It would mean more debt. But it was her job, which made it her problem to solve. She placed the call. The Flymotic was silent, a holographic double helix the only indication that a connection was attempting to be established. Then a click and the two halves of the helix merged.

'Speak, Mia.'

'Mantis, I need a technocrat. Off grid, no tyros or husks. Able to slide and guide. SynSult dope plate, Series Four or above.'

'How fast?'

'The sooner, the better.'

'Your credit is still maxed out.'

'I know. I have information to sell if you're buying.'

A pause.

'Tell me.'

'My job is Luc Benz. Elimination. Good enough?'

'Good enough.'

'So make it worth my while.'

Another pause, this one longer.

'I have someone. Owen Resler. Graduate of Humboldt Tech Academy, nine-O-ninth percentile. Junior data fracker, Scopo Industries, made redundant five days ago for opening the door to Scopo's takeover by Sun-woo Holdings. Used to work for a grey-area hackwork contractor that folded in the wake of the Athos collapse. A city-wide bulletin was issued for his arrest this morning. He's wanted for systematic data theft. Whereabouts unknown at this time.'

'He's too hot.'

'He's what I have for you. Resler wears a SynSult Series Six. In the right mind, that'll stand up against any building's central control, Nerthus excluded.'

Mia stifled a sigh. 'Fine. What lead can you give me on his location?'

'He has a sister, Ina, office manager for the New Dawn legal clinic at Zoologischer Garten. She's close to him. I'm sending you a recent bullgrab.'

The screen changed and Mia found herself looking at a young man embracing a younger woman in the middle of a packed street. Slim build, thinning hair swept back, face pinched with exhaustion.

'Thanks,' she said.

'You got it.'

The connection cut and Mia shut down the Flymotic. She changed into a charcoal collarless shell top, non-print skingloves and high-waisted pants with biometrically sealed pockets. From a dull black case she pulled out a freshly cut Hyperion, its plastic sides filed and smoothed, and slotted it into her shoulder holster.

There was a knock on the door. Ramirez. Stiff, ashen-faced, pores streaming. He nodded toward the cot and she gestured to it and he sat.

'Mantis?' he asked.

'Right.'

'Got someone?'

'Heading out now.'

'Quick work.' He winced as he made to rise. 'I'll come with you.'

'Sit down. I'll take Johnny.'

Anger diluted the pain in his eyes. 'You think I can't handle it?'

She threw a white suncoat over her shoulders and buttoned it. 'Pick a fight if it makes you feel better, but you'd be smarter saving your strength for the real job.'

Ramirez stared at her, his jaw screwed down. Then the muscles in his neck became taut and he rubbed at his temples. 'Jesuchristo, maldito infierno. That hurts.' He closed his eyes. 'Johnny's still in the hall. He's been hitting the pills pretty hard though. Keep it in mind.'

She paused at the door. 'You need me to get you some meds?'

'A Betaubalin pump if you can get one. Pills if not. I'm running low.'

'Right.'

She followed the corridor back to the hall, deserted now save for a tense figure smoking a Djasalm that coated the room in its stink.

'Johnny.'

His gaze took a couple of seconds to focus. 'Yeah?'

'You up for taking a ride with me?'

Trembling fingers removed the cigarette from between his lips and he tossed it to the ground. 'Sure. Beats listening to the crazies in my head.'

Mia hadn't been to Zoologischer Garten since the third wave of climate refugees had come up from the south. Now the area was unrecognisable. Tents and shanties and containers and inflatables choked the streets. Illegal fires burned in makeshift pits. Garbage, unrecycled and untouched, lay piled at kerbsides and made the air taste of malicious decay. Frayed clothes dried on lines slung across the entrances of boarded-up commercial buildings. Improvised screens displayed deals and prices and odds, blared music, broadcast Wraptstar streams to people who hunkered in scraps of shade. Children no older than ten waited on corners, whispered myriad services to anyone who looked like they might have a few neweuro to spare. Mia saw it all from the window of the S-Bahn, the place they called Amerika, and kept her hand on the Hyperion at her hip.

Escorts lounged in the station foyer with their weapons of choice, playing bones to kill time. They looked up when Mia and Johnny appeared, but when they saw how the pair moved they resumed their dice.

'Hell on earth,' said Johnny as they emerged from the south exit and followed a winding thoroughfare between the hovels. From a familiar tin he took a pill and swallowed it dry. Mia blinked sweat from her eyes and said nothing. She didn't want to know what effect the new pill would have on him. He was already halfway to the stars.

Faces watched them from behind tarps and emergency sheets. A kid ran over, told them he could help them find what they were looking for, but Mia shook her head and walked on. The air was stale and static and she wondered how these people could stand the heat that the city absorbed like a sponge during the day and leaked out only at night.

Then they were through, over the line that demarcated the temporary Amerika from its permanent nu-crete counterpart, and a bull wearing the yellow livery of S13 trained its lens clusters on them and scanned their ID chips and found no discrepancies. Kinetic pavement took them past the destroyed Memorial Church and an endless raft of entertainment advertorials and touts and electric impressions, and then they ducked into a side street where cheap ink on walls broadcast political slogans and doomsday messages in different tongues. The entrance to the New Dawn legal clinic was on the left. People loitered there, and they turned hungry eyes onto the two newcomers.

A man with an Ital-tech respirator in his throat disengaged from the rest and approached. The whites of his eyes were yellow. 'Help you?'

'Help yourself,' said Mia.

The man smirked. 'Tough lady. Let's see how tough.'

His hand went to his belt, and Mia clocked the handle of the butterfly blade and stepped back. Before she could do anything else, she heard a low whistle and the man's gaze shifted in time to see tanned fingers close around his wrist. He was yanked forward and a knee found his groin and he went down. Johnny, now suddenly awake and alert like Mia had never seen him, plucked the knife from the man's belt and dropped it into a pocket.

'You want this back, come and find me,' he said.

The man lay still, breathing alley dirt. None of his cohort moved to assist him.

Mia led the way inside the building and followed hand-posted signs up a scabbed stairwell to the fourth floor. A rent-a-guard with anabolic arms, a riot baton and cheap padded armour lounged in front of a rail-mounted barricade. Behind him was a Plastex door with the words 'New Dawn' etched on it.

'Whaddaya want?' His voice was slow, and Mia saw scarring around the sides of his shaven head.

'We're here to see Ina Resler.'

'Got an appointment?'

'No.'

'Gotta get one to see Ms Resler.'

Mia nodded, then pulled the Hyperion free and aimed it at the rent-a-guard's head. 'I haven't got time for this. Open the door.'

'Better aim it at his chest,' said Johnny, already doing so with his own printshot. 'Big boy's got an endo-plate up there. It'll stop a cartridge or two.'

The rent-a-guard looked from Mia's gun to Johnny's, the consternation plain on his face.

'We ain't gonna hurt her, chief,' said Johnny. 'Believe me. Just gotta confab for a minute.'

The rent-a-guard nodded slowly. On the wall behind him was a hand scanner and he palmed it and the Plastex door rattled open. Johnny slid the barricade aside and Mia stepped past the man, then covered Johnny as he followed.

'We're going in now, chief,' said Johnny. 'You close this door after us, okay?'

The rent-a-guard nodded.

They stepped into a dingy reception area. Linoleum, LED strips, walls whose stucco was hidden under political posters and fibre-paper instructions. A family of refus warming a bench looked up in alarm at the armed man and woman. Seated behind a round desk was a reception mannequin, its silicon exterior sun-bleached and ragged.

Once the rent-a-guard had closed the Plastex door, Mia holstered the Hyperion and made her way over to the mannequin, whose mouth stretched into a vague approximation of a smile. 'I need to see Ina Resler.'

'I'm sorry, but Ms Resler has no appointments scheduled for today.' The voice synthesiser must have been old, because the mannequin sounded like it was speaking from the bottom of a pit.

'You must be mistaken.'

'I rarely made mistakes. Make, I mean.'

Johnny shook his head and went to the corridor adjoining the reception area and cupped his hands. 'Ina Resler,' he yelled. 'We're here about your brother.'

Doors opened and harried faces poked their heads out and saw the tense, tanned man with the shaven head and understood that trouble had arrived at the clinic. They retreated back into their rooms.

'Please don't shout, sir,' said the mannequin, still grinning but trying to frown.

At the far end of the corridor another door opened and a woman emerged. Young, choppy haircut, dressed in a dull jumpsuit and heavy black boots. Her skin was wan, but there was no fear in her face as she strode toward Johnny and Mia. When she reached them, she stood with her feet planted wide apart and her hands on her hips.

'Good day, Ms Resler,' said the mannequin. 'Boy, it's a hot one, isn't it?'

Ina Resler ignored it. She glared at Mia. 'Who are you?'

'My name is Mia Warsaw.'

'Yeah, right. What do you want here?'

'We need to find your brother. He stole trade secrets from his employer to sell on the black market. Scopo knows, and they're after him.'

Ina Resler laughed without humour. 'Sure. And why would Owen throw away his cushy job to do that?'

'Because they fired him five days ago.'

'Bullshit.'

'Check the slabs. A bulletin was issued for his arrest this morning.'

Ina Resler's gaze became slack and Mia waited as she used her eyeover to access Vertoo. When she gasped, Mia knew she'd found the information.

'I don't believe it,' Ina Resler said, alert again. 'It says he is to be considered "extremely dangerous". Owen? He's never hurt anyone in his life.'

'Matter of interpretation,' said Mia. She couldn't help it.

'They use descriptions like that to get citizens' attention,' said Johnny. 'It doesn't matter if it's true or not.'

'Would you like me to arrange a meeting?' asked the mannequin.

'Shut up, Annie,' said Ina Resler. Her composure was gone. She looked past them to the refus who waited on the benches, watching the exchange in silence.

'Look, kid,' said Mia. 'Your brother's in trouble and even if he thinks he's safe, he isn't. The bulls have eyes everywhere. If we can get to him first, we might just be able to help him disappear.'

'Why? Why would you do that for him?'

'Because we need him for a security job.'

'Are you kidding me? You want him to work for you?'

'It's not how it seems,' said Johnny, raising a placating hand.

Ina Resler shook her head. 'You goddamn mercenaries. You can both go to hell.'

'Hell is other people,' said the mannequin.

Behind them the Plastex door flew off its hinges and the rent-a-guard dropped onto the linoleum with the back of his head missing. Ina Resler screamed and Johnny grabbed her and dragged her to the closest door and into the room beyond it. Automatic fire from the stairwell turned the mannequin into mulched silicon. Mia threw herself behind the reception desk and an electric pain ran through her as she landed on her bad shoulder. She pulled out the Hyperion and aimed it at the doorway and fired four times, then ducked back and pushed home a fresh clip. From the offices she could hear people shouting in different languages. When she peered around the desk, she saw smoke and blood and Plastex splinters. Then came more gunfire and she ducked back into cover. Bullets shredded the desk and rounds whistled past her.

You're going to die here, said a voice in her head.

Through a hole she saw a man and a woman enter the room and step over the rent-a-guard's body. Black tunics, black pants, black boots. They moved like professionals, carried weapons only a corp-bankrolled cleaner could afford. The man kept his automatic trained on the refus who cowered on the floor by the bench. The woman edged toward the ruined reception desk, a green tac laser sweeping the area.

Mia told herself not to be afraid, not to think. She jumped up and aimed the Hyperion, and in that split second she saw the flash of the laser and knew the woman had beaten her to it.

Two shots rang out. The woman and the man dropped without a sound.

Johnny swept into the room with a hot printshot in each hand and went to his targets and checked them. When he was satisfied, he reloaded each weapon. Smoke curled around him.

'Are you okay?'

Mia breathed, willing the beating in her chest to slow. The air tasted of copper and nitro. Odd to be ready to go, only to be yanked back at the last moment.

'I thought I was done. Thank you.'

He waved it away.

Ina Resler inched into the room, her gaze moving from the destroyed mannequin to Mia to the three bodies leaking out their last on the linoleum. 'Shit.'

'They were here for you,' said Mia. She went to the body of the woman and dragged the automatic from her hands. Red digits against black carbon fibre indicated the magazine had seven rounds left. She turned the woman over, found another two magazines on her belt and pocketed them. Johnny did the same with the man, but saw his weapon was biolocked. Ina Resler stumbled over to the rent-a-guard and stared down at him.

'Benny,' she said. 'Jesus Christ.'

'We need to go,' said Johnny. 'Those were slavenet liquidators.'

'What does that mean?' asked Ina Resler, looking up.

'It means Scopo isn't messing around,' said Mia. 'You're not safe. They want your brother, and if that means torturing or killing you to get what they want, they'll do it. You need to get out of town.'

'But this is my home.' Ina Resler shook her head. Her gaze found the refus who were now picking themselves up off the floor. 'My life.'

'That was over the moment your brother ripped off a concern.'

Ina Resler blinked, looked around at the destroyed reception. 'What do I do? Oh God, what do I do?'

'You come with us.'

Footsteps sounded and both Johnny and Mia spun around and sighted on a man in a too-large hemp vest and shorts who threw his hands up and trembled.

'Not him,' said Ina Resler. She went to the man. 'Nic, get these people out of the building,' she said, gesturing at the refus. 'Then call the Alliance. They'll help you sort this out.'

'What about you?' asked the man. 'What's this about, Ina?'

For a moment she was silent. Then she brushed something from her eye and squared her shoulders. 'I have to go,' she said.

'Is there another way out of this place?' asked Johnny, keeping his attention on the doorway.

She turned to him. 'The rooftops. Then we can double back to the S-Bahn.' She nodded at the automatic in Mia's hands. 'I'll get you a bag for that. Where do we need to go?'

'A safehouse,' said Mia. 'Then you tell us where we can find your brother and we get you out of Berlin.'

'But I don't know where he is,' said Ina Resler.

'So call him.'

***

They spent the night at the Delphi, where Mia sent word to a network that specialised in smuggling wanted bodies out of the city and shrouding them in the gritty cloak of the dust. The green light came the following evening, when Ina Resler was speaking to her brother. By the time she killed the call, her body had been drained of its energy, and she had to lean against the threadbare theatre seats to hold herself up. Mia gave her a few minutes to collect herself, then came to her in the gloom.

'You ready to go?' she asked.

'How can I be?' said Ina Resler. Her voice was hoarse. 'I didn't think he could be that selfish. Stupid from time to time, yes. But not this. He claimed he didn't consider Scopo would come after me. That's bad enough, but it was the way he said it. Like it was anyone's fault but his. I told him my life was over. He didn't even apologise.'

'Where is he?' asked Mia.

Ina Resler stiffened. 'You really want him?'

'Yes.'

'Fine. It's what he deserves.'

Mia learned that Owen Resler was in a biotecture pod rented by a friend of his in Karlshorst. That was new money territory, a miniature Eden protected by bulls and private security and who knew what else. Not for the first time Mia wished Mantis had given her another name, because so far Owen Resler was indirectly doing everything he could to get her killed.

'Grab your pack,' said Mia. 'Let's go.'

With night coming down they rode a brute-forced electric bike to the city's western limits, where nu-crete overlapped with blasted earth. They parked in the shadow of a crumbling derelict, next to a tarmac road that unspooled into the ether. The structures around them were more like bunkers than buildings. Scoured by sandstorms, bleached by the sun, afforded none of the mechanical, structural or meteorological protection that kept the city proper ticking over. The few ragged people in the vicinity kept their distance when they saw the automatic cradled in Mia's hands.

'I can't believe this is happening,' said Ina Resler, wrapping her arms around herself.

'It'll get easier.'

'That's supposed to help?'

'You can come back, in time. A year, two maybe. But if you make it as far as Prestige, I'm guessing you won't want to. They have refugees. You'll be one to begin with, too. But more will come, and you can be there for them. This city is lost, no matter how hard good people work to try and save it.'

Ina Resler said nothing. Mia held the automatic and kept her eyes on the night.

A half-hour later, blue headlights pricked in the darkness. Mia hugged the wall of the derelict and aimed the automatic, but when the sinewy dodecahedral shape of a polytruck fitted with desert tires materialised she relaxed.

'Here's your ride,' she said.

Ina Resler stared at the vehicle, still mute.

Mia stepped out into the road with a hand raised and the polytruck stopped. When the wing door opened, Mia found herself looking at a familiar face. Harder, less youthful maybe, but the same insolence oozing from every pore.

'Putain,' said Faustine. 'I thought you were dead.'

'Not yet,' said Mia with a half-grin.

Faustine jumped out of the truck and embraced Mia, then stood back and appraised her.

'Wait until Mara hears about this. She'll go feng feng.'

'When did you last see her?'

Faustine scratched at her cheek. 'A month ago. I've been kicking around a camp outside Stendal for a couple of weeks running parts to a new agri-robotics setup. When they got your call, I volunteered to go.'

'And Prestige?'

'Holding its own, or at least it was before I left. We're eating well. No attacks for a while. Things are locked down tight.' She looked at Ina, who was inching into the glare of the truck's headlights. 'Tell me it's not just you and her?'

'It's not,' said Mia. 'She's coming alone.'

Faustine pursed her lips, her eyes losing some of their humour. 'Long drive from camp for one pax. You know the rule.'

'This is an exception.'

'They won't like that.'

Mia gestured with the automatic. 'Will this get them off my back?'

Faustine took the weapon, held it against the light. 'Très jolie. Where did you find it?'

'On a body.'

'That figures. But listen: what's stopping you from riding along with us?'

'I have some debts to pay.'

'So? Who's going to come looking in the big wide nowhere?'

Mia shook her head. 'There's more to it than that.'

Faustine shrugged. 'As you like.' She called to Ina. 'On y va, lady. But ride upfront with me, will you? I need you to keep me awake.'

With her foot on the truck's alloy steps, Ina paused, turned, took Mia's hand and shook it.

'Don't count on my brother to save anyone except himself,' she said. She threw her pack into the truck and followed after it.

Faustine embraced Mia again, then climbed into the cockpit.

'I'll come back any time to pick you up. Think it over. À tout.'

The wing doors came down and the polytruck's oversized wheels dug into the tarmac as it made a U-turn and headed back into the dust. Mia watched the headlights until they were swallowed by the dark, then jumped onto the bike and guided it onto a two-lane road heading east.

Toward the city, toward Owen Resler

13 When the call came from Ina, Owen wasn't ready for it. Esteban had taken him in with a few words of caution but none of reproach. For two days he'd sat in the designer pod in Karlshorst, watching the well-tended neighbourhood through a curved window. He'd barely eaten, barely slept, the full weight of his actions heavy on his shoulders. He'd ripped off a corporation, and now that corporation was gunning for him. He'd heard tales of grey-market repo units that stalked rogue suits like prey through the city, sweeping them into unmarked transports and spiriting them to their former employer for cognitive deprocessing. Until Mantis collected the bidders for the data auction and he had the carbon to build a new identity, he was a prisoner.

It was while considering this reality in the early hours of the morning that a notch blinked on his eye-over. When he saw Ina's ID he opened the channel immediately.

'Ina?' he asked. 'What's wrong?'

Silence for several seconds, no camera link. This is it, he thought. This is where it all comes crashing down.

'I can't believe what you've done.'

Her voice contained a tone unlike anything he'd heard before.

'Where are you?' he said, trying to control his rising panic. 'Are you okay?'

'You're asking me that now?'

'What do you mean? Is someone there with you?'

'Yes, someone's here. A mercenary.'

Resler paced the pod floor. 'Oh Christ, Ina.'

'Not what you think. She saved me. From two people who came to New Dawn with guns. They murdered a colleague of mine and destroyed the clinic. They would have killed me, too, if two others hadn't arrived to get me out of there.'

He tried to make sense of what she'd said, but couldn't. 'What do you mean?'

Ina's voice rattled in his head, loud and ugly. 'Cut the shit. I know what you did, Owen. Data theft. All your supposed abilities, all your moral superiority, and you use them to become a thief.'

'Who told you that?'

'You acted out of self-preservation and now I'm paying the price for it. When you stole that information, did you ever think, even for a moment, that the repercussions might be felt beyond you? That they would come after me to get to you? Or your friends? These aren't human beings you're dealing with, Owen. When are you going to understand that? Econopaths care about nothing except their own gain. Just like you.'

'That's not true,' Resler said, clenching his teeth. 'I did it to get back at them. I did it to show them they can't just cast human lives aside like they're nothing.'

'If only you were so noble. That's how you'd like people to see you. But I know you better than anyone, big brother. When you went underground, you did it for the thrill. You thought you were better than everyone else. You wore a look in your eye that had nothing to do with revolution or justice. It was about gilding your own ego. This is no different. I'll tell you why you did it: it was because you made the wrong choice going to work for the suits and you didn't want to accept that they'd won. That they'd outsmarted you. You've always got to be the smartest one in the room, don't you, Owen? But the fact is your life is worth no more than anyone else's. Now you've taken mine from me. And a man is dead, which means you have blood on your hands.'

'Ina,' said Resler, barely able to speak. He stared hard at the window. Drone lights winked back. 'I didn't want this. I didn't think this would happen.'

'That's right,' said Ina. 'You didn't think.'

'Look, I'm at Evo's place. Come here and we can talk properly.'

More silence. He checked the connection, saw it was still strong.

'I only hope Ivo won't end up regretting his decision,' said Ina. 'I'm leaving Berlin, Owen. That's the option you've left me with.'

'What? To where?'

'Into the dust, where I'll be safe.'

'How can that be safe?' He was almost shouting now. 'You don't know anyone. You can't just go out there.'

'You do this to me and still you presume to tell me what to do? You really are like them, aren't you? You belong in their world.'

'I don't. I hate them just as much as you do.'

'I know you believe that. And that's why you'll never understand. I have to go.'

'Please,' he said. 'Don't. I can fix this. I can find a way out of it. Don't just disappear on me.'

'Have a nice life, Owen,' she said. 'You've earned it.'

Resler clutched at his chest. 'Wait.'

The connection cut. Ina's ID disappeared from view. Frantically, he tried to call her back, but his pings bounced. Blocked, unanswered.

She was gone. His only ally in a callous world, turned against him because of his selfishness and self-sabotage. He looked around the pod, hoping this was just a dream, that the last two years hadn't happened, that when he woke he would be back off grid, only this time his work would have purpose and Ina would see him for the person he had always tried to be.

On leaden legs he went to the couch and sank into it and put his head in his hands and sobbed.

***

'Owen?'

Resler looked up, brushed the wetness from his face. Esteban stood in the doorway, clad in a sleeping robe.

'Yeah.'

'What happened?'

In a listless voice he covered the beats of the conversation with his sister. Without speaking, Esteban went to the pod's compact kitchen, where a dispenser prepared two cups of coffee in clay mugs. He brought one to Resler, who cradled it between pale hands. The coffee was real, not ersatz, and he hated himself for taking comfort from the scent.

'You know where she's headed?' asked Esteban.

Resler shook his head.

'Give me her ID and I'll call her.'

Another shake. 'Not now. Not until she's cooled off.' He put the mug down and groaned. 'I didn't think they would come after her.'

'Different game you're playing now, amigo.'

'You think it was Joel who told them?'

'Forget Joel,' said Esteban. 'He's a shark. Has to keep moving or he'll die. Besides, he'll be under suspicion now. He got you the Scopo interview, right?'

'Yeah. Sekhmet. What if they do something to him?'

'Don't tell me you feel bad? He was ready to sell you out.'

'And you? Why are you helping me?'

'Because I'm your friend, Owen. That still counts for something, at least for me.'

Resler nodded, closed his eyes, saw Ina running frantically through sodium-tinted streets with a pack of hunter killers at her heels. No, he told himself. She can handle herself. You're the one who's taufed.

'So what now?' asked Esteban, his voice soft. 'That black market contact of yours been in touch since you uploaded the files?'

Resler answered in a monosyllable and hoped the next question wouldn't come.

It did. 'Think you've been ripped off?'

'There would be a certain poetry to it, wouldn't there?'

'Maybe. But listen. You're not safe here, Owen. Not now. We need to get you out.'

'Where can I go? I have nowhere and nothing.'

'There's an automatic dive in the GenuSstadt. Hotel Babette. They don't ask questions, don't scan your chips. Neweuro payment only. It's about as off-grid as you can get while being in the middle of the city.'

'How do you know about it?'

'It's where I go to unwind.'

Resler didn't know what Esteban meant and decided not to ask. 'When?'

'The morning rush. The more people there are on the streets, the more you'll be able to blend in.'

It made sense. Resler stood and went to his duffel, which he'd stashed in a recess near the front door, and pulled out a lightweight jacket with an anti-surveillance print that he'd bought from a Moldovan vendor in Nistria-Town. There were eyes on every street corner from Karlshorst to Alexanderplatz, but a little protection was better than nothing.

Ivo went into his bedroom, returned with a sleek black slate the size of a palm. He handed it to Resler. 'There's enough on there to cover your food and board for a few nights. Get a kingCab to Alex. No point pushing your luck on the S-Bahn.'

Resler looked at him with gratitude. 'Once my carbon comes through, I'll pay you back.'

'It ain't about that, Owen. It's never been about that.'

'I know.' He shook his head. 'I'm sorry it had to be this way. I've put you in danger, too.'

An easy grin appeared on the other man's face. 'One of us had to do something. Better to push back than let yourself be pushed.'

Esteban went to the door of his room and paused. 'Get some sleep. You're gonna need it.'

Resler settled down on the couch and closed his eyes and his sister followed him into uneasy dreams.

***

Esteban left at six sharp. Their embrace was brief, the words exchanged few. Then Resler was alone. He tidied the living space and went to the wet cell, where he washed his face with drysoap, brushed his teeth and put on a pair of drab pants, a vest and the anti-surveillance jacket. After placing a call for a kingCab he went to the window, its curved surface tinted to diffuse the hard morning sunlight. A heat shimmer softened the lines of distant towers and he watched Berlin breathe in and out. Below, people moved like insects sharing a hive mind. A few days ago he had been one of them, clinging to the bottom rung, but now he'd let go and was in freefall and didn't know where he would land. Had he failed the city or had the city failed him? The only certainty was there was no way back.

Then came the ping on his eye-over to signal the arrival of the kingCab, and any further thoughts were pushed from his mind. He grabbed his duffel, waved his hand over the door sensor and stepped into a leaf-filled corridor.

A man and a woman stood at the far end, blocking the elevator doors. They were dressed in the drab khaki of building maintenance, but their overalls didn't sit right on their frames. The man carried an oblong box at his side. Both stared at Resler through blank augmented eyes.

'Don't run,' said the woman.

Resler ran.

His shoes slapped against ersatz wood as he made for a service porthole at the opposite end of the corridor. He leapt toward it, grabbed the locking bar and turned it, and when it popped open a blast of air rushed in. He glanced over his shoulder, saw the woman calmly coming for him, noticed now how her left arm ended in a long multi-tailed electrified flail.

'Stop,' she said.

He swung his legs through the porthole and onto a ladder that was warm to the touch. The city blared and moaned below. He followed the rungs down to a narrow gantry that ran along the underside of the branch from which Esteban's designer pod hung. A glance to the end of the gantry revealed another service porthole embedded in the building's main trunk. A couple of suspension cables offered scant protection against losing his footing, but he clutched at them anyway and shuffled forward. Don't look down, he told himself. Keep your eyes on the trunk and put one foot in front of the other. They won't kill you. They need you alive to get paid.

Half a minute later, the gantry trembled as boots sounded against metal. Resler turned to see the woman striding confidently toward him, as though one misplaced step wouldn't send her plummeting to her death. When she was close enough to be able to reach him with the tails of the flail, she halted.

'You have nowhere to go, Mr Resler,' she said in a bloodless voice. 'My partner is waiting at the other end.'

Resler looked down at the tapestry of buildings, roads, transports, automatons and people below. No way out. There never had been.

'Will they kill me?' he asked.

'That isn't my concern.'

He nodded, the decision made quicker than he would've thought possible. He turned his body toward the void, his gaze finding a bio-tecture tower some five-O metres distant. No one watched from their windows. He sank to his knees, still white-knuckling one of the suspension cables. You can do it, he told himself. It's better than the alternative.

'Don't,' said the woman, realising his intention, and she raised the arm that ended in the flail.

Then Resler smelled ozone. It felt like something had just brushed past his face at high speed. But he hadn't been touched. He looked over his shoulder, saw the woman's flail was on fire and her face was a mask of pain. She took a step back, her head arching toward the sky. Then she was gone, through the wires, her fall a silent one.

The gantry vibrated with fresh weight and Resler watched as another woman approached him, this time from the building's trunk. The service porthole gaped open behind her. She wore a white suncoat and had no visible augmentations. One hand was closed around a chunky device with a yellow dish on top, and when she was within a few paces of him she stopped, flipped a switch on the rectangular body and clipped the thing to her belt.

'Planning on learning to fly, Owen Resler?' she asked, squinting in the morning light.

'Who are you? Are you with them?' His voice sounded twisted, unnatural.

'I'm here because of your sister. Two contract killers came for her at the New Dawn clinic in Zoologischer Garten. We got her out. She gave up your whereabouts to me in exchange.'

A wave of nausea passed over him. 'Can you prove that?'

The woman shrugged. 'Call her.'

I can't, he wanted to say. 'Are you here to collect on Scopo's bounty?'

'No. I have a job for you.'

He frowned. 'What?'

The woman said nothing.

'I don't know you.'

'No, but Mantis knows us both.'

Resler gripped the suspension cable. The wind plucked at the sad anti-surveillance jacket he'd thought would hide him. He hadn't even made it out of the building.

'What did you do to that repo agent?' he asked.

'I shorted her augmentations with an ESD stream-eye before she could charge her defences.'

'There's another one up there. A man.'

The woman shook her head. 'There was. Now, are you coming or would you prefer to jump?'

'You know my name. Tell me yours.'

'Mia Warsaw.'

He stared. 'You're kidding.'

'We haven't got time for this.'

On trembling legs Resler rose and followed her along the gantry to the service porthole in the trunk, which transported them into a wire-rich maintenance recess. Waiting there was a sun-burnished man in an olive-drab vest whose piercing gaze locked onto his.

'You look just like your sister,' he said by way of greeting. 'I'm Johnny.'

He took Resler's arm and steered him out of the recess and into the main corridor. The other repo agent in the khaki overalls was laid out on the floor. He looked like he was asleep.

'You ever wanted to know what a professional killer looks like, there you go,' said Johnny.

Resler allowed himself to be dragged into the elevator, which dropped through the building's core without stopping, and as they emerged into the lobby he saw that every camera had been disabled. None of it seemed real. He knew only that he was alive when he should have been dead.

Then they were outside, in the brutal heat of the morning, and they were walking fast. Two eVelos sat in the tower's short-stay park, and from a pocket the woman who claimed to be Mia Warsaw retrieved what looked like a mirror and passed it over the interface of both vehicles. The systems booted up and the bikes uttered a greeting to a Mr Tae-sik and a Mr Chi-gon.

'Get on,' she said, and Resler did as he was told.

The wide, fat wheels of the eVelos squealed as they bit into the ground, and Resler hung on to Warsaw as they punched a hole in traffic, threading past kingCabs and privates and shuttles. They joined an eight-lane artery heading north. At an exit ramp Warsaw yanked the handlebars hard and Resler squeezed his eyes shut and tried to breathe, and when he dared to open them again he saw they were surrounded by the perfunctory grey of Pankow. An under-maintained road brought them to a lot filled with rubble and twisted rebars, where they ditched the bikes.

'Stay close to me,' said Warsaw.

With Johnny at his heels, he followed her through deserted twisting alleyways that stank of garbage and dried-out rain until he no longer had any idea which direction he was facing. Finally, Warsaw paused at a nondescript metal door and took out an old keycard and swiped the lock. The door yawned open.

'In here,' she said.

Resler shuffled inside, and as the door slammed behind him low yellow lights clicked on and he saw they were in a beige-walled hallway whose air was undercut with mould. Warsaw led the way, taking a left followed by another left and then up a short flight of steps into fresh darkness. The ground creaked underfoot. Resler looked down, thought he could make out wooden floorboards.

Blinding light. He threw an arm over his eyes. Panic took hold. They had brought him here to torture him, and he'd followed them without hesitation.

'Welcome.'

He lowered his arm and blinked. He was on a stage. Before him were rows and rows of threadbare seats occupied by an audience of four: an old man in an expensive suit, a bare-chested giant with the face of an angel, a bearded type with a savage stare, and a girl dressed in technicolour threads.

'So,' said the girl. 'From that clueless look on your face, you gotta be our suit.'

THREE
THE CLIP JOINT

14 When the girl played, time stopped. Her instrument was a suspension bridge built from glass by an off-planet civilisation, a collection of translucent rods, silver-petal parachutes and placid water. The girl was as delicate as her instrument, and as she touched the rods with the tips of wet fingers they produced sounds that crystallised into the Gnossienne No. 1 by Satie. Her eyes were closed, the dust on her lids the colour of a chalkhill blue butterfly's wings, and when a tear fell onto her cheek the only surprise was that it was so self-evident. Motifs looped, tied themselves to the ends of the ones that came before. The girl's fingers remained in perpetual motion, water dripping from glass to the floor, and the music became throatier and more monumental as the Gnossienne reached its end.

Then the hands froze, the sound ceased and Lulu Mao and her Cristal Baschet dissolved into nothing.

Owen Resler deactivated his eye-over. He was on a canvas cot in a windowless room stacked with dust-thick tarps, dressed only in a white vest and black pants. The precocious kid, Janeane, watched him from the other side of the room, one leg hiked up against a piebald wall.

'She plays nice, huh? Played, I mean.'

'Yeah,' he said, and stood. 'She did.'

He'd heard of Luc Benz through his carbon offsetting projects, even thought he'd glimpsed the man once at an exclusive bar De Witt had insisted on taking him to after he'd passed the Scopo interviews. Aside from his own business, which specialised in sweeping corporate emissions under whichever rug was big enough, Benz was the heir apparent to the Habanik throne, groomed and protected by his father Eccard since the senior Benz had taken the entertainment giant's reins firmly in hand a decade prior. All senior suits had unique quirks — it was part of the starter pack — but Resler had never dreamed Benz's would amount to performing backstreet surgery on girls.

'So what do you think?' asked Janeane.

He sighed, rubbed his eyes. He still hadn't slept and was running on fumes. The attempted abduction at Esteban's place, the flight through charged city streets, the whirlwind introduction to a disparate crew of mobsters and mercenaries. It was a dream he could neither commit to nor rouse himself from.

'I don't know. I don't even know what the plan is.'

The kid shrugged. 'Neither do we. The fat man likes to play God.'

'Volante, you mean?'

'Right. The one who looks like he's stuffed his face with celmeat every day of his life.'

'You don't like him.'

'You're very perceptive, Resler.'

'And you've got a real chip on your shoulder.'

She shrugged. 'It keeps me spicy.'

'How did you even get mixed up with these people?'

He listened as she told him about a life of being exploited by anyone she'd ever placed her trust in, about her assumption six months ago that the only way to escape the cycle had been to pull her own plug, and about a woman who had stopped her and inspired her to live a different way. The same woman who had saved Resler a few hours previously.

When Janeane was done talking, he wanted to put an arm around her. Instead he said: 'No one should have to go through what you did.'

'It is what it is,' said Janeane, waving it away. 'I'm still kicking.'

He hesitated. 'I have a question about Mia.'

'Shoot.'

'Is she actually a freedom fighter? Or just a mercenary?'

Janeane laughed. 'You're such a suit.'

He looked down at his pants and vest. 'Sure looks like it. Vertoo said she assassinated Minister Bülow.'

'The Minister of Transport? The army fragged his palace. They killed him, not Mia.'

'How do you know that?'

'Because she told me.'

'And you trust her?'

'I'd say of all the people I've met in my life so far, she's one who has had the least reason to lie.'

'And you said she was also part of the group in the dust that is taking in my sister?'

'Right. And that's where I'm going when we're done here.' She cocked her head. 'Guess it makes sense for you to come along, too. We can buy some supplies and schlepp across the plain like a couple of pioneers.'

'You sure about leaving it all?'

Janeane nodded. 'City's full, man. It's a pressure cooker. When it explodes, I don't wanna be here. Surely you could see that better than me from your pedestal.'

He thought of the windowless floors in Hell. 'I wasn't on a pedestal.'

She shrugged. Resler's thoughts drifted to the girl Lulu and the man who had tortured her. During his time at Scopo, he'd been part of the environment that had helped to create Benz. He'd paid into it, devoted his time and energy to it, even defended it in conversations with Ina. He'd bought into the lie of the system because there had been no other way to survive within its embrace. He'd told himself repeatedly that if he kept his head down and worked his way up then he could, eventually, change things for the better. But the rot started at the top and moved down through the tiers, infecting everything that came the other way. There was no changing it. There was only a pandemic with an onedred percent mortality rate.

He sighed. He wasn't assured like Mia Warsaw, he didn't have the boundless resolve of his sister, and he definitely didn't possess the wry grit of Janeane. His resumé could be summed up in a single sentence: he'd failed at swimming against the tide and he'd failed at floating with it. If he could just speak with Ina. She would give him perspective. But his calls were still being blocked. Warsaw had told him her chips would be nixed for good when she made it to the camp. If he ever wanted to speak to her again, he would have to go there.

A rap at the door brought him out of his reverie. Janeane called out a greeting and a man dressed in black with wild salt-and-pepper hair entered. Lucky Ramirez, the setup king. That was how the girl had described him. Resler thought he looked like an Alexanderplatz fixer.

'Now that we have our technocrat, Disco's ready to tell us the plan. He wants everyone there, including you, mijita.'

The girl rolled her eyes. 'Génial.'

Ramirez looked at Resler. 'How are you doing?'

'Still a little turned around.'

'That figures. Listen, we gotta replace your ID chip as soon as possible. Otherwise you'll set off every detector on the street. After Disco's finished his briefing, you and me are gonna take a ride to a workshop I know in Container City, owned by a real aug artist called Jimmy Chee. Gonna cost you a couple of stacks for the switch. Are you good for it?'

Resler nodded. He had the cash slate from Esteban. He hoped it would be enough.

'You know a chip switch hurts like hell, right?' asked Janeane.

He shook his head. He didn't know that.

'If you want my advice, ask Johnny for an oblivion pill. That'll take the edge off when they make the cut.'

'Don't listen to her,' said Ramirez. 'Jimmy Chee was born with a CT chip rail in his hands. Now come on.'

***

The stage was illuminated by the blue light of three floating screens. Disco Volante stood in complete silence as he waited for his audience to take their seats. Resler lingered at the end of a row so he could keep an eye on the others. Warsaw and Janeane sat together. Johnny stood in an aisle, smoking. Ramirez occupied the front row with the mass of muscles they called BB.

Volante brought his hands together, touched his index fingers to his lips.

'I am not one for hyperbole, but I believe this may be my greatest creation yet. Provided everyone follows my plan to the letter, Luc Benz will have breathed his last by the end of this week. To the outside world, his death will appear natural, a rising star that winked out due to forces greater than himself.'

'Disco, we ain't here for a soliloquy,' said Ramirez.

A wrinkle appeared on Volante's brow. 'I take your point, however crude. This Friday we shall intercept Mr Benz after a Habanik function arranged to honour his father. Mr Eccard Benz is set to become the proud recipient of a Twelve Leaves Award for Services to Humanity. Benz Junior despises such events, which is why, during the ceremony, I shall invite him to an address that is more to his taste: Toltec, a members-only psybin bar.' He grinned. 'I have been a member since Toltec opened.'

'What makes you think he'll go for it?' asked Warsaw.

'Oh, honeyed promises and gilded incentives. The usual. For example, Benz has always wanted to possess a private celestial residence. It just so happens that my character has one and wishes to offload it without incurring the city cabal's extortionate transfer fee.'

Volante turned to the floating screens. When he waved a hand, they displayed a squat cylindrical tower of polished black stone. 'This is the exterior of Toltec. Good access and exit points, roads suitable for electric bikes and privates.' He waved a hand and a schematic of the interior appeared. As he spoke, each section lit up in turn. 'The bar is located beneath ground level. Foyer, communal lounge, time-out area, kitchen, utilities. There are private synaesthesia pods two floors underground. I have reserved one such pod for the evening of the Habanik function. This is where we shall perform the Shuffle.'

'What's a shuffle?' asked Janeane.

Volante plucked a handkerchief from his breast pocket and wiped his neck. 'My dear, if you would hold your tongue for a few seconds, I will tell you.'

Janeane extended her tongue, held it between two fingers.

'After I arrive with Benz,' said Volante, 'I will place an order for a custom psybin program, as complex as possible. While it is being pre-pared we shall retire to Toltec's communal lounge, which, as you saw, is located one floor above the private pods. Shortly thereafter, Lucky will arrive with Ms Janeane, decked out in all the finery to which our limited resources can stretch, and likewise take up residence in the lounge. I am certain Benz's attention will be drawn to her singular beauty.'

Resler glanced at Warsaw. There was what looked to be a cold fury in her eyes. He was sure she'd mentioned to him not two hours previ-ously that Janeane wasn't part of the job.

'Although Lucky and Janeane may seem like the perfect match, all that glitters is not gold between our two lovebirds. Following a heated argument, Gian will vacate the premises, leaving our gossamer-spun beauty sans amant. Fortunately for her, a certain heir will be waiting in the wings to sweep her off her feet.'

Volante looked from one face to the next. The light from the screens illuminated the fresh sweat on his brow. The man was at home on the stage, thought Resler.

'Oh, I almost forgot. Before this little scene plays out, our data ma-ven, Mr Resler, will seize control of Toltec's central security system from an off-site location and lock out the employees without raising any alarms.'

'That'll require a false front interface,' said Resler, surprised by his own voice.

'I'll let you work out the details,' said Volante, waving a hand. He shifted his attention back to Janeane. 'And now the Shuffle, my dear. Once we are safely ensconced in the pod with Mr Benz, Mr Resler will clear the way for the psychedelic refreshments to arrive. My initial idea had been to rig the microdots in a way that would send Benz into an eternal slumber, but BB discovered our man has advanced augmentations that will ringfence his mind once they register abnormal stress values. But no matter, because it turns out that Benz has an underlying heart condition.'

Ramirez turned to the hulking bodyguard. 'How did you find that out?'

'I'm not the only refugee from the island,' said BB. 'A few others from the Consort programme turned up here. One of them works as muscle for Benz. I asked, he told.'

'What'd you give him for it?'

'Nothing. I saved his life twice. He owed me.'

Resler watched them. Speaking Whicolla at Scopo was one thing, but this was another level of impenetrable. They all talked so tough, as though a single wrong word would have them reaching for the guns they wore at their belts. They apparently called Johnny the one-man army, but the moniker would have fit for any of the bodies in the room, himself and Volante excluded.

Volante cleared his throat. 'Instead, the psychedelics will be brought to my pod by Ms Warsaw, who will be installed in the kitchen. On her way to us, she will sprinkle the microdots with a pro-arrhythmic synthesising agent.'

'You're joking,' said Warsaw.

'On the contrary. I had to pull many strings to secure you a shift at Toltec. It is a highly sought-after place to work. I'm certain you can swallow your pride for the sake of the performance. Besides, it will be down to you to excise Janeane from Benz's clutches after delivering the platter. You will eject her for being underage. If Mr Benz is reluctant to part with the girl, you will call BB to assist.'

There was a faint smile on BB's face. 'Did you get me a job there, too?'

'No need, dear boy. I have made you the plus one on my membership. You need only to swipe my biometric key. I want you to wait in the lounge until it is time for you to make your entrance. I believe Mr

Benz is more likely to give the girl a secure channel over which to contact him and let her go rather than make a scene. If, however, he does prove stubborn, I expect a rousing performance from you. Shock and awe.'

BB nodded.

'And then?' asked Ramirez.

'Once Ms Warsaw and Janeane have withdrawn, Mr Benz will partake in the microdots.' He glanced at Janeane. 'That is the Shuffle. We move one way while the world spins in a different direction. Benz will still be thinking about you. His mind won't be on double-crosses or poisoning or danger. He'll be envisioning the moment he brings you to his suite.'

'And if he has one of his people test the dots first?' asked Ramirez.

Volante shrugged. 'Providing they don't have a heart condition, the arrhythmic agent will not affect them. Besides, it has a delayed onset of approximately thirty minutes. I'll use my newly installed tonin chip to mimic Benz's symptoms. Mr Resler will place a bogus call to StadtMed for assistance. Cue Johnny in a commandeered medevac, who will spirit us to a clinic with whose management I am on friendly terms. Sadly, it will be too late to do anything for Mr Benz. For my part, I will be declared deceased on arrival. '

Volante placed a hand on his heart. 'This is to be my final performance,' he said. 'By feigning death, I can disappear. There are plenty of locations where I can live out my days in luxurious anonymity.'

'You sure about that?' asked Ramirez.

'I have to say I don't place much faith in your notion that Eccard Benz will turn heaven and earth in pursuit of those responsible for the death of his son. The youngblood's demise will cause a power vacuum immediately below the top chair. A few board members may even be sufficiently emboldened to try to seize control from Eccard. No, I think when this performance is over, it'll spell war at Habanik.'

Resler shook his head. This was how people rationalised such acts. 'You make it sound like we're about to perform a civic duty,' he said. When Warsaw looked around, he reddened.

The old man nodded. 'That is one way of putting it.'

'It's murder. Plain and simple.'

Ramirez turned to him. 'You said you were in.'

'I am,' said Resler. 'But I don't want to dress it up as something it's not. That's all a suit ever does.'

Volante offered him a thin smile. 'There is only one person in this room with a track record as a suit. Perhaps before you start making moral judgements, you should ask yourself whose conscience you are seeking to appease.' He turned away, clapped his hands. 'Over the next twenty-four hours I'll speak to each of you in detail about your roles. If you have any questions you would like the group to hear, the time is now.'

Resler gritted his teeth. He had plenty of questions, but they could wait. He wanted to be out of the hall with its foul air and posturing bodies and tough words.

Mia Warsaw stood. She hadn't spoken at all during the presentation. 'You're banking on a chain of decisions going your way, Disco.'

Volante smiled. 'That is the nature of the game. But it is all within the realm of prediction and probability.'

'I don't like it.'

'Allow me to remind you that I have been putting together jobs of this calibre since well before a few bystanders elevated you to a status you scarcely deserve.'

Warsaw's eyes were white slits. 'I asked you to leave the girl out of it. It was my only request.'

'She is the keystone,' said Volante, his voice calm. 'Without her, we have no shot.'

Beside Warsaw, Janeane grimaced. 'Sekhmet, Mia. This ain't no different to what I handled onedred times on the Spree.'

Warsaw shook her head. 'It's a different game.'

'Like you'd know.' Janeane jumped up. 'What have you done so far except find Lucky? Nothing. If you'd wanted to run the show, you shoulda planned things yourself. But you didn't, so you don't get a say in what I can or can't do. You got that? I don't need another god-damn mother. Thanks to the last one, I ended up on the street.'

Without another word, she vaulted the row and followed the next one to its end, then disappeared through the door that led to the back-stage rooms. Warsaw made to follow, but Ramirez blocked her path.

'Leave it,' he said, placing a hand on her shoulder. 'Let her calm down.'

Warsaw shook off Ramirez's hand, turned to Volante. 'If anything happens to her, I'm coming after you.'

'Is there anyone you don't think you can intimidate?' asked Volante. 'It's your arrogance that irks me. Once, a long time ago, you got lucky with a fireworks show. Fine. But like the girl said: what else have you done?' He gestured to BB. 'Unlike Gian, my survival in this despicable world is not the product of good fortune, but due to the company I keep. And so I say this to you: when you wish to make your move, go ahead. But know you'll have a mountain to climb first.'

Warsaw squinted at them both, the impresario and his star. Then she made for the stairs, following them up and out of the theatre. The door slammed shut behind her.

'Was that necessary?' said Ramirez.

Volante wiped his brow. 'I don't take threats to my person idly.'

'You'd better hope she comes back.'

'She will. You heard her. She won't leave the girl to fend for herself.'

Volante muttered a command and the floating screens died and the display bars settled on the floor. BB climbed onto the stage and picked up the bars, and together they went to the curtain at the rear and disappeared behind it.

Johnny ground out his latest cigarette, started up the stairs. 'I'll go see if I can find her.'

Resler stared after him. He thought of the girl, Lulu, playing the Cristal Baschet like an angel, and he thought of his sister and then of Ngozi and Janeane, and he knew they were all connected. Each, in their way, had done their bit to bring him here, to this place where he didn't know the rules and rage governed everything.

Don't allow yourself to be overwhelmed by it, he told himself. You have a part to play. Focus on that.

'Okay,' said Ramirez, the only other person left in the hall. 'Drama's over for one afternoon.'

'And now?' asked Resler.

'Container City. Let's get you a new name.'

15 When Tempelhofer Feld's developers turned the old city park into a self-sufficient cleantech campus, they hadn't counted on the Greek Epirus mafia or the Bulgarian Mutri infiltrating the streets around it to sling diluted krokodil and blitz to fixers with pinhole eyes and rotting skin. No amount of hi-vis signage or cut-rate offers from desperate property men could drown out the frequent gunfire born of a drug turf war, and so the cleantech campus had died on the vine. Even so, a few semi-legit businesses with enough liquid carbon to pay for bleeding-edge security had popped up in Tempelhof in recent years, and Toltec was one of them. It was located underground, beneath a cylindrical concrete monolith that had been installed well over a century prior to test the stability of Berlin's marshy ground. The concrete was now encased in polished black stone, and the gang soldiers and the dealers and the fixers steered clear of the place because it was fitted with rail-mounted cannons and sur-veillance eyes that saw everything.

Though they had barely exchanged a few words since the theatre bust-up, Mia had asked Janeane to go with her to Tempelhof to scope out Toltec and find an access port from which Owen Resler could cre-ate his false front for the club's system. The girl had shrugged, thrown on an anti-surveillance coat that went from her throat to her shins and followed her out the door. On a brute-forced eVelo they slalomed through fast-moving electric traffic toward Potsdamer Platz, passing the ten rotating scraper stacks that were the Nerthus towers, before swapping the flawless roads of central Berlin for disused asphalt ribbons that unfurled between squatted biotectures and crumbling old stock. The wind was as strong as the sun, and both women had to wear sand visors to protect their eyes from grit.

On an overpass overlooking the neighbourhood Mia eased the bike to a halt and took her Galileo monocular from her coat and scanned the streets. The lens came to rest on the stone-clad cylinder that was Toltec's calling card and then on a hollowed-out prefab opposite and to the left of it. Eight storeys, windows gone, likely abandoned. The roof looked intact. It was worth a try.

She guided the eVelo through a maze of dead streets and into an alley directly behind the building, where illegal refuse collected in its seams and pools of dirt-flecked water sat undrained. After Janeane jumped clear of the bike, Mia rigged a pulse boobytrap to the eVelo's starter and made sure to disable the setting that would shoot an SOS to the nearest polizei precinct if the system was tampered with. The pulse wouldn't do much if someone was determined to strip the bike, but it would deter casual slingers.

A rusting fire escape offered access to the prefab's roof. The wind was more acute on top of the building, and as Mia looked out on a bruised sky she could taste dust in her throat. At the prefab's edge she panned her monocular over the cylinder, taking in the laser-guided, rail-mounted cannons which sat ready and deadly on its flat top. Its Torggler doors were shut up tight, the diffuser gate switched off, and there was a blast shield buttoned into the ground. She watched the place for several minutes. Nothing moved. Volante had the schematics for Toltec back at the theatre, but she'd wanted to see the place for herself, hoping it would dispel the doubt in her chest.

It didn't.

The schematics showed there was a single main entrance plus an escape chute at the rear. A near-bottleneck, the opposite of ideal. Benz would need only a few men with automatics to turn the place into a charnel house if the situation became taufed. Due to how Volante had his deception set up, she and BB would each be going in with a two-shot printbuild tucked into the small of their backs. Also not ideal.

'Deja vu.'

Mia lowered the scope. Janeane stood with her arms folded, her face barely visible above her coat's collar guard.

'How do you mean?'

'Another roof, another dead neighbourhood.'

'Berlin has enough of those.'

'No Lucky for us to save this time, though.'

'Right,' said Mia. 'The only contribution I've made so far.'

The kid had the grace to look uneasy. 'I only said that because you were making me look baichi in front of the others.'

'What do you care?'

'You're joking, right? A room full of guys, all with ten-ton egos. You know why they tolerate me? Because I push back. When you tell them they should cut me out, you undo all my work. I ain't you, Mia. I ain't got a glittering list of achievements to fall back on.'

'Neither do I, according to Volante.'

'The fat man's just scared of you. You can see it in his eyes.'

'So why do you want to dance to his tune?'

Janeane shook her head. 'I don't. I just wanna do something that leaves the right mark. Part of life involves using people as a leg-up to get to where you wanna go, right? That's all Disco is. A leg-up. If his theatrics get us a shot at Benz so we can level the score for Lulu and her mom, that's enough for me. All that time I spent down by the Spree? This'll make up for it. I can't say exactly how, but it's how I see it.'

Mia was still. Dust and grit flew around the pair of them.

Janeane pointed at the black monolith. 'Four nights from now I'm gonna go in there and play my part the best I can, and Benz is gonna be a dead man. Then I can leave.'

'Where will you go?'

'Same as you. Prestige. I'm done with Berlin, Mia. I ain't gonna be able to heal until I'm long gone.'

'It's a different life in the samizdats.'

'Good. Can't be any worse than the one I've had so far.'

Mia glanced at the sky, now darker still. Dust storm, a large one. They hit the city every few months, katabatic winds flinging red-brown against the buildings until every surface was the same colour. Afterwards, automated compressed air units blasted the dust clear from the glass and nu-crete in the good parts of town. The bad parts were left to dig themselves out.

She looked at the kid again. 'I'd say had it wrong back there. Okay? I had you wrong.'

'You had it different, not wrong.'

They stood, facing each other. Mia wanted to reach for her, pull her close, tell her she was sorry. But it wasn't her way. It wasn't what she did.

Janeane broke eye contact first. 'Storm's coming.'

I know, thought Mia. The wind flung dust against her visor. 'Let's get inside,' she said.

***

The fire escape took them back down to the alley. At the eVelo, Mia popped the side wing and retrieved the basic toolkit that citizen riders could use to perform rudimentary repairs. With visibility dropping and her visor becoming overwhelmed, she gestured for Janeane to follow her to a door that was padlocked shut. She took a joust from the kit and slotted it between the padlock clasp and the door's deadbolt and leaned on it with her full weight, and the clasp clicked and came free. A couple of kicks jolted the door from the rusted frame and it swung inward and she and the kid hauled themselves inside and dragged the door closed against the storm.

Mia coughed to clear the grit from her throat. 'Reminds me of Prestige.'

'You want to look for Resler's access port in here?' asked Janeane.

'He told you about it?'

'Yeah.' The kid slid her collar guard open. 'He said to try the basement.'

They eased their way along a corridor that smelled of ammonia until they found a set of steps receding into an underground void. The kid made to go first, but Mia touched her on the shoulder and activated an illuminator at her wrist and took the lead. Janeane's anti-surveillance coat had miniature LEDs in the seams, which, when combined with Mia's light, bathed the basement in a soft green. Roaches skittered away from the intruders as they made their way further through the underground. Empty doorways yawned at them and they checked rooms that were stripped and crumbling. Then, at the end of the void, they found a door that was locked shut. The metal bore marks from where scavengers had failed to force their way inside. When Mia tried the eVelo joust, the tool snapped in the frame.

'Probably should step back,' she said to Janeane, withdrawing a button-sized black Plastex case from her pocket.

'What is it?'

'A door-opener. Courtesy of Johnny.'

The case was magnetised with a single primer switch, and after Mia tacked it to the door and flicked the switch she and Janeane hustled to the nearest empty room and pressed themselves against the wall and waited.

Hot breath licked along the corridor. The floor rumbled. Plaster flakes fell from the ceiling.

Johnny's device had punched a hole clear through the metal, and it took Mia only a few seconds to work the door open. The room beyond was home to rust-encrusted pipes and three electrical cabinets. One cabinet had been gutted, but the other two were intact and Janeane went to them and opened them up and the light from her coat shone onto breakers and ports and buses and wires.

'There,' said the kid, pointing at a hexagonal port. 'That's the one.'

Mia squinted. 'You sure?'

'It's what he figures from the schematics. This building is close enough to Toltec that if he boosts the wireless range of your Flymotic via a duck hawk repeater on the roof, he'll be able to overlap with Toltec's mesh network, replicate the system's heartbeat and divert it to his own façade interface.'

Mia looked at her. Janeane shrugged.

'I learned a little about the ones and zeroes from polygon security.'

'You told Disco you had no idea.'

'Better to keep the fat man in the dark about some things, non?' Also, Resler gave me a refresher to take his mind off the pain while he was recovering from his chip swap.'

Mia nodded. 'What do you think of him?' Ten minutes ago, she wouldn't have asked the question. But ten minutes ago she'd regarded the kid as just a kid.

'He ain't like the growthers I had to deal with on the Spree, but he ain't like you or me either. He told me he used to work underground before he suited up. Maybe he was just dusting me, trying to get me on his side, but he sounded genuine enough.'

'He's telling the truth about that. Mantis confirmed it.'

'So what's your take?'

Of the entire group, thought Mia, it wasn't Owen Resler she was worried about. 'He ripped off a corporate and he's still breathing. That's good enough for me.'

'Sure, but he has you to thank for being able to suck down oxygen.'

Mia held back a smile. 'Something else to add to your list.'

She swung the door to the cabinet shut and retrieved a bioseal from her belt and tamped it down over the locking mechanism. Old tech from a different time. Only Resler's biometric ID — the new one Jimmy Chee had put inside him in Container City — would open it. If anyone came down to the basement and tried to crack the lock, it'd turn the contents into slag. That was why few slingers used bioseals anymore. These days, petty vindictiveness made people more likely to set one off than leave it alone. But it was all she had, so she was going with it.

They backed out of the room and Mia closed the door, but she could do nothing about the hole where the lock had been. At the steps, they could hear the storm still working its way through the glassless building above. Mia took a seat.

'It'll blow clear eventually.'

Janeane slumped against a wall. Her hands disappeared into the sleeves of her coat and she shook her head to dislodge a strand of platinum hair that had become caught in her lashes.

'You think the fat man's dreaming in colour, don't you?'

The question was spoken without her usual sing-song confidence.

'I didn't say that.'

'But?'

Mia hesitated. She owed it to the kid to be honest. 'He hasn't pulled a job in three years. He's still got vision, but I don't know if that vision matches reality.'

'How about the others?'

'The ice there isn't the thickest, either. Johnny hits his pills like a cancer patient, though I admit he's done his job so far.' She paused. Gian's on his way out, she wanted to say. But he'd asked her not to tell Janeane. 'Ramirez is a pro. And we both know BB can handle himself.' She shrugged. 'That's all there is to it.'

'Lucky's sick,' said Janeane.

'How do you know?'

'Even Resler knows. You only gotta have eyes.'

Mia stared ahead of her, at a point in the concrete where a crack met a gouge. 'Don't worry. On the night he'll do what he needs to do.'

'So will you,' said Janeane. She pushed herself away from the wall, pressed her hands together in the shape of a pistol and took aim. 'Because when I go in there, I've got Mia Warsaw at my back.' She pursed her cupid lips and the pistol bucked as she made a noise like a shot being fired. 'Even if it all goes to hell, we'll find a way to walk out clean. You and me.'

Mia became cold. 'Wait a minute, kid.'

Janeane ignored her. Her dust-coated boots shimmied over stone as she turned and aimed and fired, downing invisible enemies that came for her in the gloom. Then she swung her clasped hands around and pointed them at the ground. 'Say goodbye, Luc,' she said, the words emerging from the corner of her mouth.

'Stop, goddamn it.'

Janeane sighed. Her hands dropped, the fantasy over.

'Look,' said Mia, her voice tense. 'This isn't some holostream where no one gets hurt in the end. If you don't screw it down tight and do everything expected of you, there's no guarantee you'll live past Friday night. And you can't rely on me if trouble starts. You just can't. Your survival is on you before it's on anyone else. You got that?'

The kid grimaced. 'Oui.'

'Do you? Benz murders people — girls — for pleasure. Keep that fact in your head. Don't be cute with him. Don't get flashy. And don't back yourself into a corner.'

'You're really worried about him, aren't you?'

'It's not him who scares me. It's you, thinking you're invincible.'

To stop herself from going too far again, Mia stood and made for the top of the stairwell. The dust storm was moving on, leaving behind walls caked in red and a gauzy film in the air. She called for Janeane to come up and they left through the jacked door. Mia wedged it closed behind them and threaded the chain from the broken padlock back through the deadbolt, then used a plastic slat to erase their boot-prints in the dust.

The eVelo waited untouched in the alley, its wheels jutting out from a stout underframe, every inch of it painted the same desert brown as everything else. Mia deactivated the pulse boobytrap and wiped a gloved hand over the control panel to reveal the instruments under the Plastex. Janeane vaulted onto the back with the grace of a dancer, and Mia swung a leg over the frame and the bike sank on its suspension, and she waited for the interface to read her falsified bio-metric ID. There was a low hum as the eVelo fired up, and Mia backed it out of the alley and onto a road that was eerily empty in the after-math of the storm.

As they made their way back to Pankow, Mia was more aware than ever of Janeane's body against hers. Gripping her coat, whooping when a transport veered too close to the bike, moving when she moved. No fear, all confidence, complete faith in her accidental guard-ian.

Whatever happened inside Toltec on Friday night, thought Mia, the kid had to walk out of the place. She would make sure of it.

16 Night in the city was as bright as the day. Even in a kiez as rough as Tempelhof, the streets were lit up in artificial oranges and pinks and blues and greens, and young punks mixed with old hands as they clustered under the lights to drink and snort and smoke. Vehicles of two, four and six wheels flitted between buildings like sonic butterflies, most taking shortcuts through the neighbourhood on their way to leech town or the GenuSstadt or some ritzy gated community. A few tooled-up war wagons patrolled the minor alleys, each loaded with gang members itching to find enemy heads to shatter. From an abandoned lot came the sound of blood being let as some fringe Epirus members were ambushed by a group of Mutri associates armed with bats and poles. The screams ceased only when the ground looked like the floor of a charnel house.

Owen Resler saw none of it. He sat with his back to cold brickwork, his hands dancing in front of Mia Warsaw's Han Flymotic console as data streamed across the three floating screens that had previously been in the Delphi Theatre. His hackwork kit lay beside him on the floor. He didn't expect to have to use it, but it brought him comfort to know it was there. He carried nothing else with him. When Johnny had tried to press a printshot into his hand, he'd refused.

It had only been ten days, but it felt strange to be wearing a wrist shackle again. It peeked out from under his sleeve and disappeared into the back of the Flymotic. His SynSult plate was doing its thing, blowing an ice-cold wind through his mind, and when he looked at the holographic data swirling around him he could see gaps in the system like they were traffic lights. These were the spaces he moved into, filling them with his own code until Toltec's central control was locked inside a straitjacket without even knowing it. The club's AI wasn't smart, not by a long shot, and he found it easy to keep the curious program at arm's length as he issued the command to create a false front. Toltec's staff would think they were still running the show, at least until he needed them not to.

When he dissolved his eye-over the data streams disappeared and the SynSult plate eased up. He wiped the sweat from his brow. The back of his head still throbbed, courtesy of Jimmy Chee and his chip killer tools. On the roof of the building he was under, Johnny Seven was hunkered down with a small arsenal of weapons next to the duck hawk repeater, keeping watch over the entrance to Toltec until it was his time to arrive in the medevac he and Ramirez had stolen the previous night. Resler wanted to ping the soldier to check he was still there, but nixed the impulse.

The Flymotic issued a single low chime. The false front was ready.

The SynSult plate kicked into gear again as he activated his eye-over. Data unfurled across the floating screens, so much smaller than the transparent walls he'd become used to at Scopo. First, he accessed Toltec's cameras, drew up all tentwo feeds on one of the screens. A handful of people occupied the lounge, a wide, low space lit in soft green. BB was one of them, lying in repose on a padded recliner. His lab-ravaged body was concealed in a long haori coat with a houndstooth pattern that was buttoned to the throat. On the kitchen feed Resler saw Mia Warsaw cleaning out a rolltender. She wore a uniform, black pants and black shirt with a fluorescent blue staff stripe across the front, and a clear full-face visor.

A low whistle sounded inside Resler's ear.

'Heads up,' said Johnny.

A message for the whole team. He, BB, Volante, Johnny and Ramirez received it through their eye-overs. Warsaw and Janeane, both non-auged, were on in-ear comm beads.

Resler magnified the camera that clung to the side of the black stone cylinder. A private limo, its arching chassis accentuated by a mesial window and V-shaped guard irons at the front, poured itself along the road and pulled up outside the club. Its rear door slid open on a guide and a compact man with ocular grafts stepped out and swept the street with his gaze. He was followed by the unmistakable form of Disco Volante, resplendent in a midnight-blue tux and a pleated silk shirt. On leaving the limo, he flicked his hand out and a pencil-thin cane appeared from inside his sleeve. He leaned on it, waiting.

The next man was Benz.

He was around the same age as Resler, but that was all they had in common. Tall, sweeping white-blonde hair, porcelain skin. Designer body perfectly encased in a dynamic-thread smoking jacket with a gleaming cross-chain. All traits typical of the hyper-rich. But it was the eyes that made Benz someone to remember. They seemed to glow, two pools of bioluminescence surrounded by flawless flesh, and when they found the camera's lens Resler shivered because he was certain the man was looking directly at him.

Benz was accompanied by two other suits, similarly attractive and attired, who held themselves like peers rather than bodyguards. One glanced up and down the street and made a comment, and the other laughed. Benz didn't react. Volante, leaning on his cane, said something to the Habanik heir and waved his hand at the black cylinder.

'Party of five,' Resler heard Johnny say. 'Disco, Benz, one ronin, two tagalong suits.'

Volante stumped over to the scanner and had his credentials scanned. The Torggler doors rolled aside and the quintet passed through the diffuser, and Resler switched cameras and watched as they entered a spacious silver-plated elevator and descended two floors to Toltec's foyer, a generous cavern whose centre was dominated by a fountain of razor-sharp stalagmites. As Volante checked in with a lean man wearing a pattern-rec fluid plant in his left eye, Resler cycled through the other camera feeds. BB was still in the lounge, drinking something turquoise from a fluted glass. Warsaw had retreated to the staff bathroom, and Resler watched as she hiked up her shirt and retrieved the Agitator that had been taped to the small of her back and checked it over.

Resler sweated. This was real and it was happening. The easy part—penetrating Toltec's wireless mesh and building the false front around its central control—was done. Now he had to monitor everything, together, all at once. He'd never run a building's eyes before, not that he'd told the others. He was an imposter again, like at Scopo, but this time any lapses on his part could mean catastrophic failure. He wiped damp palms on his pants.

The Flymotic issued another chime. He checked the readout, saw that Volante's preferences for his synaesthesia pod had been logged and were now being turned into a program of visuals and aural cues. He let it run.

On the foyer feed, a Japanese woman in a micro-check suit with peak lapels that reached her shoulders greeted Benz's group and led them through to the lounge. Resler switched feeds again, watched them make their way over to a sprawling gelcouch island. He clocked Volante steal a glance at BB, but the giant stared straight ahead, his beautiful features placid. The other guests, paired off in twos and threes, paid no attention to Benz's crew.

Resler glanced at another floating screen. Volante's spec synaesthesia program was almost ready. Toltec's software was way too fast. Ramirez and Janeane hadn't arrived yet.

He rattled off a few commands, and on the screen Toltec's central control twisted itself into a knot, then cut out and began to reboot. On the foyer feed, he watched as the lean man with the pattern-rec fluid plant tapped the foyer console and frowned, then raised his head and muttered words that Resler couldn't hear. He was soon joined by a woman, taller than him and with a serious demeanour that reminded Resler of a teacher he'd endured at Scopo Academy. She listened with narrowed eyes as the man told her the building's control was in the process of resetting itself, then stalked away in the direction she had come.

In the lounge, Volante was perched on the edge of a couch, deep in discussion with Benz's colleagues, while the bodyguard stood off to one side, forever scanning the lounge through artificial lenses. Benz himself sat with his hands clasped in his lap, silent as he contemplated the Sustainable Moderne decor. The Japanese woman appeared with a tray of beverages and handed each man their order. Volante raised his glass in a toast, then leaned forward and spoke to Benz. As the latter listened he produced a cigarette case from his jacket pocket and when he opened it Resler saw the cigarettes inside looked much different to the Djasalm smokes that were available on every street corner. These, he realised, contained real tobacco.

Resler's comm channel clicked. 'The happy couple is pulling up,' said Johnny.

The outdoor camera showed a kingCab slide to a halt outside the monolith. The door opened, Janeane stepped out into the tinder-box night, and Resler found himself staring at a stranger.

Her hair was dyed International Klein Blue, cresting like a wave over her face and covering one eye almost entirely. Her lips were the same colour, and painted on each temple was a delicate geometric design. She wore an asymmetrical blood-red dress, shoulderless, with reflective black leggings that disappeared into high boots. She looked ten years older than she was.

'Be careful in there, kid,' whispered Johnny, and Janeane blew a kiss at the air.

Ramirez emerged next, stoic in a well-cut black Korean frock coat, formal pants and dress boots. There was more colour in his face than Resler could remember seeing at any time previously, and when he walked toward the entrance it was with a quickness he'd lacked at the theatre. Ramirez turned, as though speaking to Janeane. 'Are they in the lounge?'

'Yes,' said Resler, hearing the hollowness in his voice.

The door eye scanned Ramirez and the leaves rolled aside and he and Janeane stepped into the silver-plated elevator. Resler checked the foyer camera. The man with the pattern-tec fluid plant was anxiously watching the system finish its reboot, but as the elevator doors slid open and Ramirez and Janeane emerged his face became a professional mask and he moved to intercept them. Ramirez handed the man a slate, an exec pass courtesy of Volante, and the man smiled with just the right amount of servility. Then the Japanese woman in the peak-lapel suit was there again, appearing seemingly from nowhere, and only now did Resler notice the way she moved. A little too smooth for a human being, as though hesitation didn't exist in her psyche. He ran a check in Toltec's system, found the woman's ID, noted the four-character suffix that could only mean one thing: she was a mimic. IG Band, Pyrmont class. Top of the line.

A private-channel notch winked at Resler on his eye-over and he accepted it.

'How's it looking inside?' asked Johnny.

'Ramirez and Janeane are still in the foyer. No fireworks yet.'

'How are you holding up?'

'Hanging in.' He could hear a faint noise in the background. 'It's not raining, is it?'

'Just started. Rather be down there than on this roof.'

The comm went dead and Resler breathed. Despite chain-smoking and throwing back pills like a fixer, Johnny seemed like he had things locked down. It gave him a little comfort.

The mimic walked Ramirez and Janeane past the stalagmite fountain to the lounge. From there, Janeane led the way to a pair of wing chairs in direct line of sight of Benz. The mimic took their drinks order and withdrew to a compact mirrored bar, where she whispered instructions into a synthesiser unit.

A pair of luminescent eyes from across the room found the girl and a smile played on cruel lips.

Resler swallowed the unease that had suddenly built in the back of his throat.

***

Ramirez made his move ten minutes later.

He jumped out of his seat, his hands tugging at his frock coat as he said something to Janeane, and Resler could tell it was loud because everyone in the lounge except BB turned to watch. Ramirez began to gesture as Janeane, still seated, dead-eyed him, and when the mimic appeared at his elbow he spun around and jammed a finger into her chest. It was a good performance. The man's eyes were wild.

On the other lounge camera Resler noticed Volante mutter something to Benz, who stood and made a beeline for the couple. Ramirez was ready for him, whirling to face the interloper and the red-lensed bodyguard who shadowed him. Benz stopped a few paces short of the wing chairs. When he spoke, Ramirez shook his head and snarled.

Resler rubbed his eyes with the palms of his hands. Being deaf like this was useless. He keyed his comm, isolated Volante's channel.

'Disco, disable the audio filter on your eye-over.'

The voices came through a couple of seconds later.

'You don't have any idea who you're dealing with,' said Ramirez.

Benz put his hands in the pockets of his suit pants and the luminescent eyes played over Ramirez.

'Neither do you,' he said.

The words sent a shiver through Resler. He moved and spoke more like a core-grown Savant than an honest-to-god human being. His voice, at least, was auged, made to sound deeper and more commanding than it likely was.

Ramirez didn't seem deterred. 'Your muscle had better stop looking at me through those discs of his or I'm gonna break both of them.'

The bodyguard took a step forward, but Benz raised a finger and he stopped in his tracks.

Volante called over from the couch. 'Son, a little piece of advice.' His voice and attitude were different. Softer, more restrained. 'Quite while you're ahead and go home with your lady.'

Janeane rose. The blood-red dress rippled, a built-in effect of the fabric. 'I'm not anyone's lady,' she said. 'He just lost the right to take me anywhere.'

'You can all shut your mouths,' said Ramirez. He didn't take his eyes off Benz. 'What's your play, suit?'

Slowly, Benz raised his hands, palms out.

'You should calm down,' he said. He stared at Ramirez with a renewed intensity, and though the cameras didn't give Resler the perfect view, he could have sworn Benz's eyes flashed blue as he spoke.

Benz smiled. 'I'd like to invite you and your friend to join us in our private pod. Let's get to know each other.'

Ramirez grimaced, like he was in pain, then nodded.

'Ah,' said Volante, using his cane to rise from the couch. He hobbled over. 'I'm not sure we have enough room for so many guests.'

'We'll make room,' said Benz, his attention still on Ramirez.

Resler stared at the screen, frozen. Something was happening.

'I'm sure this man has other places he'd rather be,' said Volante.

'Let's ask him.' Benz turned back to Ramirez. 'You seem like you could benefit from a little cognitive relaxation,' he said, and this time Resler was certain the man's eyes had flashed blue. 'How about it?'

Ramirez nodded. Slow, robotic.

'Then it's settled.' Benz looked at Janeane. 'How about you, independent lady?'

Say no, thought Resler. Turn him down and get out of there.

'Sounds fun,' said Janeane.

Benz addressed the mimic, who was hovering nearby. 'Is Mr Finnerty's pod ready?'

She smiled, glad to be of assistance. 'Indeed it is.'

'Good. Lead the way.'

Resler could feel the sweat on his back. The threads were fraying. He looked to BB, who was still lying in his recliner, his eyes on the digital ink patterns that swirled across the ceiling.

'Uh,' said Resler, keying the comm. 'We've got a problem here.'

Johnny sounded dead sober in his ear. 'What kind?'

'Something has happened to Gian.'

'What?'

'I don't know. I can't explain it. But he's going to the pod with the others. Benz insisted.'

'Do you think Benz knows?'

Resler glanced at the screens. 'I don't see how. He'd have to be clairvoyant.'

Warsaw's voice broke in. Low, tense. 'Can we abort?'

'Not if you want to get them both out in one piece.' A new voice, soft and childlike. Resler glanced at the lounge feed. BB's lips barely moved as he spoke. 'Ramirez being there changes nothing. We stick to Disco's plan.'

'He's right,' said Johnny.

Warsaw said nothing. Resler watched her, standing stock still at the rear of Toltec's kitchen, and switched to a private channel.

'Mia,' he said.

She clicked off without responding.

On the screen, Benz, Janeane and the others had left the lounge and were heading for the pneumatic that connected the foyer with the private pods. Ramirez walked with his head down and shoulders hunched. Benz wore a serene smile. Janeane looked unconcerned. The anxiety was clear on Volante's face as he stumped along behind the rest. His grand plan was falling apart.

In the basement of the prefab, Resler watched it all from the console, his knuckles white.

***

–He realised there were no pod cameras only when Janeane, Ramirez, Benz, Volante, the two suits and the bodyguard filed into theirs. He cycled through the feeds, found that the only lens in the vicinity was a ceiling-mounted camera in the corridor. He maximised the feed in time to see the mimic withdraw from the pod with a bow. As the door closed she spun on her heel and made her way back to the pneumatic.

'They're in the pod,' said Resler. 'The bodyguard, too. Coast is clear. But I'm blind. Audio only.'

The order for a microdot platter came through on the façade interface a minute later, as Resler was listening to Benz's two buddies make lewd remarks to Janeane.

'Mia, they placed the order,' he said. Then he remembered she'd switched off her comms.

He glanced at the kitchen feed, saw her already standing at the order monitor. She swiped the order onto her wrist key before another Toltec employee could take it. He watched as she shared a brief conversation with what looked to be her supervisor, a fluid with a dynamic star tattoo that exploded across their cheek, and the supervisor nodded. She was in the clear.

In the pod, Volante was speaking.

'The microdots here are of a different class. A smooth, well-rounded journey, like a wellness bath for the soul. I'm delighted to be able to experience it with you all.'

One of Benz's associates uttered a few words of agreement.

Benz's augmented voice followed, and Resler's blood ran cold all over again. 'How old are you?'

Janeane came through clear. 'How old do you want me to be?'

A laugh without humour. 'Not yet old enough to have learned that impudence rarely pays off.'

'Is that right?'

'How did you meet your partner?'

'He ain't my partner. He paid for me for the evening.'

'You're a Munroe?'

'On occasion.'

'Which agency?'

'I work for myself.'

She was smart. Smart and quick. Not a word from Ramirez. Resler looked to the prep room. Warsaw had a slate-grey platter balanced on one hand and was making for a single-person pneumatic that would take her the three floors down to the pods.

He opened all comms. 'Mia's on the move.'

A notch on his eye-over. Johnny again.

'What's the sit-rep inside the pod?'

'I don't know. I have no feed.'

'This is taufed. I'm about as much use as a glass nail up here. Should I move?'

Why are you asking me? Resler wanted to say. He was a tech guy, not a mercenary. 'Try Mia.'

'I already did. No answer.'

'Then I'd say sit tight. I need to focus.'

'Yeah.'

The comm went dead. Resler tuned back into the conversation in the pod.

'Did you ever hear of a man named Luc Benz?' asked Benz.

'He a Wraptstar?' asked Janeane.

Laughter from Benz's friends. Still nothing from Ramirez.

On the lounge screen, Resler caught sight of BB heading for the exit, but he had no time to wonder where the man was going because Warsaw had exited the pneumatic and was in the corridor. Platter in one hand, the other hanging loose, her features set.

Resler gave the false front interface the once-over. No cracks, everything holding steady. The building AI didn't even know he was there anymore. Whatever else happened tonight, he thought, at least he'd done his job properly.

Warsaw halted in front of the pod door. Resler could only see the back of her head. The Plastex full-face visor had disappeared somewhere along the way. In the camera feed, it looked as though she was frozen. Then, like a puppet on invisible strings, her body became tauter, her shoulders straighter. She waved her free hand over the sensor, alerting those in the pod that she was outside.

The door retracted into the lintel.

'Mia Warsaw,' Resler heard Luc Benz say before his comm abruptly died. 'I've been looking forward to meeting you.'

17 It was over and Mia knew it.

The pod was padded fabric and moulded furniture, geometric patterns rolling in beautiful sync across dynamic threads. The curving ceiling consisted of a single expansive lightwall on which an undersea loop-vid played in hyper-resolution. Even without any mind-altering substances, the décor cast a spell of its own.

Luc Benz watched Mia from the seat opposite the pod doorway, legs apart and his hands on his knees. Angular jaw, strong nose, full-blooded lips, throat respirator, skin that seemed to bleed health. He was perfect, except he wasn't, because when he smiled at her there was nothing that suggested warmth. She'd met mimics who showed more genuine emotion than Benz.

There was one more thing about him. His eyes were augmented.

They glinted when he turned his head. A typical by-product of optic nerve braids. Beijing tech, illegal in Europe because of its ability to manipulate neurons when configured right. But it wasn't her he was trying to control; she had no plants other than her ID chip. Janeane didn't either. Then she realised.

Ramirez.

Intracortical interface, neurotrophic electrodes. A disintegrating subcutaneous enclosure that was gradually killing him. Somehow Benz had known about it. When she glanced at Ramirez, he was already staring at her, and she could see the man trapped inside a body that was now being controlled by another.

Benz spoke.

'Please. No need to stand on ceremony. Come and join Mr Volante, Mr Ramirez and our polygon star here.'

Mia moved faster than she ever had in her life. The microdot platter crashed to the floor and as she drew the Agitator from the small of her back she knew she would have him, because the bodyguard was slow to reach for the automatic at his shoulder and the two suits sitting on either side of Janeane were slower still. Benz didn't move a muscle. She stared into eyes that were like hammered steel and aimed and squeezed.

Her arm was yanked upward and the bullet smashed into the ceiling and the lightwall sputtered and died. Before she could move, a fist slammed into her rebuilt shoulder and she screamed. As she buckled under the pain, a hand plucked the printshot from her grasp and crushed it, then grabbed her by the uniform and threw her bodily into the pod. She hit the side of a recliner with her ribs and electricity coursed through her body. As she turned onto her back and tried to breathe, she looked up at the figure who now stood in the doorway.

'No,' said Volante.

BB had lost his haori coat. The pod spotlights illuminated an exposed torso of taut flesh and metal and scars. He rolled his neck from side to side and the cracking sound carried into the room. When he grinned it soured his beautiful features. His attention shifted to Volante.

'Sorry, Disco,' he said. 'I received a better offer.'

There was no colour in the old man's face. 'Why?'

'I warned you not to take the job.'

'What have you done?' said Volante.

'I've found my place.'

'Billy. Please, Billy.'

'Don't call me that,' said BB, the words emerging as a high-pitched scream. 'You did this. You alone.'

He swept into the room, leaping over Mia as if she wasn't there, and made for Volante, but before he could close the gap the old man swept up his cane and a hypodermic needle slid out from its curving handle. His gaze found Janeane.

'I'm sorry, my dear,' he said.

He plunged the needle into his thigh. Even as BB grasped his shirt and pulled him to his feet, Volante's eyes were sliding into the back of his head. Bloody foam bubbled in the corners of his mouth and his arms and legs became slack.

BB let Volante fall to the ground and stood over him, head cocked, as if he'd never seen a dead man before. Casually, he brought a heavy boot down against the body and there was a noise like roaches being crushed. The boot came down hard again and again, on the head, the chest, the stomach. Then BB dropped to his knees, his breathing ragged, and his fists became a blur and Mia was unable to look away as the man who had been Disco Volante was turned into an unidentifiable mass.

Throughout it all, Benz didn't move.

When BB dragged himself back to his feet his hands and forearms and chest were soaked, and he whirled around and stared at Mia with the same madness that had taken control of him in Charlie's.

'Calm yourself,' said Benz.

BB continued to stare.

'I mean it.'

Manic eyes blinked. BB's breathing slowed and he shook his head. When he looked down at the mess on the floor, he seemed surprised. From the recliner closest to him he tore off a length of fabric and used it to wipe his bloodied hands.

'My apologies,' he said.

'Accepted,' said Benz. He glanced at his bodyguard, whose automatic was levelled at Mia. 'Do you have her?'

The bodyguard nodded.

'Good.' Benz stood, adjusted a shirt cuff, went to where Mia lay. His gaze wandered over her, and she had to struggle not to flinch. A manicured hand opened the smoking jacket to reveal a holster, and Mia recognised the sleek polymer body of a six-round automatic Bolo. No chance of heat-warping or becoming jammed, more expensive than an entire production hall of industrial 3D printers. She tensed, suddenly unprepared for the end.

'Stand up now, Gian,' said Benz.

A bead of sweat ran from Ramirez's temple to his jaw. His mouth moved, but no sound emerged. He rose on unsteady legs.

'Come over to me.'

Benz released the Bolo from the holster, flipped it over in his hand and held it out in invitation.

'Take this pistol and shoot yourself in the head with it.'

Janeane tried to jump up, but Benz's suits grabbed her and pinned her to the seat.

Ramirez's wavering fingers closed around the butt and the Bolo left Benz's hand and twisted through the air until the barrel was pressed against a salt and pepper temple. His pleading eyes found Mia.

'Don't do it, Gian,' said Janeane, tears tracing lines in glitter.

'Fire,' said Benz.

A growl sounded low in Ramirez's throat. His finger wrapped itself around the trigger.

There was a click. Nothing happened.

'Lucky,' whispered Janeane.

Ramirez looked at her, and with a supreme effort managed to smile.

Benz stepped forward and wrested the Bolo from Ramirez's grip. He opened the action and racked the slide until a round flew out. Then he took a step back, aimed and fired.

There was a smell of burning hair and copper.

Mia could hear Janeane screaming but she kept her eyes on Benz. If the man planned to execute her next then she would stand and die on her feet.

But Benz slid the Bolo back into its holster. 'You ladies shall be my guests at my private residence for the foreseeable future. A car is waiting upstairs. BB, help Ms Warsaw up.'

Before the ronin could obey, Janeane wriggled free from Benz's lackeys and dropped to the floor and pressed herself to Mia's side, and Mia wrapped her arms around the kid and held her. When one of the suits tried to pull Janeane away, Mia balled her fist and swung and sent him reeling. From his belt the other suit yanked free a hinged club and swung it at the back of Janeane's head.

BB caught the club before it connected. A swift jerk pulled the suit off balance, and he was forced to relinquish the weapon. BB pushed him back, into the centre of the pod.

'That is not how we treat guests,' said Benz. The Bolo was in his hand again.

'Wait,' said the suit.

Another shot. One more body joined the two on the floor. Benz's other lackey looked on, his face drained of colour.

Benz holstered the Bolo again. 'Oh, BB,' he said. 'Before I forget. Dispatch the drone.'

For a moment Mia didn't know what he meant. Then she saw Johnny on the roof and Resler in the basement. She let go of the now-mute Janeane and touched the stud at the back of her ear.

Benz smiled. 'Don't bother. All communications were cut the moment you entered the room. BB saw to that.'

BB slid back a metal plate in his forearm and pressed his thumb to a sensor. His gaze lost its intensity as he took command of a drone that was flying through the Tempelhof night, and Mia wanted to scream. Her eyes scanned the room, searching for something, anything, that she could use against her captors. But it was futile. She had walked into a trap and she had lost.

BB cleared his throat and slid the forearm plate closed.

'Payload delivered. The roof has been razed. I've dispatched the crew to secure Resler. Scopo's seek unit has been alerted for the hand-over.'

Benz nodded. 'Then it is time for us to leave.'

BB grabbed Mia and Janeane in either hand and hauled them to their feet. Mia kept hold of the kid, shielding her with her own battered body. She shivered when she felt BB's breath against her ear. His voice was barely a whisper.

'If you try to run I won't kill you. But you'll wish I had.'

A push in her back and she was in the corridor with Janeane. BB, Benz, the lackey and the bodyguard followed, and the pod became a grave. They made their way to the pneumatic that waited to take them up to the lobby and out of Toltec. As she held onto Janeane, Mia could see it all already. The club employees looking the other way and getting a tip for their discretion. The limo journey to Potsdamer Platz. The arrival at Benz's private residence. The casual violence from BB if either she or the kid breathed wrong. Then the sadism of Benz as he cut each of them open in turn, hollowed them out and sewed them shut, over and over, until their minds and their bodies failed utterly. Before the end, they would wish they had died with Gian and Volante.

Mia Warsaw had no cards left to play.

And she was afraid.

18

Resler heard Johnny shout something about a drone. Then the building exploded.

When he picked himself up off the floor, he had to cough brick dust from his lungs. The floating screens were buried under a piece of the ceiling and the wrist shackle had come free of his forearm port. The Flymotic was lying on its side, but it looked to be in one piece. More importantly, the doorway was intact. He still had a way out.

'Johnny?'

No answer.

After Benz had uttered Mia Warsaw's name, Resler had watched the Shuffle go wrong on the screen. Warsaw had drawn her gun, BB had run the length of the corridor at an improbable speed and ripped it from her grasp, and then he'd assaulted her and thrown her into the pod. Resler had relayed the scene to Johnny, who had told him to keep his attention on the feeds while he came up with a plan. The breathless warning about the drone had sounded in his skull a few minutes later and a shockwave had jarred the backbone of the prefab.

Resler tried each of the team in turn. Warsaw, Janeane, Johnny, Ramirez, Volante. Aside from the ringing in his ears, he could hear nothing. No voices, no clicks, no ambient sounds.

The Flymotic. He righted it, blew the dust from its casing, plugged the wrist shackle back in and had the machine project a holographic interface into the dead space of the basement room. Then he shifted the camera feeds from the destroyed floating screens directly to his eye-over. The feeds were too small to view collectively, so he had to cycle through each one. As he lingered on Toltec's exterior camera, a fresh sweat broke out on his brow. The building he was under was on fire. Rubble dotted the street. The arched limo idled at the kerb, its tinted mesial window reflecting yellow flame. Rain came down like a steel curtain.

He continued cycling through the feeds, then stopped. Warsaw and Janeane were in the elevator that connected the pods with the lobby. The arms of the older woman were wrapped around the younger one, and Janeane's face was streaked with tears. Benz's bodyguard with the red oculars flanked them on their left, one of the suits on their right, and a placid BB stood in front of the pneumatic doors. Benz loomed behind the two women, his eyes burning into the back of Warsaw's head. There was no sign of Ramirez, Volante or the other suit.

A voice whispered to him, told him what it meant.

The group emerged into a foyer that was all activity. The employee with the pattern-rec fluid plant and his manager stood open-mouthed by the reception block, their eyes glued to screens embedded in Plastex, no doubt watching the destruction outside. Unnoticed, Benz's group made its way past the stalagmite fountain toward the silver-plated elevator that would take them to street level.

Do something, Resler told himself. Anything.

His hands danced as they locked out the elevator, then launched a search of Toltec's schematics and indexes and data files for something to work with. The SynSult plate kicked in and cooled his mind and guided him through holographic streams. He could hear parts of the building he was under crashing to the street, but he did his best to ignore the noise as his augmented brain scanned the information being projected from the Flymotic at hyperspeed, in search of something that could give Warsaw and Janeane a chance to break free from Benz's grip.

He found it in the HAMR files.

The mimic. She was in the lounge, speaking to anxious guests who had felt the explosion and wanted to know if they were in any danger. During his time underground, Resler had read up on the ethics of hacking a mimic brain and learned how, despite their limited functionalities, it was torture for them. Once a mimic was programmed, that was it. They didn't want to be interfered with. At the time, he could conceive of no scenario in which he would need to take control of a mimic brain. Now things were different. His hackwork kit lay covered in brick dust on the ground, and he unzipped the bag and rummaged around until he found a small black cylinder, which he plugged into the Flymotic. A set of software tools appeared and he accessed the Henzai activator and used it to drill into the HAMR files until he reached the DAIEI master codes. These he fed into Toltec's central control, and when the system isolated the mimic and the Flymotic displayed its decision tree prednet, he saw that he had only to issue commands at the superordinate level and it would do his bidding.

'Forgive me,' he said.

His hands became a blur.

In the lounge the mimic stopped speaking to the guests mid-sentence, spun on her heel and left the room. She began to run, picking up speed as she headed into the foyer, and she didn't break stride as she snapped a razor-sharp glass stalagmite off the fountain. The bodyguard with the red oculars barked a warning and his auto-holster propelled his pistol into his hand, but the mimic had already launched the stalagmite, and as the suit who stood next to Janeane turned around it impaled him in the chest.

Then all hell broke loose.

The mimic slammed into the bodyguard and sent him flying into Benz, and the three went to ground. Warsaw moved, pulling Janeane after her, but BB was quick to wrap his hand around the girl's wrist and yank her from Warsaw's grasp. On the floor, the mimic's hands found the bodyguard's face and pushed her thumbs through his oculars into his skull. Then her movements became jerky, her eyes fluttering, and Resler saw that the prone Benz had a pistol in his hand and was emptying it into the mimic. A final shot split her head apart and she slumped on top of the unmoving bodyguard. Benz swung the weapon around as Warsaw made a run for the reception block.

Resler, desperate, killed the lights.

The camera feed dissolved into green. The bullet from Benz's pistol hit the fountain, shattering several stalagmites, and an unscathed Warsaw vaulted the reception block and almost landed on top of the two Toltec employees who cowered there. In the new darkness, Resler watched as Janeane buried her teeth into the knotted flesh of BB's hand and tried to wriggle free, but the man slapped her across the face with a strength that knocked her unconscious. As she slid to the floor BB went to the dead bodyguard and retrieved the pistol he'd been holding. He said something to Benz, who rose to his feet and nodded. In the darkness, the two men looked directly at the reception block.

Resler found the building's loudspeaker settings, selected a high-frequency pitch and dialled it up to an ugly volume. On the feed, Benz clamped his hands to his ears. He shouted something to BB, who shook his head and started for the reception block. Resler switched cameras and saw that the Toltec employee with the pattern-rec implant was holding open a hatch as Warsaw's spectral green figure eased into it. Resler brought up a holographic schematic, found the hatch was an entrance to a crawlspace that terminated in a utility area, and unlocked the door at its far end. On the feed, BB rounded the reception block, took one look at the open hatch and shot both Toltec employees between the eyes. Before he could follow Warsaw, Resler punched a command, and the hatch closed and sealed itself. Undeterred, BB crouched and ran practised fingers around its outline, then rose and stamped on it hard enough to make a dent. Before he could continue, Benz was by his side, his hands still pressed against his ears, shouting something that prompted a nod from BB. The two men made for the silver-plated pneumatic, BB pausing to scoop Janeane off the floor and sling her over a shoulder, and when they found the elevator locked Benz led them to the emergency stairs with his pistol drawn.

Resler manipulated the holographic schematic some more, found the command to lock the street-level Torggler doors and set the diffuser gate to incapacitate all implants. He didn't know what else to do. Even as he contemplated placing a call to the closest polizei unit, his eye-over showed BB and Benz emerging from the stairwell into Toltec's antechamber. Without dropping Janeane, BB uncoupled the third finger on his left hand to reveal a spiker, which he inserted into a wall port. The diffuser gate died and the Torgglers rolled aside, and BB eyed the street and then ran out into the oily rain and to the limo that idled with its rear door open. Benz followed a moment later, darting out from under Toltec's canopy and diving head-first into the car. The door closed and the limo flashed high-beam headlights as it accelerated away, taking Janeane with it.

Too late, Resler realised why they had made a run for the car. The rail-mounted cannons on the building's exterior. A weapon he could have used to free the kid. He felt the adrenaline in his chest and choked back a sob as he threatened to go to pieces.

Get a grip, he told himself. Right now.

He cycled through the Toltec feeds, breathing hard, but Warsaw was nowhere to be seen. Only bodies remained. There was nothing more he could do. He disconnected the wrist shackle and shut down the Flymotic console, and the rudimentary night vision on his eye-over kicked in as the room became like pitch. With fumbling hands he threw the console into his duffel together with his hackwork kit and slung it across his back. He made for the door, then paused.

The sound of boots echoed outside.

He pressed himself against the wall, felt the finality of the bricks through his shirt. The utility room was a one-way-in, one-way-out deal. No windows, shafts or holes. Everyone else had been taken care of. Now it was his turn. The question was whether they intended to take him alive or make this place his grave.

He would have preferred the latter.

A voice rattled outside.

'Owen Resler. We just wasted a lot of sweat digging out the back door to this shitbox, so get your ass out here right now, 'cos we ain't in the mood. You got a date with Scopo.'

Resler squeezed his eyes shut and breathed too much air.

'You got five seconds, puta. Then we're comin' in.'

More voices, speaking different languages. Ugly laughter.

'Cinco.'

Don't let them take you.

'Cuatro.'

Run at them. Attack them. Give them an excuse.

'Tres.'

Open your eyes. Move your legs. Do something.

'Dos.'

But he could only stand and wait to die.

'Uno.'

Gunshots drowned out the final word. Resler dropped to the floor, hugging his knees to his chest and screaming expletives he couldn't hear over the noise. These were his final moments, blind and dumb and terrified, and he wished it could have been different.

The firing stopped.

When Resler opened his eyes and looked toward the doorway, his eye-over illuminated an apparition. Clothes charred, skin blackened, ear and neck bloodied. A snaplight hung from a sash belt. Trembling hands cradled two heat-warped printshots.

'Well,' said Johnny. 'You ain't dead.'

***

It took Resler a couple of tries to find his voice. 'Neither are you.'

Johnny looked down at himself, as if surprised. 'Not yet.'

'What happened?'

'I was at the stairwell when the firebomb hit. Blew me clean down the stairs, knocked me out for a while. Are you hurt?'

Resler scrambled to his feet. 'I don't think so. No.'

'Good. The bulls are on their way. We need to go.'

'The others.'

Johnny held up a hand. 'It can wait.'

The corridor was a mess, all chipped stone and scorch marks and claret splashes. Resler had to step over five bodies that had been chewed up by Johnny's guns, and as the taste of blood built up in the back of his throat he wanted to retch. He followed Johnny up the stairs and through the remains of the building to an exit carved out of the rubble. Outside, he could hear the whine of drone motors far above, an automatic voice issuing a warning for all humans and automatons within hearing range to remain where they were. Rain drummed against concrete, heavy and apocalyptic. As they made their way along the narrow backstreet, Johnny stumbled and clutched at his side and groaned.

'Sekhmet. Are you hit?' asked Resler, knowing how foolish the question sounded.

'Keep going,' said Johnny with a grimace. 'The bike's just around the corner.'

They found it with the boobytraps disabled and the body and wiring half-stripped, but when Resler touched his index finger to the port the eVelo warmed up and the lights flickered on.

'Good morning, Mr Pleasance,' it said.

After Johnny eased himself onto the pillion, Resler took the stick and guided the bike onto a soaking potholed road. No drones buzzed them as they went, and before long they had put some distance between themselves and Toltec. Resler turned off at the intersection preceding Tempelhofer Feld and merged with the traffic slipstream on Innenbahn Zwei. Despite having half its parts missing, the eVelo held together, though he had to fight to keep it steady.

'How are you doing?' he shouted behind him.

'Hanging on,' said Johnny. 'Tell me what happened.'

'BB betrayed us. He's working for Benz.'

'Son of a bitch. Volante, too?'

'No. I think he's dead. Him and Ramirez, back in the pod. I didn't see them come out.'

Johnny muttered a few words Resler couldn't hear. A prayer, an oath, something.

'What about the girls?'

'Benz has Janeane.'

'Christ. And Mia?'

'BB roughed her up but she got free. The last I saw of her, she was still inside. I don't know.'

'Where are we going now?'

'The rendezvous.'

'No, man. Think about it. BB knows the address.'

Resler gripped the bars tighter, shook his head. Wake up, Owen, he told himself. Wake up or you're dead.

Then he had an idea.

'Hold on.'

He pulled the bike off the Innenbahn and plunged into the grid-like streets of New Kreuzberg. The rain continued its bombardment. Efficient newbuilds abruptly gave way to container stacks, nu-crete prefabs, failed biotectures and old pre-Act blocks. Signs and holographics and lightwalls burned like flash fires on the steppe. Citizens sheltered under haggard Plastex canopies, while dayglo escorts flaunted their flesh under the broken sky. They were in the Ge-nuSstadt, where lowlifes thrived and dreams died.

When Resler tucked the bike into an eVelo dock, the system issued a warning for him to remain there until a maintenance employee arrived to assess the damage. Johnny's skin was like fibrepaper and blood leaked through the hand that was pressed to his side. Resler went to take him by the arm but the soldier shook his head.

'Where?' he asked through gritted teeth.

'I know a place that's safe,' said Resler. He hoped it was true.

In the rain-soaked dawn, Berlin's entertainment district looked like the memory of a collapsing dream. They followed a rubber strip choked with pepped suits and spectral blue-collars, past graft parlours and vial vendors and carbogen bars and fleshhouses with roller gauze covering the windows. Chancers clocked the duffel at Resler's shoulder and he held it tight. He followed arrows only he could see on his eye-over, into a deserted lane barely wide enough for two people to stand shoulder to shoulder. Halfway down was a shuttered door with a name spelled out above it in sad lights: Hotel Babette. He punched the intercom, prayed Ivo's information was good.

The screen flickered and a woman's face appeared.

'I need a room,' he said. 'The name's Pleasance.'

'How long?'

'A night. Maybe two.'

'Alone?'

'No.' He stepped aside so the woman could see Johnny in the intercom's eye.

'Payment upfront.'

'Okay.'

'If you're trying to rip this place off —'

'I know, it's an automatic,' said Resler. 'We just want to be out of the rain.'

The screen died. There was a click and the shutter retracted and the door opened. Resler ducked inside, followed by Johnny. In a narrow hallway, Johnny dug a neweuro card from his blood-soaked jacket and settled the room fee. A creaking staircase took them up to the first floor. Six rooms, one whose door was open. Scuffed walls, disinfectant smell, no windows. The room contained a single bed, a chair, a sink and a screen. A four-bladed fan hung motionless overhead.

Johnny half-fell onto the bed and he closed his eyes. A trickle of blood began to dirty the sheet. Resler remained standing in the doorway, panic rising.

What are you gonna do now, Owen? asked the voice of his sister in his head.

Her question echoed without answer.

FOUR

WOUNDED ANIMALS

19 There was a staircase in Berlin that descended into the old train tunnels underneath the city. It was unremarkable except for two things. First, it was one of only three entry points that had not been claimed by a gang, rendered impassable by a barricade or become lost to a cave-in. Second, there was a rusted metal sign over the entrance to the stairs that bore a quotation: 'I carry the bars within me'. None who used the staircase paid any attention to the words. In subterranea, the only language that counted was survival, and survival came from being quiet and being quick and keeping to the shadows. Underneath the world there were no bulls, no suits, no drones, no all-seeing eyes. Only the forgotten and the lost.

Mia Warsaw was the latter. She had to hold on to the wall as she took the stairs down into the tunnel system. Her bad shoulder burned. Glass had bitten her face, her arms, her torso. After escaping from Toltec via a disposal chute, she'd lain low in a nearby derelict, sleeping fitfully until the polizei had withdrawn from the area. Then she'd walked for hours, too afraid to risk public transport, too broke to order a kingCab, until she'd reached the staircase. Now, at the bottom of it, she found herself in a tunnel painted orange by illegal strip lights, and the slingers and the hustlers who loitered there gave her the once-over and saw she was not a woman who had anything to offer them. She had made the same journey through the tunnels only once before, but even in her exhausted state the directions came to her without prompting. It took another half-hour to reach her destination: a utility tunnel unmarked by gang colours. The blast door was open, the autocannons bowed. She was expected.

Her skin crawled as she hobbled along the shaft. Invisible eyes watched her from every angle, hidden amid rusting pipes and junked tech boxes and colourless girders. At the end of the shaft was an airlock, sealed tight. She leaned with one hand against a brick wall shored up with graphene netting and waited.

A generic AI voice spoke. 'Please state your purpose.'

'Mantis, I need your help.'

'I must ask for specifics,' said the AI.

'The job fell apart. Everyone is dead. I'm hurt.' She hesitated before she spoke her next words. 'If you patch me up and give me what I need, I'll work it off. Any way you want.'

Silence followed. Mia's body throbbed.

The AI spoke. 'Step back.'

Locks clicked and clamps released and the airlock door arched open. Mia stepped into a small chamber and the door closed behind her, and there was the sound of air being recycled. Two nozzles emerged from hatches to her left and right and sprayed her with an odourless disinfectant that made her want to sneeze. The next door yawned open and she crossed into a spherical chamber that bled hardware. Consoles, tools, robotic arms, a graft bed. Condensation dripped from the walls and collected in recycling trays. The air tasted too clean. Screens displayed codes, data streams, status bars, Wraptstar content.

Standing at the centre of it all was Mantis.

Puller of strings, architect of data, gambler of lives. Conductive ceramic fingernails, bloodless lips, pale skin, a deep graft-induced scar at their temple. They wore a bacteriostatic graphene suit that shimmered under ultraviolet diodes and a pair of oversized magniX goggles. Mia had been to the chamber once before, and then, as now, she'd been hurt bad. Mantis had paid people to stitch her up and change her chips and hide her until the law cooled, and Mia had promised to pay them back.

Life had a habit of repeating itself.

'You look like you wrestled with a bale of razor wire and lost,' said Mantis.

'I need your help.'

'You said that already.'

They gestured at a padded chair stacked with junked devices, and Mia went to it and cleared it and sat. She closed her eyes, saw Janeane dancing in darkness.

A robotic arm chased a rail along the top of the chamber and swooped down with a cup in its hand.

'Please drink this,' said the AI.

Mia didn't ask what was in it. Even as she tipped it back, she could feel the liquid working its way through her. After a few moments her shoulder stopped burning and her head became clear.

'I need you to run a trace for me,' she said.

Mantis peered at her, eyes weakened by years spent under artificial light.

'Before I do anything for you, let us agree on what you mean by working off your existing and future debt.'

Mia tried to stay calm. 'Wetwork, theft, erasure. Anything you want. After I get Benz.'

'Can you?'

'Can I what?'

Mantis's voice had an edge of irritation to it. 'Can you get him?'

'I have to. He took someone from me, and I need to get her back.'

One of the screens behind Mantis was tuned to Wraptstar. On it, a samnite fighter entered a packed amphitheatre. The name Ace Alessi flashed up alongside his vital stats.

'The girl Janeane.'

'Yes,' said Mia. 'She's just a kid. Please.'

Mantis held her gaze. 'Give me the trace input.'

Mia reeled off Janeane's falsified bio-identification key.

Mantis went to a console that was twice the size of anything Mia usually saw on the surface and brought up a holographic topography of the city. With their ceramic nails they lifted the hologram and threw it into the centre of the chamber, and the topography expanded until its undulating lines lapped against the walls.

'Run the trace, InTen,' said Mantis.

Red dots were for chips inside people who were still alive. Grey chips belonged to the dead.

'ID found,' said the AI.

'Show me.'

A pulsing red dot appeared amid the lilac web. Mia breathed.

Mantis manipulated the topography until Mia found herself looking at a grid-like representation of Potsdamer Platz. The red dot was in one of the Platz's ten superscrapers, Nerthus IV, approximately halfway up.

'Benz's suite,' said Mia, more to herself than to Mantis.

'If you're planning on going in there, the deal's off.'

Mia watched the dot and tried to keep her mounting despair at bay as she ran through a list in her head. Volante, dead. Ramirez, dead. Johnny Seven, dead. BB, at large. Resler? The suit was the only one she wasn't sure about.

'Run another trace for me. The data fracker you put me onto.'

She spoke Resler's new ID aloud and Mantis's AI began a new search.

The suit's chip was red. And it wasn't where Mia expected it to be. The holographic topography zoomed in and lingered on an automatic rack-and-stack in one of the GenuSstadt's abscesses.

'Would you like me to place the call?' asked Mantis.

'Please.'

The topography faded almost to nothing and a screen floated across to Mia and resized itself until it was slightly larger than her head. The screen glowed blue and a double white helix spiralled in a digital sea.

On the Wraptstar channel, the samnite Ace Alessi stalked his opponent.

The helix fused and the blue field dissolved into a grainy image of a sparse, windowless hotel room. Resler filled the centre of the frame. Johnny Seven lay on a bed behind him, eyes closed.

'Oh, thank Christ,' said Resler.

'Is he alive?' Mia asked.

'Yes,' he said. 'But he's hurt and needs a doctor. I don't know what to do.'

She squinted at Johnny and thought she saw his eyelid twitch.

'Where are you, Mia?' asked Resler.

'Underground. Why Babette?'

He frowned. 'How did you know that?'

She waited.

'Someone I trust put me onto this place,' he said. 'But I'm scared, Mia. Anyone could have seen us come in here.'

I don't give a damn, she thought. Janeane's the one who needs help. You can't even get it together enough to put out a call for StadtMed to pick up Johnny. She allowed her irritation to boil over. 'What would you have done if I didn't contact you, Owen? Would you have just left him like that?'

'I don't know. Christ, I don't know.'

He pressed a knuckled hand to his forehead and shook. As she watched his anguish, her anger faded.

'Okay, okay. Be calm. We need to get both of you away from the GenuSstadt. It's way too hot.' She paused. The Delphi was out. 'I'll charter a kingCab and pick you up. You just have to get streetside.' She checked the map. 'The corner of the Mardi Marquis and Shishido Carbogen.'

'Where are we going?'

'Wait.'

Mia muted the sound and looked past the screen. 'I need a clinic.'

Mantis barely hesitated. 'There's a place called Weltschmerz in Gesundbrunnen. Good doctor, used to work at New Charité before he was canned. It's going to cost you, though.'

'Like I said, I'll work it off.'

'You'll have to survive first.'

On the Wraptstar feed, Ace Alessi swung his short sword, missing his opponent by a hair.

'I aim to.'

'Same as a lot of people. Doesn't always pan out that way.'

'Extend me the credit line or don't. I haven't got time for this.'

They held each other's gaze, too many seconds elapsing for Mia to know what the response would be. Then Mantis shrugged, a human gesture that didn't seem right coming from them. 'It's yours. But this is your limit. Don't ask for more.'

Mia exhaled, relief softening the pain that was slowly returning to her body. She unmuted the screen. Resler was looking behind him, at the prone form of Johnny.

'Owen.'

He shivered, turned to the screen with a silent question in his eyes.

'We're taking Johnny to a clinic. Get to the corner of the Mardi Marquis and Shishido Carbogen. Okay?'

A nod. 'How long will you be?'

'An hour. I'll have the cab ping you when I'm fifteen minutes out. That should be plenty of time. Wake Johnny up now. Find something to wrap his wounds with. You don't want him bleeding in the street. Can you do that?'

Resler nodded again. 'And if the bulls stop us?'

Then enjoy the rest of your life on a slavenet, she wanted to say. 'They won't. Trust me.'

She winced as heat radiated along her side. The restorative was definitely wearing off. 'Look, Owen. I need you to keep it together for a little while longer. You managed to get out of Tempelhof without dying. That's harder than what I'm asking you to do now. Be smart, don't attract attention and keep your head down. See you in an hour.'

She cut the feed. The screen dissolved and the bar floated across the chamber and deposited itself in a recess. Mantis had moved over to a visualisation table surrounded by a patchwork quantum whose hardware took up one quarter of the chamber. Boxed Josephson junctions bearing the crimson markings of a famous Beijing corporate stood side by side with dark green milspec Plastex, under which optical components — photon emitters, beam splitters, photoresistors, pulsed laser diodes, interferometers — produced, split and changed the phase of photons. Condensation streamed into run-off gullies, cycling liquid into the quantum's central cooling system whose throat was always parched. Mantis studied a labyrinthine wire-frame holographic cylinder through their magniX goggles. Mia recognised the cylinder as a Mercy door. Unbreakable, supposedly, though only until the future proved otherwise.

'I'm going,' she said.

Mantis flipped the magniX goggles up, threw her a hard look. 'In-Ten will order a kingCab for the nearest exit. That's Bismarck. The slingers controlling it will give you safe passage. I'll add that to the bill, too. Need an escort?'

Mia shook her head. 'I'll be fine.' She looked down at the ripped and bloodied Toltec uniform she was wearing, then at the datatect in their bacteriostatic graphene suit. 'I don't suppose you have any spare clothes lying around?'

'Sure,' said Mantis, gesturing at the tech-lined chamber. 'Pick anything off the rack.'

'I'm a little short on humour right now.'

The AI arm swooped down and handed her a flashlight and a Daisy baton, fully charged.

'These are on the house,' said Mantis. 'The slingers at Bismarck will give you something to wrap yourself in.'

'Thank you.'

They eyed each other, one a desperate mercenary, the other a minor deity of the underworld, and each saw respect reflected back at them. Maybe that was why Mantis allowed her to push it so far, thought Mia. Either that or they simply knew a good deal when they saw one.

'Do you think you have a chance?' asked Mantis.

Mia saw Benz and she saw BB and she saw the Nerthus towers rising like skeletal fingers from cemetery soil. 'Not yet. But I'll make one.'

'Then good luck.'

Mia nodded, limped to the airlock. On the Wraptstar feed, the match was ending. Ace Alessi stood over his battered opponent, the short sword poised. The crowd in the amphitheatre was frenetic. They wanted more. They demanded a blood sacrifice to the entertainment gods. And as Mia waited for the door to unlock he gave it to them.

Mechanical sounds were followed by a hiss of escaping air and the door opened and Mia left Mantis and her solitary, sterile world behind. As she made her way through the cramped tunnel, the reassuring weight of the Daisy in her pocket, Mia heard the kid's voice echo in front, behind and around her.

'When I go in there,' Janeane said. 'I've got Mia Warsaw at my back. Even if it all goes to hell, we'll find a way to walk out clean. You and me.'

20 Gesundbrunnen carried traces of the old city in its blood. Electric opportunity in the streets, the promise of carbon and neweuro by whatever means. Families spanning multiple generations were dug into brutalist blocks, unable to be prised out through incentive or coercion. Hardy businesses flouted climate rules, selling everything from polyester threads spun over the border in Poland to cuts of celmeat grown illegally in vats outside the capital. There was no love for bulls or growthers or the Preservation Act in the neighbourhood. If the kiez honchos could've had their way, they would've excised Gesundbrunnen from the rest of Berlin and let it thrive as a miniature free state, unburdened by the debts amassed by the hyperrich. But that would've taken an army.

Resler had never been inside a clinic as filthy as Weltschmerz. Run by a slender-faced Brit who was already blind drunk when they arrived and who continued to drink while he cut and sewed, there was dried blood on the walls and on the floor and the stink of old death in the air. The lights were pharmacy green, which lent everything a sickly glow. Resler kept to the edge of the operating room and watched the surgeon work first on Johnny and then on Mia Warsaw. Now Johnny was out cold on a vinyl graft bed, his exposed torso mummified with bandages, bloodied gauze littering a trolley top. When the surgeon clicked two red fingers, a clean-up bot trundled out from a wall recess and swept the contents into the opening in its side and then withdrew.

'This chap was certainly on some junk,' said the surgeon, casting bloodshot eyes at Johnny. 'Even if he hadn't sprung a leak, it would have only been a matter of time before he blew a gasket.'

He went to a locker and tried the door, and when nothing happened he thumped the side of it and it sprang open. From within he produced a bottle of clear liquor and took a long pull. He held it out to Warsaw, who declined. Resler accepted the bottle and drank and did his best not to choke on the taste.

'My own brand,' said the surgeon, noticing his grimace. 'It has been said that it packs a veritable punch.'

'Will he be okay?' asked Warsaw.

'He lost enough blood to fill a bucket, but he'll be fine. He has a couple of high-grade internals that will help repair his body swiftly enough. Was he military, by any chance?'

She nodded.

'Thought so. One can always tell.' The surgeon plucked the bottle from Resler's hand and drank again. 'Still, those internals only work properly when the body isn't reliant on certain other substances, so I performed a full flush.'

Resler stirred. 'What does that mean?'

'Oh. Evacuated the toxins, introduced a little transmitter trimix. That's disulfiram, anticonvulsants and receptor antagonists, you understand. He'll wake up with a headache, but his cravings should be broken long enough to get himself shipshape.'

'Right,' said Resler. He wasn't sure what shipshape was supposed to mean or if Johnny had ever been that.

'How much do we owe you?' asked Warsaw.

The surgeon waved his hand. 'Your benefactor took care of it. They're a good sport, no? They send plenty of business bleeding through my doors.'

But not enough to pay for someone to clean the place up a little, thought Resler.

The surgeon belched and wiped his mouth with the back of his hand and threw the bottle back into the locker. 'Pardon. Would you excuse me for a few minutes? Your friend's repairs required a lot of juice, so I have to reset the auxiliaries for the graft beds. It's upstairs, you see.'

'Fine,' said Warsaw.

The surgeon lurched toward a narrow staircase at the back of the room and took the handrail with both hands. With the sound of his footsteps receding, Warsaw rose and checked on Johnny, then retrieved a black ripstop nylon bag from a corner and started to strip off her ruined Toltec uniform.

Resler turned away. 'What do we do now?'

'I told you already.'

'You said what you plan to do. What about me? What about Johnny?'

'You're free to go. You did your job. Johnny will decide for himself when he wakes up.'

He shook his head. It wasn't enough. He couldn't just wave good-bye and hit the streets. The panic he'd felt back at Hotel Babette was dwindling with every moment he spent in Warsaw's presence. It wasn't over.

'Come on.'

'What is it you want from me?' she asked.

'I don't know,' he said, and realised he didn't. 'How do you know Janeane is still alive?'

'Mantis had a map. Her bio-identification key is still red. She's in Nerthus IV.'

Resler listened to the sound of fabric tearing.

'Besides,' she said, her voice colourless. 'Benz keeps his victims alive for days. That's his kink.'

'What if he's duplicated the key? He knows you're not dead. It could be bait. A mirror trace.'

There came the buzz of a zip being pulled up. 'I'll take that chance. Hey, Resler.'

He glanced over his shoulder, saw she'd changed into a grey jumpsuit with bioseal pouches on the sleeves, legs and chest, and a pair of heavy boots. Maintenance-wear, robust and reliable.

'Pass me that baton, would you?'

He looked where she was pointing. A Daisy, weighted at the handle, lay on a counter flecked with brown. He handed it over.

'Did you give Volante or BB your neural ID?' she asked.

He shook his head.

'Good. Now, you're going to think this is above your pay grade, but I've got another question for you. What's the best way to get into Nerthus?'

He stared. 'How should I know?'

'Because you aren't as dumb as you look. Let's take it step by step. What kind of security would I be up against if I hit the main entrance?'

He thought of Scopo's defences, mapped them onto Nerthus. 'All of it. Mimic guards, drones, diffuser gates, organic-enhanced security, and a central control AI that'll bring down the iron curtain and alert the bulls the moment it senses danger. It's likely each tower has its own in-house rapid response team, too. Humans, automatons or both.'

'And if I enter a different way? Say, via a landing pad?'

'By glider? It's smarter, at least. Suits look down for danger, not up. But there's one major obstacle.'

'Which is?'

'Money. Do you know how much you have to pay for a seat on a glider?' Resler laughed softly, listening to his own question. 'I do. How much cash do you have left?'

'Zero.'

A thought bubbled its way to the surface, pushed his fatigue into the background. He watched as Warsaw slid the Daisy into a hip pouch.

'Then I find another way,' she said. 'A back door.'

He wanted to tell her again that it was suicide. That she might as well ask the surgeon to give her a lethal shot now. But he only looked at her and wished he had her resolve.

'I'll come with you.'

The voice was rough. They both turned. Johnny was sitting up on the graft bed, his green eyes alert. An exploratory hand reached to the side that had been ripped open and sewn shut.

'How are you feeling?' asked Resler.

'Dead awake,' said Johnny. He nodded at Warsaw. 'If you want my advice, we find a vantage point, set up with a rifle and wait until he comes out. Then we blast away until he stops breathing.'

Resler shook his head. 'There are more eyes on Potsdamer Platz than anywhere else in the city. Vantage points don't exist. Even if you wrapped the gun in plumbition weave, the drones would be on you the moment you made a suspicious move.'

'And that won't get the kid out,' said Warsaw. 'It has to be from the inside.'

'Okay,' said Johnny. He eased himself off the bed and reached for his jacket, which lay on the dirt-streaked tile. The tremble in his hands was gone.

'Take it easy,' said Warsaw.

'I'm fine. And don't try to talk me out of anything. I liked that kid.'

There was silence as he pulled on his jacket. Resler waited, then waited some more. He heard his sister again: what are you gonna do now, Owen? Because it turned out there was something he could do. Something they couldn't.

'I may be able to get you onto a glider,' he said.

Warsaw raised an eyebrow, questioning.

'The Scopo data. Mantis is still holding it for me, or at least I assume they are. They auction it off and we use the carbon to get you set up. If it's enough, that is.'

Warsaw shook her head. 'Whatever you make from that deal is yours. You can use it to change your face, get another chip, begin again.'

Resler looked down at himself, then at her. 'I've started over more times than I care to count. I'm not a suit, I'm not a growther, I'm not a radical and I'm damn sure not like any of you. I'm not anything except what I am. Now, I'm cashing in and you're taking the carbon.'

'Owen,' said Warsaw. 'You don't have to do this.'

'You won't change my mind. If there's one of us that deserves a second chance, it's the kid. I'm not leaving her with Benz any more than you are.'

'Then I accept,' said Warsaw, and Resler wasn't sure if he'd imagined her voice waver.

'You're a good man, Owen,' said Johnny.

Resler hesitated. 'Just one thing.'

'Yes?' asked Warsaw.

'How do I get in touch with Mantis?'

***

The call to Mantis was swift. The full deck of bidders wasn't ready, but there were enough standing by who had expressed an interest in the data and would be keen to broker a deal quickly. Resler asked the datatect to extract a solitary file and send it to him, then sell the rest. Another idea was forming.

When he dissolved the eye-over, he saw Warsaw coming down the narrow staircase at the back of the room.

'The doc's sleeping off his libations,' she said by way of explanation. 'What's the verdict?'

'Mantis expects to have a buyer within the next three-O minutes.'

'That data must be white hot,' said Johnny, who was back on the graft bed. He cradled a mug of quickheat vitamino Warsaw had found in the surgeon's locker. 'No wonder they sent their best cleaners after you.'

'I had a thought about the security in Nerthus IV,' said Resler, changing the subject. 'One of the Scopo files contained information about a man called Falko Wagenknecht, the chief data scientist at a company called Ynside. It does all the upkeep for the Yuanrang Ten control systems in the Nerthus towers.'

'You've lost me,' said Warsaw.

'Wagenknecht will likely have access codes to those control systems. If I can get hold of them, I might be able to take control of Benz's floor and isolate it.'

'Why not the whole building?' asked Johnny.

'Because my brain would fry in less time than it takes to cook an egg.' He tapped the side of his head. 'But with my SynSult plate and the codes, a few floors should be possible. Theoretically, at least. In any case, I'll need to meet Wagenknecht in person.'

'I can do it,' said Warsaw.

'And wave a gun in his face? It won't work. He'll just make up some bull, sell it to you and go straight to Benz. Suits understand a different kind of threat. I'll contact him straight, spin him a headhunter story, then use the information in the file to prise the codes out of him.' He glanced around the green-hued clinic, saw no windows. 'What time is it, anyway?'

'Nine-midi, evening,' said Johnny.

'I'll ping him tonight with an aim to meet tomorrow lunchtime. In the meantime, I'll hook up the Flymotic and start creating an infiltration program for Nerthus IV. My hackwork kit has an index of old programs from my underground days I can work with.'

Warsaw looked at him, the surprise clear on her face. 'Could it be you're taking charge, Owen?'

He managed a weak grin. 'Maybe. Do you feel up to a job?'

'Depends what kind.'

'I'll have to enter central control locally. Remote wireless meshes and false fronts won't work on Nerthus. I have to be on site, and to get through the door I need apex shrouds.'

Warsaw shrugged.

'Artificial ID-locked retinas. They bluff the entrance scanners. Believe me, I'd rather avoid it. The insertion procedure is supposed to be agony. But I can't get inside without them.'

'Okay. Where?'

He fell silent, thinking. Then he clicked his fingers. 'Amerika, over by Zoologischer Garten. There's an eyetech engineer named Henrietta Bes. If you can find her, she should be able to take care of it. She has my VCF. Maybe she'll remember my name. If she agrees, she can take a cut from the Scopo carbon when it arrives.'

Johnny let out a soft laugh. 'Refus trade in neweuro, man. How would they benefit from keeping their carbon footprint in the minus?'

Resler felt the blood prick in his cheeks. 'We don't have any neweuro right this second.'

'I can be persuasive,' said Warsaw.

'I don't want her exploited. It doesn't matter who we're doing it for.'

'I didn't say anything about exploiting,' said Warsaw, frowning. 'We aren't all lowlifes, just like all suits aren't econopaths.'

More embarrassment. 'Sorry. Tension's getting to me.'

He went to a desk at the back of the room, rooted around in the drawers until he found a scrap of fibrepaper and a pencil. He had his eye-over perform a dimensional scan, then wrote down the measurements and handed the scrap to Warsaw.

'My pupillary distance and prescription. Give it to Bes.'

Warsaw glanced at the figures, stuffed the fibrepaper into her jumpsuit. 'If that's all, I'll head out now.'

'Want me to come with?' asked Johnny.

Warsaw shook her head. 'When the surgeon wakes up from his nap, ask him to give you a once-over before he starts drinking again. If you're fit, I want you to do something for us.'

'Tell me.'

'We need guns.'

'What kind?'

'The killing kind.'

Johnny nodded. 'I'll take care of it. But bear in mind we're gonna need to get them through airport security if we're taking a glider.'

Resler, listening, recalled a conversation he'd had with De Witt what seemed like a lifetime ago. 'Some bodyguards travel under an exemption pass,' he said. 'Honto expensive, but you can go through the detectors without having to open your case.'

Warsaw shouldered the nylon bag and nodded. 'You're full of surprises, Owen. Keep it up.'

'Before you go, we need a new meet,' said Johnny. 'I'm not walking around Gesundbrunnen weighed down with hardware.'

Warsaw thought for a moment. 'We'll rendezvous tomorrow at Jimmy Chee's graft shop in Container City. He owes me a favour.' She went to a wall cabinet, opened it, tipped several blister packs of pills and vials into the bag. 'Reimburse the doc for these,' she said. 'And good luck, both of you.'

Then she was gone.

'Better wake the sawbones,' said Johnny.

Before Resler could reply, a notch blinked on his eye-over. The ID was scrubbed.

Mantis.

'Yes,' he said. Only now was he gripped by the fear that the theft of the data, the danger he'd put Ina and Ngozi in, everything he'd endured since being fired, had been for nothing. Why would anyone want the Scopo files? Every corporation knew their competitors played dirty. That was what gave them the excuse to do it themselves. The only interested groups would be activists and journalists, and their accounts tended to be painted red rather than black.

Mantis's tone was calm, disinterested. 'The data is sold.'

'For how much?'

When they pinged him a banco-file, he wanted both to laugh and to cry. Instead, he forced himself to think of Janeane. The carbon wasn't for him. It was an ugly means to a better end. Or at least he hoped it was.

'You're rich, Owen Resler.'

'I see that. Who bought it?'

'Scopo's main rival. A subsidiary of Faber that works on suprasubliminal technology.'

'Go ahead and take your cut.'

'I already did.'

He coughed. 'I need a clean account in the name of Mr Amsden Pleasance. Can you do that?'

'Yes. You'll have the details shortly.'

'Thank you.'

'It was a pleasure doing business with you, Owen Resler.'

The connection cut. A few seconds later he received the information for an account at a small holding bank he'd never heard of, coded to his false ID.

He dissolved the eye-over and went to the surgeon's locker and found the bottle of homebrew and took a pull.

'Good news?' asked Johnny, watching him.

'Better than I could ever have hoped for,' said Resler. He plugged the bottle and set it down, then looked into the unsettling eyes of the career soldier. 'We're going to die doing this, aren't we?'

'Probably. Best to decide now how you face it. Dignity or despair.'

'Easy to say.'

'Easy enough to do, too.' Johnny went to Resler, laid a hand on his shoulder. 'You've done great up to now. Don't go pretending you lost your spine, because I can see it just fine.'

Resler nodded, more to himself than to Johnny.

'Let's get to work,' he said.

21 A spit-shined moon was hung up on display, artificial orange fuzz rising to meet it. The S-Bahn train flitted between darkened biotecture scrapers on tracks that should have been condemned, every corner accompanied by the scream of metal on metal. Generic lightwall billboards touting subscription medication services and high-risk, high-reward LINK programmes threw colour onto sun-faded carriages. Inside, chemical hawkers whispered their wares, the better to take the edge off the day, and many passengers gave in to the temptation and snorted, swallowed or drank their purchases and wished to be home already.

Mia Warsaw stood with her back to a window at the rear of the train, her gaze taking in the faces without settling on any one. Slavenetters, cleaning crews, mimics: Benz could have activated one or all or none of them, depending on how much of a threat he considered her. BB likely would have counselled the Habanik heir to hunt her down, but BB was hired muscle, so who knew if Benz would listen? Either way, caution was her strongest ally.

She hoped Janeane was hanging on.

The S-Bahn followed a long, lazy curve that brought it parallel with Hauptbahnhof, where short-flight gliders rose on tiltrotors from illuminated pads, joining flight corridors that snaked through downtown to Potsdamer Platz, Brandenburg Airport and the heavily guarded IG Band plants at Ahrensfelde. The only trains that ran to Hauptbahnhof now were maglev bullets linking Berlin with Hamburg and Frankfurt and beyond. The S-Bahn didn't stop there. Anyone riding it had no business at glider central.

After the gliders the S-Bahn plunged back into the jungle, weaving between nu-crete and glass and metal and graphene composite. There were many building sites populated by exoskeletal baggers and AI-assisted cranes. Rubberised pedestrian strips were awash with the crowds of night. The tinny automatic voice of the train spoke the station names at the same time as they appeared on an overhead screen in Latin, Cyrillic, Chinese and Greek script. Westhafen, Turmstrasse, Bellevue, Tiergarten. Then one more: Zoologischer Garten.

On the platform, Mia moved through the crowds, down gum-caked stairs and into a swirling foyer, where refus with tired eyes held out tablets to commuters. Scarred guardians lined the walls, waiting for their services to be called on. She approached a tall man holding a bo staff whose midriff was swathed in blue-dyed wraps. Irezumi tattoos extended from his wrists to his pectorals. He held out his hand, palm facing her, in greeting, and she did the same.

'Dae yill want tae gang intae Am-town?'

She nodded. 'Who do I see if I need to find someone?'

'Hae tae praat tae Tagawa.'

'A honcho?'

The man shook his head. 'Kens refus.'

'Will you take payment in pharma?'

He shrugged.

She handed him the nylon bag of drugs she'd ransacked from the clinic, and he took one look inside and nodded. He swung the bo staff around and rested it against his shoulder, then beckoned for her to follow.

They took the east exit, which opened directly onto Amerika. Lights strung up on poles, running on leeched juice, dictated a path through tents and huts and shelters. It was late, but the heat of the day lingered on the ground. Unshaven men with wild eyes looked at Mia, some with curiosity, some with disdain, and she kept one hand on the concealed Daisy. Her hire-guardian moved lightly for a large man, the bo staff nodding against his shoulder, and he glanced behind him every few metres to check she was still there.

A fork in the path led them deeper into the refu sprawl. Left alone by the corporate-sponsored police precincts, Amerika was governed by its own set of laws. The air was alive with languages, mixing and separating like oil on water. Lookout kids whistled when they spied Mia with the hire-guardian, and the piercing sounds carried through to the turf leaders who controlled the drink, drugs, prostitution, gambling and digital opiates in the camp and who fought wars with each other because it was the only power they had left to cling to.

The hire-guardian stopped at a modest structure made of polymer-reinforced bamboo sheets, its entrance concealed by a mosquito net.

'Tagawa,' he said.

Mia pulled back the net and was greeted by the smell of jasmine. The interior was lit by candles and the glow of multiple floating screens. An incense stick dropped ash onto a plinth made of stacked red bricks. At the centre of the hut was a recliner and in it was a man with a spiky blonde cut and white ocular lenses. He wore an elaborate red and gold jacket with flowing black pants. His face seemed to be pulled down on the left and the corner of his mouth twitched.

When he spoke it was in a language Mia didn't understand. She said nothing.

'You don't have a lingua chip.' His words were heavily accented.

'No.'

'You are not from this camp.'

'No.'

'What do you want?'

'I'm looking for an eyetech engineer. Henrietta Bes is the name.'

Tagawa shifted in the recliner. 'Are you here to kill her?'

Mia squinted at him. 'No.'

'But you are a mercenary.'

'Of a kind.'

'Which kind?'

'The kind that doesn't ask a stranger to point them in the right direction if they're planning to end someone's life.'

The corner of Tagawa's mouth twitched. 'Can you get her away?'

'From here?'

He nodded.

'Does she want to go?'

A shrug. 'I do not know. But she is being threatened by a gang.'

'Why do you care?'

'She has done good work for me. I have looked out for her, but I cannot keep doing it. My partner has had a child. I will not put my family in danger for someone else.'

Mia bit her tongue. She didn't care about the man's story, but saying so wouldn't get her anywhere. 'Where can I find Bes?'

'Tell your guardian to take you to the aviary. Her workshop is there.'

'Thanks.'

On the threshold of the hut he called a single word. 'Mercenary.'

She turned.

'Come and find me,' he said, 'if you ever need a job.'

'Doing what?'

The light from the candles reflected off his ocular plants. 'Getting people out before it happens. There are those who will give up everything to live another day.'

'Before what happens?'

'The collapse,' he said with a small shrug. 'It is coming, and it is closer than many think.'

Mia squinted at him, questions crowding her mouth. But she kept them to herself and threw aside the mosquito net and ducked into the night, where the hire-guardian waited with his bo staff in hand and a patient blankness in his eyes.

***

The aviary was a steel obelisk whose sides were carved with images of extinct birds. At its base was a spout that disgorged yellowed water.

Day or night, there was always a queue of people holding jugs and bottles and jerry cans. Some refus earned money from standing in line all day for customers who appeared only when it was their turn to collect water. The spout worked on a timer, and after touching a bar-coded arm to the scanner the refu had threeten seconds to line up the throat of their receptacle and catch as much liquid as they could before a shutter cut off the stream. There were no second chances, because the barcodes allowed access to water only once a day at any single water point in the city. Tales of gangs cutting off other refus' arms and pressing them to the scanner weren't uncommon.

Mia stood with the hire-guardian and scrutinised the patchwork of structures that flanked the obelisk. Bug lights burned blue and crackled when mosquitoes landed on their surface. She'd heard that malaria and dengue were rife in the camp. The vaccine roll-out had been slow in Berlin, and refus were way down on the list. When Mia felt something land on her neck she slapped at her skin, and the sound was loud enough to draw a glance from her hire-guardian.

'See anything that looks like a workshop?' she asked.

'Yin steid, ayi.'

He pointed. Mia's gaze settled on the top of a container behind a row of shanties. As she moved closer, she saw that the container was mounted on breeze blocks, with the double doors at the front thrown open to the night to reveal an interior congested with hardware. She was no expert, but the stuff looked jerry-built, a mishmash of Bulgarian and Chinese and South African parts that had no business being run together. At its centre, a tall woman wearing stained gloves and magniX goggles shuttled between two workbenches on a bubble chair that hung from an overhead rail. When Mia approached the container's ladder, a sticklike sentry automaton that she'd dismissed as junked parts shook itself awake and levelled a lupara at her chest. The hire-guardian grunted a warning.

The bubble chair came to a dead stop and the woman flipped the goggles up and peered out and down at Mia.

'One more step and my Waakhond will put enough electricity in you to light up leech town,' she said.

'Are you Henrietta Bes?'

'Who's asking?'

'Do you remember the name Owen Resler?'

Her eyes narrowed and she thought about it for a moment, or at least seemed to.

'Nope.'

'He said you do retinal stuff. Plants, screens, interfaces. I need something.'

'What?'

'Apex shrouds. Male, able to interface with a SynSult Series Six. I have the eye measurements.'

'Who's the suit aiming to crack?'

So you do remember him, thought Mia. 'I'd say the less you know, the better.'

Bes nodded. 'Probably right. It ain't gonna be cheap. How do you want to pay?'

'That depends. There's a rumour you're having trouble with a gang.'

Bes sighed and stripped the gloves from her hands. 'By rumour you mean Tagawa. I didn't ask him to get involved.'

'But he's right,' said Mia.

Bes opened her mouth to respond, then looked past Mia with her eyes narrowed. Mia turned to find four men approaching. Gang colours, sleeveless shirts, subdermal augmentations that could have been practical or cosmetic or both. All wore metal spikes in their skulls. Mia had seen their kind many times. Appearance over substance. They would've been easy to handle if not for the weapons. One had a machete honed to a point. Another who looked to be the leader brandished a crude two-shot printjob. Hanging from the wrist of another was a large tessen fan, its ribs closed. Only one, a short guy with oculars that glowed aquamarine, was unarmed.

'Easy,' said Mia to the hire-guardian, who gripped his bo staff in two hands.

The leader, all sinew and muscle with grid lines across his cheek and forehead, called out to Bes.

'Collect.' His voice had a nasal twang to it.

'I ain't got anything for you,' said Bes.

The man shook his head. 'No more excuses.'

'I ain't giving you any. I work for what I have. What do you do?'

'Protection.'

'From whom?'

The man raised a finger, the nail encased in chrome, and wagged it at her. 'Had this conversation already.' Now he glanced at Mia. 'Friends of yours?'

'Customers.'

'You smell like outside,' said the tessen-holder.

The man whose eyes glowed nodded. 'Look like it, too.'

'What do you want here?' asked the leader.

'Business,' said Mia, thumbing the Daisy's mechanism to bring it to full charge in her pocket. 'But not with you.'

She weighed them up. The hire-guardian would probably go for the machete boy. She would tackle the leader. That left the tessen fan. If it was a spring-loaded design that fired flechettes, she would have to be quick.

'All business goes through me,' said the leader.

Mia narrowed her eyes. 'Not from where I'm standing.'

His lip curled into a sneer. 'Lemme show you what I mean.'

It happened fast. As he brought the printshot up, she threw the Daisy at him and it connected with his chest and loosed the full charge into his body. Then she was blind, her world turned white by a lucky narrow-range beam emitted by the man with the oculars, and on instinct she dived to the ground. There was a crackle from behind her followed by shouts of pain, and she felt rather than saw her hire-guardian lumber forward. Then came a metal breath, and she heard flechettes whistle overhead. Another scream was followed by the snapping of bone.

Silence.

As the white faded and her vision hardened into solid shapes, Mia saw that the four men were down and her hire-guardian was still standing. He came to her and held out his hand, and when she took it she saw his arm had a gouge deep enough to reveal the yellow-white of fat.

'Are you okay?'

'Theen fan,' he said by way of explanation.

She looked at the men. The leader lay unmoving, clearly dead, the printshot unfired in a rigid hand. The man with the oculars was face down, his clothes smoking slightly. The machete boy was curled in a ball, wrists and fingers smashed beyond use, while the tessen-holder sat with his legs splayed in front of him, red dripping from an ear. She went to him and picked up the tessen and closed it and slipped it into a pocket. Then she called out to Bes, who was studying the holes made by the fan's metal flechettes in the container door.

'Turn off your sentry, would you? I'm coming up.'

'I only had one charge left for the lupara,' said Bes. 'You're safe.'

The stick automaton cradled its empty weapon and watched with unblinking eyes as Mia climbed the ladder. Her ribs and shoulder ached. On reaching the top Bes extended a hand and she took it.

'Those boys were beginning to suspect I didn't have much in the way of personal defences,' said Bes. 'You've done me a favour. What was it you wanted?'

'Apex shrouds—'

'For a SynSult Series Six, right.' She gestured to the incapacitated men. 'That doesn't cover the kind of tech you're talking about.'

'Resler can pay you on delivery.'

Bes shook her head and sighed. 'I just want to live my life in peace.'

'Look around you. They're not going to be claiming protection any time soon.'

'More will come. All you did was create a power vacuum.'

Mia grimaced. This was taking too long. 'Would you leave the camp?'

'Why?'

'I can get you on a transport heading east a few days from now to a samizdat chain in the dust. You can ask the driver to take you as far as Prestige. It's a farm operation. Safe as can be out there.'

'I don't know. I ain't a farmer.'

'They need engineers more than anything. Aeroponics, vertblade setups, vehicles. If you want peace, that's where you'll find it. Not here.'

Bes looked at the men and sighed. 'Sure seems that way. Got any proof you're not bullshitting me on that transport?'

Mia shrugged. 'You have Resler's contact vcf. Ping him.'

'I will.'

Bes went to the rear of the container, out of Mia's earshot. Mia watched as her hire-guardian tore a blue wrap from his midriff and expertly bound the wound at his arm.

The eyetech engineer returned several minutes later.

'Okay,' she said. 'That Resler guy sounds on the level. I'll take your deal.'

'How long to make the shrouds?'

'I have a sheet already. I just need to tailor it to his emmetropic dimensions. An hour, tops.'

'Fine.'

'What is it you're planning to do? Really?'

Her patience was at an end. 'Do as I've asked or don't. But stop wasting my time.'

Bes said nothing. Then she flipped the magnix goggles down over her eyes. 'Wait outside.'

***

By the time Bes was done cutting the retinal shrouds to Resler's parameters, the foot soldiers had been carted away on a trolley by a man wearing a bloodstained apron and a kid who was the spitting image of him. Whether they were allies or opportunists, Mia didn't know.

'Maens is naan mediciner,' the hire-guardian said.

When Bes called Mia's name, she climbed into the container once more, where the air smelled of chemicals and cauterised thermoplastic. The engineer handed her a dull metal box no larger than the palm of her hand.

'Tell him it's normal for them to hurt like hell when they go in. Also let him know he should rest his eyes for at least ten hours before going out into natural light.'

Mia pocketed the box. 'I think you should leave camp tonight. Safer that way. There's a flop house, the Walfisch, in the Tirolerviertel, which will take you without a chip. I'll have Resler buy you a room for the next few days. He'll ping you with instructions on where to go to catch the transport and when.'

Bes nodded slowly. 'I hope you're being straight with me.'

'I am. I'll see you in Prestige. Good luck.'

The hire-guardian led Mia back along the winding pathways of Amerika, to where the reassuring brick outline of Zoologischer Garten loomed. Inside, the forgotten and the hopeless lay on stained tiles with their eyes closed and chemicals twisting their blood.

'Thank you,' said Mia to the hire-guardian.

'Welcome.' He gave her a short bow, then went to a pharma-dispenser in the corner of the station and cycled through the catalogue for what he needed for his arm. He didn't look in her direction again.

Mia went up to the platform and blended into the crowd waiting for the next train. A malfunctioning lightwall switched itself on every few seconds, called out the name of a beer that was supposedly safer to drink than the city water supply. As yellow digits ticked down and a red dot on an overhead fauxgraphic map tracked the S-Bahn's journey to the station, Mia wiped the fatigue from her eyes and tried not to think of Janeane. She saw the tattooed face of the man she had killed, the Daisy's full charge stopping his heart, and tried to recall what number that put her on now.

When the train arrived several minutes later, she still didn't know.

22

Resler knew he wasn't going to like Falko Wagenknecht when the man insisted they meet in an adrenal bar. The concept of adrenal exhaustion had taken hold among the elite in recent years, and various enterprising snake-oil purveyors had opened establishments claiming to be able to replenish the body's glands for a mildly extortionate fee. Located on floor three-O of a bamboo scraper in suit town, the bar was close enough to Potsdamer Platz that Resler could see the ten light-studded rotating scrapers known as the Nerthus towers from the bubble window in the bar's anteroom. Ever since Athos had gone under, the middle section of tower XII, known as the Pharma, had been dead, and the blacked-out windows were like a mourning band fitted around a giant limb.

Standing behind the Pharma was Nerthus IV.

The bar was upmarket enough to employ a human being as a host, and the man's smile was slick as he greeted Resler. His sculpted brows rose slightly at the mention of Wagenknecht's name, and he led Resler from the anteroom into the bar proper, a miserable synthesis of dark wood and polished chrome spotlighted in turquoise. The conditioned air was too cold to be comfortable. As they passed low-slung private tables that were mostly empty, Resler squirmed in his dynamic-thread jacket. He'd had the whole suit laser-cut at great cost early that morning by an Armenian tailor in Gesundbrunnen, the better to make an impression. Back at Scopo he would have killed for such an outfit. Now the textile sat claustrophobic against his skin.

Wagenknecht was already seated at a table for two in a VIP area hidden behind an elaborate folding screen. He was heavyset and balding, and wore a mint-green kurta with a synthetic fur collar and cobalt jewellery on his fingers and in his ears. In a golden rack next to him was a row of colour-coded adrenal bottles. On the table, two lacquered wooden mouthpieces, connected to silk-clad hoses, rested on padded mats.

'You're Pleasance?' asked Wagenknecht, making no effort to rise.

'Pleased to meet you,' said Resler.

The scientist waved a hand at the vacant chair and Resler sat. He saw now that Wagenknecht, too, wore a SynSult plate, though it was seventh generation.

'I ordered a selection,' said Wagenknecht, gesturing at the adrenal bottles. 'I don't know about you, but I'm long overdue for a top-up. The plebiscites wear me down with their mere existence.' He laughed.

Resler forced a smile.

'How about this décor? I adore Nu-Chinoiserie. It's so bold. Better than the supposedly authentic dross coming out of Beijing these days. Don't you agree?'

'Sure,' said Resler. His initial suspicion had been correct. He didn't like the man. On his eye-over he boosted the volume so Johnny could hear everything.

'Allow me,' said Wagenknecht. He slotted the silk-clad hoses into two bottles, then brought one of the mouthpieces to his lips and inhaled sharply. 'Bliss,' he said.

Resler did the same. Whatever was in the bottle had no taste. And he felt no effect.

'So you're one of Mr Portnov's men,' said Wagenknecht

'His director of operations.'

'Never met the fellow, but I know his reputation, of course. Everyone does.' Wagenknecht took another hit from the mouthpiece. 'Between you and me, I am loyal to Ynside. But there is always a higher table to sit at, as you well know, and it is most flattering to hear a place has potentially been set for me. Care for a beverage? Something to eat, perhaps?'

Resler set the lacquered mouthpiece on the mat. 'A water.'

'My tab, you understand.'

'A water is fine.'

'Clear head, clear decisions. Je comprends parfaitement.'

Wagenknecht fell silent for a moment as he placed the order on his eye-over, and Resler took the opportunity to regroup. The scientist liked the sound of his own voice, so he would let the man talk. And when he'd said too much, that was the time to bring up Scopo.

The centre of the table slid open and a bottle of the clearest water Resler had ever seen rose on a platform. With a little prompting from Wagenknecht he picked it up and peeled back the bio-top and brought it to his lips. It was like nothing he'd ever tasted. He'd read that good, pure water had no taste, but this did. An electric sweetness made its way to his brain, and he closed his eyes and allowed himself a quiet moment of ecstasy.

When he opened them again, Wagenknecht was watching him.

'I like a man who appreciates the finer things. Sadly, such individuals are few and far between.'

Resler said nothing, setting the bottle on the table.

'In our call you mentioned a need for a quantum machine learning expert. Care to tell me what Mr Portnov has in mind?'

'Until we sign an NDA, not much.'

'The broad strokes, then. There is so much cloak and dagger surrounding Blue Elk that it's difficult to parse fact from fiction.'

'Well,' said Resler. 'As you probably know, we work at the intersection of government and corporate interests within the context of military spending. At present, we're seeking to expand on our AI capabilities in defensive and offensive scenarios by accelerating the learning process based on a hybrid quantum-classical model.' Resler paused, then smiled. 'I shouldn't say this, but there are plans afoot to topple a certain rogue state's leadership in the foreseeable future.'

Wagenknecht's eyes bulged. 'France? It's France, isn't it?'

'I'm not at liberté to say.'

The scientist slapped his thigh. 'I knew it. As soon as they started messing around with fusion drives, I told myself the cabal wouldn't let it lie. Oh, how I'd love to be part of that. Show the Blanquist scum who they're dealing with.'

Before Resler could respond, the centre of the table opened again. On the platform this time were razor-thin slices of celmeat resting on cut blocks of dry ice. A silver-tipped sprinkler spat droplets of hot water onto the ice blocks, creating a fog that wafted over the table. Wagenknecht put his hands together in admiration.

'Excuse me for a moment,' he said, and one of his eyes flushed a ruby red.

Resler hid his surprise at the fact that the chief data scientist for the city's leading IoT firm had a Wraptstar implant. After a few moments Wagenknecht's eye lost its artificial hue. An apologetic half-smile followed.

'I have onedredthou subscribers to my little channel,' he said. 'Addicts to the lap of luxury, every one of them. It started as a joke among friends, but the plebiscites failed to pick up on the subtext. They seem to think I'm giving them a glimpse of a world they should strive for.' He laughed. 'Even if they toiled for a century, they wouldn't be shown through the front door of a place like this. Carbon is meaningless without class.'

He seized a pair of chopsticks and swept a slice of celmeat into his mouth, then followed it up with three long pulls of adrenal air. 'All so invigorating.'

Enough, thought Resler. No more of this man.

'I have a file. Text-only. Narrow band. I'd like you to read it.'

'A non-disclosure agreement?'

'Of a kind.'

'I must warn you that I don't sign anything without my lawyer casting his reptilian gaze over it first.'

'That's not an issue.'

The scientist's mouth curved into an indulgent grin. 'Then send away. My channel is open.'

Resler fired the file Mantis had ripped for him across the narrow band to Wagenknecht, whose eyes lost their focus as he opened it on his eye-over. Resler watched as the man's fleshy body stiffened.

When Wagenknecht next spoke, his voice was quiet. 'Where did you get this?'

Resler steadied his nerves. The moment of truth had arrived. 'That is not your concern. What matters is that if you fail to do as I say, the information in that file will be released across Vertoo. You and the rest of Ynside will be ruined.'

'This is blackmail.'

'In a word.'

Wagenknecht shook his head slowly. 'You realise I'm quite prepared to defend myself against any and all of the baseless claims in that file?'

Anger spiked in Resler. 'By baseless you mean the containment tests that led to the deaths of twothou people in Haushofer Blocks One, Two and Three. The story was all over Vertoo.'

'I have no knowledge of such tests.'

'Bullshit. You signed off on them. The ink trail leads to you. It's all there. Answer me this: what value could such a test possibly have?'

Wagenknecht eyed him with something approaching amusement. 'Hypothetically? It may lead one to conclude that in the event of state collapse, martial law or a climate-induced catastrophe, it is possible to confine certain subsections of society to their residences until further notice. Without major civil unrest, that is. That's something with which I'm sure Blue Elk is familiar.'

'"Further notice" meaning until their oxygen supply runs out.'

'That is one eventuality. But think about it this way, if your imagination permits it: when the barbarians arrive at the gates, what would be the benefit in presenting them with more foot soldiers for their army? Wouldn't it be better to lock down the animals for their own safety? And if supplies run low, whose stomachs should be filled first? Those who create problems or those who solve them?'

'These are not animals. They are human beings.'

'I believe you and Mr Portnov are overestimating how much the death of a few plebiscites will affect the way we do business. Let me be frank: break this on Vertoo and it'll be a talking point for a day. Then the city will move on. Do you know why? Because anyone who matters in this world won't care, so the traction simply won't exist. Oh, there'll certainly be a few riots on the fringes and some disgruntled workers will set fire to a building or two that no one gives a damn about. But guess what? That gives us the excuse to send the polizei in, weed out the ringleaders and strike fear into the remainder. So, in fact, you'll be doing our people a favour by releasing the file to the great unwashed public.'

'You aren't God,' said Resler in disbelief. 'You realise that, don't you?'

'Do you know the name of a single citizen who perished in Haushofer One, Two or Three? No? I thought so. There is not a Von Grebner, Zilverhuizen, Gongbao, Benz or Skelton among them. So why should there be any uproar? In fact, I'd wager that if I broadcast the contents of your file on my Wraptstar channel, my net subscriber rate would go up rather than down.'

Resler blinked. 'Are you taking Scopo right now?'

'Of course.' Wagenknecht shrugged. 'Every morning, midday and evening. The recommended dose.' His eyes lost their focus again as he returned to the file.

Resler glanced around the near-deserted adrenal bar in desperation. This wasn't how it was supposed to go. There was no bargaining with a sociopath. He'd said to Mia Warsaw that suits understood a different kind of threat, but being held responsible for the deaths of twothou innocent citizens apparently wasn't it.

On the table, the ice blocks were melting and the celmeat cuts were turning grey.

'Wait,' said Wagenknecht.

Resler turned his attention back to the scientist. And he saw fear.

'You know about Meyer.'

Resler opened the text file on his eye-over, scanned for the name. Julian Meyer, former chief technology officer of Ynside. A conversation between him and Wagenknecht, one of the last recorded before Meyer's death, revealing that Wagenknecht had recommended Meyer visit a brothel, the Seven Wonders, where the CTO had been strangled and had his chips cut out by an unknown assailant.

'I didn't kill Julian,' said Wagenknecht in a small voice.

Resler thought fast. 'Of course not. You had someone else do it.'

The word was little more than a whisper. 'No.'

'I'm sure the Seven Wonders has a record of its clientele, especially elite profiles such as yourself. I'm guessing you were a regular customer right up until Meyer's death. How about this for a wager: I bet I can find a Munroe there who knows more about what happened to Meyer than they let on to the polizei. Perhaps even the same one you paid off. Your pockets may be large, but Mr Portnov's are larger.'

Wagenknecht's pupils were dilated. 'You can't prove anything.'

'I won't need to. In business, suspicion is the same as death by a thousand cuts. No one will trust you. Not your superiors, not your subordinates, not your competitors.'

'This can't get out. It can't.'

One life compared to twothou, thought Resler. 'That's up to you, isn't it?'

'What is it you want, Pleasance?' asked Wagenknecht. He ran a jewelled hand through what little hair remained on his head.

'Your firm oversees security for Nerthus.'

'Yes,' said Wagenknecht.

'When did you last work Nerthus IV?'

'I don't know exactly. Around three months ago. That's right. We performed a full system upgrade for the central control. An intricate job that—'.

Resler held up a hand. 'I want the Yuanrang Ten override code for floors five-O-one to five-O-four in Nerthus IV. And I want an employee retinal pass keyed to my neural ID.'

Wagenknecht looked at him. 'You must be kidding. Yuanrang Ten is one of the most sophisticated all-in systems in the world. Do you realise how many fences we have to put up just to be able to work inside it safety? The moment you enter, the AI will rip you to shreds. Nerthus ghosts aren't like the rest. They don't play nice. They're sadistic.'

'Then it won't matter if you give me the code.'

'I can't. It's more than my life's worth.'

'And your colleagues finding out about Julian Meyer's demise isn't?'

Resler put his elbows on the table and picked up a piece of celmeat and tossed it into his mouth. It was cold and wet and tasted of nothing. 'I'll level with you, Falko. I'm going into that tower and I don't expect to come out alive. You can either give me the code and trust that I'll be dead within two-O-four hours, in which case you'll be in the clear. Or you can leave yourself to the mercy of the kind of people who salivate at the prospect of a high-up prick like you falling from his perch.'

'How can you be so ruthless? All I've ever wanted is to do my job well.'

'Take it or leave it.'

'What if I give you a job instead? A mind like yours will fit right in with us. C-suite. I can swing it. I've got clout with the rest of the board.'

'No.'

'Okay, so you want to get paid. Who doesn't? Name your price. Carbon, neweuro, crypto, metals. I can do all of them.'

Resler stood and sealed his suit jacket. A rich blue wave rippled across the thread. 'I'm leaving.'

'Don't make me do this.'

'I'm not making you do anything.'

He turned, held his nerve, started to walk away.

'Wait.'

Resler planted his heel on the polished floor.

'Okay,' said Wagenknecht, hatred and defeat radiating from every pore. 'I'll do it.'

'Narrow band. Same channel as the file.'

He waited as Wagenknecht's eyes lost focus. The ping arrived on his eye-over a minute later, and he opened the narrow-band communication to find the codes. Stamped and chained and encrypted and impossible to be anything other than what they were. He forwarded them to Warsaw's Flymotic console and dissolved the eye-over.

Wagenknecht grimaced. 'I must say this has been a thoroughly disagreeable lunch, Pleasance.'

'I'm glad,' said Resler. On an impulse, he reached for the bottle of water on the table and drank the remainder. It tasted even sweeter than before.

'What do you intend to do inside Nerthus? Tell me that, at least.'

'If I succeed then you'll know.'

'The moment you walk out of here, I could inform their security.'

'But you won't,' said Resler. 'Because you stand to gain more from watching and waiting and making your move once the tipping point is reached. Instability and crisis are fertile soil for scum like you.'

Then Wagenknecht did something unexpected. He smiled. Predatory, ugly, all teeth. 'Quite right,' he said.

Resler walked away, the man's face burned into his mind, passing table after empty table, and the bile rose in his throat and he wanted to scream. As he stalked through the anteroom, the front-of-house man raised a perfectly bladed eyebrow.

'Monsieur is paying,' said Resler, and he stepped into the elevator and the doors slid shut without a sound.

***

Outside, away from the air-conditioned reality of the restaurant, Resler joined the stream of citizens on the slidewalk heading in the opposite direction to Potsdamer Platz. As he weaved between people he looked in front, behind and around him, half-expecting to see a bull on his tail. But his assumption seemed to be holding true. Wagenknecht was content to wait and see if opportunity could be conjured from chaos.

When he had put enough distance between him and the bar, he took a seat on a spotless bench in the shadow of a bulb-shaped scraper and opened a comm channel on his eye-over and placed a call. Audio only, ID withheld.

Three dots became a hard blue line. 'If this is another ad, I'm gonna be pissed.'

'It's me, Ngozi. Owen Resler.'

'Owen. Are you okay?'

'Hanging in.'

'Where are you?'

'Still in the city for the moment. How are you doing?'

'You mean between losing my job and redlining carbon and having to work on a microbial farm? Pure geznet.'

He winced. 'That's on me.'

'You said it. What is it you want, Owen?'

He didn't answer straight away. He didn't answer because he didn't know.

'I just wanted to hear your voice,' he said.

Dead silence on the line. Then: 'My shift is starting soon, Owen. I have to get across town.'

'Wait.'

'What is it?'

'Your cut.'

'You actually sold it?'

'Right. I need an account number.'

A ping came through on his eye-over, and he accessed the account Mantis had set up for him and transferred half as a banco-file.

'I've sent it.'

He waited.

'Owen.' Ngozi's voice was like paper. 'This is huge.'

'We did okay.'

'You can say that again. Sekhmet, Owen. I'm rich. No more microbials. Oh, my shift leader's gonna have an aneurysm when I tell him I'm not coming in.'

Resler smiled to himself.

'This is unbelievable. Why don't you come by my place tomorrow? We can talk things over.'

Because I'll either be inside Nerthus or already dead, he didn't say. 'I'll try. Look, I have to go. There's a few things I need to take care of right now.'

'I bet. Take care, Owen. Stay in touch.'

'You, too.'

The connection died and Resler stood and adjusted the cuffs of his jacket. Then he walked, just another suit in the stream that swirled under the light of a thousand artificial moons.

23 Nepenthe. A thread so rotten it had no place even in the chemically saturated social fabric that clothed modern-day society. Nepenthe was a drug that had been developed two-O years previously in an underground lab by anarchists who had wanted to wipe the minds of the elite, but who had been caught before they could put the wheels in motion and then died without surrendering their recipe on how to synthesise it. It wasn't designed to stop a person's heart. That was too simple. It had been engineered to burn through the limbic system — the thalamus and the hippocampal and reticular formations — and disrupt the individual's memory so severely they wouldn't even remember their own name. They would still breathe, but they wouldn't know they were alive.

There were only nine vials left in existence. Johnny Seven had one of them.

He'd spent the morning running from safe house to deposit box, retrieving weapons and supplies, and in the bottom of one drawer he'd found the Nepenthe. Fluorescent blue liquid in a glass vial, itself housed within a plastic cradle. A nipple at the top for a needle to spike its way inside and suck out the poison. He'd traded a life for it long ago, saved a suit who hadn't been worth saving, and the suit had given him the Nepenthe in payment. It was worth a lot to the right bidder, but even when his funds and his pills had been running low he'd kept hold of the brain burner for a rainy day.

When he looked to the sky now, the clouds were charcoal.

While Resler was in the restaurant, Johnny had waited at a chow stand across the street and listened to Wagenknecht over his eye-over. He'd heard the complete lack of remorse in the man's voice as he spoke about the deaths of twothou people, ground his teeth as the scientist had casually justified his actions. Standing there at the imitation wood counter, he'd fingered the plastic cradle in his pocket and glanced at the black bag on the stool next to him and made his decision.

An eye for an eye didn't make the world go blind if a third person was dispensing justice.

***

From the chow stand Johnny watched as Resler emerged into the street, collected himself and melted into the crowd hurrying along the slidewalk. He dissolved his eye-over, then clicked his finger and a box on a guide rail swung around the counter and stopped above his head. A periscope node extended from the box and Johnny buzzed it with a nitingalvate credit slate. There was just enough on it to cover his tab. He slung his bag over his shoulder and stepped into the street, exchanging semi-conditioned air for the warm ripe wetness of the city, and found a spot where he could lean with his back to a wall and keep an eye on the bamboo tower.

Wagenknecht appeared some ten minutes later. Balding, overweight, wearing some kind of fur-trimmed dress, he was nothing to look at, but he drew looks of admiration from the suits on the street anyway because of the cobalt that dripped from him and the SynSult plate at his temple. The man was well aware of the attention, and upped the ante by withdrawing a gold case from his pocket, cracking it open and slipping an ephedra sachet into his mouth. Then he joined the crowd, heading in the opposite direction to Owen.

Johnny followed at a distance. He felt alert, determined, in a way that had evaded him for the longest time. Being torn open by a drone and put back together by a backstreet blade merchant had done something to his brain. He had no desire to open his tin of pills, heard no voices in his head, saw no shadows at the edges of his vision. Whether it was permanent or temporary didn't matter. All he knew is that he would ride the snake for as long as he could.

Wagenknecht crossed the divide into leech town on foot, and now the pedestrians around him stopped to stare. For a moment Johnny wondered how the scientist wasn't afraid. Then he realised no one would dare do anything to him because his bulk and his clothing were proof enough of his power. His ego was astounding, even for Berlin. Johnny had known a woman like Wagenknecht during the First Water Conflict, around the time when Wrocław, Dresden and Prague had been celestial-bombed into slag within the space of a few excruciating days. Back then he'd been new to Lepage Company, which had been ordered to go into Prague, dig up the command bunkers to see if anyone of rank had survived the onslaught, and execute them. They had flown over the devastation on tiltrotor gyros, flimsy things with AI pilots that were barely smart enough to schlepp agri-tools, let alone human beings. As they'd hit Prague proper a storm front had drawn in and a couple of NCOs had recommended turning back, but the company's new captain, a woman named Maskavich, had ignored the advice. She'd wanted the first boots on the ground to belong to Lepage, because then she would go down in history as the fighter who had destroyed the last of the Bohemian resistance. Her ego had cost them: the wind had thrown the gyros around like wheat stalks, downing two and killing nine. Maskavich had been written up for it, but in the end she'd moved on to better things on the back of Lepage's reputation. Her and Wagenknecht were the kind of people who saw the world as dead clay waiting to be shaped, not an assemblage of life.

In leech town Johnny dodged pedestrians and ignored the light-walls and advertorials and graphics. His movements were loose and easy, and he imagined he could hear the Nepenthe sloshing inside its vial. His gaze clung to the back of Wagenknecht's fat neck, where chevrons of black hair pointed toward his shoulders. They passed alleys clogged with trash, dark spots into which he could have dragged the scientist and made him disappear, but he didn't want to do it that way. He wanted to send a message.

After taking an escalator up to a pedestrian bridge, Wagenknecht made his way toward a lightwall that burned a Rothko yellow. On it was an impression of an impossible woman. Hourglass shape, koga-rashi bob, oversized where it counted. She beckoned to the scientist, and he waddled through an outsized entrance whose doors slid shut behind him. Above the entrance was a sign: Rainy Taxi. A glo-doll ho-tel.

Johnny repositioned the bag on his shoulder and, after taking a ten count, followed Wagenknecht inside. The only light came from a belt of blue circular lamps set into the floor. A shadow peeled away from the wall and moved to intercept Johnny. Male, grey-haired but in shape, wearing a cheap bionic arm prettied up with an imitation stone veneer. He muttered something in a language Johnny didn't under-stand.

'What's the story, chief?' he asked.

'Can you pay, vet?'

'Sure.' Johnny pulled out the empty credit slate and flashed it at the man.

'Had trouble with your kind before, vet. Violence trouble.'

'Not me, chief. I'm just here for the girls.'

'What's in the bag?'

Johnny looked down, as if surprised to see it. 'My life, brother. My whole damn life.'

The one-armed man eyed him, then stepped aside and waved his organic hand. 'Follow the lights, vet. Enjoy yourself.'

Johnny raised a finger to his temple in salute. The blue lamps in the floor took him around a corner into a low-ceilinged fishbowl lobby, which branched off to the left and right to individual cabins whose doors were all closed. There were eight in total, and notches above two of them indicated they were occupied. He went first to a vacant cabin. It was small, with barely enough space to accommodate a queen bed. A glo-doll waited inside, seated upright with her hands on exposed knees, and when the cabin door locked it woke and a low golden light shone from the ceiling onto its artificial skin and hair. A pair of blank eyes found him.

'How would you like me?'

Johnny ignored her. The phrase was pre-recorded. The doll wasn't a mimic. Those could only be found at high-end places, the kind that wouldn't allow him within five-O metres of the door. This one was nothing but moulded silicon and electronics, a softcore puppet, dated tech that still served a purpose for hard-up hard-ons and aficionados. Johnny guessed Wagenknecht was the latter.

'Let's have a good time together,' said the glo-doll.

Johnny slipped the Nepenthe vial from its plastic cradle and re-trieved a single-use syringe with a wicked needle that he'd lifted from Weltschmerz. He prepared the dose, sucking the fluorescence into the cylinder, then held it between his teeth as he took a tool set from his bag and pried open the lock casing on the door. It took just a few sec-onds to unlock the mechanism. That was good. The door slid open and he was back in the fishbowl lobby. He looked around, his gaze sweep-ing the corners of the room, and saw only a single surveillance puck watching the adjoining corridor rather than the fishbowl. He went to one of the two occupied cabins and crouched down and applied his tools to the lock.

When the door opened Johnny found himself staring at the rear end of a pale man whose face was obscured by the thighs of a purple-skinned glo-doll with a spiked tail. He was so engrossed in the act that he didn't look up. Silently, Johnny stepped out and punched the but-ton and the door swept shut. He walked over to the other occupied cabin and once again crouched down and jimmied the lock. The door opened.

Falko Wagenknecht writhed on top of a glo-doll three times smaller than he was, his eyes screwed shut and his mouth twisted half-way between a grimace and ecstasy as the doll told him he was a king. His jewellery jingled with every thrust. Johnny took the syringe from between his teeth, flicked it once with his index finger and squirted a tiny amount of Nepenthe from the needle. Then he stood and watched as Wagenknecht, the man who had signed off on the deaths of thousands of innocent people, continued to pump away at the doll. Panting, gasping for breath, sweat running down his matted back. The doll threw out platitudes that barely made sense and the scientist's cries reached a crescendo and his body shook.

As he rolled off the glo-doll he saw a stranger standing over him.

The needle found flesh and Falko Wagenknecht's eyelids fluttered and closed.

'That was wonderful,' said the glo-doll, staring at the cabin ceiling. 'Let's go again.'

Johnny removed the needle and capped it and threw it into his bag. Among the scientist's possessions he found a credit slate loaded with neweuro and transferred it to his own. He watched the man for a moment, wondering if the Nepenthe was still as potent as it had once been, then stepped out of the cabin and punched the button to close the door behind him. He followed the lamps back around to the front of house, half-expecting a welcome committee, but the one-armed man was alone and he was grinning.

'You quick, vet.'

'Gotta be in this world, chief.'

'Ain't that the truth.'

The man laughed and Johnny paid him and he left.

He moved with the crowd along the leechtown walkways until he clocked the multi-lensed conical head of a polizei automaton, then rode the next escalator down to ground level. From there he headed to the nearest S-Bahn station. As he walked he activated his eye-over and placed a call to Resler.

'Johnny.'

'How goes it, chief?'

'I've been trying to ping you. Are you okay?'

'Never felt better,' he said, and realised it was the truth. 'How about those codes?'

'They're legit. Did you hear everything Wagenknecht said?'

'Yeah. Now there's a growther on an entirely different level of feng feng.'

'I'm not so sure. In fact, I'm beginning to think they're all that way, at least at the top.'

'You could be right about that.'

'I'm heading to Container City now. Mia has the shrouds. Where are you?'

'Near Anhalter Bahnhof. I'll meet you at Jimmy Chee's place in an hour. I have one more hardware stop to make for Mia.'

'Right.'

Johnny fished out a carton of Djasalm cigarettes and lit one. Anhalter burned bright at the end of the street. A dispatch drone flew too low along the centre of the strip, barely missing the signs that protruded from every facade. A kingCab pulled up outside an austere residential tower, disgorged two women wearing threadbare Maintenon suits who clung to each other as they made their way inside. Engineered cloud cover hung in the sky like a fleet of mothballed airships. Johnny took it in, understanding that this was it, that this was all there ever needed to be. No more guilt, fear or pain.

In that moment he was content.

24 Jimmy Chee's chop shop was easy to overlook. Located in a couple of old shipping bricks in the heart of Container City, the only indicator that it was home to one of the best grafters in Berlin was Chee's name engraved on a brass plaque on the side facing the thoroughfare. Even the entrance didn't advertise itself, hidden behind a polymer mesh caked in layers of grime.

Jimmy Chee was in the rear of the shop, detangling hyperthreads on an outsized Bastille console, when Mia Warsaw arrived to collect her favour. A year back, the grafter had been stiffed by a local syndicate member in Container City after auging the man to three-O percent. Mia had taken on the debt, secured Jimmy Chee his payment.

They exchanged a few words before she handed him the shrouds that had been sliced, ground and polished by Henrietta Bes.

'Good cutwork,' said Jimmy Chee. He was a young man, tall and broad-shouldered, with permanent half-moon oculars of his own design and a nose plug to filter the bad air that hung like a curtain over Container City. He wore an apron, its many pockets holding the essential tools of his trade. 'You let whoever it was know if they want more jobs, they can come to me.'

Mia shook her head. 'They're gone.'

Chee placed the shrouds back in their sleek black box and returned to his hyperthreads. 'There's a cot over there, behind the junk. If you want to get some rest.'

She followed his directions, finding a strip of foam hidden by fibreboard boxes that were stamped with the red seal of Henzai Corp. She removed her outerwear, lay down, stared at the unpainted container roof. A stale smell rose from the foam. Her bones were heavy with fatigue. She surprised herself by thinking about Gian Ramirez, allowed herself to miss the closeness he had provided, long ago, during one of her many lives. She was not so fatalistic as to believe in an afterlife, but if one did exist then she hoped Gian had found his peace there.

After a time she closed her eyes, and when she did she could see Janeane dancing in the darkness on blades that cut up an ancient theatre floor.

'You don't really think I'm alive, do you?'

There was a smile on the girl's face as she spoke. She stopped with a flourish and raised her arms to the sky.

'Yes,' said Mia. 'I do.'

'Geznet. Gotta admire your tenacity. But let's say I am. You reckon they'll have left me alone? Think I'll be all in one piece?'

'Don't ask me what I can't know.'

'I think you got a feeling though, right? And let me tell you something else: guys like Benz don't have patience. They don't wait. Know how I know that? It was the same at my window on the Spree. Ah, Mia. When you saved me at the Trident, I thought I'd left that world behind. But you opened the door and let me right back in, didn't you?'

'That wasn't my choice.'

'It isn't as though you put up much of a fight against the fat man.'

'Stop it.'

'Stop what? You're okay. You get to play the hero, like in those old kinofilms the glitz channels yammer on about. Gun in one hand, one-liner in the other.'

'I'm not okay.'

'Come on. Just answer my question and I'll leave you in peace. What if Benz has already cut me open and had his fun? What do you do then?'

'He won't get away with it,' said Mia, and she knew she was dreaming because there were tears on her cheeks. She turned away from the kid, unable to look at her any longer, and there was only the stage and blackness. When she looked down she saw metal protruding from her arms and realised she was the one Benz had worked on, not Janeane, and instead of horror she felt release because if she was already in the tower then she wouldn't have to ask the soldier and the suit to risk their lives and go with her.

'Hey.'

A hand touched her shoulder. She opened her eyes. Jimmy Chee, standing over her, expressionless.

'What is it?'

'You were out for a long time. They're here.'

She rose, feeling the ache in her bad shoulder. An old digital clock hanging from a wall showed that it was almost ten. She rounded the boxes, found herself looking at two men. Owen Resler, leaning against the chop shop counter in a dynamic suit whose thread shimmered from midnight blue to black. And Johnny Seven, veteran of a thousand wars, who placed a large black ripstop nylon bag on a tarp-covered graft station. When he saw her, he smiled.

'Sorry to wake you,' he said. 'But we have some fellas to kill.'

***

Jimmy Chee brewed a pot of chicory coffee, which he doled out between the four of them. The men found places to perch amid the dust-coated electronics and sipped from glass beakers as they waited for Mia to speak.

'Last chance to bail,' she said.

Resler shook his head.

'Not a chance,' said Johnny.

'Okay, then. Let's go over the plan. Owen?'

'I've booked you two jumpseats on a Vlyt D37 glider from Brandenburg to Nerthus IV at seven-midi. Tentwo-minute flight, fully occupied, passengers coming in from West Paris. I'll make my entry into the tower two-O minutes before take-off. If I fail, then you'll know in good time and you can abort. I had a look at the schematics for the tower. The third floor is all utilities, so that's where I'll mount my system strike. After your arrival, I'll lock out security and isolate floors five-O-one to five-O-four. Then it's down to you.'

'How about the exemption pass?'

'I'm still working on that. They're like gold dust on Vertoo trading portals.'

'How far is it from the landing pad to Benz's suite?'

'Three floors.'

Mia grimaced. That was a long way, even with weapons.

'You're going to have to come out of that glider ready to fight,' said Resler, looking from her to Johnny. 'The Yuanrang system is more sophisticated than anything I've ever engaged with. Once the building AI discovers I'm in the system, it'll try to shut me down as quickly and brutally as possible. Threat hunters, IDS, hackbacks, inoculation, you name it. I'll start fires wherever I can, get it looking in different directions, but to tell you the truth I have no idea what I'm dealing with. If my SynSult plate can't handle it — if I can't handle it — you're going to have to take care of everything yourself. Security, access, surveillance guards. The whole shebang.'

'Understood,' said Mia. 'Johnny?'

The soldier put down his cup of chicory, went to the bag, pulled back the zip and began to place items on the graft station bed. Mia counted four gov-issue Agitators, a dull orange Nylon automatic with its stock folded, and the Göl-Tek carbon-fibre carbine she'd last seen in Johnny's container in the forest. He'd also brought enough ammunition to feed the guns ten times over, and a couple of magnetised cases of gelignite. It was an arsenal.

Jimmy Chee cast his augmented gaze over the weapons. 'Are you staging a revolution?'

'Of a kind,' said Johnny.

'Explosives, too?'

He grinned. 'Last resort.'

Resler turned to Mia. 'There's one thing we haven't discussed. And we need to. Once you find Janeane, how do you plan to get out?'

She nodded. He was right. She hadn't said anything about it because she didn't want to tempt fate. She stood and went to the corner of the chop shop where she'd stashed them, and returned with three rectangular grey bags, each with an orange tongue hanging from the back.

'Chutes?' asked Johnny.

'The pneumatics will be locked out and any gliders attempting to leave will be shot out of the sky. We don't know what state the kid is in or if she can walk. This is the only way I can figure it. Either Janeane wears her own or I'll take her on mine. We can drop into leech town and then make our way underground from there.'

Johnny's gaze shifted from the parachutes to Mia and back to the parachutes. He laughed. 'You're feng feng, man. Onedred percent crazy.'

'It's all I've got.'

'It's good enough.'

To cover her nerves, she pulled out a parejo and bit off the end. Jimmy Chee threw her a lighter and she sparked it. The sharp scent of synthetic tobacco filled the space. Overhead, a ventilator switched on.

'You ever jumped with one before?' asked Johnny.

She shook her head. 'Pull here?'

'Right.'

'Looks easy enough.'

'It is. Word of advice: don't wait around after you jump. It might seem like we're high up, but the ground comes at you quick. So just pull. Gravity will do the rest.'

She nodded and exhaled smoke. 'Got it.'

'What about you, Owen?' Johnny asked. 'Walking out the way you came in?'

Resler glanced at him. 'Walking out of where?'

'Nerthus. When we're done.'

'Right. Yeah.'

Mia frowned. 'What's the problem?'

'Nothing.'

'Don't do the timid thing. Spill it.'

'You want to know?' He scratched the back of his neck.

'Yes.'

He smiled, a weak one. 'The chance of any of us making it out is minimal.'

Mia looked at him, wondering if he was about to back out. 'Once you open the door for us, you can unplug and get out of there.' She nodded at the guns on the graft bed. 'We'll manage.'

'How about if you get cornered by building security?' asked Resler. 'What if you use all your explosives on a single door? What if you can't get inside Benz's residence? No, I need to stay and that's all there is to it.'

Mia tried to keep control of her anger. 'Don't make it sound like I'm forcing you to do this. Because I'm not.'

Now it was his turn to be annoyed. 'Sekhmet, you're missing the point. That kid was the only one out of any of you who acted and sounded like a human being. I haven't got a problem with what we're doing, but don't ask me again how I'm getting out. It's insulting. Okay?'

He looked from Mia to Johnny. The soldier nodded.

'Fine,' said Mia. 'I understand.'

'Good. Do you have the shrouds?'

Jimmy Chee retrieved the case from the back of the shop and Resler took it and looked them over. A spotlight above him caught the surface of the shrouds, made them look like moons half buried in a black injection-moulded sea.

'Nice job,' he muttered. 'Perfect.'

'Like MR glass,' said Johnny. 'We used to wear them in training. Cheaper to put holes in virtual targets with virtual bullets. Doesn't look so bad to me.'

Jimmy Chee stirred. 'It doesn't sit on the eyeball. Shrouds are attached to the socket. As in the bone. Makes them undetectable.'

'Oh.'

'Let me get set up.'

Resler handed Jimmy Chee the shrouds and the grafter went to a bed and pulled back the tarp and switched on the machines around it. A low hum filled the can.

'How did things end up with Henrietta?' asked Resler.

'She's in a flop house right now, waiting for a transport to take her out of the city. Maybe she'll end up in Prestige with your sister.'

'What happened?'

'Some trouble in the camp. Wouldn't have been safe to leave her there.'

For a moment he looked at her strangely, and Mia wondered what she'd said. Then he smiled. 'Thank you.'

She folded her arms across her chest. 'It wasn't for you, Owen.'

He shook his head. 'I know. But someone had to say it.'

'Ready,' said Jimmy Chee.

The smile vanished. Resler went to the graft station and lay on the bed. A mechanical arm unfolded itself from a recess in the metal roof and slid over until it was positioned above him. Its metal fingers clicked together twice, testing its responsiveness. Jimmy Chee tapped at a screen.

'Ready?' he asked.

'No,' said Resler.

Two more mechanical arms rose from either side of the graft bed, these ones smaller, and they made for Resler's face. Their ends blossomed into prongs, and the prongs touched his closed eyelids and drew them wide open and held them there. He ground his teeth together as the full whites of his eyes became visible. Jimmy Chee swiped at the screen and the main arm came down from the roof, central piston hissing, and pincered the shroud for Resler's left eye between steel fingers. It swung around toward the bed, and Resler's body tensed and his eyes became frantic. The shroud touched his exposed lens. The mechanical arm, controlled by Jimmy Chee, pushed hard, and Resler cried out, a long gurgling release of pain. The arm rotated on its ball pivot as it slipped the shroud around the eye and anchored it to bone with microscopic staples. It released and pulled back and Resler's sobs filled the chop shop, and Johnny turned his head away. Mia kept watching. The mechanical arm glided over to the shroud case and plucked the second shroud free and returned to Resler, whose cheeks were wet with tears. This time, when he saw the arm coming, he braced himself, gripping the arms of the graft station and clenching his teeth, and when the shroud came down against his right eye he screamed. The arm moved the shroud into place, stapled it to the bone and pulled back. The smaller arms released Resler's eyelids and retreated into the graft station. Resler turned his head to the side with his eyes closed and retched, then slumped back on the bed.

Jimmy Chee glanced at Mia, nodded.

It was done.

***

While Johnny checked over the weapons, Mia booted her Flymotic console and ran the trace program Resler had prepared. It loaded for a minute, then displayed the results on a floating screen Jimmy Chee had hooked up for her.

Janeane's dot was red, located on floor five-O-three of Nerthus IV.

She stared at it.

'The kid's hanging in,' said Johnny, looking over.

Mia closed the program and glanced at the unconscious Resler on the graft bed. What would she have done if the dot was grey? Forget the whole thing, tell the other two to stand down, start working off her debt to Mantis as though nothing had happened? No. Even if Janeane was gone, she had no choice but to go in there. That place was the source of it, the rotten dying heart, and she needed to cut it out. It wasn't about whether the dot was grey or red, not now. It was about facing up to the reality of things and doing something about it, just as Faye Mao had put it to her back in the condemned residential block.

Jimmy Chee appeared from the shop's kitchen module with a gelwater pouch and a coldmed kit in hand and took it over to Resler. He cracked the coldmed kit and unwrapped an epinephrine patch and slapped it on the fracker's chest.

Five seconds later, Resler was awake and breathing hard.

'Am I dead?' he asked.

'Not yet,' said Jimmy Chee.

He tore the cap off the pouch and pushed it into Resler's hand, and Resler squeezed gelwater between thin dull lips.

'That hurt,' he said. 'A lot.'

'You handled it well,' said Jimmy Chee.

'How do I look?'

Jimmy Chee thumbed a button on the graft bed and a mirror rose from the foot of it. Resler leaned forward and checked his appearance. Aside from some redness to the sclera and a lack of colour in his cheeks, it wasn't possible to tell he'd been auged.

'It feels like my eyes are on fire.'

'That'll wear off soon enough,' said Jimmy Chee. He gestured at the coldmed kit. 'Painkillers and adrenals. Take what you need as you need it. For now you should keep your eyes closed and rest.'

'There's a cot behind there,' said Mia, nodding toward the fibreboard boxes stamped with the Henzai Corp seal.

'I'll give you a hand,' said Johnny. He threw Resler's arm over his shoulder and eased him off the bed. 'Let's go, chief,' he said.

Mia glanced at the clock above the counter. Five hours before final prep.

'Mia?'

She turned to look into the half-moon oculars of Jimmy Chee.

'You need me for anything else?'

She shook her head. 'Thanks. You've done plenty.'

'There's a pajatso den a few cans down. I'll go there now, stay a while.'

'We'll be out of here by six.'

He nodded. 'Good luck. I hope you pull it off.' He manoeuvred his tall frame around a shelf of old tech and disappeared from view. A few moments later the container door creaked and clanged shut.

Mia went to the graft station vacated by Resler and adjusted the bed until it was flat, then lay on the stiff vinyl with her hands clasped behind her head. Nerves plotted in her stomach. She didn't believe in telepathy, but she spoke two words in her head over and over and hoped the girl would hear them: I'm coming.

Johnny appeared from behind the Henzai boxes, wiping his hands on his fatigues.

'Is he okay?' asked Mia.

'He's out again, but he's a strong kid. He'll survive. How about you?'

For a moment she wanted to tell him. Her doubts, her fear of BB and Benz, her guilt at still drawing breath when Gian was dead, her self-loathing at having failed to protect Janeane despite her promise. But she tamped it all down inside her and looked into the unwavering green eyes of Johnny Seven and nodded. 'Let's get some rest.'

He reached out, squeezed her good shoulder. 'You're gonna do fine.' He went to the other graft bed, threw back the tarp and climbed onto it.

'Lights out,' he said, and the chop shop fell into darkness.

25 The arrivals lounge at Brandenburg Airport was a Plato's cave of central Berlin. Its furnishings brutally efficient, its processes streamlined and orderly, its lounges occupied by those who trusted the system to steer them toward prosperity. No transients, no nongrowthers, no subterraneans, no offgrids, no refus. In the dawn light, red-eyed suits touched down from Frankfurt, Munich, Hamburg, the Conurbation and elsewhere, bound for meetings in the tech capital. After passing through diffuser gates and security controls they were intercepted by slick reps who whispered instructions and kept time like an atomic clock. They hurried the new arrivals to the airport's local transfer hub, where short-hop hydrogen gliders waited to boost human payloads to Potsdamer Platz, Friedrichshain and Kreuzberg.

Mia Warsaw and Johnny Seven had been standing in the arrivals lounge for three-O minutes with several metres of polished flooring between them. Each was dressed in standard wear for bodyguards: charcoal two-button suit with no lapels, blood-red collared shirt, polymer tie. Each also wore a set of streamlined tac webbing concealed underneath their shirts. They were linked by in-ear beads, but said nothing for fear of attracting the attention of the many surveillance eyes that watched the space. Even so, as the minutes stretched and the faces around them were recycled, no human, mimic or auto rep gave the pair a second glance. Above the arrivals doors was a plant-sensitive screen that adapted its display to the passengers' augmentations.

For Mia and Johnny, his eye-over disabled so as not to set off any alarms once inside Nerthus, the screen showed only static flight details against a blue background.

An alert flashed across the screen, indicating that an eVTOL had arrived from West Paris, British sector. Mia and Johnny shifted their weight, smoothed their suits, made ready. When the arrival doors slid open and a fresh stream of bodies filled the lounge, the pair joined the crowd and followed spectral yellow arrows in the floor to the transfer hub.

Mia ghosted between passengers until she was at Johnny's shoulder and focused on her breathing. The suits around them looked harried, fatigued, wan. She tried to imagine their lives and the sacrifices they made but found that she couldn't, and realised it was because she didn't care. The only thing she and Johnny had in common with them was the pace of their footsteps. In Johnny's hand was the bag of dismantled weapons and gelignite, all sealed in plumbition-weave boxes. Resler had secured a carry-on permit on Vertoo at the eleventh hour, shortly before they'd boarded the maglev to the airport. The only thing they had to do now was to get on the short-hop glider to Nerthus IV.

A connecting tunnel brought them into another lounge with huge floating screens and panoramic windows, and Mia looked out onto a spotless departure apron, where row after row of chevron-shaped gliders waited, their three-bladed dual tiltrotors unmoving. Automatic guides accompanied human passengers to the foot of their transports, where they were met by uniformed flight attendants with faces set in surgically enhanced smiles. Mia had never flown before and the idea of stepping onto a glider made her anxious. She glanced at Johnny, took solace from his calm expression. He'd been in the air plenty of times with the army.

Another passageway disgorged them into the transfer hub, a large round space whose centre was given over to a curated tropical rainforest encased under a dome. Emerald leaves pressed up against clear Plastex, a living sculpture ignored by passengers searching for their gates. Lightwalls displayed generic ads for purewater, celestial timeshares and dreamtank subscriptions. A group of suits broke away from the main pack and made for a gate whose glider was bound for Nerthus IV, and Mia and Johnny followed. Overhead, a disembodied AI voice assured passengers their safety was paramount and requested their compliance in all security matters.

Body scanners framed the gate, flanked by armed mimics with obvious facial grafts. Mia sweated, though she was unarmed. Her bag contained the three compact parachutes that Johnny had checked and rechecked that morning. Johnny extricated himself from the group and entered the deserted immunity lane, and was about to pass through the gate when a mimic blocked his path. Green-grey uniform, slender frame, a neat chrome strip across the forehead. One hand rested on the butt of what looked to be a modified cisuto, the pulse weapon carried by polizei automatons.

'Greetings, Mx Wheeler. This lane is for immunity pass holders only.'

Johnny stopped. 'I have one.'

A moment passed. 'You have a single boarding pass, basic grade.'

'Check again.'

Another moment, this one longer. 'Single pass, basic grade. No immunity.'

Mia watched from her queue. A few suits ahead of her glanced at Johnny, curious. She willed him to keep his cool, knew the mimic would rather shoot first than take a chance on compromising the security of the airport.

Johnny shrugged. There wasn't a bead of sweat on him. 'Employer mistake, I guess. You know how it is.'

The mimic said nothing. Johnny's lean face reflected back at him from the chrome strip.

'Actually, maybe you don't.' He nodded at the other queue. 'Over there?'

'That is correct.'

Mia cursed. Resler had paid several stacks of carbon for a bogus pass. The fracker was on the comm as well, but she said nothing to him. She looked around. An emergency exit sign glowed two gates down. If she had to run, that was where she would try for.

Then it was her turn at the scanner. A mimic waved for her to step forward and she placed the bag containing the chutes on a conveyor and stood between two semi-circular walls, and a light flickered from red to green and back to red. She left the scanner and was stopped by another uniform, this one recognisably human from the way she moved and spoke.

'Security detail for Ynside?'

'That's me,' said Mia.

'How's that working out for ya?'

'It keeps me in carbon.'

'No other reason to get up in the morning. Where are you comin' from?'

'West Paris.'

'I ain't never had the scanner read pure organic for muscle before. How come you ain't got any grafts?'

'An airport's not the only place that'll scan a girl from all angles,' said Mia.

The uniform wrinkled her brow.

'Sometimes I need to go places where people don't know what I am,' she explained. 'Having a one-shotter grafted onto my forearm gives my occupation away real quick.'

The uniform grinned, pleased with herself. 'Not just muscle, then. I thought so.'

Mia winked. 'Don't tell anyone, eh? That's between you and me.'

The uniform waved her through into a seating area with a rank of gelchairs. She retrieved her bag and took a seat and glanced at Johnny at the back of the short queue. She brought her hand to her mouth as if to stifle a yawn, spoke as quietly as she could.

'Johnny, turn around and go.'

He showed no sign that he'd heard her.

'Go back to the city. Find another way in.'

Nothing.

The three passengers in front of Johnny went through the scanner without fanfare and then it was his turn. The mimic from the immunity lane waited beside the machine. Mia couldn't tell if there was tension in the air or if it was just her. Johnny held the bag out. Blacker than his suit, bearing an insignia on the side that Mia didn't recognise.

'Please place the bag here, Mx Wheeler,' said the mimic, gesturing toward a conveyor band and a pearl-shaped machine whose open mouth was marked by the blue tint of a diffusion wall.

Johnny did as he was asked, then stepped between the two semi-circular walls. On the other side he adjusted his cuffs and waited, not a care in the world. The machine chimed and spat the bag out the other end, and the mimic retrieved it and placed it on a brushed steel table and beckoned for Johnny to approach. Every suit on the flight was watching him now.

'Please open the bag,' said the mimic.

'Sure,' said Johnny, and he pulled back the double zips in a movement that was all confidence.

The mimic peered inside, enhancements working overtime. Johnny glanced beyond the mimic's head, at the screen above the departure portal. The glider would be ready to board in less than a minute. Using both hands, the mimic lifted a long rectangular box from the bag and placed it on the steel surface.

'What is this?'

'It's a resuscitation unit for my client,' said Johnny. 'He has a weak heart.'

'It has plumbition weave running through it.'

'Of course. It needs to be protected.'

'Please open it.'

'If I do that, it'll be useless.'

'Plumbition items are not permitted to be carried on board.'

Johnny nodded as though he expected the answer. 'No problem. I'll tell Mr Benz I had to leave it here. Next time he orders a unit direct from Beijing, I'll inform him that he'll have to check it as cargo.'

The mimic didn't speak for a moment. 'Mr Luc Benz, CEO of Chastity Carbon, board member of Habanik Entertainment Corp.'

'That's correct,' said Johnny.

'The resuscitation unit is for him.'

'Sure is. Or was. I'll let him know it wasn't permitted. I'd appreciate it if you could give me your ID number. He'll want his internal team to investigate, see how a situation like this can be avoided in future. Of course, he did supply me with an immunity pass precisely for that reason, but you assured me there is no record of one.'

The mimic glanced at his human coworker, who directed her gaze elsewhere. He placed the box back in the bag and pushed the bag toward Johnny. 'Enjoy your flight, Mx Wheeler.'

Johnny zipped up the bag. 'I will.' His tone of voice hadn't changed throughout the conversation.

The light at the departure portal blinked green before Johnny could sit, and the passengers formed a line and began to pass through the circular door. Mia hung back, making sure she was second to last. She and Johnny crossed the threshold and the door closed behind them, and she offered a silent thanks to the mimic's creator for putting its mind on such narrow rails. The woman in front of her wore a suit that rippled from red to burnt orange with every step, and Mia followed her into the black confines of a glider that smelled of recycled air and synthetic pine. The seats were set out in two banks of two, five rows total, and her ID chip's name was displayed above a seat in the rear left row. Johnny was next to her.

She stashed her bag, then belted herself in, throwing the straps over each shoulder. Johnny took his seat.

'Relax,' he murmured, looking straight ahead.

'I am.'

'When you're tense, a vein jumps at your temple.'

She resisted the urge to check if he was right. 'You did well back there.'

'Mimics. Gotta love them. Easy to work around if you know the patterns. We used to bring back all kinds of contraband through civilian airports with Lepage.' He paused. 'You just need to trigger its fear module and you're home and dry.'

A neutral voice announced take-off, and there was a brief jolt as the glider disengaged from its holding arm and rolled over the apron to an illuminated take-off square. Mia gripped the armrests as the tiltrotor engines fired up. The glider vibrated and began to ascend, following its departure funnel to the height allotted by the airport tower.

'Sekhmet,' said Mia.

Johnny touched her arm. 'It's okay.'

When she glanced through the viewport, she could see where the city petered out to become scrub and dust and flotsam. The glider tilted forward and picked up speed and the airport slipped from view altogether, and Mia's mind cooled and the tightness left her chest. The machine was smooth, the noise of the rotors low. It wasn't so bad. No worse than slaloming through automatic traffic on an eVelo or traversing a non-serviced skybridge that swayed in the breeze. The part she hadn't been able to control was over, which meant she could now steel herself for what was to come: confusion and killing and death and, if her luck held, the chance to see the girl whose face refused to leave her mind's eye.

The glider raced across a sky made of hammered gold. Already the city was building itself in the viewport, lozenges becoming stacks becoming storeys. And at the heart of it all lay the towers.

'Beautiful day to die,' said Johnny. There was a faint smile on his lips.

'Owen,' muttered Mia.

'Right here.' Resler's voice was clear and steady.

'We're in the air. On schedule.'

'I'm approaching the Platz.'

'Good luck.'

'Same to you.'

Through the viewport Mia observed the grey-beige city that was laid out like a gigantic circuit board. Organic on artificial, animate against inanimate, a fortress beset on all sides by threats, but which had nevertheless managed to hold out so far. Soon enough, though, a wave would come that would be too large for Berlin to withstand. And everything within it would be drowned.

The glider cut the morning in half. They were on their way.

26 Owen Resler's eyes hurt. It was a raw ugly pain that saturated his cheeks and electrified his jaw and made him want to groan. That worried him, because he couldn't allow for any distractions inside the tower. As it was, he was having trouble holding any thought in his head that didn't involve the staples that had been fired into his orbital sockets.

He kept his eyes closed on the maglev, listening as stations and business centres were spoken aloud by the train's dumb AI. Mia and Johnny had made it through the airport without being stopped and were in the skies above Berlin. Now he had to do his part. If he failed they would be killed and so would the girl. Adrenaline spiked in his chest. How could everything have changed so much since Frankfurt? Had there been a chance to play it smarter? Would he have wanted to, knowing what people were capable of in the suit world? There were no answers. He was where he was, and he would do his best to see it through. It was all he had left.

'Nerthus IV concourse,' said the AI. 'Exit for residential units, HydroVessel Industries, Holborn, Diadochi and rapid transit to Nerthus III and V.'

Resler reached for the briefcase at his foot, rose and made for the door. In the ballistic glass a stranger stared back at him. Clean-shaven, hair slicked back, clad in the last suit he would ever wear. His eyes looked fine. A touch of redness, perhaps, but healthy.

The maglev slid into a station designed to look like a Kyoto forest, quiet and placid, with a frosted nu-crete path twisting between thatches of bamboo trees. Strategic lighting painted the stems turquoise, and lightwall ads spoke to the commuters in low, respectful tones as they walked by. Station announcements were opt-in, activated via neural link, and there were no floating screens to display departure times or company messages. Resler walked at a brisk pace, all too aware of the seconds ticking by, and hopped onto a slidewalk that carried him at a fourtenfive-degree incline directly into the mezzanine of Nerthus IV. He'd never been inside one of the towers before, but he'd watched enough feeds on Wraptstar to have an idea of what to expect.

Even so, the tower's lobby made him forget the pain in his eyes. Because the place soared.

Circular with teak floors polished to a mirror shine, the space was dominated by white columns sculpted into floral shapes and a false ceiling daubed with brand-sponsored frescoes in gold and blue and cream. Gigantic chandeliers hung overhead, crystal prisms splitting LED light. At the centre was a chrome fountain, interlocking rotating plates that mimicked the design of the Nerthus towers, spewing water clearer than any Resler had ever seen in his life. It was one big advertisement to power and wealth, nothing more, and it soured Resler's stomach because it was a joke. A bad joke.

A wall interface tucked away where it wouldn't disrupt the lobby's aesthetic blinked the word 'Assistance' into the gilded void. Resler went to it and the letters resolved into a humanoid impression. Female, sober dress, eyes blank, shoulders slightly hunched. The perfect servant for the men in the high tower.

'How may I assist?'

'Pleasance, executive operations at Ynside. Routine check of central control. Data scan.'

'No appointment is scheduled.'

'I know. Part of our new policy. We have received reports of data tampering prior to our visits. This is in direct violation of the Climate

Preservation Act. Failure to provide permission to conduct a scan may result in legal consequences.'

'To which floor do you require access?'

'Unknown. I require a DX5 control interface.'

'Floor nine.' The impression gestured toward a livid red lens next to the interface. 'The retinal scan, Mr Pleasance.'

Moment of truth, thought Resler. Either he'd be in or he'd be dead. He placed his briefcase on the floor, stooped to line himself up with the scanner, forced himself not to blink as the machine beamed his left eye and then his right. The red light dimmed and Resler straightened up and clenched his teeth against the fresh pain that radiated from his sockets. The impression was motionless except for wisps of hair that trembled in a non-existent breeze.

It blinked.

'Access granted to floor nine, operations. May I sync your neuro-optical superimposition interface to the building's downstream iden-tification code?'

'Please do.'

'I have reserved a console in cubicle tenfour. Take pneumatic bank beta and follow the arrows as they appear on your interface. If you require anything else, I will be pleased to assist you. Enjoy your stay at Nerthus IV, Mr Pleasance.'

'Thank you,' he said, and he turned away and made for a bank of brass-fronted pneumatics marked with a lowercase beta symbol. He spoke aloud the number nine and waited for an elevator to touch down. Before it did, a name boomed through the lobby.

'Hoffman?'

He turned. A man around his age, making a beeline for him. Face fleshy and without visible implants, suit functional rather than de-signer, a hand raised in greeting. Resler heard the brass-fronted doors slide open behind him, but he stayed put. Whatever the man wanted, it was better to settle it in the lobby.

'Hoffman,' said the man again, his shoes landing like bullets against the polished teak. 'Thought I saw you there.' He broke into a grin. 'Remember me? Collins. The Prosydius summit.'

Resler smiled back. 'Of course, Collins. Great to see you.'

'What a geznet coincidence. Nerthus, of all places. So how are you getting along?'

'Same old, same old.'

The man laughed. 'Must be doing something right. Sharp suit you got there.' He looked closer. 'Anti-surveillance?'

Resler shrugged. 'You can never be too careful.'

'I hear that.'

'So what's your sentence?'

Another grin. 'Here to tinker with a few service bots up on two-O-four. Swipe, wipe and type.'

Resler raised an eyebrow. 'No blue-collars to take care of it?'

The smile faded. 'Come on, in here? You gotta have two PhDs before they even let you through the door. Nah, but it's okay. I don't mind doing gruntwork in a ritzdiamond like this. Seen that fountain?'

'Sure.'

'It's something.' The man winked. 'Snapped a couple on my eye-over to show the kids.'

'How are they doing?'

'Ah, you know. The way things are? Wish I could give them more of a chance, like we had. But they're going up against the savant schools and the damn refu streams and everything else. How's a homegrown white-collar supposed to compete with cheap labour and helots?'

'Search me.'

'Sometimes I think they'll be lucky to find a job running pajatso in Container City.'

'Not if they have you in their corner,' said Resler. 'That's one edge the refus don't have.'

'I suppose,' said the man. 'Hey, Hoffman.'

'Yeah.'

'Why don't we split a bottle when you're done? I could wait right here.'

'Wish I could,' said Resler. 'But the deadline for this job is razor.'

'Old man giving everyone hell, is he?'

'You'd better believe it.'

The man laughed again. 'Okay. I'll be in touch. Where are you living now?'

Resler hesitated, then went for it. 'Biotecture pod close to leech town. The Croft.'

'So far away from work?'

'Closer to the action.'

'Must have set you back.'

Resler shook his head. 'Clearance. Last guy died in there after being logged into Wraptstar for too long. Agent said if I dealt with the smell, she'd take half off.'

The man wrinkled his nose. 'Some deal.'

'It is what it is.'

The man glanced at the bank of pneumatics. The elevator for floors two-O to three-O sat waiting. 'Time to ride. Good speaking to you, Hoffman.'

Resler raised two fingers in a lazy salute. 'Don't get into trouble.'

Then the man was gone, into the tube and up through the bowels of the tower, and Resler composed himself and sent a prayer of thanks to whoever was watching over him. He stepped into his own idling pneumatic and rode it to floor nine, then followed streaks of yellow imposed on his eye-over through a hallway whose walls were a tapestry of preserved moss and bark. The entrance to cubicle tenfour lit up like a landing pad and a scanner read his retinal shrouds, then the door slid open and Resler stepped inside. From the briefcase he unzipped his hackwork kit and ran a joy scalpel through the local door control. He killed the surveillance eye, then stepped back into the hallway and locked the door.

He returned to the pneumatic, which hadn't moved.

'Third floor,' he said.

The eye-over was telling him to go back. He ended the sync to the building and continued on, down a nondescript, green-tinted corridor, past sealed doors hiding the artificial organs that kept the great tower alive. There was no one else around. Surveillance eyes stared blankly, the premium anti-surveillance fabric in his jacket shielding him from their gaze. As he walked, he felt the weight of Nerthus IV around him. Then it began to press against his chest until it was difficult to draw breath, and he had to stop and rest his briefcase on the floor and lean against a spotless wall with his head bowed until the panic had subsided. He wanted to rub his eyes but they were still far too raw, so he stuffed his hands into the pockets of his suit pants and told himself to get it together.

The door he chose was like the others he had passed, green-white with a scanner, identified by his infiltration program as the room least frequented on that floor. From his hackwork kit he withdrew a U-shaped device that curled around his index finger, and he thumbed a button on the side and held it to the scanner, and the device bombarded its sensors with invisible information until it froze. During the reset, the device fired an override command into the gap and the door opened.

A notch blinked on his eye-over and he opened the channel.

'Owen,' said Mia Warsaw, 'we're on approach. I can see the tower.'

The man in the lobby had waylaid him. He was behind schedule.

'I'm still setting up,' he said.

The response came after several seconds of dead air. 'Be quick.'

The room was compact and low-lit, with four chunky wall-mounted back-end consoles for engineers to perform spot patches and scans. Resler ignored them. He thumbed the door shut and locked himself in, then shrugged off his jacket and unbuttoned his sleeves and rolled them up. The locks on his briefcase made a popping sound and he pulled out Mia's Flymotic console, its EVA case still bearing the marks from where it had been knocked over in the drone strike on the

Tempelhof prefab. He booted it and withdrew the only other item in the briefcase, a spider bot, which he activated and put to work unscrewing the housing on one of the wall-mounted consoles. When the cover came free, a jungle of cables and wires spilled out onto the floor and Resler's eye-over identified the ones he needed and he disconnected the ends and plugged them into the Flymotic. He extended the console's wrist shackle and slid it into his forearm port.

He was about to swim in the lifeblood of Nerthus IV.

A breath. Then he launched the infiltration program.

The Flymotic's rear holographic projection eye opened and a wireframe representation of the building's central control appeared in the room. Resler's SynSult plate kicked in as an endless holographic stream of data swirled around the room. He could hear himself choking on the scale of it, feel the SynSult struggle to cool his brain enough to handle the data. The stream was blue, purple, pink, yellow, each colour representing a different basic type of information, but there was simply too much. His mind couldn't cope. Sweat poured from him. His eyes burned. Gasping, he paused his program and yanked the wrist shackle from his forearm port. The stream disappeared. His overheated mind buzzed. According to his eye-over, he had been inside for approximately three seconds.

He closed his eyes. I can't do it, he thought. I'll die before I can get it under control.

'Landing in two-midi,' said Mia in his head.

A plea for more time became stuck in his throat. His thoughts were fragmented, irritated. Even the best frackers at Scopo wouldn't be able to do this.

Another incoming message. Johnny's calm voice. 'Owen?'

He managed to squeeze out a word. 'Yeah.'

'Are we ready?'

'Not yet.'

'You can do it.'

I can't, he wanted to say. I can't help you. You're going to die.

The Flymotic sat before him, a circular brain inside a rectangular skeleton, smarter than he was but unable to function without his input. Isolating a few floors was a task that usually took a matter of seconds, but every second inside central control came with the risk of his brain shutting down on him. What he needed, he thought, were shields to deflect the data onslaught while he worked.

'Hold on,' he said, unsure whether he was telling Mia and Johnny or if it was for his own benefit.

As the time ticked by, he drew on all of the knowledge he'd learned underground and at Scopo's academy to amend the infiltration program he'd written. His hands flew over lightkeys projected toward him by the Flymotic, lines of code appearing in the air as the barriers took shape. He sent a hypothetical, asking the machine how long they would last based on his previous attempt. The answer was slower to arrive than he expected: ten seconds. It would have to be enough.

Mia and Johnny hadn't pinged him again. He checked his eyeover. The time was up. Either they were on the landing pad or already in the tower, which meant they needed him. He breathed deep and took a seat on the cool utility room floor, the wrist shackle pinched between his thumb and forefinger and the hexagonal forearm port exposed. He glanced at the ceiling, saw no sign from the gods.

Resler plunged the shackle into his arm and went again.

This time he knew what to expect, but the stream still hit him like a road train on a flat highway. The data came from all sides, the DNA of a steel and nu-crete megalith, and already he could feel his barriers crumbling under the onslaught. With hot pain radiating from the base of his skull, he worked to pull pertinent threads from the never-ending stream and find the hole through which to escape. Somewhere, part of him registered that he'd seen no sign of Nerthus IV's AI. Too insignificant to matter, maybe, a new light winking on only to burn out moments later. All around him was data and more data, grains of sand containing galaxies. Shadows appeared at the edges of his vision, telling him he was losing consciousness, and a tear fell from his maimed eye. His body vibrated with the effort to stay in one piece.

Then he saw it, the handle he needed to open the door, and as the shadows surrounded him he reached for it but it was too late, too late, and he wished he could say sorry to Mia and Johnny for failing to survive for only ten seconds inside the machine, and he gave himself up, ready to be digested, ready to become nothing.

The maelstrom stopped. The shadows receded.

'Oh no,' said Mia, a world away.

Resler blinked. He was still there, just. Data threads hung like curtains in the utility room, still oppressive but no longer smothering. He checked his infiltration program. In his delirium he'd managed to slot the last command home and isolate floors five-O-one to five-O-four. The readout said he'd been point-zero-seven of a second from fatal information overload.

But he was inside.

He wiped the sweat from his face and felt a deep ache in his legs and arms and knew he would have difficulty walking out of the room without limping. He shook the thought away. Though he'd accessed the floors, he still had to gain control over them. An exploratory finger touched the dope plate at his temple. Warm, but still functioning. He trusted it to hold.

An incoming ping. Johnny. 'Owen, help.'

The Yuanrang Ten central control wasn't something he was familiar with, but its basic structure was the same as the high-end systems he did know, and when his infiltration program isolated the master command list and prompted him to enter the override he nearly shouted with joy. He pulled Wagenknecht's codes from his eye-over and transferred them to the Flymotic. For a moment nothing happened and he cursed the data scientist. Then a confirmation. Control over floors five-O-one through five-O-four was his. He locked the pneumatics to prevent anyone from ascending or descending, then had the security cameras by five-O-one's external entrance routed to his eye-over.

He found himself looking at a rainforest. Emerald leaves spilled from moss-covered boughs and vines wrapped themselves around brown-orange trunks. A small waterfall cascaded from an open ceiling into a pool, sending blue-tinted mist into the air. Carbon steel floor panels cut a path through the foliage. A double set of glass doors offered a glimpse of a deserted landing pad.

And Mia and Johnny stood frozen between three liquidators.

The automatons were identifiable from their bulbed craniums, cylindrical bodies and blade-like arms. Superior security for a top-level building. Standard programming was to subdue perpetrators by detaching their hands and cauterising the stumps. Sometimes the hands were reattached later. Usually they weren't.

Mia flinched as a liquidator raised one of its blades.

Resler swept through the master command list. The SynSult pulsed at his temple. He found the command line and yanked it as the liquidator brought its blade down. It shivered and froze, the weapon stopping a finger's breadth from Mia's wrist. The pulse light on the craniums of all three automatons blinked out.

Mia and Johnny looked at each other.

'Door's open,' said Resler. He could hear a terrible strain in his voice. 'Get going.'

27

The rainforest was a wonder, a lab-grown pyretic dream born of a single-minded desire to control nature down to its individual leaves, but Mia Warsaw didn't have time to admire it. The flora concealed all manner of threats. She scanned the green for movement while Johnny unpacked the weapons they would use to launch their assault on Luc Benz's residence three floors above.

'Here,' said Johnny.

He threw her the tessen fan that she'd liberated in Amerika and thrown into the bag at the last second. She held it ready as Johnny assembled the guns, casting a glance at the disabled liquidators behind them. She'd been frozen by fear. That couldn't happen again. The kid was close and she was damned if she was going to fail now. Three hostile floors separated them, but she had a one-man army at her side and a ghost in the system.

'Owen,' she said. 'Do you have things under control?'

'Yes.' Resler sounded tense. 'But I don't know for how long. There's a hell of a lot of data up there, even for just those three floors. And I can feel the AI now. It knows I'm here.'

'Where do we need to go?'

'Straight ahead, three-O metres. In the forest on the right is an emergency exit that will take you into a service stairwell. You can head up to Benz's residence from there.'

'What about the other passengers who came in with us?'

'The ones who didn't get to a pneumatic before I took over are in the antechamber adjoining you. I've locked them in. They aren't going anywhere.'

The sound of a magazine clicking home cut short any further conversation. Johnny passed her the short-stock Nylon, which she slung on a strap over her bad shoulder, and two of the Agitators. She hung the tessen fan from a loop on her webbing. He picked up the Göl-Tek carbon-fibre carbine and cradled it between his arms. The two gelignite cases, their last resort, were strapped to his back.

'Ready,' he said.

'I'll lead.' She adjusted the straps of the bag containing hers and Janeane's chutes, and held the Nylon flush against her so she could direct the orange muzzle toward any threat that might be hiding the trees. Then she moved out. Her boots clicked against carbon steel floor panels, incongruous in their deadness.

Resler kept up a commentary as they walked. 'I'm working to disable the defences on each level, but each command is wrapped in a host of other commands. I've never seen anything like it. The system's been designed not to shut down. Like, ever. And each floor is its own complete ecosystem, set up to run without interruption. It's not supposed to be touched.'

Mia was only half-listening. Leaves brushed her exposed arms, left a faint dampness on her skin. The air was more humid than she would've expected. The amount of juice that had to go into keeping the forest alive wasn't worth thinking about.

'It's like the tower knows itself,' said Resler in a tone of wonder.

'You mean it's self-aware?' asked Johnny.

'Not quite. It's like the earth. No single brain or consciousness. More like thousands of them, working together. And the AI is a product of that collective awareness. It doesn't like me being here, I can tell you that.'

The leaves ahead parted and Mia had only a second to aim before two liquidators were on the walkway, lethal blades slicing through the air. The Nylon boomed and the Göl-Tek buzzed and the two machines hit the floor and lay smoking amid twisted roots. Mia dropped to one knee as Johnny moved past her.

'Ah, now I see,' said Resler. 'Sorry.'

Johnny rolled the head of one of the liquidators over with a boot. 'Where now?'

'The door's two-O paces ahead to your right,' said Resler. 'I'm trying to find the command to open it. The system's a jungle.'

'You're telling me,' said Johnny, eyeing the leaves. He took the lead and Mia followed, and after a few metres they left the path and moved between densely packed trunks. The air dripped with life and Mia pulled down a breath of it to calm herself. The further they went, the darker it became, and they had to use their carbines to push the leaves out of the way.

'There,' said Johnny, and Mia squinted and saw a door, smooth with no handles and only the barest trace of a frame.

'Owen?' she said.

'Working on it.'

Then a new noise. A hiss of escaping air, multiple sets of boots moving fast over pressed metal, the swish and clink of serious weapons, voices speaking in a shorthand Mia didn't recognise or understand. Humans, come to do the job where the machines had failed. She and Johnny crouched with their back to the door and their rifles ready.

'Security blackshirts,' said Resler. 'They came in from outside, Daedalus jets from five floors down. They're sweeping. Don't speak and don't move.'

Get the door open, Mia wanted to say, but she knew Resler was doing his best.

Through the trunks she caught a glimpse of a man. An implant protruded from the base of his skull. She imagined the rest of them moving down the pathway, lending enhanced eyes and ears to the fauna. A drop of condensation fell from a frond and landed on her neck. She shivered.

It was enough.

The blackshirt whipped around, weapon raised, and Mia saw the sneer on his metallised face in the second before Resler killed the lights and the floor went dark.

An alarm split the air. Mia loosed the Nylon in the spot where she'd seen the blackshirt and then dropped to her stomach and felt cold mulch seep through the fabric of her pants. Explosions followed flashes and she rolled and snapped up and fired at what had to be a muzzle flash. The return came fast, shredding the trunk next to her, and she edged back through the leaves until she was touching wall. Bullets continued to fly, either from the blackshirts or Johnny or both. At a sound to her right she turned and fired and then the Nylon was empty, so she let it hang and drew an Agitator. Voices competed to be heard over the alarm, gruff, authoritative, metallic. In a splinter of automatic light she saw a man with a razor-sharp face take aim at her, and she barely had enough time to duck before a chrome fist flew past and buried itself in the wall. She whipped the Agitator up and squeezed and the man dropped. She looked around, trying to find Johnny in the pencil-sketch jungle, and realised she couldn't hear the singular pop of the Göl-Tek. A new dread started in her chest as she reloaded her weapons. An incendiary round set fire to a branch close by, but the flames barely had time to take hold before a spiderbot crawled down the trunk and doused the fire with foam. Its chemical smell mixed with the scent of heated plastic and the forest's own perfume.

Then, from the trees on the other side of the pathway, came a guttural yell, issued not in pain but in anger. A rifle fired controlled bursts as the blackshirts shouted to each other in panicked voices. Then came the terrible sound of screams being methodically cut short. When the shooting stopped, the forest was enveloped in an unsettling silence.

'Mia?'

'Yeah, Johnny.'

'You okay?'

She patted herself down. The man with the chrome fist had come closest. 'All clear. You?'

'I'm good.'

'Ah,' said Resler. 'Found it.'

A rectangle of muted light illuminated the forest as the emergency exit door rumbled open. Johnny appeared beside her, his skin streaked with dirt and moss and life from the trees. He looked ancient and ageless at the same time.

'Their weapons are biolocked,' he said. 'Think they heard that upstairs?'

'I wouldn't be surprised if each floor was soundproofed,' she said.

'That's correct,' said Resler. 'I've locked the landing pad doors now, by the way. I didn't realise they would be so enterprising.'

Mia and Johnny went into the stairwell with their weapons primed. It was deserted. Nu-crete, oblong and austere with a void at the centre. No sound of footsteps ascending or descending to meet them. There was a manual door control on the wall and Mia brushed the sensor and the forest disappeared.

Johnny went to the handrail and looked down and then up.

'See anything?' asked Mia.

'Lots of stairs.' He turned to her. 'We're alone for now, but we should probably count on company soon enough. Got any water in that bag? My throat's full of grit.'

She shook her head, eyed the stairs. Three floors between her and the kid.

Then two words in their ears, sounding as though they had been ripped from Resler's mouth. 'Oh God.'

'Owen?' said Johnny.

'The tower AI is trying to override my program,' said Resler. He was breathing fast. 'White blood cells coming to combat the virus. It's holding for now, but you need to move. Tech's minimal in the stairwell. I have no eyes on you or the floors above you, so watch yourselves. The back door to Benz's level isn't listed in the index. I'll keep looking.'

Johnny pushed a finger into his ear to mute the bead's ultrasensitive mike and Mia did the same. 'The boy doesn't sound too stable,' he said. 'If he loses control of the floors, they'll seal us in here, lob a few concussion grenades our way and dispatch the wireheads to clean up.'

I know, she wanted to say. I know it as well as you do. Instead she moved, her footsteps loud as she followed the curve of smooth nucrete up through the tower. The air was ultra-purified. No dust, no humidity, not even the metallic edge of recycled oxygen. On the landing above she waited for Johnny to join her. His Göl-Tek covered the door as she took the next flight. She could feel the sweat from her fingers against the Nylon's plasticated body. No blackshirts, no liquidators. No sound except their boots and their breathing.

They halted on the landing of five-O-three. Two more twists of the stairwell, thought Mia, and they would be there.

'Owen,' she said.

It took several seconds before he responded. 'This AI. It's relentless.'

'We're one floor down from Benz.'

'The door isn't anywhere in the system. I can't open it. I'd say he probably has air-gapped computers running the show up there.'

'So what do we do?'

'I have the command for the door on five-O-three.'

'What's behind it?'

'System says it's a vacant apartment. Opens into some kind of storage room. The power is off. Once you get to the pneumatics, I can take you up.' The last word was cut off as Resler hissed in pain. 'Sorry.'

'Do you have any eyes in there, at least?' asked Johnny.

'No.'

'What if we go via the floor above Benz? Five-O-five.'

'No. I don't have it isolated.'

'Then we'll take our chances with the vacant,' said Mia. 'Open the door and seal it once we're inside.'

'I will,' said Resler.

The door shivered and loosed a rind of dust and then it was open. Mia led, stepping into a room loaded with shelving units and boxes. The air was warm, non-ventilated. Johnny used a knife at his belt to lever open a box and withdrew a silver-gloss package stamped with five words: Synthesised Chemical Replacement As Nutrition. He checked another, found that it contained gelwater pouches. He ripped the cap off one and drank until it was empty.

'Thirsty?' he whispered.

Mia didn't respond.

An open door brought them into a large kitchen that was dormant and spotless. In the corner was a Torggler door with its frame lights extinguished. Mia lowered the Nylon and went to the manual control and waved her hand over the sensor. The leaves didn't budge. She glanced at Johnny and he shouldered the Göl-Tek and gripped the Torggler's left leaf and the muscles in his arms jumped as he pulled. After a few moments of struggling it moved reluctantly on its rail, and Mia ducked through and Johnny did the same.

A lounge, oppressively large, with beige walls and floors and ceiling. Neo-deco flowlights, squared-off furniture cloaked in drop cloths, ornamental marble columns, a sunken floor accessible via a short flight of steps. Floating at its centre was a semi-transparent man. Tall, muscular, coldly attractive, dressed in a black Tang suit. He turned to Mia and Johnny and spread his arms wide.

'Welcome,' said Luc Benz. 'I'm glad you could make it.'

Then the firing started and the room became death.

28There were shots and there were shouts and then there was silence.

Resler blinked aching eyes and felt a sense of déjà vu.

'Mia? Johnny?'

The two were still there as nodes of light on his eye-over. He dialled the sound to maximum, but he couldn't even hear them breathing. He broke the contact, connected it again.

'Can you hear me?'

Still nothing. Something was interfering with the beads.

There was another thing, too. He'd been gritting his teeth and sweating buckets with the effort of repelling Nerthus IV's AI, but it had backed off the moment he'd lost contact with Mia and Johnny. What did that mean? Did it govern itself or was it acting on someone's orders?

He opened indexes and schematics for floor five-O-three, searching for surveillance eyes he could co-opt and finding none. All he had was a manifest confirming it was vacant and control over the main and rear doors. No owner ID, no custodian sweeps, no system logs. Like Benz's residence above it, the floor was a void.

Or a tomb.

He had the Flymotic transfer the feeds from the surveillance eyes on floor five-O-two to his eye-over. It, too, was a residence, its interiors a melange of synthetic teak and glass and slabs of obsidian. The owner, a silver-haired man with flawlessly crisped skin, lounged in a newcentury chair in the living area, eyes closed, while a mimic played a cello for him. Aside from the obscene wealth, there was nothing out of place that Resler could see. He switched to five-O-one and saw the junked automatons and the blackshirted bodies of the men Mia and Johnny had cut down. Nothing breathed except the trees.

Then a notch blinked on his eye-over. ID scrubbed. Frowning, he accepted the ping.

'Mantis?'

'Hello, Mr Pleasance.'

A man's voice. Round and resonant and augmented.

'Or perhaps I should call you Owen Resler.'

Resler didn't trust himself to speak.

'Do you know how many first-time visitors this tower has on any given day, Mr Resler? I'll tell you: between five and ten. We are very much a closed ecosystem here, so it doesn't take much of a leap in logic to determine that whoever is mounting an attack on central control came from outside. Alas, you aren't where you were told to go. Floor nine, cubicle tenfour. So where are you?'

All he had to do was cut the connection. One command and the voice would be gone.

'I know you're there, Mr Resler. BB knows it, too. The textile knight, come to save little Janeane.'

Anger, hot and uncontrolled, at hearing the girl's name.

'Go to hell,' said Resler.

'Ah, he speaks.'

Panic rolled in like a wave.

'I have a proposition for you, Mr Resler.'

'You have nothing I could want.'

'Hear me out.' The voice was compelling, soothing, and Resler realised he wouldn't cut Benz off until he'd heard what he had to say.

'Every Nerthus tower has its own unique AI. Nerthus IV's resident is named Themis. You may have noticed it has decided to leave you in peace.'

'What of it?'

'I am giving you a single chance. If you extricate yourself from central control, you may walk out of this building alive. No one will stop you, no one will follow you. You'll be a free man. What's more, you'll have enough carbon credit to last several lifetimes.'

Resler's eye-over blinked and an encrypted banco-file appeared in his retinal view.

'The file I just sent you contains the information to an account only you may access. The balance is large enough for you to settle wherever you want. Berlin, Hamburg, the Conurbation, Frankfurt, abroad. It will be topped up every month. Leave now and I will send you the decryption code.'

'Why? Why would you do that?'

'Because this isn't your crusade, Mr Resler. You aren't a—what is the term they use—a nongrowther. You know how the game works and you know it can't be won. The best you can hope for is insulate yourself from the miseries of this existence. Those who aspire to be subversives, like Ms Warsaw or the soldier or even Ms Janeane, are destined to fail. They will be subsumed into the whole or they will be expunged. There is no option to operate outside the social system humankind has created for itself. This is what we have and what always will be. I'm giving you the chance to reclaim your place within that system.'

A thought came to Resler. 'Let me speak to Janeane first.'

'I'm afraid that is not possible.'

'Why not?'

'The girl put up a good fight, more than most. But even her mind and body had a limit.'

His chest emptied itself of fear and in its place there was rage. 'She's dead?'

'And you will be too if you fail to do as I ask.'

'You first,' said Resler, and he killed the comm.

A perfect grey wall stared back at him and he screamed. He had no more tears left to shed.

Janeane. A girl whose life, from what little he'd understood of it, had been a battle from start to finish. Questions with no answers filled his mind. How had she spent her final moments? Had she been in agony? Had BB touched her? What had Benz done with the body?

The coldness of the floor seeped into him, cooled his anger, cooled his mind.

The only question that mattered now was why Benz had pinged him. Why he'd offered him a way out. A man who was sure of his position wouldn't do such a thing. It told him two facts.

Mia and Johnny were still kicking up on five-O-three.

And Benz saw him as a threat.

He glanced at the door. Locked, sealed, not safe. He wouldn't remain undetected forever. What he needed was to throw off the mantle covering Benz's floor. Penetrate the void and get eyes and ears up on five-O-four.

He had an idea.

Back when he was doing hackwork, one of the top minds, a woman with teneight years' experience under her belt, had worked out a way to use a building's ventilators to send commands to air-gapped computer systems. It involved taking control of the fans inside the ventilators and adjusting their speeds to create different sound frequencies, each of which represented a letter or number. By putting together a string of frequencies, the fans could send commands to nearby microelectromechanical systems accelerometers used in consoles to keep their holographics steady. Resler had watched the woman give a full demonstration of how it worked. A few weeks later Athos had collapsed and the group had dissolved, and he'd forgotten all about it.

It could work, he told himself. That was, if his hunch about the electronics being air-gapped was correct.

The AI, Themis, continued to keep its distance. Benz must have been giving him a few minutes to think the proposition over. Resler brought up a wireframe of the building on the Flymotic and the holographic display filled the room. Five-O-four was represented in green and he isolated it and banished the remainder and saw that although the floor itself was dark to him, its perimeter wasn't. The outline was there, and he could see the myriad systems that lived in its walls. Door control. Fire safety. Lighting. Water. Slab rotation. Solar capture. Pneumatic.

Ventilation.

He got to work creating an alphabet and digit key for the fan frequencies, using his infiltration program for the heavy lifting. He felt the steadying influence of the SynSult at his temple, wondered how much longer Benz would give him before he let Themis loose. He needed more barriers, more protection from its onslaught. In between sewing together lines of code he glanced at the notches on his eye-over, which remained lightless. His infiltration program produced the digit key at the same time as he put the finishing touches to a scutum shield script. The holographic representation of the floor, black in the centre and green at the edges, hung before him.

'Launch it,' he said to the Flymotic.

The program went to work.

And Benz's patience reached its limit, because Themis came at him again.

29 The room had been empty and then it was full.

Johnny moved first. When the mercenaries with high-tech weapons slipped from their cover, he brought the Göl-Tek up and sprayed in a low arc, and instead of taking their shots the mercs were forced into evasive action. One woman was too slow and dropped with a cry, and Mia saw everything in slow motion before her legs connected with her brain and she jumped behind a bar cabinet overlooking the sunken floor.

The shooting started in earnest. The noise was its own beast, violent and terrifying, and Mia felt it in her bones as she struggled to release an Agitator from her webbing. Bullet holes studded the Torggler door behind her like a string of dead LEDs, and the bar cabinet shook and she knew she didn't have more than a few seconds before a round hit its mark. To her left, Johnny stood with his back pressed against a ruby-coloured pillar that was being ground into bloody dust. When a lull in the firing came he aimed and the Göl-Tek barked and there were screams. A round plucked at his arm and he dived back into cover and glanced at her, features tight but with no trace of fear. He mouthed something but she couldn't make it out, and in the back of her mind she realised something was blocking the beads, which meant Resler couldn't help them.

Then her Agitator was free and cradled between steady hands, and she listened to the shots and imagined the angles. The joes out there weren't standard security. They were professional killers hired to do a job by a man who always seemed to be one step ahead, all crowded into a luxury lounge that was now a killing floor.

'Come out and die,' said the Benz hologram.

She popped up and fired and felt the pistol buck and saw a man with brass plates in his cheeks clutch his throat and go down, and then she was running, away from the scant protection of the bar cabinet to a column on the other side of the room. The noise reached fever pitch and a round smashed into the Agitator in her hand and sent it flying. Then she was behind the column, but she had only a moment before a tattooed woman whirling an electrified weighted chain was on her. Mia barely avoided the chain and planted a fist in the woman's face, then swung the Nylon around on its strap and fired. The woman fell with a look of surprise before her eyes closed. Her tattoos continued to swarm where she lay.

On the other side of the room the Göl-Tek buzzed.

Mia looked at her hand, saw splinters of blue embedded in the palm. Blood dripped onto the spotless floor. She took a graphene bandage from her webbing and wrapped it around the wound and felt it apply pressure and get to work sanitising the lacerations. Desperately, she tried to reach Resler. The light was on but no one was home. There was another lull in the firing, and she poked the Nylon out from behind the column and let off a burst and knew she wasn't hitting anything but hoped it would keep the mercs' heads down while she came up with her next move.

'You're too late for the girl,' said the Benz hologram.

Mia slammed a new clip home and told herself not to listen.

From the other side of the room Johnny shouted her name. He pointed forward and she nodded, and as he made a run for it she covered him as best she could, but another bullet found its mark and he stumbled and fell behind a nu-crete plinth that held a twisted iron sculpture. A man with a blade where his left arm would have been seized the chance and ran at the plinth, and though Mia pulled the trigger nothing happened because the Nylon was dry again. The bladed man jumped, clearing the iron sculpture with an ease that suggested augmentation, and Mia screamed a warning before a flurry of shots forced her into cover. She couldn't see Johnny, didn't know if he'd heard her. Her eyes found the embossed millwork on the ceiling as she tried to think of a way out. But her mind was blank. This is where it breaks, she heard a voice say. This is where you fall.

The Benz hologram spoke. 'Cease fire,' it said, and the shooting stopped.

***

This hiss of hot metal. The smell of burning plastic. The sloughing of stone onto polished floor. A man whimpering in pain. Somewhere, a dust cloth smouldered and smoke drifted without direction.

Mia peeked out from behind the column and watched as the Benz hologram surveyed the damage to the room. Then it turned to her and she knew the man of flesh and blood was looking at her through the construct's eyes.

'So much sound and fury, signifying nothing.'

She waited.

'Warsaw,' said the hologram. 'To avoid further destruction, I am in favour of ending this here. I didn't believe you would be foolish enough to come for the girl, but your erstwhile colleague BB convinced me otherwise. Allow me to briefly summarise the situation. The girl is dead. Owen Resler has been apprehended. You are surrounded and all doors leading into that room are locked. You're alone. Now, if you surrender, I promise your death will be quick.'

Mia brought Janeane's face to her mind. Sparkling dancing girl, too world-weary for her age. A tear appeared in the corner of her eye and she let it fall. That kid had meant more to her than even she had allowed herself to acknowledge. Now it was over, not that she'd ever believed she'd stood a chance of getting her back. Benz had won.

Then came another man's voice. 'She isn't alone.'

Johnny.

The Benz hologram turned. 'Ah, the soldier. You of all people must realise this is a fight you cannot win.'

'I knew that coming in.'

'And yet it is never too late to be smart. I'm willing to let you walk out of here right now if you put your weapons down and leave Warsaw to her fate.'

'Why don't you offer me a job while you're at it?'

'If that's what you want,' said Benz.

'Deal of a lifetime.'

'That's one way of putting it.'

'I'll think I'll pass.'

'Brave. Brave but pointless.'

Behind the Benz hologram, Mia saw a man with an anabolic body break the barrel of a thump gum over his leg and shove home a fat cylindrical round, then snap it shut and prop it on the backrest of a chair. The thump gun's mouth pointed directly at Mia's column. She slid down the stone, the parachutes on her back cushioning her, until she was on her haunches. She cuffed the tears from her eyes. Her injured hand throbbed.

'My people are prepared to turn that room into a wall of fire if they have to.'

'You're the one who'll have to foot the bill,' said Johnny, and despite her misery Mia smiled.

Then she heard a low whistle. She glanced around the column, saw, by the plinth, a man's hand clutching a black case. Gelignite. The last resort. For a moment she felt fear, then acceptance. It wouldn't bring the tower down, likely wouldn't even destroy the room, but when it detonated the man himself would feel the vibrations one floor up and know how close they had come. She whistled back.

'My patience is at an end,' said the Benz hologram.

'You drive a hard bargain,' said Johnny. 'Count of three. And we'll come out.'

Mia closed her eyes and wrapped her arms around herself. A calmness washed over her. If there was something after this, she hoped she would be seeing the kid shortly.

'One,' said Johnny.

A narrow band of light on the case glowed green.

'Two.'

Mia took a breath, held it.

'Three.'

The gelignite case flew in a parabolic arc, over the top of the Benz hologram, and landed just short of the surviving mercenaries. All hit the deck except one man who suspected the black case was nothing more than an ESD, and he boosted his antistatic bucklers in anticipation and kept his weapon trained on the plinth.

When the green light became red the man was vaporised.

Mia felt the touch of superheated air on her arms, and then she was knocked to the floor and her world turned black.

30

When the Flymotic nudged Resler, he stopped wrestling with Themis and stared.

The infiltration program had found a computer on five-O-four. A roll of the dice in the dark and he'd hit double sixes. He checked the data readout to confirm it: the computer was air-gapped. Disconnected network. Total physical, electromagnetic and electronic isolation. But the fan frequency gambit had worked all the same and the bridge was built. He was in.

With his attention drawn to the readout, Themis attacked with full force. The Flymotic's holographic display lit up like a lightwall, the defences breached in several places at once. He scrambled to repair them, using every trick he knew to force the AI back. The SynSult plate was warm at his temple as it worked overtime to keep his mind from overloading. His body was rigid, his muscles cramping. He wanted to scream, but he couldn't afford to waste the energy. As the infiltration programme searched for and destroyed the rogue elements within his sphere of control, Themis retreated. He sealed the holes behind it and breathed.

He issued a command via five-O-four's ventilation system for the air-gapped computer to activate its wireless network. It took several minutes for the fans to cycle through the frequencies, and he used the time to throw up as many fresh barriers as he could. Then he ordered the Flymotic to forward the surveillance feeds for the floors under his control to his eye-over. The glider passengers who had arrived with

Mia and Johnny were still trapped in the antechamber on five-O-one. Another blackshirt security team equipped with Daedalus jetpacks was on the landing pad, trying and failing to open the exterior door with prisebars. Explosives would have done it, Resler reasoned, but setting off bombs inside a hyperscraper was the last thing anyone wanted to do.

Then, without ceremony, the breached computer appeared on the Flymotic's display with its wireless enabled. He sent an exploratory command and found he could access it like any other terminal. No encryption, no further defences to deal with. Its isolation had been its protection. A few more targeted instructions connected the computer to the other systems under his control and he routed all data to the Flymotic.

The black void of five-O-four disappeared, replaced by a holographic wireframe.

The first thing he did was lock the floor's emergency exit door. Then he set about restoring sound and vision, identifying the cameras and microphones inside the suite and throwing the digital switches required to turn them on. Eight feeds were sent to his eye-over and he cycled through them.

The residence he found himself looking at was a work of art. It drew the outside in, made the interior feel infinite. Each room was flooded with light, encouraged by vast windows that were like frozen glass lakes turned on their sides. Wood met stone met textile in perfect balance. Most impressively, it was all functional. Everything served a purpose; nothing existed purely for the sake of ornamentation. The furniture, all Beijing Zhu right angles and isosceles triangles, was of a quality Resler had never seen before. The colour palette was muted, but rich: gold, aqua, ash, copper. There was tech everywhere, but it was integrated into the furnishings. No one element stood out, with the effect that the whole did.

And at the heart of it all, in what looked to be a conference room, were Luc Benz and BB.

Benz sat at one end of a long black bioceramic table, in a Løvgren wrap chair, with a coupe glass in hand. He wore a perfectly tailored black Tang suit without a tie, and from the angle at which he was seated Resler could see the butt of a pistol hanging from a holster inside his jacket. A patch of graphene gauze was affixed to his perfect cheek. BB stood behind him. Stripped to the waist, holding the same monstrous gun he'd forever been cleaning at the theatre in Pankow. Both watched a giant floating screen that showed a kinofilm of suited men and women destroying an apartment with automatic weapons. The sound was turned up to a deafening level. Neither man spoke.

Resler drummed his fingers against the floor of the utility room. He could see them and he could hear them, but as of yet he couldn't hurt them. He continued cycling through the feeds, looking for something he could commandeer to make his presence felt.

Then he found Janeane.

She lay unmoving on a raised slab in the smallest of the residence's rooms. Dressed in a simple green sleeveless upper layer and pants that were too large for her, she looked tiny, like a bird with broken wings. Her blue-tinted hair fell around her face, obscuring it from view. Mechanical devices and bladetech on rollers crowded around the slab, as if trying to get at her. The walls of the room were padded, the wipe-clean fabric spotted. When he saw the wide-set grooves in the floor around the slab he guessed at their purpose and his stomach heaved.

The girl stirred.

As Janeane turned her head, her hair moved to reveal what was underneath and Resler cried out, because there was the barbarity of the world laid bare on a child's face. Her eyes opened, and he saw that they were myopic and absent of spark. She sat up with a wince.

He ran through the systems list, found that the mic attached to the surveillance eye in the room had been permanently disabled. I'm here, he wanted to say to her. I can see you. You're not alone.

The command to unlock the door to the room flashed up and he hit it. The door swung open and Janeane turned toward it in fear, but frowned when neither Benz nor BB appeared. Resler dimmed the lights twice in quick succession, and when Janeane looked up he did it again. Her eye became focused, and as she swung her legs off the slab he cycled back through the feeds to the main room. Before he could think of a way to distract the two men and give Janeane a chance to escape, the kinofilm they were watching dissolved into flames and cut out. Benz stood and threw the coupe glass across the room and it shattered against the wall.

BB set the Gauss rifle on the conference table. His childlike voice came through clear.

'We should leave.'

Benz spoke through a snarl. 'Why? They're dead.'

'Even so. That bomb could have shaken one too many rivets clear of their holes.'

'This is a Nerthus tower. It cannot collapse, especially not from anything cooked up by that soldier.'

'You continue to underestimate them. '

Benz raised a finger. 'Watch your tone. Remember who's paying your wage. Now, I want you to go down there and find out if anyone is still breathing.'

'How? The fracker still has control.'

'Ever heard of the stairs? Your spiker can override the circuitry in the service door.'

'What if they're alive?'

'They won't be.'

BB folded his arms across his scarred chest.

'If Warsaw is still breathing,' said Benz, 'I want you to bring her to me.'

'Fine. Let me go and check on the kid first'

Resler's blood froze.

'There's no need,' said Benz. 'She's dosed to the eyeballs.'

'That's what you said last time.'

Benz's hand strayed to the graphene gauze at his cheek. 'Just go.'

BB picked up the Gauss rifle and slung it over his shoulder. 'Better call in a tilt to come and pick us up, just in case. I saw enough bad things in London to know that brute force can trump even the best laid schemes.'

'If it appeases you, fine,' said Benz with a shrug.

Resler shivered. That had been no kinofilm. It was a live feed of floor five-O-three. Mia and Johnny had been in a fight for their lives and he'd sat and watched and cycled through his damn feeds like he was watching Wraptstar. Now they were gone, and BB had been dispatched to bring back their bodies.

The Flymotic flashed a warning and then another. Themis had forced another gap and was pouring through and his infiltration programme was buckling under its power. He watched his barriers crumble, felt the sweat run in lines down his face as Nerthus IV's AI came straight for him.

Resler's box of tricks was empty and he was alone.

It was the end.

31

When Mia woke, she was lying on her stomach and the Nylon was on the floor in front of her. She sat up, tried to think beyond the ringing in her ears and the taste of copper in her mouth. There was smoke, and when she looked around she saw the room was on fire. No spiderbots had appeared to put it out. There was a crash as part of the ceiling collapsed and the lights went out.

Move, she told herself. Pick up the gun and move.

In a room lit by flames she dragged her battered body over the polished floor, making for the plinth where Johnny had been. She saw organic shapes in the smoke, realised she wasn't the only one who had survived, and before she could reach fresh cover she heard a grunt and turned to see the anabolic with the thump gun. Blood ran from lacerations in his head, but his eyes were alert as he brought the squat barrel around for the killing shot. Before he could fire, the snap of a rifle sounded and he crumpled. Johnny emerged from the smoke with the Göl-Tek against his shoulder, and he grabbed Mia by the webbing and pulled her into cover behind a half-destroyed column.

'Still dancing?' he said, a pained grin on his face. His shirt was wet with blood.

'Still.' She brought the Nylon around and checked the clip and saw it was empty. Her hand reached into her webbing, found nothing. She let the weapon fall to the floor and pulled free her last Agitator. It was becoming difficult to breathe. There were flames in front, behind and around them, scorching the ceiling and turning the contents of the lounge to slag.

'We need to go,' she said over the noise. 'Right now.'

Johnny surveyed the destruction through red-rimmed eyes and nodded. 'Wait here.'

Before she could protest he lurched away from the column, fired into the smoke, then disappeared into it. The snap of the Göl-Tek was joined by other sounds. Automatics, single-shots, desperate words uttered in different languages. Thuds and screams. Follow him, she told herself. But she could only hold her Agitator in a wavering hand and watch the space where she'd last seen him.

The firing stopped. Somewhere behind her a window exploded. Then she heard her name being called.

She moved, feeling the hurt in her body with every step. Smoke found its way into her lungs and made her eyes stream. Her name rang out once more and she used the sound of the voice to orient herself. She stumbled over something and looked down to see a body. Then another and another, strung out like breadcrumbs for her to follow, all the way to the locked Torggler entrance. It was there that she found Johnny.

He was sitting on the floor with his back to the wall and his legs out before him, staring at nothing. When she approached he managed a weak grin.

'I love what we've done with the place.'

She holstered the Agitator and dropped to her knees and ran her eyes over his body. He'd been hit in more places than she could count. From her webbing she pulled out a can of spray dressing and discharged foam into the wounds that looked the most serious. Johnny hissed.

'We gotta get out of here,' he said, slurring his words.

'We will,' she said, exchanging the can for graphene bandages, which she slapped over the foam-filled holes. She grabbed him under the armpits and pulled him upright. 'Can you stand?'

'I can lean.'

'Good enough.'

She stood him by the wall and went to Torggler. The flames were at her back now, insatiable and terrifying. She saw how the gelignite explosion had jolted the door off its bearing, and through the gap she could see a pristine antechamber with a security desk and a giant cut-glass chandelier. She put her shoulder against the leaf, the metal hot on her skin, and pushed until she screamed.

The leaf yielded, just enough for a body to fit through.

Blind now, Mia groped through the darkness with one hand against the wall and when she found Johnny still standing she threw his arm over her shoulders and dragged him with her.

They were burning.

She found the gap again and pushed Johnny through first, then followed after him. She emerged choking on the other side, and when she had put enough distance between her and the terrible heat she sank to the ground and sucked down oxygen. Then she wiped her eyes and, with a strength summoned from deep within her, clambered to her feet and dragged a stricken Johnny over to the bank of brass tubes at the end of the antechamber. Their clothes smouldered on their backs. She waved her hand across the pneumatic sensor. Nothing happened.

She looked back down the antechamber, saw the smoke pouring through the gap in the door. They had escaped the inferno only to die anyway. 'Resler,' she said, not daring to hope. 'Can you hear me?'

She turned to the pneumatic once more, tried to dig her fingers between the brass doors. The skin on her hands was a violent red. The doors didn't move an inch.

'Try him again,' said Johnny, his voice little more than a whisper. 'Owen. Please, Owen.'

She checked her webbing. All she had left was her Agitator, the parachutes and the baichi tessen fan. She contemplated firing off the printshot's two rounds at the pneumatic, but knew the doors were designed to withstand that kind of force.

'The security desk,' said Johnny. 'Maybe it still has power. A tool. Something.'

She ran over to it, only to find every shelf and hole empty. The console built into the surface was blank and didn't respond to her commands. When she prodded the manual buttons on the underside of the desk, nothing happened. The antechamber was dead, a coffin, and theirs were the bodies to fill it.

Returning to the bank of tubes, she found Johnny slumped on his side with his eyes closed. She couldn't tell if he was alive or dead, didn't want to know. She looked at the ceiling, her lips twisting in readiness to mutter a prayer. 'Goddamn you, Owen Resler,' she said instead.

Then there were spiders and there was rain.

32

'I hear you, Mia,' said Resler.

With shaking hands he closed the command list for the spiderbot fire system and activated the pneumatic bank on five-O-three. The Flymotic's display wavered, the holographics rippling with colours that didn't match the system levels. The SynSult was a mini sun at his temple. His infiltration program was still online, twisting code into last-ditch walls that were swept aside almost as soon as they were put up. His head was clouded. The data streams projected by the console's holographic eye had lost all meaning, become continuous lines that wrapped themselves around his throat and wrists and ankles. Pain was a constant, and he couldn't tell if it was physical or mental or both.

'What's the situation?' It took great effort to speak.

'Johnny's hurt. We need to get off this level right now.'

He glanced at a schematic, swept at the console with a tense finger. 'Elevator's coming.'

The pneumatic's feed transferred to his eye-over, and he watched as the door opened and Mia Warsaw pulled a bloodied and seemingly unconscious Johnny into the tube.

'Up or down?' he asked, though he knew the answer.

She looked directly into the surveillance eye. 'Up. I'm finishing this.'

He did as he was told and the elevator rose. On the feed, Mia searched through Johnny's webbing and pulled out a coldmed kit, then opened his shirt slapped an epinephrine patch on his exposed chest. His eyes shot open and he gasped.

'Sekhmet,' he said.

'Why are the beads working again?' asked Mia, her voice raw.

'They must have had sonic dampeners set up all around the suite,' said Resler. 'Once you made it out of there, I could hear you again, clear as a bell. It took me a moment to find the right command.'

'Perfect timing,' she said. 'And now?'

'Benz is alone. BB went down to five-O-three via the service stairwell to check you were dead. I don't see him on the feeds, so I guess he's still down there.' He shook his head, struggling to shift the clouds. 'Themis. The Nerthus AI. It's taking back control.'

'How long do we have?'

'A couple of minutes, maybe.'

Then she voiced the question he didn't want her to ask. 'What about Janeane?'

He hesitated, struggling for words.

'Owen?'

'Yeah.'

'Just tell me.'

'She's alive.'

He watched as she closed her eyes and pressed a fist to her forehead. 'How is she?'

'Later,' he said. 'You're on five-O-four now.'

As the pneumatic slowed to a halt, Resler cycled through the feeds and found the surveillance eye for the floor's antechamber. A burst of noise distorted the image. The brass door rolled open and Mia emerged into the room with the printgun held out in front of her. Johnny limped behind, his face ashen, one hand pressed to his side. Mia dropped the parachute bags onto a checkerboard floor and her gaze swept the room, taking in a levitating water feature, a collection of majesty palms and yuccas, a huge inactive floating screen and a C-shaped lounge sofa that looked as though it had never been sat on.

'The entrance is to your left,' said Resler through gritted teeth. Another burst of static. 'Once you're in, you need to head right. That's where Janeane is. Small room.'

He fought through the fog and found the command to open the door, but as he was about to swipe the lightkey it opened of its own accord.

BB loomed in the doorway, the Gauss rifle cradled between thick hands.

For a moment no one moved. Then two things happened. The Gauss rifle bucked with a sound piercing enough to make glass shatter, and Johnny shoved Mia aside and took the ferromagnetic projectile full in the chest.

Mia returned fire with the Agitator, but BB twisted his body at an augmented speed and the subsonic bullet rattled off the body of the Gauss rifle. In a single fluid movement, he allowed the gun to fall and yanked something from his belt and his hand made a snapping motion. A glittering length of barbed tape snaked through the air, catching Mia on the back of the hand that held the printshot and digging deep into her flesh. Mia screamed and the weapon fell.

BB walked toward her, a smile on his angelic face.

'Last one standing,' he said.

Resler did the only thing he could think of. He accessed the floating screen in the antechamber and patched in the top Wraptstar vid on Vertoo.

'Incoming,' he said to Mia.

A half-naked Falko Wagenknecht, chief data scientist of Ynside, appeared on the screen, and Resler watched as he jumped from a nucrete walkway into moving traffic with a smile on his face.

As BB turned to it, an unspoken question on his lips, Mia's free hand shot to the fan hanging from her webbing. When she flicked it open, five metal flechettes flew from hollow ribs and for the first time BB was too slow. One missed, but the other four impaled themselves in his chest, throat and eye. He staggered back, useless fingers tugging at the steel in his face, until he reached the C-shaped couch. He collapsed onto it and looked up at the ceiling as red pooled onto beige. His breathing slowed and the angelic face became a rigid mask, terror etched into every line, and he shook his head as he tried to fight against the black. But there were no augmentations in his body that could stave off death.

BB's chest heaved a final time and he became still.

Mia dropped the fan and picked up the Agitator. The hand that had been raked by the barbed tape was streaming blood, but she ignored it. She went to Johnny and turned him over and Resler could see there was nothing to be done. Her hand brushed his face and she unclipped something from around his neck.

'I'm going in,' she said.

Then the feeds died and he could no longer see her. The SynSult burned like a supernova and he cried out and felt hands that were no longer his scrabbling at his temple to prise it free. Themis was there, isolating him, inhabiting him, scouring his brain from the inside.

In the split second before the pain took over every centimetre of his body, he saw a light, and he believed that light belonged to God.

33 Mia Warsaw still stood.

Silence surrounded her. The door to Benz's residence yawned open, revealing a lounge much like the one she and Johnny had destroyed. She had no plan. Only a beat-up Agitator and a single cartridge to finish a job that had started in a rotting room on the bad side of town. She transferred the printshot from her dripping hand to her bandaged one Don't hesitate, she told herself. Whatever's in there, whatever he's done to the kid, pick your shot and fire and don't miss.

Over her in-ear comm bead came a scream that was abruptly cut off.

'Owen?'

Nothing.

She ghosted inside, making sure to hug the wall. Instead of a sunken space at the centre, there was a black bioceramic table screened off by slabs of glass lit in aquamarine. The pulse bar for a floating screen rested in a gold cradle on the table. Beyond it, floor-to-ceiling windows were hidden behind velvet drapes. A huge triptych painting adorned one wall. There was no sign of Benz. She followed Resler's instructions, padding softly along an austere hallway that turned nine-O degrees and terminated in an open metal door. Her hands throbbed. At the threshold she paused and shifted the Agitator for a better grip, then swept into the room.

A padded cell with a stone floor. Compact, but with dimensions enough to house multiple machines that stood in a row along one wall. Wicked blades and other implements hung from hooks suspended from the ceiling. Perfectly angled LEDs painted the cell a butter yellow. Janeane lay on a slab in the centre of the room, her head turned away from Mia and her hair covering her face. An irregular line of sutures closed a long gash on her left forearm. Benz stood next to her, immaculate in his black Tang suit, with his hands in the air. His bland-beautiful features remained placid even when she aimed the Agitator at his face.

'Well,' he said. 'You got me, Ms Warsaw.'

The voice-enhancer was switched off. His voice was thinner, more pinched, like a boy trying to imitate a man.

'BB?' he asked.

'He checked out,' she said.

Benz nodded, as though the news was expected. She glanced at Janeane. Her chest rose and fell. She was still breathing.

He smiled, lowered his hands.

'A remarkable girl. She managed to hold out long after others gave up. What my patients never understand is that I am trying to help them. The technology I introduce to their bodies is intended to make them more resilient citizens, to give them an edge in the cutthroat day-to-day existence that constitutes this city's calling card.'

'Shut up,' said Mia.

Benz sighed. 'I remembered you from back in the day, Ms Warsaw. That old pinyin Bülow deserved his fate, even if you never meant it to happen that way. What you can't know is how thankful I was to you for making his death so public. Shall I tell you why? Bülow was a corrupt soul, but he had his limits. He wasn't one for mindless human suffering, not after what he experienced first hand during the Water Conflict. And so when he followed up on the rumours about me and discovered my predilection for surgery, he was ready to go both to the chancellor and the press about it. It would have ruined me. Fortunately, you swooped in like an avenging angel and removed him from the picture. I recall toasting your name at a dinner with my inner circle when the news came through about his body being found under the rubble of his home.'

Nausea took hold in Mia's stomach. 'I told you to shut up.'

His hand reached for a pristine white cuff, jerked it out from underneath the sleeve of his jacket. The Agitator twitched.

'Just making sure I look my best when you execute me,' said Benz.

'Put your hands by your sides,' said Mia. Shoot him, said a voice. Why would you wait? Shoot him now. But still she hesitated.

His hands fell. 'I have one final request.'

'You aren't in a position to request anything.'

'Correct. But it pertains to the girl. You came here for her, so I hope you'll at least hear what I have to say.'

Her gaze shifted to Janeane on the slab and then back to Benz. 'What is it?'

'The medical staff who see to her should know that I implanted an experimental mastaba conscience isolator inside her. I don't yet know if her body will reject or accept it, which is why I have left the wound open except for a triple-skin seal. It may need to be debrided if it becomes infected.'

Mia took a step closer to the slab. 'Where is the implant?' she said, her voice barely audible.

'Right here,' said Benz, and he reached over and tucked Janeane's hair back over her ear and Mia saw it and understood why Resler had held his tongue. Her gaze froze and her body trembled and the muzzle of the Agitator dipped.

Benz was on her before she could recover. He ripped the printgun from her hand and threw it across the room. A balled fist struck her in the face and she felt her nose break, and then her legs were swiped from under her and she went down onto cold grooved stone. A boot found her side and the air left her lungs. Then he was on top of her, his strength far superior to hers, and her arms were pinned at her sides and she could do nothing except look up into a leering face that was far more alive than it had been seconds ago. His hand dipped into his jacket and emerged holding the Bolo pistol that she'd last seen in a blood-spattered pod in Toltec, and as he pressed his weight into her he used the muzzle to stroke the hair at her temple.

'You came close,' he said. The voice-enhancer was activated again, his words unable to be dampened by the padded walls. 'Closer than anyone.'

He gazed down at her with illuminated eyes.

'I know I could never persuade you to join me, not after what I did to the girl. But I wish there had been some way. Escaping the club and then having the audacity to come here? This is the first time in a long time I felt afraid of someone who wasn't my father. Thank you for that. I needed it.'

He pushed his knee into her elbow and she grimaced but refused to make a sound.

'I considered operating on you, but you're simply too dangerous to keep around. Instead, I intend to use your death for my political gain. My father doesn't have long left, despite his trips to the regeneration chambers at C-State. The Habanik board is waiting for me to make my move. What better way to demonstrate my mettle than to present Berlin with the head of the terrorist who killed a decorated minister? I'll be celebrated from here to Switzerland. They'll be begging me to take the reins.'

His enhanced voice filled her ears and clouded her mind, torturing her in her final moments. She hated this man like she'd hated no one else, and she wished he would pull the trigger and give her peace.

Then Benz screamed and his blood was on her skin.

He rolled off her, the Bolo clattering against stone, and when she wiped the stickiness from her face she saw Janeane. The kid wielded a wicked scalpel, which she stabbed into Benz's back and neck over and over without remorse. He managed to turn, catching her by the wrist and bending it until the scalpel fell from her hand. He rose on uncertain legs, his Tang jacket torn to shreds, and flung her over the slab, and she hit the padded wall and lay still. With his face a mask of anger and agony, he cast around on the ground for the Bolo.

'Hey,' said Mia, the Agitator in her hand.

When he looked into her eyes she fired.

***

Janeane stared at her from where she'd fallen.

'Mia?'

'I'm here, baby.'

She stood, unsure of which blood was hers and which had belonged to Benz. Her body shook as she made her way over to the kid. The wound on Janeane's face glared at her, a technological horror held back only by three layers of acrylic adhesive, and she wished she could brush the kid's hair over her cheek so she would never have to see it.

'You came.'

'I promised.'

'Are you alone?'

She shook her head. 'Johnny and Owen were with me. They didn't make it.'

Janeane closed her eyes. 'I saw Gian in my dreams. He told me you were coming.'

Mia dropped to the ground and Janeane's arms wrapped themselves around her midriff and she didn't know what to do except press the kid's unharmed cheek to her chest and hold her. She felt tears against her skin.

'My face.'

'We'll fix that,' said Mia. 'We'll fix all of it.'

They sat together, quiet and exhausted, and Mia decided it wouldn't be bad if this was the last thing she experienced on earth.

Eventually, Janeane stirred. 'Can we go?'

'Yes.' Mia helped the girl to her feet. 'We can do that.'

She led the way out of the operating theatre, the girl's wrist in one ravaged hand, the non-locked Bolo in the other. The lounge was still empty, the main entranceway wide open. In the antechamber BB's body remained seated on the couch. Janeane grimaced and turned away.

'Did you get him?'

Mia nodded. 'Only because Johnny gave me the chance.'

On the far side of the room, between a crack in the velvet drapes, the sky was pencilled grey. A storm was coming. Mia didn't know how long she'd been in the tower. It felt like forever.

'How are we gonna get out?' asked Janeane.

'I have chutes. We're jumping.'

The kid shivered.

'Be right back,' said Mia, and she went into the antechamber. The black bag containing the chutes was lying on the checkerboard floor, near Johnny, and she slung it over a shoulder and returned to Janeane. She guided the kid through the lounge, then swept aside the drapes and found a door leading out onto a huge, plant-heavy deck. Both women breathed in clean, moist air. The deck terminated in a vacant pad for tiltrotor aircraft.

'Wait,' said Janeane, struggling to shake herself free from Mia's grasp.

'You'll be fine. All you have to do is jump.'

'Not that. Something BB said.'

Mia paused, one foot already on the tiltrotor pad. 'Tell me.'

'He was worried about you parachuting onto the deck.'

'Too slow. Sentry drones would have shot us out of the sky as we came down.'

'Right,' said Janeane. 'But Johnny was trained in freefall, wasn't he? A fast descent, low opening wouldn't have been out of the question. That's what BB said.'

Mia could feel the seconds ticking away. 'And?'

'And Benz said he'd installed an Odachi close-quarters system to counteract threats like that.'

'So?'

Janeane clicked her tongue. 'Mia, come on. If we jump, ain't there a chance of setting off the Odachi?'

Mia considered it for a moment. 'Sekhmet.' She looked around the deck, seeing no sign of hardware, then out at the city with its needles and spires and blocks.

'Owen,' she said, not daring to hope. 'Can you hear me? Are you still there?'

Nothing.

'Speak to me, Owen. Please. We need you now.'

A single word in her ear. 'Mia.'

She breathed, the relief strong enough to bring a gleam to her eyes. 'We're on Benz's deck. Can you see us?'

'No.' There was a pause. 'I can't see anything.'

Mia tried to ignore the crawling sensation on her skin. 'Benz is dead, but we need your help. There's an Odachi close-quarters defence system installed somewhere on the exterior of the tower. If we jump, it'll track us and blow us out of the sky.'

No answer.

She raised her voice. 'Owen, do you understand what I'm saying to you? You have to disable that system.'

The response, when it came, was slurred. 'Themis has control now.'

'I don't care. Think of a way to shut it down.'

Silence.

'Owen, wake the hell up. We're nearly home. You need to do this now.'

Janeane stirred. 'He's using the Flymotic to access the system?'

'Yeah.'

'Tell him to do a data overload. Prep the command to disable the Odachi on his eye-over, then send it at the same time as he opens the floodgates on the Flymotic with everything he has. It should take the AI a second or two to sift through the data before it overrides the eye-over's command. That's all we need to evade the Odachi's tracker.'

'Owen.'

This time Resler answered. 'Yes.'

Mia relayed the message to him.

Silence. Then: 'That could work. When I give the word, you have to jump.'

'We will,' said Mia.

'Get ready. Good luck.'

She turned to Janeane. 'He's going to try it.'

The kid nodded. 'He'll manage.'

Mia dumped the chutes on the deck and grabbed one and eased it onto Janeane's frame. She adjusted the harness and fastened the buckles and gave the rig the once-over, then made sure the kid knew where the ripcord was.

'As soon as you jump, pull it.' From the bag she handed Janeane a violet-tinted visor, which she slipped over her face. 'Then use the handles and follow me as best you can. We're aiming to clear the plaza and reach leech town. If we can make it that far, we can disappear underground. Then we're home free.'

'You ever do this before?'

'Sure. Loads of times.'

'Really?'

'No.'

'Geznet.' The girl's lips came together in a familiar grin, and for a moment the ravaged side of her face lost its horror and to Mia she was whole again. 'I'm ready.'

After putting on her own chute and fastening it, she led Janeane onto the tiltrotor pad. A cold wind whipped at their skin. The whole of Berlin was laid out before them, cramped yet boundless, extending to the horizon and beyond.

'Owen?' said Mia, but there was no response.

The rain started, driving its way up from the south and slaloming between the Nerthus towers. Surveillance and delivery drones in operation around the Platz lowered their trajectories accordingly. Mia took Janeane by the hand and squeezed it, and the kid squeezed back. Whatever happened next, they would be okay.

'Don't be afraid,' said Mia.

Janeane looked out at the city. 'I'm not.'

Then a single word, barely decipherable. 'Jump.'

Their hands parted.

From the deck of a hyperscraper, two women threw themselves into the void.

34 Owen Resler was done, almost.

He knew, because the AI allowed him to know, that his final command to switch off the Odachi defences around Nerthus IV had been obeyed. And he knew, because the AI allowed him to know, that in the second before Themis had reactivated the system, Mia and Janeane had jumped from the tiltrotor pad without being vaporised.

Fragments of information passed through his mind like bolts of silk on the wind, and he could only snatch at them and guess what they meant. Now that the AI had its system back, Themis ignored him. It wasted no processing power sending a surge that would overload his mind and flatline him. There was no need. It was content to repair the damage he had wrought and let nature take its course.

Because he was dying.

The SynSult had burned out. If he still had eyes, then they were closed. There was no pain in his body, no feeling at all. Even if he had wanted to raise his hand, he couldn't have done it. He could no longer feel the shackle disappearing into the port whose metal-silicon veins led to the chip implanted at the base of his brain. His mind had decoupled itself from his body, the luminous distinct from the material, and because he was freed from the flesh he had no fear and he could look back over his life as an impartial observer. There had been many false starts, wrong turns, disappointments and betrayals, but he'd had a purpose at the end. It had counted for something. There had been the kid who had needed help, and he had given everything to free her. As the compartments of his brain shut down one by one, lights switching off in a vacated building, the realisation gave him satisfaction.

There was one thing he had to do before the final bulb winked out.

Somewhere, buried within the fog, was his eye-over, his last link to a world that already seemed trivial to him. He reached into the fog, searching for it, calling for it, willing it to come to him so he could deliver a message. It was there, because it needed to be there.

White lines on grey. A bead of light connected to a name. The eye-over stood by, waiting for his command. He opened a channel. When he spoke, he couldn't feel his lips move, but he could hear the word formed by them.

'Mia.'

The silence stretched like a thread. He held on, not hoping, not expecting, because such sensations were no longer part of him.

'Mia.'

Themis was there, more present again. The torturer turned observer, learning from him in death. He didn't want to know what the AI would do with the information. He did not care. He communicated to it only that it should let him speak when the moment came, and he felt its acquiescence.

'Owen?'

A woman's voice. Faint, but it appeared to him as a lantern. The fog rolled back.

'Are you safe?'

'The chutes carried us through. I'm taking Janeane into the tunnels. We'll be able to lose the bulls down there. Then I'll get her out of the city.'

The tunnels. The city. Concepts he no longer understood. 'Will she recover?'

'In time.'

'Tell her.' He paused. Words were inefficient, insufficient. 'Tell her from me.'

'I will.'

'And.'

'What is it?'

The suggestion of a face, a light in her eyes.

'My sister. I want her to know I took a different path, like she said.'

'I'll tell her. I'll tell her everything.'

For the briefest of moments, his mind reconnected with the body that sat broken on the floor of a utility room. He could feel his head nodding and the tears on his skin and the saliva in his throat. Then the link broke and he floated free again. The white lines of the eye-over faded.

'You did good Owen.' Mia's voice was almost gone. 'Will you be okay?'

He tried to respond, but the comm channel collapsed and the eye-over dissolved and there was no more Mia. The part of Themis that had listened to the conversation drifted away, its curiosity — if an AI could be deemed to exhibit such a quality — satisfied. He was glad of it, because he wanted to face the next part alone. He did not know what to expect, but as his mind's darkness brightened to a field of the purest light he could see the faces of the few who had loved him and the few he had loved in his turn, and his life played backward and forward at different speeds and depths and intervals, and he watched it all because here was infinity and the chance to find a definitive peace with himself. Over and over again, in as many constellations as there were stars in the universe.

Yes, Owen Resler thought. He would be okay.

E pilogue

The settlement was called Prestige. Once it had been nothing more than a collection of walls and roofs, abandoned to the dust. But a woman in black had brought people and life to the place, and after her death another woman who was said to have two minds had continued the task, and now it was a free town where none carried a carbon debt and money did not exist and its residents owned, managed and controlled everything as a collective. All had jobs that they worked without complaint. Nurturing aeroponic fields that stretched to the horizon. Repairing systems that turned the sun and air into electricity and purified water and kept the dust at bay. Teaching and hunting, guarding and driving, cooking and creating.

A few led.

Janeane didn't yet know where or whether she fit among the people of Prestige. Her body was still repairing itself, and she was tired and irritable much of the time. At night her dreams spoiled to nightmares. She saw Gian putting a pistol to his head with a terrified gleam in his eyes. She saw Benz standing over her with a serrated blade in perfectly manicured hands. She saw Owen suffocated by cables while he screamed her name. In the mornings, she stared at her reflection for minutes at a time, scrutinising the repaired left side of her face, the skin there a different colour, too perfect to be real. The implant—not, as Benz had said, a mastaba conscience isolator, but a cheapjack antistatic with a Hong Kong serial number—had been removed, as had the two that had been buried deep in her arm. It wasn't the disfigurement that bothered her so much as the fact that she would never be able to forget the man who had done it to her.

More than that, she was alone.

Mia hadn't joined her. After Benz's death was splashed all over Vertoo, Lulu Chao's mother had paid what she owed. Mia had used the carbon to shift old debts and cover the surgery for her face and body, and there had been little left when the bladists were done with their work. And it would have been fine, except Mia was now in fresh debt with Mantis and that, too, had to be paid. She had begged Mia to come with her anyway, but Mia had refused, pushing her into a poly-truck and pressing Johnny's bloodstained ID disk into her hand and telling her to bury it in the ground when she arrived in Prestige.

'I'll be along,' had been the last words Mia said before the poly-truck door had swung shut.

After being bounced from settlement to settlement, Janeane had arrived in Prestige, where she had asked to see Ina Resler. When a woman with soft eyes and a hard mouth had entered the room, she had seen the resemblance and a shiver had passed through her body and words had failed her for the first time in her life. But she recovered enough to tell Ina about her brother and the part he had played in freeing her and the words he'd relayed to Mia. Ina had listened in silence, and when Janeane was done she had grasped her hand and thanked her. There had been no sadness in Ina's eyes, only reassurance, and Janeane had clutched at her until she had no more tears left.

A few days later, Ina had signed out a two-seater transport from the vehicle pool and driven Janeane out of the camp and beyond the fields to a forest that had survived the dust. After Ina had dug a hole among twisted roots, Janeane dropped Johnny's ID disk into the hole, and together they used their hands to push the soil over the top. Then they walked back to the transport and drove to Prestige in comfortable silence.

Janeane hoped Johnny would have approved of the spot.

Death woke her.

The air was thick and her sweat turned the cot's canvas dark. She got up. The clothes she put on had been made in the town: a loose collarless shirt that reached her thighs, wide-legged pants and sandals. The fabric had been brushed, but it was still rough and she wished she had brought more personal effects with her from Berlin. Mia had tried to warn her about home comforts, but she'd wanted to make a clean cut with the city and had packed the bare minimum. She didn't exactly regret leaving, didn't miss the action or the ads or the noise, but there were many aspects of her new life that would take time to understand and accept.

She left her room and followed darkened corridors until she was outside. It was dawn and it was cool and there was no dust. In a yard of sun-baked mud, she wandered past dead fire pits and the two-storey canteen building and the garage that housed the vehicle pool, then climbed a ladder to the top of the fortified wall that encircled Prestige's sleeping quarters. A sentry nodded at her and she nodded back, then moved off a way so she could be alone, and when she found a good spot she sat with her legs dangling and looked out over the aeroponic fields and saw green leaves protected by translucent dust tarps. The faces and forms of her nightmares faded in the peaceful air, and she listened to her body and felt older than she believed she had any right to feel.

An hour passed and the sun rose and warmed her neck. She did not move. The landscape soothed her. There were no lightwalls, no holographics, no drones, no skeletons of steel and nu-crete. Of all the things that could have been disorienting, being clear of the jungle wasn't one of them. It was already fading, as though the life she'd led — that of an orphan, a polygon girl, a thief, a grifter — had belonged to someone else and she had been told about it in passing. Better that way, she thought. Better to begin again without having to live up to an expectation of how she should act.

When the sun became too cruel, she swung her legs back over the wall and stood. A woman walked toward her along the rampart.

Young, but with deep scars on her face and arms. If she had been in the city, she could have had them repaired. The woman had helped her to settle in during her first days, but she'd been out of camp for more than a week, driving relief missions to other settlements that didn't yet have a crop yield close to rivalling Prestige.

'Janeane.' Faustine had an accent the Wraptstar advertisers would have paid for and the kids would have died for. She raised a hand. 'Tu vas bien?'

'Near enough.'

'Couldn't sleep?'

'Not tonight. Not any night.'

'It'll get better with time. If you need a little assistance, you can ask Monshiro to prepare a tonic for you.'

'I don't want to forget.'

'No one said anything about forgetting. But a pause from time to time has its benefits.'

Janeane stuffed her hands into the pockets of her pants, wondered why the other woman had sought her out.

Faustine raised a hand, brushed Janeane's cheek with her finger. 'It has healed well.'

'It doesn't hurt anymore.' That was a lie, but she wasn't ready to acknowledge the pain aloud yet. 'Was there something you needed?'

'I just came from Xi Yang. A dragonfly arrived.'

She didn't dare to hope. 'Any word from Mia?'

Faustine shook her head. 'Not yet. But a message from Mantis.'

Janeane squinted at her in the sunlight. 'What did they say?'

'That others are coming. From the city. And that we should be ready for them.'

'What others?'

'Who can tell?' Faustine shrugged. 'Ones like you, ones like me. Maybe even ones like Mia.'

Janeane shook her head. 'There isn't anyone like her.'

'C'est juste. Did you know she trained me to shoot?'

'No.'

'Oui. Right here in Prestige. She was mean.'

'That sounds like her.' Janeane smiled.

'Did she teach you?'

'No.'

'Then I will.'

She shook her head again. 'I've hurt enough people.'

'It's not about causing hurt,' said Faustine. 'It's about protection, starting with yourself. Let me tell you this: when you're surrounded by the blind, it's easy not to see. That's how it is in the cities. But the fact is more and more people are leaving for settlements like these. The dam of lies they've been propping up for so long is disintegrating. When it breaks, a flood will come, and all of us need to be ready for it.'

The question Janeane asked herself every day came to her lips. 'Why should it be my problem?'

'You're standing here, aren't you?'

'I'm tired.'

'I know. Moi aussi. And so is Mia. But we do it anyway. You understand?'

'I think so.'

'Bravo.' Faustine squeezed her arm. 'So now go and get some rest. You're going to need it.'

She made to leave, then paused. 'You know her better than I do. Do you think she'll make it out this way again?'

Janeane turned away, toward the fields, and felt the sun touch different skins. Until Faustine had asked, she hadn't known the answer. But there was only one truth.

'She'll be along,' she said.

ACKNOWLEDGEMENTS

I wish to thank the following people for their ongoing support: Liam and Jemma Price, Sigrid Storla, Elsa Monsch, Martin Stabler, Henning Claussen, Martin Meir, Christian Reuter, Matthew Hills, Sebastián Becerra Lukauskis, Hannes Wegener, Hendrik Thiele, Reagan Rothe, Fraser Patterson, Emma Hall, Daniel Johnson, Ciarán Fleck, Simon Jansky, Finnuala Quinn, Ashley Godfrey, Noah and Sophia Gordon, Fabio Frittoli and Neil Mathews. If I have forgotten anyone, please call me up and hurl abuse at me, and I'll be sure to cite your name at the end of the next book.

OTHER WORKS

Reality Testing
ISBN-13: 978-1-68433-797-2
Welcome to Berlin. Population: desperate. In the throes of the climate crisis, the green tech pioneers are king, and if you aren't willing to be their serf then you're surplus to requirements.

Carbon credit for sleeping on the job. That's the offer a dreamtech puts to Mara Kinzig and she jumps on it. After all, the city ain't getting any cheaper.

Then someone changes the deal while she's dreaming in the tank.

Now Mara has a body on her hands, an extra voice in her head, and the law on her tail. Only the Vanguard, a Foreign Legion of outcasts seeking an alternative path in the dust between the city states, might be able to help her figure out what went wrong. First, though, she'll have to escape the seething streets of Berlin alive…

Available in paperback and ebook format.

By the Feet of Men
ISBN-13: 978-1-78904-145-3
WANTED: Men and women willing to drive through the valley of the shadow of death.

The world's population has been decimated by the Change, a chain reaction of events triggered by global warming. In Europe, governments have fallen, cities have crumbled and the wheels of production have ground to a halt. The Alps region, containing most of the continent's remaining fresh water, has become a closed state with heavily fortified borders. Survivors cling on by trading through the Runners, truck drivers who deliver cargo and take a percentage. Amid the ruins of central Germany, two Runners, Cassady and Ghazi, are called on to deliver medical supplies to a research base deep in the Italian desert, where scientists claim to be building a machine that could reverse the effects of the Change. Joining the pair is a ragtag collection of drivers, all of whom have something to prove. Standing in their way are starving nomads, crumbling cities, hostile weather and a rogue state hellbent on the convoy's destruction. And there's another problem: Cassady is close to losing his nerve.

Available in paperback and ebook format.

ABOUT THE AUTHOR

Grant Price is the author of *By the Feet of Men* (Cosmic Egg, 2019), *Reality Testing* (Black Rose Writing, 2022) and *Pacific State* (Black Rose Writing, 2023). He has translated several books ranging from photography to religion, and his essays and short stories have appeared in The Daily Telegraph and elsewhere. He currently lives in Berlin.

Website: grantrhysprice.com

GRANT PRICE
"A rip-roaring cyberpunk novel... it's definitely science fiction, but it's frighteningly plausible."
—The San Francisco Book Review
REALITY TESTING
THE SUNDOWN SERIES : BOOK ONE

NOTE FROM THE AUTHOR

Word-of-mouth is crucial for any author to succeed. If you enjoyed *Pacific State*, please leave a review online—anywhere you are able. Even if it's just a sentence or two. It would make all the difference and would be very much appreciated.

Thanks!
Grant Price

We hope you enjoyed reading this title from:

www.blackrosewriting.com

Subscribe to our mailing list – *The Rosevine* – and receive **FREE** books, daily deals, and stay current with news about upcoming releases and our hottest authors.
Scan the QR code below to sign up.

Already a subscriber? Please accept a sincere thank you for being a fan of Black Rose Writing authors.

View other Black Rose Writing titles at
www.blackrosewriting.com/books and use promo code
PRINT to receive a **20% discount** when purchasing.